The Final Thaw

Also by Karl J. Hanson

The Third Thaw

Before the Thaw

The Final Thaw

Book 3 in The Third Thaw Series

Karl J. Hanson

E. L. Marker
Salt Lake City

E. L. Marker, an imprint of WiDo Publishing
Salt Lake City, Utah
widopublishing.com

Cover design by Steven Novak
Book design by Marny K. Parkin

ISBN 978-1-947966-53-6
Printed in the United States of America

To Lisa, Julie and Paige

Part I:

Present Day Earth

Chapter 1

WHEN TOM JOHNSON PULLED THE LINCOLN NAVIGATOR into the Arabella Hotel's parking lot in Sedona, Arizona, he immediately caught sight of his customers, an older couple, sitting on a bench under the porte cochère. Tom usually gave group tours, but today's tour was going to be private. He thought it strange the couple hadn't just rented a car, but Greg, his boss, said they had insisted he should be their guide.

Taking off his Ray-Bans, he glanced at the rearview mirror. His new front teeth looked good. *Getting dental implants was the best decision I ever made!* He got the implants after his two upper front teeth snapped off while he was eating a Skor's bar.

Tom was in his early sixties. He was still a handsome man—especially with his new teeth. To reinforce his "western tour guide" persona, he typically dressed as a cowboy, sporting bison leather boots, a silver belt with a big metal buckle saying "*Arizona,*" and a red checkered shirt. As a nice touch, he wore a little bolo shoestring necktie, just like the one Colonel Sanders used to wear. He was especially proud of his leather Stetson cowboy hat, which had cost him $495 in Santa Fe.

Grabbing his Stetson, his clipboard, and a Bic pen, he stepped out of the luxury SUV to greet his clients.

"Howdy, folks!" Tom said in a boisterous voice, turning on his cowboy charm to maximum effect. "I assume you folks are Charles and Elise Timoshenko."

"That would be us, Tom," said the man, with a half-grin.

"Hi," said the woman in a flat voice, without looking up. She seemed preoccupied with her rings, which she was repeatedly twisting.

Tom looked Charles straight in the eye, giving him a vigorous handshake. "Pleased to meet ya', Charles. I'm Tom Johnson, your guide."

He noticed Charles had a wimpy grip, was just a smidge over six feet tall, and had salt and pepper hair. He appeared to be in his early seventies. Elise looked younger and was perhaps in her early sixties. She got up and walked directly to the car, without saying a word.

Charles watched his wife, then looked at Tom, giving him a forced smile; then he followed her to the car. They sat in the row behind the driver's seat.

Am I losing my charm? Tom wondered. His customers tended to be happy vacationers who loved his cowboy spiel. It looked as though he was about to have a tough day, cooped-up for the next eighteen hours with two duds. He saw himself as a performer of sorts, one who offered witty commentary, kept things rolling, and was constantly "on." There was a lot of material to cover: Arizona's geology, Indian culture, fishing stories. . . .

Tom slipped into the driver's seat and turned to face his passengers.

"So, my instructions are to first take you to an appointment in Winslow. Then, after your meeting, I'll take you—it just says 'here.' I suppose this means I'll take you wherever you want to go."

"Yes, that is correct, Tom," said Charles. "We are meeting someone by the name of. . . . Excuse me, just a second. . . ."

Charles searched in his pocket for a scrap of paper.

"His name is Hototo of The Little Bird Clan. I was told he specifically asked to see you in Winslow."

"*Hototo?* Well, I'm flattered to hear that!"

Why the old Indian wanted to see him was a mystery. He had barely spoken more than five words to him, in all the tours he had given at Homolovi State Park.

Tom looked for the ignition but seemed unfamiliar with the controls of the rental Lincoln SUV. "Sorry, folks, but I seem to be having a problem here. I usually drive a Ford Econoline van. I can't find where the keys go."

Charles said, "It's a keyless ignition, Tom. There's a button."

"A button?"

Charles reached forward and pointed at a button next to the steering wheel.

"See, that one."

Tom pushed the button, and the Lincoln started.

"Thanks, Charles."

"Your van must be an antique. Most new cars have keyless ignitions."

"Yep, the van is old, for sure. Keyless ignition! Think of that! When I picked up this buggy at the rental place, it was already running. Next time I'll need to pay attention to what they tell me."

It was just after eleven a.m. when they pulled out of the hotel onto Route 179, heading north through downtown Sedona.

Tom pointed ahead at the red rock formations.

"Spectacular, isn't it? That's Cathedral Rock, up ahead, one of the most beautiful sights in the world. It's good we're getting an early start before the tourists get here. This stretch of road will be jammed with traffic at about noon. Happens every day, like clockwork.

"Sedona has changed a lot since I arrived in these parts. Not too long ago, this was a remote location. They used to film Hollywood westerns here, with big stars like John Wayne and Jimmy Stewart. Now it's a trendy tourist destination. See all these souvenir shops and pink jeeps! There's a Starbucks, just like 'Anyplace, USA.' Fortunately, we don't have waterparks—*yet*," he laughed. "But it's beautiful, isn't it?"

"Indeed, it is," Charles said. "The rock formations remind me of New Mexico."

"Whereabouts?"

"The Jemez Mountains. They're not as red as these mountains. It's amazing that at one time, this entire area was under the sea."

"Sounds like you know quite a bit about geology, Charles. What do you do for a living?"

"I'm a structural engineer. Actually, I'm semi-retired—well, I suppose *officially* retired, given the circumstances," he said, pausing to look at Elise, who was staring out of her window. There was a vacant expression in her eyes, as if she were taking in everything yet seeing nothing.

"I've read many geotechnical reports in my career," continued Charles.

"Geotechnical reports?"

"You know, geotechnical reports for designing foundations. They provide recommendations for engineers to design foundations. When Elise and I were first married, we lived in Los Alamos, New Mexico. That's where I got interested in geology."

"So you worked at Los Alamos National Labs?"

"Uh-huh, worked on the supercomputer there. They always have the latest, most powerful supercomputers. They've got a Cray XC40, one of the most powerful computers in the world. When I was there, I helped develop code for simulating structures in real-time."

"*Simulating structures,* you say? In *real*-time? Not sure what you mean by that," Tom said, his brows furrowing. "So, you're no longer there?"

"Oh, we left a long time ago. Now we live near Chicago."

"Chicago! I'm originally from that area myself."

"Really? Whereabouts?" asked Elise, suddenly turning away from her window.

"Lived in Rockford, Illinois. Been here the past twenty-four years. In all this time, I haven't been back once."

Tom didn't want to talk about Rockford. If pressed, he'd give his usual answer: Business had dried up. There was no point discussing his divorce from Donna. It was so long ago, he had almost blocked-out that part of his life, except for the memory of his boys.

"Basically, I've learned about geology by giving tours," said Tom. "I'm not into books or computers, but there've been several times when I've given tours to geologists visiting Arizona and Nevada. I've had a ring-side seat listening to the experts. One geologist became a friend of mine, and we used to keep in touch."

Tom scratched his chin, leaving one hand on the wheel.

"His last name was—let me think... Scott... yeah, that was it. Professor Scott, from Cal Tech. Said he studied moon rocks. I don't know why this sticks in my mind, but he said Chicago has a lot of clay underground. Is that true?"

"Yes, in the Chicago area, most foundations are on hard clay that was compressed by the glaciers. The soils are sedimentary deposits."

Charles leaned over the empty front seat and pointed at a rock formation several hundreds of feet above them. "You see, up there, those layers of different colored rocks?"

Tom looked up and saw a distinct pattern of layered seams, tilted at about thirty degrees from horizontal.

"Yep, see 'em."

"I would conjecture those rock layers are probably the sedimentary remains of ancient coral reefs. I wouldn't be surprised if those rocks have fossils of ancient sea life."

"Every time I hear this stuff, it amazes me!" said Tom, shaking his head. "I still can't wrap my head around the idea most of the United States was underwater at one time!"

"It blows my mind, too," said Charles, smiling.

Tom decided he liked Charles. They both had lived in the Midwest; they were both interested in geology. Maybe the day wasn't going to be too bad, after all—except for Elise. *What was going on with her?* "Don't you just love science?" he continued enthusiastically. "I'm sure you're aware there's going to be a lunar eclipse tonight."

But Charles did not respond.

The SUV continued on through the canyon on Route 89, along Oak Creek. Sometimes, when Tom was driving hundreds of miles between stops, he thought about his former life in the Midwest. He and Donna had fought all the time, mostly over money. His drinking was out of control. Jeff and Tom, Jr., were only nine and six when things went bad. He had moved into a trailer—God, how he hated it there! It was a lonely life, pretending to have a normal relationship with the boys, seeing them every other weekend, taking them bowling, or to movies and mini-golf, acting as though everything was normal. He was in a dead-end job, selling washers and refrigerators at Polk Brothers. That's why he had chucked it all and moved to Arizona. It was the hardest decision of his life. His boys hated him for leaving—and he couldn't blame them.

He looked in the distance, at the magnificent scenery. *I gave up being a dad for this. Was it worth it?*

They had now reached an altitude of about 8,000 feet. At this elevation, the landscape suddenly changed, becoming heavily forested with towering conifers.

"All these ponderosas remind me of Los Alamos."

"Never been there," said Tom. "The ponderosas must like this elevation. We're getting closer to Flagstaff."

"It almost looks like Colorado. It's amazing how different this part of Arizona looks from lower elevations."

"Right you are."

An hour later, they reached the outskirts of Flagstaff.

"Do we have time to make a detour to see Meteor Crater?" asked Charles.

Tom looked at his watch. "Your meeting in Winslow is at four p.m.?"

"Correct."

"We have plenty of time. Meteor Crater is on the way. It's only fifteen miles from Winslow. It's Arizona's 'other hole in the ground,'" he laughed.

"Other hole?"

"Don't tell me you don't know what's the other hole in the ground?"

"Of course—I forgot. The Grand Canyon!"

"Yep. Well, Meteor Canyon is a wee bit smaller than the Grand Canyon. It's 4,000 feet in diameter and 600 feet deep."

"4,000 feet!" Charles whistled. "Almost a mile—very impressive. Can't wait to see it."

Tom looked in the mirror at Elise, who had been quiet the entire time.

"Are you okay, Mrs. Timoshenko?"

"Yes, perfectly," she replied, in a voice devoid of emotion. "Everything's hunky-dory."

They turned east, taking Route 40 toward Winslow. It didn't take long before they came to Meteor Crater Road. Near the entrance to the road, they saw a peculiar geodesic dome structure.

"What's that building, Tom?" asked Elise, sounding slightly more animated.

"Oh, that's the Meteor City Trading Post. Was abandoned for years. It's famous among Route 66 buffs. You know the history of trading posts, don't you?"

"Nope."

"Well, I have just enough time to tell you a story before we get to the crater. You know about the Indians and the Long Walk?"

"Can't say that I do," replied Elise.

"During the 1860s, American troops were sent to Arizona to capture Navajo Indians and place them on a reservation in New Mexico, called Bosque Redondo. The Navajos were forced to walk the entire journey from Arizona to New Mexico, in what became known as the Long Walk. Many of them died along the way.

"Eventually, in 1868, the US Government allowed the Indians to return to their homeland in Arizona. Now, after living eight years on the reservation in New Mexico, the Indians had developed a taste for the white man's food. This was when trading posts began to appear."

"What did they trade at the trading posts?" asked Charles.

"Things like sugar, salt, coffee, white flour, pots and pans, and bridles and saddles."

"No frozen pizzas?" asked Elise, with a sarcastic edge to her voice.

Tom laughed. "I'm not even sure if anyone but the Italians were eating pizzas in those days. Originally, only white men owned these trading posts. They were called 'traders.' Many of these trader men married Indian women."

"Interesting," murmured Elise.

They arrived at the parking lot of the Meteor Crater Visitors' Center. Charles paid for three tickets to see the crater; then they took an elevator up to the second floor where there were exhibits and lecture halls. There was a large meteorite on display, the Holsinger Meteorite, identified as the largest fragment found at the site.

Exiting the Visitors' Center, they headed to the viewing platform at the edge of the crater. The wind whipped around them mercilessly. Bracing themselves, they gripped the handrails, gazing down into the massive hole in the ground, unlike anything on Earth.

"Amazing, isn't it?" Tom shouted over the wind.

"Absolutely!" Charles responded. "Does anyone know when—"

"Can't hear ya', Charles!" interrupted Tom, getting closer.

"DOES ANYONE KNOW WHEN THE METEOR HIT?"

"THEY ESTIMATE IT WAS 50,000 YEARS AGO."

Charles gave the "thumbs-up" signal.

"HOW BIG WAS THE METEOR?" shouted Elise.

"FIFTY METERS IN DIAMETER."

"Fifty meters?" repeated Elise, but her words were lost in the wind.

The couple continued to look over the edge of the observation platform. As Tom held himself back, Elise and Charles began whispering to each other; their conversation became louder and more animated, but Tom could not understand much of what they were saying on account of the wind. Charles seemed to be explaining that fifty meters was about half the length of a football field. Suddenly, Elise began gesticulating wildly.

"Damn it, Charles! Look at this hole! A one-hundred-fifty-foot asteroid did this!" Then she stormed off toward the parking lot, in tears.

For a few minutes, Charles hunched over the railing, staring down at the crater; then, he straightened up and turned toward Tom, who was standing close by.

"Sorry about this, Tom. Perhaps it was a mistake coming here."

"Yeah, sure. No problem," said Tom. He followed Charles back to the Lincoln, confused by the entire outburst.

They left Meteor Crater without further conversation. Soon they hooked-up with Interstate Route 40—formerly known as Route 66—and drove east toward Winslow. Glancing in the rearview mirror, Tom could see the couple were sitting as far apart as possible. Elise was dabbing her eyes with a tissue while Charles had a pained expression on his face.

Not the best time to interrupt them, thought Tom, but he needed to explain a few of the ground rules about dealing with the Indians.

"Charles, you mentioned you will be meeting Hototo."

Lost in his own thoughts, Charles finally responded.

"Sorry, Tom. What were you were asking?"

"I said, you mentioned you're meeting Hototo."

"Yes, that's the man's name. You said you know him."

"Can't say I 'know' him: Hototo and I are just acquaintances. I'm not even sure to which tribe his clan belongs. I've run into Hototo a few times at Homolovi State Park. He's an old man who seems to like hanging around there."

"Excuse my ignorance, but what's *Homolovi* State Park?"

"It's an ancient village, north-east of Winslow. It's where the Ancestral Puebloans once lived. I bring tours there all the time. The Indian guides provide walking tours through the village."

"Are they still called Indians?"

"Well . . . it depends who you ask. Some of them are okay being called 'Indians,' but others aren't. You see, the word 'Indian' is a white man's label. To be politically correct, I try to say 'Native Americans' when I'm around them. Anyway, while the *Native Americans* are giving walking tours, I stay behind and talk to the locals who are selling jewelry and blankets. That's how I met Hototo."

"Does he sell jewelry?"

"No, no. He's just an old man who likes to hang-out in the village."

Tom looked at Charles in the rearview mirror. "Are you familiar with the ancient tribes that lived in this area?"

"I have a vague understanding, based on a few things I've read on Wikipedia."

"Well, I'm no expert, myself, but I can explain some of the important points. The ancestors of the Hopis, Pueblo, and Zuni tribes came here thousands of years ago. Homolovi is one of many ancestral villages. It's one of the newer ones, dating back to 200 AD."

Tom made a quick adjustment to the rearview mirror, then continued.

"Let's go over some basics about the Indians—I mean the *Native Americans*. Most of the Native Americans in Arizona are Navajos, but just to the north is where Hopis live. They're a small segment of the Native population. Just across the state line, in New Mexico, you'll find Pueblos and Zunis, who also claim to be descendants of the ancient ones."

"Does . . ." began Charles, then he paused to read a note, "Excuse me—I forgot his name. . . . Does *Hototo* look like a Hopi, Pueblo, or Zuni?"

Tom scratched his chin. "Tryin' to picture him. . . . No, come to think of it, Hototo doesn't look at all like a Hopi. They have a very distinctive appearance. And he's certainly not a Navajo."

Tom quickly turned to look at Charles. "I assume you're interested in the *Anasazi* people?"

Charles did not respond immediately. "Ah . . . yes. We are interested in only a piece of information left behind by the Anasazi."

"Only *a piece of information*?"

"Yes. Suffice it to say, only a piece."

"Oh? Well, it's been my experience that many people, especially archeologists, are quite interested in the Anasazi. The disappearance of the Anasazi people represents one of the greatest mysteries in archeology. For more than 10,000 years, the Anasazi people lived on the Colorado Plateau, then, *whish!*" He snapped his fingers.

A highway sign indicated they were approaching Winslow.

"Looks like we're getting close. Just a word of warning: The word '*Anasazi*' is a Navajo word, meaning 'Our enemy's ancestors.' The Navajos and Hopis were enemies at one time, and there seems to remain some animosity between the tribes. We need to play it safe, so, if we talk about the Ancestral Puebloans, please use the Hopi word '*Hisatsinom*' which means 'ancestors.'"

"Okay. Thanks for the warning." Charles repeated *Hisatsinom* several times under his breath. "Kind of a tongue twister."

"Good that I warned you. Sounds like you got it," Tom said. "As I was saying, the Anasazis—whoops, slip of the tongue!—I meant the Hisatsinom, were here for more than 10,000 years."

"Did they know those other Indian tribes in Mexico, Central America and South America?"

"You mean the Mayans and the Aztecs?"

"I don't remember their names."

"Well, it's interesting you ask. There is evidence of trade between the Ancestral Puebloans and the Mayans and the Aztecs. Before we *Pahanas* came here—white men—there seems to have been a vast system of commerce in these parts between tribes."

"What did they trade?"

Tom pinched his lower lip. "Well, with the Aztecs, you're asking? I think they traded chocolate, for one. Ya' see—here's an interesting thing, Charles—chocolate can only be grown near the Equator, where the Aztec lived."

"Interesting. But what did the Aztec want in return?"

"Oh, they got things like turquoise and silver, we have a lot of that stuff in these parts."

Tom quickly turned toward Elise, and said, "The Indians sell jewelry made with turquoise and silver. Would you like to go to a trading post to shop for some jewelry?"

But Elise was staring out the window, seemingly lost in her own world.

"No shopping, Tom. We're really here for a meeting," said Charles. "Our interests are quite specific."

Chapter 2

AT THREE THIRTY-SEVEN P.M. THEY CAME TO THE WINSLOW exit.

"Here's our turn," announced Tom.

"We're scheduled to meet someone at the Best Western. Do you know where that is?"

"Of course."

Tom drove the SUV to the Best Western parking lot, which was almost full. He found a spot next to a van with an accessible chair lift in the back. When Tom opened his door, he was hit by a blast of hot air.

"*Whew,* it's a hot one! Good thing they have air conditioning inside the hotel."

Charles and his wife got out of the vehicle and walked quickly toward the building. Tom followed at a leisurely pace, this time keeping a safe distance from them.

As he was about to enter the hotel, Tom saw a car driving into the parking lot. It was a black Mercedes Benz A-Class kicking-up dust. The car pulled into an empty spot near the entrance, and a middle-aged man stepped out. He had long black hair pulled back into a ponytail and wore a brown embroidered suit coat and a white felt cowboy hat.

The man brushed off his sleeves and adjusted the fit of his fancy suit; then, he went to the trunk and removed an aluminum briefcase. He walked briskly past Tom, who was standing near the hotel's entrance. Once inside, the newcomer removed his sunglasses and zeroed-in on Charles, who was talking to the hotel desk clerk.

Walking directly up to him, he said, "Charles Timoshenko, I presume?"

"Professor Day?"

The man smiled. "Please, call me Tim," he said, as he vigorously shook Charles's hand. "After so many emails, it's good to meet you in person finally!"

"Likewise, Tim. We just got here ourselves," said Charles, placing his arm around Elise's waist. "Tim, this is my wife, Elise."

"Pleased to meet you, Elise."

Smiling slightly, Elise extended a cold hand.

"The meeting is scheduled to start in just a few minutes," said Charles. "We'll be in the conference room, down this hall, to the left."

Tom, who had been standing off to the side, walked up to Charles.

"Excuse me, Mr. Timoshenko. While you're having your meeting, I'll be out in the parking lot and—"

Charles put his hand on Tom's shoulder.

"Hold on there, Tom—I don't want you going anywhere. I realize this may seem a bit awkward, but I want you to attend this meeting, too."

"You want *me* at your meeting? Ah, are you sure?" said Tom.

"We're meeting with several of the elder tribe leaders. As I mentioned when you came for us at the hotel, the chief specifically asked you be present."

"The chief . . . asked for me?"

"Yes, Hototo."

"Hototo is the *chief?*"

"Excuse me, Tom," interrupted Professor Day, "but we haven't met yet. I'm Tim Day from the University of Illinois. I've been in direct communication with Chief Hototo and The Little Bird Clan. His clan lives just west of here, near the crater."

"So, let me get this straight: Hototo is the chief of a clan—*of mixed-up tribes?*" said Tom, shaking his head. "And he wants me to sit in on this meeting?"

"Yes," said Charles. "Frankly, Tom, this is why we hired you. Hototo wants you at this meeting."

"Okay," said Tom, his mind racing. Perhaps he was to act as an intermediary, somewhat like a trader at an Indian trading post.

"I think I understand."

They walked into the hotel's conference room where four tables, two long and two short, were arranged in a rectangle. Three tribal statesmen, all of whom were quite elderly, were already seated at one of the long tables. A younger man in western dress was sitting at one of the short tables.

Charles, Elise, and the professor sat at the long table opposite the elders. Looking flustered, Tom took a seat facing the younger man whom he presumed was the translator.

The chief, Hototo, was seated in an electric wheelchair next to his two companions. In his mid-nineties, he had dark brown skin and high, prominent cheekbones. He wore a cap over his long white ponytail, and a heavy cotton plaid shirt and vest. His steady gaze took in each of the participants in the room. When his eyes reached Tom, he nodded and smiled.

"*Tikpia uala?*" [You've come?]

"*Kema,*" [Yes,] said Tom, grinning broadly.

Charles cleared his throat. "I want to thank the elders of The Little Bird Clan for allowing us to meet with you today. My name is Charles Timoshenko. To my right is Professor Timothy Day of the University of Illinois . . . and, to my left is my wife, Elise Timoshenko . . ."

Charles gestured toward Tom, ". . . and, this is Tom Johnson, whom some of you know. With these introductions, let me explain why we are here today."

He removed an envelope from his jacket pocket and held it in front of him.

"I have brought with me a letter from the President of the United States. This letter explains that Professor Day and myself are both advisors to the President on scientific matters."

He handed the letter to Tom. "Please pass this over to these gentlemen, Tom."

Staring at the presidential seal on the letter, Tom handed the letter to Hototo.

The elders each studied the letter, holding it up against the fluorescent lighting, examining the President's signature; then, they passed the document over to the translator. The translator slowly read aloud, translating each word into their native language.

Tom knew these men understood English perfectly well but was also aware they preferred to use their native language during tribal meetings and for matters of importance.

"This letter says you are members of the National Academy of Science. The elders would like to know what this means?" asked the translator, taking his cue from Hototo.

"The National Academy of Science is comprised of experts in various fields who advise the President," responded Charles. "My specialty is structural engineering. Professor Day's specialty is—"

"Ancestral Pueblo Archeology," interjected Professor Day.

"Thanks, Tim. Now, please explain exactly why we're here today."

"Let me begin with a bit of personal history," said Tim. "During the 1920s and '30s, my great grandfather, Joshua Day, owned a trading post on the Second Mesa. His store was located between the Hopi villages of *Shipaulovi* and *Mishongnovi*. He was a white man, as were all the traders in those days. It was there he met and, eventually, married my great grandmother, a Hopi woman, who was a member of the Bear Strap Clan. As a result of their marriage, I am proud to say I am one-eighth Hopi."

Tom noticed Professor Day had a slightly round face, a distinctive feature common among the Hopis.

"For the past few months, Chief Hototo and I have exchanged letters about a particular archeological artifact." The professor placed his metal briefcase on the table, directly in front of him.

"Inside this briefcase, I have brought with me something that, unfortunately, was taken from Native Americans by my great grandfather long ago. The artifact which I am about to show you has been in my family's possession the past eighty-five years."

Hearing this, one of the elders, a toothless man by the name of Chevoyo, became quite agitated.

"Stolen? Why bring it to us?"

An intense discussion between the elders developed, none of which Tom could follow.

Finally, the translator said, "As you can see, some of the elders are very disturbed by your admission of theft!"

"*Pah!*" interrupted Hototo.

The translator immediately stopped talking. The professor motioned for Tom to place the briefcase on the table in front of Hototo.

"You want me to open it, Profs?"

"Yes, if you would, Tom."

Tom unlatched the top of the briefcase and carefully raised the lid. Inside were three broken pieces of dried clay or mudstone. They were covered in faded red pictographs that depicted what appeared to be the sun or, perhaps, the stars.

Hototo and his two companions examined the artifacts and began talking loudly. Chevoyo grimaced angrily, shaking his head. Then, scraping back his chair, he stood up and hobbled out of the room, leaning heavily on a roughly-hewn cypress walking stick.

"We must wait here for Chevoyo to retrieve something from the van," explained the translator.

For several minutes, everyone sat quietly, waiting for Chevoyo. When he returned, he was carrying a hand-woven tribal blanket. Very carefully, Chevoyo placed the bundle on the table in front of Hototo and slowly unwrapped the blanket.

Inside was a large clay tablet with a missing corner.

Hototo whispered in the direction of the translator.

"What you are seeing is very sacred," said the translator. "No *pahana* has ever seen this before. But given the circumstances . . ."

This was the second time that day Tom had heard this expression, *"given the circumstances." What circumstances?*

The three elders began piecing together the broken sacred tablet pieces, as though they were solving a jigsaw puzzle. Very soon, the pieces fitted perfectly. Hototo motioned for everyone to come to his side of the table and see the re-assembled tablet.

Tom studied the imagery. The pictographs showed a crescent moon that was almost entirely eclipsed. There were three stars and a round object with a line trailing from it.

While the group studied the sacred tablet, Professor Day quickly took a photo with his cellphone. Fortunately, he had turned off the flash, and no one, except perhaps Tom, noticed.

Tom continued to study the round object with the mysterious line coming out of it.

"Is this an ancient record of Halley's Comet?" he asked.

"*Pah!*" said Hototo, frowning. He turned to Tom and said, in perfect English: "You don't understand! This tablet is not a *history* tablet! This tablet is a *prophesy* tablet! It is a prediction of our future!"

"So the ancients were predicting we will be seeing Halley's Comet again?"

Ignoring Tom's remark, Hototo turned to Charles. "Let's get directly to the point, Mr. Timoshenko. How much time do we have?"

"Only thirteen more days," replied Charles.

"We're seeing Halley's Comet in thirteen days?" asked Tom, confused.

Charles looked directly at Tom. "Forget about Halley's Comet, Tom. We're talking about an asteroid hitting the Earth in thirteen days."

Suddenly, Elise broke down in tears. She covered her ears with both hands, her face twisted in anguish. Without saying a word, Charles handed her a box of tissues that happened to be on the table.

Tom raised his eyebrows. *An asteroid? In thirteen days?*

Bypassing the translator, Charles spoke directly to Hototo.

"This tablet shows a geometrical formation. What were the Hisatsinom trying to tell us?"

Hototo studied the assembled tablet, lightly tracing a finger over the pictographs.

"This tablet shows an astronomical alignment, which you will be able to find during the lunar eclipse."

Professor Day looked at Charles. "Good, we're on the right track—that's what our people deduced."

"This is why we're here today," said Charles. "The lunar eclipse is tonight."

He looked at the elderly man sitting across from him.

"Chief Hototo, where do we find this astronomical alignment?"

"Tonight, you must go to Chaco Canyon. When you get there, go to the great kiva, Casa Rinconada. It is there, during the eclipse, you will find what you are looking for," said Hototo, slowly pulling himself up from his wheelchair.

"We must go now," he said abruptly.

With the help of the young translator, he stood up; then, shakily, he walked over to Professor Day, who was now standing next to Charles, and bowed slightly.

"It was good that you came. We forgive your ancestor."

"Thank you, Chief," said the professor, bowing in return. "We know his action has harmed your people and my people."

"Chief Hototo, you have been more than generous with your time and helpfulness," interjected Charles. "I just hope we find what we are looking for."

The chief grasped Charles's arm with both hands. Then he shuffled over to Elise, who was still sitting, with her head in her hands. Suddenly, she looked up, startled to see Hototo, peering down at her. Quickly, she scooted back her chair and stood up, facing Hototo, who reached for her trembling hands. She could feel the warmth of his grip as his gnarled fingers encircled hers. For a few seconds, he looked steadily into her reddened eyes.

"This is a long story we are in—and you are a principal player. Do not despair. The story has already been written."

Then, leaning on the arm of his translator, Hototo walked back to his red electric wheelchair. Once seated, he turned and raised his right hand, palm outward, as if in blessing. With the flick of a switch and a turn of the throttle, he drove out of the conference room, followed by the translator and the other elders.

"Do you know where Chaco Canyon is, Tom?" asked Charles.

Still stunned, Tom cleared his throat.

"Chaco Canyon? Yes, of course, I know where it is. It's in New Mexico, just across the state line."

Tom pursed his lips, considering his options. He had become uncomfortable around these people; they were, obviously, a part of a sci-fi cult! *Might as well play along.*

"Okay, everybody!" said Charles, "Let's go! We're running out of time!" He walked out of the hotel to the parking lot and the others followed. Seeing Elise was lagging behind, he stopped to wait for her.

"Are you okay?"

Elise nodded at her husband. "Yeah. Sorry I lost it."

"We're almost there, honey."

The professor meanwhile walked over to his Mercedes and opened the trunk, removing a large bag which he carried over to the Lincoln, putting it in the back.

"I brought this from Champaign-Urbana. It's a Meade 16-inch LX200 telescope, with the AutoStar II computer system."

"That's one powerful observatory telescope!"

"Of course. Nothing but the best!"

"Can't wait to use it—but we need to get out of here before we miss the lunar eclipse!"

They got back on Interstate 40 and drove east. It took almost two hours to reach Gallup, New Mexico, then another two hours of driving on rough, back roads, before they reached their destination: Chaco Canyon.

Tom said little along the way. In his twenty-four years as a tour guide, he had seen plenty of kooks coming to these parts, looking for space aliens. *All day long, he'd had suspicions about these weirdos!* However, he had to admit they had almost taken him in. They certainly acted legitimate. *A letter from the President! Good one!*

He decided to play along. Tom looked in the rearview mirror at Charles and smiled. "Okay, Charles, what's this about an asteroid hitting us in thirteen days? How long have you guys known about this?"

"We've known about the asteroid for almost ten years, Tom."

"Who are 'we'?"

"As I explained in the meeting, I am a member of the National Academy, an advisor to the President. Ten years ago, the asteroid was discovered by the satellite *New Horizons,* as it was leaving the solar system into the Oort Cloud."

The Oort Cloud?

"Most world governments have been alerted of this situation. There have been no public announcements—at least not yet."

No public announcements! Tom had to control himself from smirking.

"So, where is it hitting?"

"Based on our latest calculations, the asteroid will impact slightly to the west of Wichita, Kansas."

"Wichita, heh? And you say no one has warned them? Not even the mayor?"

Charles paused. "No, not yet, Tom. We plan to make an announcement next week. We expect there will be mass hysteria. . . . But it will be no use."

"Why would that be?"

"Let me put this in perspective, Tom. Remember today, what you said about the size of the asteroid that created Meteor Crater?"

"Well, yeah, sure. They say an asteroid fifty meters in diameter caused that. It was made of pure iron. So how big is the asteroid that will be hitting Wichita?"

"Tom, this asteroid is approximately one hundred miles in diameter. Not only will it destroy Wichita; it will destroy everything."

"Like all of Kansas?"

"No, like everything, Tom," Charles said. "This one is bigger than the one that caused the mass extinction of the dinosaurs. It will destroy us all."

"STOP IT!" screamed Elise. "I DON'T WANT TO HEAR ABOUT THIS ANYMORE!"

"I'm just trying to explain—"

"I SAID, STOP IT!"

Everyone became quiet.

~

When they arrived at Chaco Canyon, it was almost nine p.m. It was very dark because the moon was nearly fully eclipsed. There was a sign at the entrance, displaying Chaco Canyon was a national park; however, the gate was firmly locked.

A park ranger carrying a flashlight emerged from a small building next to the entrance gate. He approached the left side of the vehicle. Both Tom and Charles rolled down their windows.

"Hi, folks. I'm sorry to tell you we close the park at five p.m."

"Good evening, Ranger," said Charles. Then he handed him a letter.

"This letter explains our authority with the US government. Will you do us a favor and please call the number shown on the bottom?"

The ranger read the letter, and his eyes widened.

"Ah, yeah, sure. I see no problem with that.... Please wait here...."

"Thank you," said Charles.

The park ranger went inside the entrance kiosk. After nearly two minutes, he emerged with a stunned look on his face.

"Please proceed."

The ranger lifted the gate allowing their vehicle to pass.

"Charles, do you mind if I ask, who did the ranger call?" asked Tom.

"He just talked to the White House, Tom."

Tom stopped the car abruptly and looked back at Charles.

"The White House?"

"Yes, the President, Tom. Please, we must continue! We're running out of time!"

As they drove into the park, Professor Day studied a map showing the layout of the site.

"Okay, we're getting close. Casa Rinconada is coming up on the left in just a few hundred feet."

As soon as they reached the parking lot, they clambered out of the SUV. The professor retrieved the bag holding the telescope from the back of the vehicle.

Charles began walking at a brisk pace in the direction of the kiva. The gravel path was hard under-foot, and several steep rises made the half-mile trek no easy undertaking.

"Hurry! We need to set up fast. Look at the moon!"

"We must look for the star pattern shown in the pictograph from Casa Rinconada when the lunar eclipse occurs," panted Tim, struggling under the weight of the telescope. "We will have only a few hours. After that, we've lost our window of opportunity."

Tom looked up at the moon; it was almost entirely red. The lunar eclipse was about to happen.

They continued making their way toward Casa Rinconada. Set on a hill, half-sunk into the Earth, the vast structure was the largest of six kivas in the Chaco Canyon; it would have served as the civic and ceremonial center for nearby villages.

Tom pointed at the dark interior of the kiva.

"You going down there?"

The professor paused, wiping the sweat from his forehead with the back of his hand.

"No. This kiva had a roof at one time. People couldn't see the sky from inside the building. Let's set up the 'scope here."

Tom looked up at the sky.

"There are so many stars. Which ones are you looking for?"

Ignoring Tom's question, Professor Day removed the telescope from its case and began setting it up on its tripod. Meanwhile, Charles Timoshenko sat on a crumbling stone wall, with his laptop.

"I'm booting-up—have to use my cell phone as a hot spot. Are you about set up?"

"Yes, just about," said Tim. He finished assembling the telescope, then adjusted the tripod legs. A few minutes later, he said, "Okay, I'm ready. Please interface with the laptop."

"Will do," said Charles. "Okay. I've made the connection to the telescope. I'm retrieving the coordinates . . . now I'm pasting the coordinates into the telescope controls . . . I'm about to press 'Proceed.' Are you ready?"

"Yes—as ready as I'll ever be. Please proceed!"

The telescope slowly moved into position, then it stopped.

Charles closed the laptop and hurried over toward the telescope. Tom watched in confusion; instead of looking into the eyepiece, Charles was looking along the shaft of the telescope.

"It's really dark, Tim. I'm afraid I can't make out any rock formations," he said.

"Don't worry—the important thing is we got a fix on the coordinates. Frankly, I was worried we would miss the window."

"Me, too," replied Charles. "We'll get some more light once the moon gets out of the Earth's shadow."

Patiently, they waited until the light of the moon became brighter. Elise stood close by, shivering, as she watched her husband look down the shaft of the telescope again. Suddenly, he motioned to the professor to join him.

"Yes, I think we have a winner! Come over here and take a look!"

The professor looked along the telescope shaft. Charles asked, "You see them? The three stars, all lined-up with the tops of three different rock structures over there."

The professor took out his cell phone and looked at the photo of the pictograph head he had snapped at the hotel.

"It's a match! Tom, Elise, come over here and take a look!"

Tom looked down the shaft of the telescope, still not sure what he was supposed to see.

"See it?" asked Tim. "Those rock structures in the distance have been purposely arranged to align with this star configuration during the lunar eclipse!"

It was true. The three stars appeared to be in the same position as in the ancient pictograph, but Tom had no idea what this meant or why the others were so excited.

Elise was shaking. She looked down the shaft for nearly a minute. Finally, she spoke. "This proves it, doesn't it, Charles?"

Charles nodded and smiled, hugging Elise. "Yes, this proves it."

Tom was baffled.

"I'm not following you guys. What are you looking for?"

"We think this is a marker left by the Anasazi identifying Planet K851b," explained Charles.

"Planet K8 . . . *what?*"

"Sorry, Tom, but it would take too long to explain. Basically, we've just proven thousands of years ago, the Anasazi knew of the existence of a specific Earth-like planet located twenty-three light-years from Earth."

Elise was smiling as she continued to cling to her husband. "It's true! It's actually true!"

"I'm still not following," said Tom, baffled.

Charles wiped the sweat from his forehead.

"Tom, there isn't any point in keeping this a secret. There is a highly classified mission to save the human race from extinction by the impending asteroid."

Tom grimaced.

"I'm sensing your disbelief, Tom. I'd probably feel the same if I were in your position. Suffice it to say, four years ago, a manned space expedition was sent to Planet K851b to re-establish human civilization."

Okay—this is simply too much! thought Tom. *No more smiling, no more making small talk.* He was tired and just wanted to go home and never see these people again for the rest of his life.

They left Chaco Canyon, ready now for the long drive back to Arizona. Tom was quiet the entire time, as he chauffeured the professor back to Winslow and the Timoshenkos back to Sedona. By the time he got home, it was three thirty-seven a.m., and he was exhausted.

He could not sleep the entire night. They really had him fooled! They had the old Indian, Hototo, fooled, too! The letter, *from the President of the United States*—come on! Good one! Nice touch—it seemed so authentic!

Still, they seemed so believable.

In the morning, Tom made his coffee and ate breakfast. He would need to return the Lincoln to the rental agency when it opened at nine a.m.

He couldn't stop thinking about the unthinkable: *What if they were right, what if there were only thirteen days left! If their crazy story was true, what options did he have? Could he escape? Was Canada far enough?*

He decided the best option was to assume he had thirteen days left to live. He would take a two-week vacation. If an asteroid did not hit, great—he'd go back to work, resume his life, everything back to normal, no damage done.

Then he began thinking about his sons: *What were Jeff and Tom like? What were they doing? What did they look like? Did they live in Rockford? Was Donna still there? Had she remarried?*

At eight-thirty a.m., he called his boss.

"Hey Greg," Tom said. "Something's come-up. An emergency back home. I'm gonna' need to take a few days off."

"Can't this wait, Tom? I've scheduled you to give a tour of the Grand Canyon tomorrow!"

"Sorry, Greg. This is nonnegotiable. Marty can do it—he's retired, but he can still handle Grand Canyon tours. I'm afraid I have to leave."

And with that, Tom disconnected the call.

Part II: Planet K851b, 80,000 years in the future

Chapter 3

JANU COULD SEE FAINT VAPORS COMING FROM BEHIND THE corner of the building; there was a putrid smell that made him want to gag. The creature must be positioning for an attack, he told himself. Cautiously, Janu grabbed his helmet microphone and cupped his right hand over his mouthpiece. As quietly as possible, he messaged Steven: "Got a fix at ten o'clock." Flattening his body against the wall, he waited, listening through his headphones for Steven's response.

Finally, he heard him, but he couldn't make out the words.

"*Ah, Jay, . . . (noise) . . . Jay, . . . you're not coming in . . . (noise) . . . Can you repeat?*"

"I said ten o'clock!" Janu repeated, worried the Gorgonops might hear. "*Repeat—repeat, at ten o'clock!*"

"*Still can't copy . . . (noise) . . .*"

"*Verdamndt!*" Janu cursed under his breath.

Only twenty feet away lay the prize: the Golden Urn. It was so close he could almost touch it, but he was boxed in on all sides by the herd of Gorgonops, gigantic carnivorous reptiles! *Where the hell was Steven? What had happened to him?*

Then he saw a glint of gold, the sun's reflection bouncing off Steven's armor. He was on the other side of the street, crouched behind a brick wall. Janu watched as Steve inched his way forward, on his stomach, firmly gripping his machine gun, guerilla-style.

Suddenly, Steven rolled out from behind the wall, machine gun blazing, shooting full throttle from a crouched position at the creature. Aiming for the big alpha male's tiny brain, he fired at least twenty rounds; then he staggered to his feet and switched firing positions, aiming low, from the hip, screaming Rambo style, "*Yahhhhh!*" The bullets rattled into the massive reptile's hide, leaving a trail of bloody holes, from its shoulder to its head—until, *click, click, click*, the barrel was empty!

"*Verdamndt!*" Steve cursed.

Out of bullets and out of options, Steven looked directly at his comrade Janu, screaming, "Jay! Help! Out of ammo!"

By now, the entire herd of Gorgonops was on alert. At least thirty of them, each the size of a rhinoceros, lumbered in the direction of Janu and Steve. The alpha male, bleeding profusely, snorted loudly, signaling the herd to attack.

"Jay! Help—*now!*" Steve yelled.

Cautiously, Janu edged his way toward Steve until he was close enough to toss him his extra ammo belt. Perhaps a combined assault might turn the herd back. Taking a deep breath, Janu darted into the street only to trip and fall to the ground.

Suddenly, there was a loud squawk from a loudspeaker. "Janu—are you okay? *Ah*, sorry guys, but I think somebody from the last group left their shirt on the floor!" The store owner, Michael, came running out of the control booth and entered the virtual reality game room. He picked up the shirt.

"Wow, I'm really sorry about this, guys! We can start over if you want."

"Nah, we gotta' get going, anyway, Mikey," said Janu as he removed the virtual reality goggles, transporting himself from a colorful virtual world back to the real world: the Virtual Reality Game Room located inside Supercomputer Building 1. The room was constructed of plasticized fern particle boards, ramps, and walls, which matched the geometry of the virtual world.

The Game Room had become very popular with kids in New Munich, with various shoot-out games, such as "*Gorgonops Attack,*" "*Shoot-out at the OK Corral,*" "*War of the Worlds,*" and "*King Kong versus Godzilla.*" Each game required a complex configuration of ramps and walls that matched the virtual reality world. This task kept Michael, the game room operator, always busy moving the props around between games.

Janu and Steve were sixteen years old. They referred to themselves as "cousins," although, technically, they weren't physically related. Janu, who had been conceived by parents in Greece, had been adopted by Horst and

Ingrid Apoteker, on this planet twenty-three light-years from Earth; Steve's father was the son of Horst and Ingrid. Technically, that qualified Janu as Steve's adopted uncle!

"Jay, we gotta' get going," said Steve. "The new cadet ceremony is at one p.m."

"Plenty of time," said Janu.

The two boys left the Supercomputer Building 1, walking down the *Haupt Straße*—the Main Street—of New Munich, toward the bridge that crossed the river into the American Sector. New Munich—or *Neu Munchen,* as the Germans called it—had grown to a community of about 1,200 people since the first spaceship carrying robots and frozen embryos landed on Planet K851b some seventy-five years earlier.

The idea of colonizing a planet using frozen embryos to be birthed and raised by robots originated as a wild thought experiment between two friends, over 80,000 years ago. Charles Timoshenko and Frank Erbstoesser were quite surprised when the US and German governments adopted their idea. It was a last-ditch effort to save humanity from extinction because an enormous renegade asteroid was about to hit the Earth.

The mission, code-named the *When Worlds Collide Plan*, involved sending three rockets to Planet K851b. The rocket ships landed at three sites: the "New Munich" site, which would be colonized by German people, the descendants of sixty frozen embryos; the "New Eden" site, destined to be inhabited by American people, also descendants of sixty frozen embryos; and the "Einstein-Newton" site, which would be under the control of robots that had been programmed to manufacture necessities for the human population.

For the most part, the entire mission went without a glitch: After landing, the pioneer robots constructed the shelters and infrastructure required for raising the humans. Once the two settlements were ready, the robots gestated the frozen embryos, using German-made "birthing" machines. The embryos were gestated in groups of fifteen called "Thaws," and the members of a Thaw shared the same birthday. There was a five-year difference in age between consecutive Thaw groups.

From the day they were born, the young Thaws lived somewhat predictable lives. From an early age, they worked hard, tending fields, feeding livestock, making hand-made items for everyday living, and attending school. Before turning sixteen years old, they were completely unaware of the strange circumstances of their existence. However, their lives changed abruptly on their sixteenth birthday, when they learned the "people" raising them were actually robots and they themselves came from a distant planet called "Earth." Hearing this news was as shocking to them as it must have been for the young Clark Kent when he learned he was from the planet Krypton.

To fulfill their Earth-mandated mission, the American Thaws, at the age of twenty-one, traveled the 1,067-mile distance from New Eden to New Munich, to combine the two communities. It was a hazardous journey, for although Planet K851b had a similar atmosphere to Earth's, it was hundreds of millennia behind Earth in terms of its geological development. Along the way, there were constant threats from hostile species such as giant scorpions and dragonflies, as well as from terrifying reptile predators like Dimetrodon and Gorgonops. Unfortunately, the first two groups—the First and Second Thaws—were killed along the way. The Third Thaws succeeded in making the journey to New Munich, except for one casualty who was attacked by a monstrous placoderm fish; five years later, the Fourth Thaws also completed the trek but lost several people to attacks by wildlife.

~

New Munich had two different sectors separated by a river: the Deutsch-speaking German Sector and the English-speaking American Sector. Both Janu and Steve lived in the American Sector, although they went to high school with the Germans in the German Sector.

Alternately jogging and sprinting, the boys quickly arrived at the bridge, a remarkable engineering achievement called a "Jawerth" suspension bridge. They stopped near the center of its two-hundred-foot span and looked down into the river. As usual, they took turns spitting over the railing, counting the seconds it took for their lugers to hit the water.

Looking down, Steve saw a massive creature, swimming toward the bridge.

"Jay, look," he said, pointing at a fin piercing the surface. "You see that?"

"*Mein Gott!*" replied Janu, "Look at the size of that fish! It must be thirty feet long!"

"Yeah, I've heard about this type of fish before," said Steve, whistling under his breath. "It was a monster like this that killed a man when my parents came here. Gobbled him up in one bite."

"*Mein Gott!* What a way to die!"

Planet K851b was a perfect planet to restart modern civilization: It was about the same size as Earth; it had nearly the same gravity; there was plenty of water; and, like Earth, it had a magnetic field shielding life from harmful solar rays. There was one major difference from Earth: the sky was orange instead of blue.

Perhaps most interesting of all, the plants and animals found on this planet were similar to those found during prehistoric times on Earth. For example, the "big fish" Steve and Janu had just seen in the river was the equivalent of a thirty-foot-long fish called Dunkleosteus, which had lived during the Devonian Period on Earth.

Janu and Steve continued walking across the bridge, into the American Sector. They were not late, so they slowed their pace when they reached Chicago Street. It was springtime—almost summer—and the Earth trees and flowers that lined the streets were blooming. School was finally out, and they had the whole summer ahead, except for one thing: Cadet Basic Training, which would last six weeks.

It did not take them long to come to the American Club at the end of Chicago Street, where the ceremony was taking place. The parking lot was filled with horses and buggies, and there were also a few of the new electric cars, which had recently appeared around New Munich.

Janu walked directly to one of the electric cars. It looked a lot like a regular buggy, which was pulled by horses, but this one didn't have a buggy shaft.

Steve whistled and touched the car. "Nice. What is it?"

Janu said, "This is my dad's buggy. He bought it a few weeks ago."

"It looks like a buggy."

"Yeah, it's called a 'horseless buggy.' It has an electric battery and a motor—no need for a horse."

"Has he let you drive it?" asked Steve.

"Not yet, he says he'll let me when I turn sixteen."

"That's next week."

Janu smiled and nodded. "Yes, sir . . . next week. I can hardly wait!"

They walked to the entrance of the American Club building and opened the door. The room was crowded with the parents and siblings of the teenagers who were going to be inducted as the American Cadets.

Looking at the stage, Janu saw it was already filled with his American high school classmates, sitting three lines deep on bleachers. Though he couldn't see them, he knew his father, Horst Apoteker, and his friend, Adam Timoshenko, would be standing in the wings. They would soon be coming out on stage to direct the ceremony.

Hurrying up the steps leading to the stage, Janu disappeared behind the curtains and walked up to his father and Adam, with Steve tagging close behind.

"*Hallo, Vater und Herr Timoshenko!*"

"Hallo, Janu and Steve—you two had better take your seats," said Captain Horst, sternly. "Come on, Adam, let's roll."

Steve grabbed Janu's arm.

"*Entshuldigen* [Excuse me], Janu, we must hurry! It's about to start!"

Janu's father, Horst Apoteker, was the captain of the Third Thaw cadet group—the first of the Thaws to complete the treacherous journey from New Eden to New Munich. Once a year, he and Adam Timoshenko put on their uniforms for the Cadet Induction Ceremony: the same uniforms they had been given in New Eden, forty years ago, which were now faded and somewhat tight. At these ceremonies, Horst was, again, recognized as "Captain Horst" Apoteker; similarly, Adam was "Lieutenant Adam," a title that reflected his official rank in the Third Thaw cadet group. Both men were now in their sixties, which made them the "Elders/Wise-Old-Men" in the community.

Janu and Steve dashed onto the stage. The only available spots were at the end of the third bleacher row, almost behind the curtains. Mouthing their apologies, they pushed their way across the bleachers, stepping between the other students' knees. Once seated, Janu was happy to see the Russian girl, Olga, in the front row. Shielding his eyes from the bright lights shining on the stage, he looked into the audience. He saw his *Mutti* [mother], Ingrid, sitting in the fourth row, and waved excitedly.

Steve's parents owned the local television station in New Munich. His father was standing behind a large television camera, filming the event for the local television station news. Steve waved, trying to catch his attention, but his father was making final adjustments to his camera settings.

When it was time to begin the ceremony, Captain Horst and Lieutenant Adam walked from stage left. Horst, a tall man with greying hair, strolled toward the podium, carrying a folder. At one time, he had been confined to a wheelchair, caused by an attack by a bull elephant, leaving him paralyzed from the waist down. Thanks to nano-surgery, performed by his wife, *Arztin* [Dr.] Ingrid, and the "Genius" supercomputer, Horst had regained the use of his legs, although he could no longer move as quickly as before the accident.

The audience began to quiet down. Smiling, Horst looked around the room, holding his hand above his eyes to shield them from the flare lights; then he looked back at the new inductees and waved, giving them the "thumbs-up."

As was the proper custom, he began his address with a Deutsch greeting:

"*Wilkommen Americaners!* Welcome, everyone! We are here today to swear-in a new group of young men and women into the American Cadets. They have reached the age of sixteen."

He stopped briefly, shaking his head.

"I can remember clearly when my group, *the Third Thaws,* were sworn-in as American Cadets. And you know what? We were clueless!"

The entire audience broke into laughter, and there were giggles from the bleachers.

"Yes, you can laugh, but, honestly, we were *completely* clueless!" continued Horst. "You see, we had just learned the people who were raising us—the Guardians—were robots!"

Again, the entire audience broke into laughter, so familiar with this story they never tired of hearing.

"Wow! I mean, what a shock that was!" said Horst, looking around the audience, grinning.

"The older people here—the 'Thaws'—remember the Guardians, of course, because they took care of us, just like parents would have done. There were no 'married Guardians'; we didn't call them 'Mom' or 'Dad', we called them by their first names. Imagine our shock. Robots! Wow!"

He paused, as the room erupted in laughter, yet again, not because Horst was sharing some new revelation but because this was an occasion to celebrate. Everyone knew about the Guardians; everyone knew without them, the mission to colonize Planet K851b would have failed.

"Well, today's cadets are an exceptional group," he continued, turning toward the inductees, then back to the audience.

"I'm a Thaw, which is somewhat unique, right? And, for all these years, I've been inducting new cadets who were born the 'regular way,'" he said, making quotation signs with his fingers. "As a matter of fact, I've never inducted a single cadet who came to the planet as a frozen embryo. That's always made me kind of jealous!"

Once again, the audience laughed appreciatively.

"Yes, I've been kind of jealous of all these 'naturally born' kids, but today I'm about to induct an extraordinary group of young adults, some of whom were also thawed!"

Horst peered into the audience, holding his right hand above his eyes.

"I'm looking for Anastasia. Has anyone seen Anastasia?"

Several rows back from the stage, a beautiful blonde-haired woman in a green dress rose to her feet and signaled to Horst.

"Yoo-hoo, I'm right here, Horst . . . you didn't lose me!"

Everyone laughed.

"Anastasia, please join me on the stage."

As Anastasia made her way down the center aisle, everyone clapped. She was a popular figure in New Munich and had done much to serve the community. When she reached Captain Horst, they greeted each other with a quick kiss on each cheek, European style.

"As we all know," said Horst, "seventeen years ago, Anastasia arrived on this planet in a Russian spacecraft. She didn't speak a word of English or Deutsch; in fact, she didn't remember anything about her former life. Isn't that right, Anastasia?"

Anastasia nodded and spoke into the microphone.

"That's right, Horst. As you say, I, too, was clueless!"

More laughter.

"When the Russian spacecraft landed at the Einstein-Newton site, it carried many frozen embryos. How many do you think there were, Anastasia?"

Anastasia bent toward the microphone again.

"One hundred embryos, Horst."

"And from what countries did these embryos come?"

"Well, there were many countries which donated embryos. Most of the embryos were Russian, of course. There were also embryos from many other countries."

"Like where? Please, I never get tired of hearing about this!"

More laughter.

"Well, let me see . . . we now have children from Russia, Ukraine, Turkey, France, Greece . . . ah, let me see—oh yes, let's not forget India, China, Iraq. . . . Hmm, I almost forgot one from the island of Malta."

"Amazing! The small country of Malta!" said Horst. "And tell me, Anastasia, how many of those children have you carried as a surrogate mother?"

Anastasia laughed. "Twelve children, over the past fifteen years!"

Everyone clapped. There were even a few catcalls from the audience which the kids on the bleachers tried to imitate.

Anastasia leaned into the microphone. "I think I'm about to retire! I am happy to say many other women have also acted as surrogates. Of the one hundred embryos, fifty have already been born, and I am proud to say that some of them are with us today!"

Horst turned toward the new inductees.

"Will those of you who were frozen embryos please stand up."

Hesitantly, Janu stood up, along with Olga, the Russian girl, Marek, the Polish boy, and Reem, the girl from Iraq. The remainder of the teenagers, including Steve, remained seated because they had been born the natural "old-fashioned" way.

"Thank you!" said Horst. "Perhaps we should call you people the Fifth Thaw!"

This comment received more laughter from the audience, some of whom were now standing to get a better view.

"Okay, everyone, please be seated," said Horst. "Thank you, Anastasia!" She walked down the stage steps back to her seat, waving and shaking hands along the way.

Horst then turned to address the youth on the bleachers. They were typical of other cadets: bright, high-spirited, mostly respectful, but somewhat emotionally immature. They had so much to learn, but would inevitably have a tough time with discipline.

"As new cadets, you will be trained to explore and survive in the wilderness. You will learn the same survival skills the Third Thaw used on our 1,000-mile journey to this place. It was not all fun and games and camping out in the wild. The wilderness is a dangerous place. Just outside of New Munich, just past the perimeter guarded by dogs, there are all sorts of dangerous animals. When the Third Thaw journeyed from New Eden to New Munich, we encountered giant reptiles, amphibians, scorpions, spiders, and giant man-eating fish. You will be learning about these animals and how to protect yourselves from them.

"There were other expeditions from New Eden before the Third Thaws made it. Unfortunately, all of them, except for Farmer Jim and Mary, perished when their raft went over a waterfall. We, too, almost died going over the same waterfall! There is so much to share with you—I could stand here for hours reminiscing about all the dangerous situations we encountered. Sadly, we lost one man named Gerald—*God Bless his soul*—who was eaten alive by a huge fish!"

Hearing this, Janu whispered to Steve, "See . . . I was right!"

"For you to survive in the wild, your group must act as a unit," said Horst. "This means you will eventually be ranked according to a military chain of command. Some of you will be promoted. One of you will become the captain of your group. You will learn to respect your captain and follow orders."

Discreetly, Janu looked from the corner of his eyes at the other inductees. Would they expect him to be like his father, to become the captain of his group? Was he "leader material"?

Horst continued, "It has been forty years since we made the long journey to New Munich. Today, those of us of the Third Thaw are now Elders."

He stopped to survey the group of new cadets.

"As hard to believe as this may sound, someday you, too, will become Elders.

"This is life: it keeps going and going and never stops." Then, somewhat quietly, he added, "Life never stops . . . *except for us individually*, while the rest go on."

Janu grimaced. *Wasn't this going too far? Was his dad still sad about his friend, Gerald, who had been eaten by a fish?*

Captain Horst stepped away from the podium to exchange a few words with Lieutenant Adam. The Lieutenant walked to the edge of the stage, quickly returning with a stack of green uniforms. He passed them to an inductee in the first row, who began distributing the uniforms to all the inductees.

Thanking Adam, Horst turned once more to face the cadets, who were now holding their neatly folded uniforms.

"You have each received your new cadet uniform," said Horst. "You will be required to wear your uniform every time we meet. You will be required to keep these uniforms clean for our daily inspections.

"Beginning tomorrow at six a.m., you are expected to be here. For the next six weeks, from Monday through Friday, you will receive your basic training for eight hours a day."

Horst paused to take a sip of water.

"Okay, everyone, it's time to take your pledge. Please raise your right hand and place it over your heart, like I'm doing."

Horst placed his right hand over his heart. The inductees placed their right hands on their chests; a few of them whispered and joked, but most of the group seemed aware of the solemnity of the occasion.

"In this part of the program, we will be reciting The Pledge of Allegiance, using the original words from 1892. Every cadet from New Eden and the American Sector has recited this pledge before you. We do this out of respect for the American Planners of The Mission, whose vision and self-sacrifice made our lives possible here.

"Now, repeat after me: *I pledge allegiance . . .*" said Horst while holding his right hand over his heart.

"*I pledge allegiance . . .*" repeated the inductees, together with some members of the audience.

"*. . . to my flag and the Republic for which it stands—One nation, indivisible—with liberty and justice for all.*"

It was like reading words from an old book, like reading Shakespeare. Horst had said this pledge so many times, he said it automatically, without thinking, but many times he wondered about the meaning of the words. *What was America? What was it really like?*

"Congratulations!" declared Horst, once they finished reciting The Pledge of Allegiance. "You are now American Cadets!"

The next day basic training would begin.

Chapter 4

THE NEXT MORNING, JANU WOKE UP AT FIVE A.M., MUCH earlier than during the school year. Still groggy, he forced himself out of bed, going downstairs in his pajamas to make his usual breakfast of muesli and toast with jam. When he reached the kitchen, he was surprised to see his mother sitting at the table, sipping her coffee, already dressed for work.

"*Guten Morgen!*" said Ingrid, who was wearing her white physician's uniform. Ingrid was a Captain Practitioner at the *Krankenhaus*.

"*Guten Morgen, Mutti,*" replied Janu. "Do you always get up this early on weekdays?"

Lifting a large enamel canister off the kitchen counter, he scooped a generous amount of muesli into a cereal bowl, topped it with milk from the refrigerator, and joined her at the table.

"Well, normally, I don't. Today they needed somebody in the Emergency Department. *Arztin* Erica has the flu—I'm covering for her."

"Will *Vater* be at basic training this morning?"

"No, I doubt it," said Ingrid, placing her empty coffee mug on the table. "He usually only goes to the Cadet ceremonies. Did you notice how his old uniform is falling apart? One of these ceremonies, I expect the pants will split in front of the parents!"

Smiling, she paused for a moment, then tapped her index finger against pursed lips.

"Oh, I almost forgot—*Vater* is having his annual physical today."

"Oh, are you giving the physical?" asked Janu, looking at her slyly.

"Don't be funny, Janu! Married physicians don't examine their spouses! No, I believe *Vater* is seeing *Arztin* Karl."

She looked at her watch. "*Ich zu spät. Ich musse gehen!*" [I'm late, I must go!]

She leaned over and kissed Janu on his forehead.

"*Ich liebe dich!*" [I love you!]

"Yeah, Mom," replied Janu. "See you later."

Janu finished breakfast, stacked the dirty plates in the kitchen sink, and then headed back to his room. After taking a quick shower, he put on his new green uniform and a pair of new black "Cadet regulation" patent leather shoes. He looked at himself in the mirror, carefully parting his black hair to the side. Janu had bushy eyebrows, which were growing together into a unibrow. Compared to his friends, he was quite hairy. For the past two years, he had been shaving on Saturday mornings, but he was beginning to think he needed to shave more frequently. Carefully examining his stubble in the mirror, he decided to shave, even though it wasn't his regular shaving day.

It was still dark outside when Janu left the house. In an hour, the roosters would be crowing all over New Munich, waking up the townsfolk. For the cadets, however, training would be starting in fifteen minutes; fortunately, there was still plenty of time to walk to the American Club.

The Apoteker family lived in a two-story house on Abbey Road. Like most of the homes in the American Sector, their house was designed in the Prairie Style, based on Frank Lloyd Wright's architecture.

The American Sector, established by the Third Thaws, was almost twenty years old. The land on this side of the river was, at one time, covered in prehistoric ferns; now, Earth trees and shrubs flourished there, while flowers, oaks, maple trees, apple trees, and cherry trees lined the streets. Bees from Earth thrived within the city limits, pollinating the flowers and the fruit trees.

Janu walked at a steady pace along Abbey Road, then turned left on Penny Lane for two blocks, until he reached the main thoroughfare, Chicago Street. Soon he saw several other cadets converging in the direction of the American Club, including the red-haired Russian girl, Olga. Despite her freckles, she was becoming quite beautiful. Standing five feet four inches tall, with long wavy hair, heart-shaped lips, and deep-set eyes, she was lean and athletic. In fact, she was the fastest female sprinter on New Munich High's track team.

Breaking into a run, Janu caught up with Olga, stood at attention, and saluted her, thrusting out his chest like a soldier on parade.

"*Guten Morgen,* Olga!"

"*Ja, Guten Morgen,* Jay!" she laughed, saluting him in turn.

"Marching time!" said Janu, swinging his hands high while he set off with exaggerated steps.

Olga mimicked him, swinging her hands even higher, walking faster until she caught up with him. Then they marched together, taking longer steps until they broke into a run. Finally, they stopped, convulsed with laughter.

"You are so weird, Jay!"

"You're the weird one," said Janu, laughing. "Isn't it too early to be goofing around, wasting energy? We'll probably be doing a lot of exercises today."

Olga reached out and messed-up Janu's hair.

"You are so weird," she repeated, smiling affectionately.

Janu's cheeks burned.

"Well, we were both frozen embryos, so should we call ourselves 'The Fifth Thaw?'" he asked, half-jokingly.

"I don't get it," replied Olga. "I mean, I've heard about 'The Third Thaw,' but was there a 'Fourth Thaw?'"

"I don't know. Maybe."

"We'd better run," said Olga. "Only five more minutes!"

She sprinted off in an impromptu hundred-yard dash to the American Club Building. Delayed at the starting block, Janu chased after her. Though he was a respectable sprinter, he was no match for Olga's blazing speed.

At the entrance, Olga pivoted, hands clasped above her head.

"And the crowd goes wild! Once again, the winner!"

"Maybe we should try another form of competition, like weight lifting," objected Jay who was now leaning against the doorway, panting heavily.

"Ha, ha, very funny. Come on, let's go inside."

Janu followed Olga into the American Club. Once inside, he saw the stage curtains were drawn, concealing the podium where his father had stood during the induction ceremony. Sixteen chairs now faced a blank chalkboard, awaiting the new cadets who were casually milling around, talking to each other. Seeing his cousin, Steve, Janu walked over to greet him, momentarily forgetting about Olga.

Promptly, at six a.m., the door burst open, and two men entered the room—Fredric Timoshenko and Max Baumeister, who were both in their late twenties. Janu had known them his entire life; his father, Horst Apoteker, was best friends with their fathers, Adam Timoshenko and Hansel Baumeister. Fredric looked a lot like Lieutenant Adam. Tall and lanky, he was about five foot ten and had dark brown hair. His glasses, tortoiseshell frames with rectangular lenses, gave him a studious appearance. In contrast, Max Baumeister was a solidly built man who worked construction. About an inch shorter than Fredric, Max had blond hair, which he wore in a short crew cut; he was beginning to show signs of balding.

Since he was a little kid, Janu had clowned around with Fredric and Max, but, judging by the serious expressions on their faces, he realized today wasn't about fun and games.

"EVERYONE SEPARATE! MEN ON MY RIGHT, WOMEN ON MY LEFT!" Fredric shouted.

The cadets quickly separated into two evenly numbered groups of ten each. There was some jostling and murmuring as they did so. Janu exchanged amused expressions with Steve, who was still standing next to him. Looking over at Olga, he tried to catch her attention, but she was whispering to Reem, the girl from Iraq.

"CADETS, THERE WILL BE NO TALKING! STAND AT ATTENTION!" bellowed Max.

With perfect timing, the entrance doors opened, and Lieutenant Adam Timoshenko walked into the room. He went directly to the front of the room, where both Fredric and Max were standing at attention, saluting him.

The lieutenant returned the salute.

"At ease, Sergeants!"

Sergeants Fredric and Max relaxed, standing with their feet apart, clasping their hands behind their backs and looking straight ahead.

Lieutenant Timoshenko looked at the recruits and said, in a booming voice, "*Guten Morgen, Cadets!*"

"*Guten Morgen!*" came the weak response.

"I think we'll need to work on that," said Lieutenant Timoshenko. "You're a unit, so you need to act like a unit! I need to hear more volume! Let's try again. *Guten Morgen, Cadets!*"

This time, everyone answered loudly, in unison.

"*Danke! Ja, das ist besser!*" [Thank you! Yes, that is better!]

"Let's begin by introducing your sergeants, Sergeant Fredric and Sergeant Max."

Fredric Timoshenko and Max Baumeister stepped forward and snapped to attention.

"At ease, men!"

"YES, SIR!"

"A few ground rules," continued the lieutenant, looking steadily at the cadets. "When you are in this building, you are in a military unit, and you must follow the orders of your sergeants. Is that clear?"

"YES, SIR!"

"For the next two weeks, Sergeant Max will be training the girls' group, and Sergeant Fredric will train the boys' group. After two weeks, they will switch.

"You will be trained both physically and mentally. You will be trained hard, and you will become stronger. You will be trained to survive in the wilderness. You will be trained in the art of how to protect yourselves. You will learn how to use weapons. . . ."

When Janu heard "weapons" mentioned, he looked at Steve and smiled.

"You will learn what plants and animals are safe to eat."

The lieutenant walked over to a rolled-up screen hanging on the wall behind him, and pulled it down, displaying the drawing of a creature with a fin on its back.

"The drawings I am showing you depict just a few of the animals we encountered on our long journey to New Munich as The Third Thaw. This creature behind me, cadets, is what we call a Sail-Back. We were threatened by these creatures multiple times. They are dangerous. They look like dinosaurs, but they're reptiles—aggressive reptiles. They resemble a prehistoric Earth animal called a Dimetrodon which lived about 300 million years ago. If you run across one of these, they're hard to kill with bullets, unless you're lucky and hit their tiny brains. We were able to kill them with axes."

The cadets sat in awe, exchanging wide-eyed looks. The Sail-Backs were the real thing, *real* monsters, not the fake virtual reality monsters they encountered in computer games.

The lieutenant moved to another screen. This one showed a drawing of a massive insect.

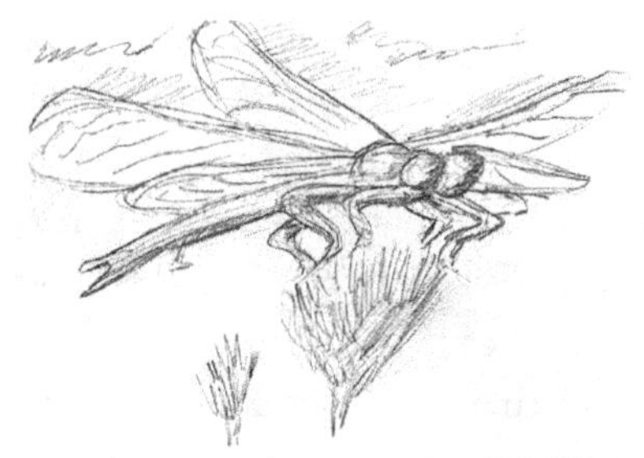

"This drawing depicts a giant dragonfly. We encountered insects like these several times. You might be asking yourself, '*What's the big deal? It's just a bug.*' Well, these 'bugs' have a three-foot wingspan, and they've got a nasty bite. They also like to burrow into hair, especially women's long hair."

Instinctively, Olga grabbed her hair and twisted it into a thick braid.

"Yes, cadet," continued Lieutenant Timoshenko, looking directly at Olga. "Dragonflies will definitely be attracted to your red hair."

Embarrassed, Olga let go of her braid, smiling slightly.

"These dragonflies fly in swarms, and the swarms move fast. When they bite, it hurts. If you are attacked by a swarm, a gun is useless: you will be wasting your ammo. For every hundred rounds you shoot, you'll hit one—maybe. Swarms tend to have a form of group intelligence, which gives them immunity. However, we have devised ways to kill swarms, which is one of the skills we'll be teaching you."

Janu was listening intently to every word. A swarm with "group intelligence" would raise the level of difficulty beyond any virtual reality games he had ever played. *How cool!*

The lieutenant moved to yet another screen. This one showed a crude sketch of two animals, about the size of a dog or cat, with big teeth.

"We called these little animals with tusks 'River Gophers.' They're not dangerous. We encountered a lot of them near the rivers. They live underground in holes, and, when it rains, that's where they retreat. Unfortunately for them, when it floods, they also retreat into their holes—and drown!"

He paused, shaking his head.

"We saw hundreds of their carcasses after big storms. I mention this because their carcasses attract swarms of dragonflies, so watch out."

Lieutenant Timoshenko walked to the center of the room.

"The three creatures I have just described are just a few of the wild animals we encountered. To be quite honest, we don't know all the animals out there."

He surveyed the cadets, from left to right.

"Are there any questions?"

Steve raised his hand.

"Yes, Cadet Steve," said the lieutenant, motioning him to stand.

"Lieutenant, after our training, will we get any field experience?"

"Yes, you certainly will," smiled the officer. "I was just about to get to that. After four weeks of basic training, you will be sent into the field for two weeks. You will be traveling to a remote region outside of New Munich, which we have been mapping for years."

He walked to a large map on the wall.

Janu studied the map. He spotted New Munich, a small area located in the lower left-hand corner. There was a red line leading from New Munich to a distant location, marked in colors and X's.

The lieutenant tapped at the map with a wooden pointer. "These areas marked with X's have already been surveyed by previous cadets. Focus your attention on this square area colored blue. This is Area 63, which your group will be surveying after you complete training."

Janu raised his hand.

"Yes, Cadet Janu."

"How big an area is Area 63?"

"Each of these rectangles is twenty-five miles by twenty-five miles or 400,000 acres," said the lieutenant. "This land has never been explored before; you will be the first surveyors. Based on limited information, we believe this area is somewhat mountainous, possibly with active volcanos."

The lieutenant walked away from the map and turned to the cadets.

"Any more questions?"

No one raised their hands.

"Okay, then this is it for today."

Lieutenant Timoshenko collected his briefcase, then turned toward the sergeants who immediately stood at attention.

"Sergeants!"

"YES, SIR!" said the two sergeants.

"I am placing this group in your command!"

"YES, SIR!" they said in unison, saluting their commanding officer.

Lieutenant Timoshenko saluted in return, then left the building.

Lieutenant Adam Timoshenko left and walked to his horse and buggy in the parking lot. His old chestnut brown mare, "Honey," had been at one time quite a beautiful horse; now, she had a slumped back. She was the best horse Adam had ever owned. He stroked her blonde and grey mane. "Good girl," he said softly, reaching into his pocket for a brown sugar cube. "There you go." The horse whinnied with pleasure, munching on the treat.

Suddenly, Honey jolted slightly, startled by the noise of an approaching machine.

Adam turned to see a horseless carriage whizzing down the street—the second one he had seen that week. As the vehicle drew closer, he saw Horst was driving, steering the contraption using a wheel. Horst waved and honked his horn, without stopping.

Amazing, thought Adam, whistling under his breath. *He must be going at least eight miles an hour!* Shaking his head, he climbed into his buggy and grabbed the reins.

"Come on, old girl! We don't need those new-fangled machines!" He clicked his tongue and gently whipped the reins. "Giddy-up!" Honey whinnied and started-off at a slow clip.

Adam leaned over, resting his elbows on his knees, wondering what it was like to drive a horseless carriage. He drove the buggy down Chicago Street, until he arrived at the bridge crossing the river. There was a rule all riders must dismount before crossing the bridge because the horses tended to get spooked.

Climbing down from his perch, he walked Honey, pulling her by the bridle across the two-hundred-foot span bridge. When he reached the other side, he jumped back into his seat and drove down the *Haupt Straße,* the three-block-long main street on the German side of town.

It was a short distance to his destination, Supercomputer Building 1. When he arrived, he tied Honey to a post next to a water trough, gave her another sugar cube, and patted her on the neck.

"Here, ya go. See you in a couple of hours."

Today was something of a milestone for Adam: He had made an appointment to have his personality simulated in the Artificial Personality Simulator or APS. Adam was sixty-two years old—the same age as when his grandfather, Charles Timoshenko, had been simulated on Earth.

80,000 years before, Charles Timoshenko was a prominent structural engineer on Earth, in a city called Chicago. He was among several people who had been selected to have their personalities and knowledge encapsulated by the APS simulation program, for the purpose of educating the remnant of humanity on Planet K851b.

When Adam was a youngster growing up in New Eden, he had formed a close relationship with his APS "virtual" grandparents, Charles and Elise. Charles, in fact, had trained him to become an engineer. He also had fun with his grandparents, taking long virtual reality bicycle trips to places like Chicago. His APS grandparents provided him with the closest possible experience of life on Earth.

When Adam entered Supercomputer 1, he saw a teenage boy, perhaps sixteen years old, sitting behind a desk, playing a video game.

"*Hallo, jungen Mann!*" said Adam, in Deutsch, the language customarily spoken on the German side of town.

The boy looked up briefly from his game.

"Oh, hi, *Mr.* Timoshenko," he replied in perfect English, purposely using "Mr." instead of "Herr."

"I was looking for Fritz Junior."

"Oh, that's my dad. He's over in the Virtual Reality game room, setting up for a party."

"You're Fritz's son?"

"*Ja. Ich heiße Fritz III.* Some people simply call me *'Dritten'* ['Third'] for short."

"*Angenehm, Dritten!* [My pleasure, Third!]. I'm here for my appointment in the APS room, *bitte.*"

"Of course, *Herr* Timoshenko. We've got you set up in *Raum* 63."

"*Danke!*"

Adam walked to Room 63 and found the virtual reality goggles. He sat down in the chair and put on the googles. Immediately, he saw his grandfather sitting comfortably in a chair facing him, smiling.

"Well, hello, Adam," said APS Charles Timoshenko.

"Hello, Opa," said Adam, using the Deutsch nickname for grandfather.

"It has been a long time since we last spoke," said the APS Opa. "Is there a reason for your visit?"

Adam paused to collect his thoughts. "I believe I am about the same age as you were when you were interviewed by the Artificial Personality Simulator in Chicago. Isn't that true?"

"Ah, the countless hours of simulation I had on Earth! I began the APS Program when I was sixty-two years old. Is that how old you are now?"

"Yes, I just turned sixty-two only a few weeks ago."

"How wonderful! Don't you think we resemble each other physically?"

"Why, yes, that thought has crossed my mind," said Adam, noting he had nearly the exact facial features as his grandfather. "What is that phrase—we're 'dead ringers'?"

"Yes, 'dead ringers' is a phrase that fits," laughed APS Opa. "Please tell me what else is on your mind?"

Again, Adam paused to collect his thoughts.

"I think it's important I also leave behind my legacy."

"Like your own APS simulation?"

"Yes, I think so."

"Well, that can certainly be arranged. Since your childhood, we've been able to collect a substantial amount of information about your personality. We currently have a larger database of your personality than my database."

"That's what I thought. I just wanted to make sure that, someday, in the future, my kids or grandkids could talk to me when I'm gone. You know, like how I'm talking to you." Adam's voice trailed off.

Recently, he had been thinking about his own mortality. His entire life had been so active and unpredictable he had never paused to reflect on its meaning. For sure, he had changed people's lives for the better, but why did he want to make an APS version of himself? *Was it to be remembered for eternity?*

"I have an interesting question," said APS Opa. "Is there anything about your life you regret?"

Adam pondered over this for a few moments. Finally, he broke his silence.

"Come to think of it, I've been very fortunate. We have done no less than re-establish human civilization! It is amazing, isn't it?"

"Yes, it is certainly amazing," said APS Opa. The virtual simulation paused. He sat back in his virtual chair, lacing his virtual fingers behind his head, deep in thought. Finally, he looked directly at Adam.

"I sense you feel there has been something missing."

Adam smiled wryly.

"There is one thing that has always bothered me: I will never know Earth. I will never see a blue sky, or experience what Earth was *really* like. The closest thing to a real Earth we have here is this—" he waved his hands around the room—"this room . . . this virtual reality room."

"Adam, you are talking to the wrong person."

"I don't understand," said Adam, frowning.

APS Opa leaned toward his grandson.

"Obviously, Adam, I will never know what it is to be human."

Chapter 5

HE WATCHED FROM THE HILL OVERLOOKING THE FIELD AS they went through their drills. He had memorized their routine: After running laps, they would take a short break, followed by the obstacle course which involved wriggling under barbed-wire, squeezing through tires, swinging on ropes, and scaling walls. Their sergeants blew little whistles, ordering the slower cadets to do push-ups when they lagged behind. Then came rifle or archery practice.

For the past few mornings, he had watched them through binoculars, absorbing every detail before he left for his shift at the factory. Chad put the binoculars down.

"Dumm Amerikaners!" [Stupid Americans!] he spat.

He had been staring at them for so long that he was getting worried the binoculars might leave marks around his eyes. *He must not leave any evidence!*

~

Chad Gurke's life had not amounted to much since his father died fifteen years before. Chet Gurke had been a famous television news announcer, a successful businessman who could afford any extravagance. When Chad was a boy, his friends called him the "rich kid" because he had so many possessions: a pellet gun, a horse, a dog, a pool table, even a motorcycle—the only one in New Munich!

But it had been a long time since Chad was the "rich kid" in the neighborhood; now that he was an adult, not many people noticed Chad at all, despite his signature long blond ponytail.

~

He looked at his watch. Soon it would be time to leave. He had been lying on a blanket, trying to keep dry from the morning dew, but his clothing already felt damp. He watched the rookies and, in particular, that toy soldier drill sergeant, Max Baumeister. *How he hated him!*

Years ago, Baumeister and his American friends had trespassed on his family's property. Chad captured the invaders and locked them inside a dog cage for hours. *Vater was so proud! Das war richtig!*

Chad instinctively touched the crooked bump on his nose, which Baumeister had broken after escaping from the dog cage. He cursed Baumeister under his breath. However, his hatred for Americans wasn't entirely due to his broken nose; he hated them for something far worse than that. When Chad was sixteen, his father had been a major investor in a vacation resort called "The Lodge." On the fatal day of his accident, Chet Gurke was visiting the construction site to watch the pouring of the basement slab. After construction workers left for the day, his father had somehow fallen on top of a very sharp reinforcing bar in the middle of the concrete. The next day, the construction crew discovered his body, skewered through the stomach.

Everyone assumed Chet Gurke's death was an accident, but a construction worker disclosed something suspicious about the pour: There was a broad trail of hardened, messed-up concrete leading away from where his father's body lay to the edge of the slab. Upon hearing this, Chad went to The Lodge to investigate. He quickly found the trail, which did, indeed, look odd; there were faint impressions that could only have been made by knee caps as well as one distinct handprint, all pointing toward the edge. It was as though someone had dragged themselves across the wet concrete—*while his Vater was dying.*

He immediately deduced the trail had been made by someone who could not walk, or there would have been footprints. At the time, a business associate of his father, an American named Horst Apoteker, was the only person in New Munich who was paralyzed. Therefore, Chad concluded, Apoteker was somehow responsible for his father's death.

~

Chad checked his watch; he had only twenty minutes to get to work. He rolled up his blanket, placing it in his backpack, along with his binoculars;

then, he walked toward the river, avoiding the American streets. *No one must notice him spying on the Americans. He must leave no traces.*

Following the riverbank in the direction of the bridge, he saw an elderly woman pushing a cartload of firewood. Patiently, he waited for her to cross the river until she was out of sight. Then, after double-checking no one could see him, he sprinted across the bridge to the German side.

Safely back on home turf, he relaxed his pace. As he entered the factory where he worked as a baker, he tried to appear calm. He went directly to the men's locker room and changed into a fresh white cotton smock. He stuffed his long ponytail inside a hair net and put on a disposable white paper hat. Finally, he washed his hands in a large circular sink, where the other bakers were also washing. No one talked, as they scrubbed their hands with industrial-strength, pumice-like soap. Chad didn't like small talk.

He walked out of the locker room onto the factory floor. The building buzzed with the activities of butchers, sausage makers, soup chefs, candy makers, pizza makers, and, of course, the condiment makers.

Both of his parents had been condiment makers. Before switching to his career in television, Chad's father was a pickle-maker in this very building—hence the family name "*Gurke,*" which meant "pickle." Chad's mother, Berta, made a variety of condiments: pickle relish, ketchup, salsa, and mustard. Even his deceased uncle, Ulrich, had been *einen Metzger*—a butcher, specializing in sausages. Coming from a long line of food industry workers, Chad seemed predestined to follow in the same tradition.

He walked over to a wall on which there was a chart listing the week's baking schedule. It was *Dienstag*—Tuesday—and the chart called for dinner rolls, English muffins, and French bread. The next day's schedule listed rye loaves and potato bread. If everything went as planned, he would need to take time off. Once he knew the exact date of the cadets' expedition, he would request leave from his supervisor.

After finishing his eight-hour shift, Chad walked home. He still lived with his mother in the big house his father had built. As Chad neared the house, he could not stop thinking about the Americans. He spat on the ground, then picked up a rock which he hurled at his cat, Shadow, who happened to be sitting near the door. The rock narrowly missed, and the cat, letting out a screech, leaped into the bushes.

When Chad opened the front door, he heard his mother's voice.

"Chet, are you home?"

"No, *Mutti,* it's me, Chad," he corrected her. For the past few years, she had gotten into the habit of calling him "Chet."

Berta walked to the foyer and kissed her son. In her middle sixties, she rarely left the house.

She had slipped into senility long ago, shortly after *Vater* died. She was the one person Chad had in his life. His sister, Greta, was now married to the local blacksmith; they lived next to the stables on *die Haupt Straße* and were expecting their first baby in three months.

"Well, you better get washed-up," said Berta. "*Vater* will be home soon for supper."

There was no use explaining to her *Vater* was dead; he had tried countless times.

"Yes, *Mutti,* I'll wash-up before *Vater* gets home," he said, wearily.

Chad went upstairs to his room, where he had lived his entire life. Now a grown man in his thirties, he still slept in a single bed, surrounded by memorabilia from his childhood. Not a bit had changed since his father's death: There were trophies from kindergarten soccer through high school swimming meets; there were many photos of Chad and Chet on the wall. *He had been so happy then.*

During dinner, Berta alternated her comments between Chad and an invisible Chet. She always made dinner for her husband, and, looking in the direction of his empty chair, would ask him how his day went, constantly nodding her head or laughing at jokes which only she could hear. Every night, Chad took his father's uneaten plate of food and gave it to the German Shepherd, Hans.

After *Abendessen* [dinner], Chad announced he had somewhere to go that evening.

"*Habst du Spaß!*" [Have fun!], said his mother.

He put on his coat and kissed his mother, saying, "*Tschüß!*" [Bye!]; then he left the house.

It was seven-thirty p.m., and the sun had already gone down. Chad, wearing a black trench coat, merged into the night. After crossing the bridge to the American Sector, he put on a black ski mask and black gloves, blending-in with the shadows. He stuck close to the riverbank, re-tracing the path he had taken in the morning, returning to the hill overlooking the field where the American cadets trained.

From the hill, he could see there was no activity. Cautiously, he walked to the American Clubhouse, which was dark. Cupping his hands against the front window, he peered inside. Then he headed to the back of the building where he found a half-open transom. Underneath the transom, there was a dumpster. Hoisting himself on top of the dumpster, he stood eye-level with the transom, which he opened further until he could look down into the restroom below.

With some difficulty, he squeezed through the transom and lowered himself onto the floor. Cautiously, he left the restroom, walking down a dark hall to the main room where the cadets trained. Closing the curtains, he turned on one of the lights.

There were various training materials posted on the walls, including sketches of reptiles, giant dragonflies, and a massive man-eating fish. There were also diagrams of camping gear, showing tents, canteens, and the basics of tying knots. Then Chad found what he was looking for: a map with many squares, one of which was marked "63."

Taking out his camera, he photographed the map. He now had the crucial piece of information he needed.

Chapter 6

IT WAS THE LAST DAY OF TRAINING, AND THE CADETS WERE running a brutally hard five-mile race. After six weeks of drills and other endurance tests, each cadet now had the stamina to carry a full backpack along with their rifle, which was to be held horizontally at all times. The course began at the American Club, then stretched to Farmer Jim's, then back again, across the river into the German Sector, before returning to the American Club.

Janu, Steve, and Olga were leaders of the pack, running neck-and-neck. They were almost an hour into the race and were on the last leg. Most of the other cadets were lagging far behind, still on the other side of the river, in the German Sector.

Janu wanted to win this one. He understood the strategy of long-distance running and was holding back, just a tad, conserving his energy. He looked over at Steve and Olga. Judging by Steve's pained expression and heavy breathing, he could tell Steve had nothing left in him. Olga was harder to read. She was a fast sprinter, but, as everyone knows, sprinters burn-out in the long run.

Janu rounded the corner and entered the American Club's oval running track. He was in the final hundred yards and could see the sergeants at the finish line. It was time to make his move and go for the gold. He kicked into a sprint, dashing away from the others, pushing himself flat-out to maximum speed. . . .

Then, quite to his surprise, Olga came up swiftly from behind, passing him on his right. Like a cheetah, she sprung across the finish line before Janu, with at least a ten-foot gap between them.

When Janu finished the race, Sergeant Max was snorting with laughter. He high-fived Janu. "Nice try, Cadet!" Then he turned to Sergeant Fredric and held out his hand. "Okay, cough-up."

Sergeant Fredric jammed his hand in his pocket and pulled out one Centra. Reluctantly, he handed over the silver coin to Sergeant Max. "This makes us even."

Sergeant Max thrust his fist in the air and kissed the money, shouting, "*Spitze!*"

Janu was both annoyed and amused the sergeants had made bets on him. Could he have tried harder? he wondered. No, he had given the race his best shot. Still, he was disappointed.

He limped over to Olga, who was lying in the grass, holding her side, panting. Janu removed his backpack and plopped it next to her. He stood doubled-over, hands on his knees, exhausted. Between breaths, he managed to say, "Since when have you . . . ever . . . beat me . . . in the five-mile?"

Gasping for air, Olga managed a laugh.

"I figured . . . out . . . your strategy."

Sergeant Max blew his whistle. "Olga! Janu! Come over here!"

Olga stood up, brushing the grass clippings off her shorts. She smiled and placed her hand on Janu's shoulder.

"Good race, Jay."

Janu's face reddened at her touch. Lately, she had this power over him, which made him feel embarrassed.

"Ah, yeah, good race, Ollie," he said, using Olga's nickname.

The two walked over to an area next to the track, facing the finish line. Just a few seconds later, Steve sprinted to the finish, then collapsed on the grass.

"Good job, Cous!" said Janu, pulling Steve to his feet. "You got third!"

Clutching his stomach, Steve winced.

"*Ich haben eine Magenschmerzen!*" [I have a stomach ache!]

The three stood "at ease" near the finish line, as the other cadets trickled in. Eighteen minutes later, the last cadet, a big guy named Hans Groß, hobbled across the finish line, using his rifle as a crutch.

"What the hell happened, Groß?" yelled Sergeant Fredric.

"*Entshuldigen,* Sarge. I tripped near the creek at Farmer Jim's," said Hans, grimacing with pain.

"Is your leg broken?"

"Nein! Aber mein Fuß ist verstaucht!" said Hans, rubbing his foot, explaining he had sprained his ankle.

"*Shade! Geh dort druben.*" [Too bad! Get over there.]

Strangely enough, Janu thrived on the physical demands and discipline of training: Long hikes and runs, culminating in today's tortuous race; obstacle courses, climbing walls, swinging from ropes, getting caked in mud; daily target practice, shooting rifles and crossbows. He also enjoyed learning about survival skills, surveying, and how to make maps.

Suddenly, they were interrupted by a whizzing sound coming from behind them. Janu turned to see his father driving onto the oval running track. The car entered the far side of the track, then sped around the turn, toward them, into the final stretch. As it drew closer, Janu saw his father, Horst Apoteker, and his father's best friend, Adam Timoshenko. Both men were wearing their officers' caps and old cadet uniforms.

"*Ten hut!* Fall in line, cadets!" roared Sergeant Max.

The cadets formed two lines and stood at attention, just as the captain and lieutenant stepped out of their vehicle. Captain Horst adjusted the lapels of his jacket, then pulled a metal telescopic cane out of his pocket, extending it full length. The two officers began walking toward the cadets. About midway, the lieutenant stopped and walked back to the car to retrieve a box.

A box of medals? wondered Janu.

He watched as his father walked slowly toward the cadets, leaning on his cane.

The captain consulted with the sergeants, then pulled out a handkerchief and blotted his forehead. Surveying the cadets who were still standing at attention, he casually instructed them to stand at ease.

"The last time I saw you was six weeks ago, at the induction ceremony," he remarked. "You have just completed your basic training. Now it is time to discuss the field mission, but before we get into the next phase, Lieutenant Adam will be presenting the merit awards. Lieutenant, please take over."

Over the next fifteen minutes or so, Lieutenant Adam presented the merit awards. There were awards for "Best Marksman With Rifle," "Best Marksman With Crossbow," "Best Survival Skills," "Best At Obstacle Course," and "Best Surveyor." The recipients of each award received small metal pins with colored bars, which were to be worn at formal military events.

Janu was quite pleased to win "Best Marksman With Crossbow" and a silver medal for that day's race. Of course, Olga won the gold medal for the race; somewhat unexpectedly, she also won the merit award for "Best Surveyor."

There were also several "joke" awards, such as "Cadet Who Performed Most Push-Ups," won by Steve Timoshenko, and "Cadet With Cleanest Uniform," won by Harriet Schuhmacher, a somewhat shy girl, whose father owned the shoe store. Hans Groß was quite pleased to win the joke award for "Best At Standing At Attention"—although he was having trouble standing at attention due to his sprained ankle.

After the awards ceremony, Captain Horst had a few more words to share.

"Now, it's time to discuss your mission: the reason behind all your training. Your mission, like all past cadet missions, will be to survey a piece of wilderness in the outskirts of New Munich."

He paused to put on his reading glasses and check his notes; then, he motioned to Olga to step forward.

"Your group will be surveying Area 63. Let's hear from our surveying expert, Cadet Olga. Please explain what we know about Area 63."

"Yes, Sir, Captain," answered Olga. "The only information we have about Area 63 are its dimensions. The region is twenty-five miles by twenty-five miles."

"Correct, Cadet."

Taking off his glasses, he cleared his throat.

"The fact is, we know very little about this planet. The original maps are based on aerial information obtained by the first spacecraft that landed here."

Leaning on his cane, he turned again toward Olga.

"Cadet Olga, please describe the survey equipment you will be using."

"Yes, Captain, Sir," answered Olga. "We will use an electronic theodolite—*a total station*—to collect horizontal topology and elevations."

"And by 'horizontal topology,' you mean north-east coordinates?"

"Exactly, Captain, Sir. We will record the north-east coordinates of the physical features we encounter."

"Such as?"

"It all depends on the topography, Sir. We may encounter streams, boulders, cliffs. There's even the possibility we may discover caves. As you say, we don't know what's out there."

"And how will you be recording elevations?"

"Certainly, Captain. When we arrive near Area 63, we will look for benchmark elevations set by previous cadet groups. We have a listing of all the benchmarks."

"What elevation datum will you be using?"

"Elevation 0.0 has been arbitrarily set to a chiseled 'X' located in front of the pretzel shop in New Munich."

"Interesting! The pretzel shop—I had forgotten. Continue."

"As I was explaining, Sir, we will determine elevations by measuring the relative height of objects to the benchmarks."

"And, from this survey data, you will make maps?"

"Correct, Sir. Over the next school year, we will draw maps using the survey data in our field books."

"Thank you, Cadet Olga. I'm confident you are ready for this assignment."

"Thank you, Sir," she said. "Captain, may I ask when we will be shipping out?"

At that point, Sergeant Max stepped forward.

"Excuse me, Captain, but we never discussed the date of departure. We're all packed and ready to go. Since tomorrow is *Samstag* [Saturday], did you want to wait until *Monstag* [Monday]?"

Captain Horst and Lieutenant Adam briefly stepped aside. Finally, the captain spoke.

"We see no reason to wait through the weekend. You will ship out tomorrow."

Janu and Steve grinned at each other. The entire cadet squad was pumped-up—except for Hans Groß, who looked worried, because of his ankle sprain.

"Just one more thing," concluded Captain Horst. "Lieutenant Adam and I will be accompanying your squad for the first few days," he said, looking directly at Janu. "Now, go home and pack your gear for tomorrow. We will be meeting here promptly at 0600."

"YES, SIR!" replied the cadets in unison.

As the squad disbanded, Horst approached Janu.

"Jay, I want to drive you home."

"Ah, yeah sure, Dad."

"How about if I let you drive?"

"Really, Dad?"

"Sure, you're sixteen. But, before we go, help me find a new uniform."

Horst pointed to his tattered shirt. "This thing has served its useful life."

"No kidding, Dad."

Father and son went inside the American Clubhouse and opened the supply closet, where the new Cadet uniforms were stored. Horst looked at the top shelf and said, "Please hand me one of those extra-large ones, *dort druben* [over there]?"

"*Ja, ich konne,*" [Yes, I can,] replied Janu. He stood on a stepstool and grabbed the uniform, tossing it down to his father.

Horst removed his old uniform tunic, stripping down to his jeans. He slipped on a new, loosely-fitting top. It was traditional for cadets to wear the same types of clothing the original settlers had worn because they served as "a connection to the past" and were "character building." Their uniforms were somewhat like potato sacks made of rough-hewn cotton, so crude that cotton seeds were visible. They had no sleeves, just holes for the arms, and used seashells instead of round plastic buttons.

They left the building and walked to the car. Horst slid behind the wheel and drove to the church parking lot, with Janu sitting in the front passenger seat. Then they switched places for Janu's first driving lesson. The new driver got off to a shaky start, at one point narrowly missing the Church Music Director, Frau Eileen. Soon, however, he mastered the controls of the vehicle.

With Janu at the wheel, they exited the parking lot and drove home along Chicago Avenue, traveling at a blistering speed of six or seven miles per hour, about the speed of a horse in a two-trot. When they arrived at their house on Abbey Road, Ingrid was outside watering her rose bushes. She watched as Janu pulled the car into the gravel driveway and brought it to a stop under the porte cochère; then, he flipped the ignition switch to "off," and the electric motor came to a halt.

She clapped her hands and walked up to the car.

"*Ausgezeichnet!* [Excellent!] I am so proud of you!" she said, kissing him on the cheek.

Janu flashed a broad smile.

"*Danke, Mutti!* It was a lot easier than I thought."

Horst patted him on the back.

"Good job, son. We have an early start tomorrow. Better go upstairs and start packing."

"*Ja, Vater!*"

After Janu went inside, Ingrid turned to Horst.

"I'm curious—what prompted you to go on the Cadet Mission this summer? The last time you camped in the wild was on your trip to New Eden before Janu was born."

"Well, I think it's important I spend some time with Janu," he said, forcing a smile. "You should have seen him driving! Eileen was in the church parking lot and—"

"Is there something wrong?" interrupted Ingrid, looking at him directly. "You have *that look.* You never told me about the results of your physical today with *Arzt* Karl."

Horst's grin quickly faded. He stared at his boot toes.

"So—you're *not* all right?" Ingrid insisted in a shaky voice.

Horst turned toward her, shaking his head.

~

The next morning, Janu's alarm clock went off at five-thirty a.m. He rushed downstairs and ate his *Frühstuck* in record time. By five-forty-five a.m., he was out the door, carrying his backpack to the car. After tying his gear to the luggage rack, he waited patiently inside the car for his father to join him.

When he finally came outside with Ingrid at his side, Horst was wearing his captain's cap and his new cadet uniform; it now had narrow blue shoulder patches, about three inches long, each bearing three white stars.

"Did *Mutti* sew those on?" Janu asked.

"*Ja.* She sewed them last night," said Horst, leaning over to kiss Ingrid. "The patches are called *shoulder boards,* Janu."

"I thought they're called *epaulets,*" interjected Ingrid.

"Ah, I beg to differ, dear. Napoleon's French Army may have worn fancy *epaulets,* but in the US Army, we call them *shoulder marks* or *boards:* take your pick."

"So, you're in the US Army now?" she said, sarcastically.

"Well, not technically. We're sort of like the US Army, aren't we, Janu? I suppose we can call ourselves anything we want!"

"*Vater,* what do the three stars mean?" asked Janu.

"I was just about to explain. The three stars represent the Third Thaw."

"Oh, I get it: 'Three stars' mean 'third.' *Vater,* I'm a thaw, too! Will my cadet group get our own insignia?"

But before Horst could answer, Ingrid suddenly hugged Horst, burying her face in his chest to stifle her sobs. When she finally pulled away from him, she looked him straight in the eye.

"I want you to be careful, you hear me?"

Horst nodded, wiping the tears from her face with the corner of his tunic.

"Yeah, sure. Don't worry. It's just a few weeks."

Janu stared at his parents. *Why were they acting so sad?*

Horst broke away from Ingrid's embrace.

"Wir mussen gehen! Ich verabschiede mich." [We must go! I'm saying goodbye.]

Ingrid dabbed her tears and took a step back. Twisting a handkerchief between her hands, she watched them get into the car.

Horst flipped on the electric switch, and the motor sputtered into action.

As they drove away, Ingrid called after them.

"Auf Wiedersehen!"

"Auf Wiedersehen, Mutti!" said Janu. "See you again, Mother!"

Chapter 7

AREA 63 WAS LOCATED ONE HUNDRED AND FIFTY MILES from New Munich. It would be an all-day excursion for the cadet squad, traveling at an average speed of fifteen miles per hour, along a rough road, which saw traffic only twice a year. The cadets traveled in two transport trailers the sergeants towed behind the SUVs they were driving. With their grey canvas tops strung over circular ribs, these trailers resembled modernized versions of Conestoga wagons, the old wagons used to settle the American West. There was also a Chuck Wagon trailer Horst and Adam towed behind their SUV.

This was the first time the young cadets had ever been outside the New Munich settlement. They had lived their entire lives there, in a small town-like setting that resembled suburban Earth, having modern streets, houses, manicured lawns, and plants and trees grown from Earth seeds.

The cadets said little along the way on the bumpy, noisy ride, as they sat on the long benches facing each other inside the wagons. Janu was wide awake and very uncomfortable; somehow, Steve had fallen asleep, with his head leaning against his shoulder.

Janu wanted to see what was outside, but the cadets behind them were blocking his view. He turned around, looking for a way to unfasten the canvas top. Noticing the system of loops and pegs holding the canvas in place, he grabbed one of the loops and tried to loosen it. Unfortunately, it was tightly fastened.

"Steve, wake up!" he said to Steve, whose eyes were still closed.

"Scoot over. Help me unhitch some of these loops."

Together, they were able to remove the canvas loops from three of the pegs; then, lifting the canvas, they stuck their heads outside.

They had never seen a landscape like this before. Towering trees with straight trunks filled the vast, flat valley, their branches extending to form a high canopy of large dagger-shaped leaves and needle-like cones. There were other, shorter trees, roughly six feet in diameter. Everywhere they looked, ferns and mosses covered the terrain, while rushes and horsetails, taller than any man, lined swampy ponds and swayed in the wind.

Suddenly, Steve screamed, gesturing wildly.

"*Schauen sie! Mein Gott!* I think I just saw a swarm of giant dragonflies!"

"*Ja, stimmt zu!*" confirmed Janu, seeing the tell-tale three-foot wingspans. The swarm moved together as if it were a vast living organism made up of smaller living organisms; fortunately, it soared to a higher elevation and was soon out of sight. On the ground, not far from their wagon, there were many enormous insects of the arthropod variety—millipedes, centipedes, beetles, spiders, and flies with wings that measured about a foot long. As Janu watched a giant fly whiz by, a small reptile-like animal on the side of the road leaped up and snatched the bug in mid-air!

The cadets had never seen animals like these before. Everything was just as the sergeants had described: A wilderness teeming with wild, primitive flora and fauna. This planet was so much like Earth—yet evidently in a much earlier stage of evolution. For his entire life, Janu's mother had talked to him about biology and evolution. Now he was witnessing all she had described first-hand.

~

After four hours of traversing this terrain, Janu, who had begun to doze off, suddenly felt the road was getting steeper. Peeking under the canvas flap, he saw they were no longer in a forest. Here, the ground was much drier, almost dusty, and the plants were small and scrubby, unlike the lush wildlife they had experienced earlier.

"We must be approaching a river," he said to Steve.

"River?" said Steve, groggily, waking up from his nap.

Indeed, they had reached a high bluff next to a river. At this point, the road became a switchback, with narrow hairpin turns. The sergeants slowed down their SUVs, pulling the wagons at a steady pace down the steep incline, zig-zagging back and forth until they reached the bottom where the caravan came to a stop next to the river.

Sergeant Max Baumeister climbed out of his SUV and stretched.

"Listen up, everybody!" he shouted. "We're taking a break! Go to the Chuck Wagon and get some grub!"

Sergeant Fredric immediately made his way over to the officers' SUV.

"Hey, Dad and Horst—I mean, Captain."

Horst laughed, "No need for formalities, Fredric."

"Thanks. We need to take a break here. You guys might as well grab something to eat."

Sergeant Fredric walked over to the river edge, where Sergeant Max was standing next to Cadet Olga, already eating a sandwich. He tossed a lunch pack to Fredric.

Max crouched down and studied the river, scratching his whisker stubble.

"Looks about fifty feet across. How deep?"

"Don't know how deep," said Fredric as he bit into his sandwich. "It's been a long time since we've been here—and this river changes a lot, depending on the rainfall. Here, Cadet Olga, please hold onto my lunch for a moment."

Handing Olga his sandwich, he kicked off his shoes, then slowly waded into the water.

"Yow! This water is cold!"

By the time he reached the middle of the river, the water was almost up to his knees.

"It's about two feet!" he shouted back.

Suddenly, Cadet Olga screamed, dropping both Fredric's sandwich and her own. Almost choking, she pointed toward a cluster of bullrushes on the opposite river bank.

"*Schauen sie! Dort druben!*" [Look! Over there!]

Startled, Fredric looked up as a massive creature emerged from its lair. About twelve feet from its long, flat head to its thick ridged tail, it was now lumbering toward the river on short stubby legs. For a moment, it stopped, surveying the cadets with protruding eyes, its sharp razor-edged teeth gleaming in the sunlight; silently, it dropped into the water and began heading toward Fredric. Submerged with only its eyes poking above the surface, it whipped its tail from side to side, propelling itself through the water.

Frantically, Fredric tried to scramble to the shore, but his feet sank into quicksand. The harder he squirmed, the more the deadly force sucked him down, and, all the while, the creature drew closer.

"Max! Do something—I'm stuck!"

For a few seconds, Max stood rooted to the spot; then, as Olga continued to scream, he sprang into action and dashed toward the SUV. Grabbing his rifle from the gun rack—a replica standard US military M16—and a satchel of ammo, he quickly loaded a clip of 0.223 bullets before sprinting back to the river. Sliding down the river bank, he forged his way through the water until he was about ten feet away from Fredric—close enough to get a good shot. Flipping off the safety catch, he set the M16 to single-shot mode and took careful aim. Though he was sure he had hit the thing, the animal appeared unfazed.

Hands shaking, Max flipped the M16's lever to semi-automatic mode. The creature was only twenty feet away and was closing in fast on Fredric. Max fired off two short rounds, but he overshot, missing his target. Then his rifle locked up.

"Damn it!" he cursed.

He hit the jamming mechanism with his palm, trying to clear the chamber. Meanwhile, the predator had switched direction. Just as the jammed bullet fell out, Max looked up and saw the monster thrashing through the water toward him, its deadly jaws gaping wide.

With no time to spare, Max flipped the M16 to full-automatic and fired a straight-up clean sweep from the hip until the clip emptied. Choking from the acrid smoke, he unloaded and inserted another clip, firing continuously until that, too, had emptied.

He was out of ammo.

Peering through the smoke, he could see the bullet-riddled carcass of the reptile floating belly-up. A pool of blood trailed in its wake as it slowly drifted downstream, carried by the current.

Max turned around to see the group of new cadets huddled together on the shore, motionless. One by one, they began to clap and whistle. Adam and Horst stood a little distance behind them, silently surveying the whole scene.

"Spitze!" [Awesome!] said Janu.

"Großartig und grauenshaft!" [Awesome and gruesome!] said Steve.

"Janu! Steve! Stop gawkin' and get me a rope!" yelled Fredric, whose legs were now completely invisible.

Janu ran to the SUV and rummaged through the trunk; fortunately, underneath the vehicle repair kit, there was a coiled hemp rope about fifteen feet in length. When he returned, he gave one end to Steve and three other cadets; then, wading into the river, he tossed the other end to Fredric.

Grasping the rope, Fredric knotted it around his waist, keeping his hands and arms free. Then, at a signal from Max, the team began to pull in unison, their feet planted firmly in the sand near the water's edge. Staggering backward, the rope blistering the palms of their hands, they heaved with all their might. Gradually, Fredric broke free from the treacherous sand, and the cadets were able to haul him back to shore.

When Sergeant Fredric finally stepped onto the shore, his legs were caked in mud.

Max walked up to him and patted him on the shoulder.

"Hey, buddy, are you okay?"

"Man, that was close . . ." said Fredric, unable to complete his sentence.

"Yeah," said Max. "It was damned close for me, too—damned close!"

Regaining his composure, Sergeant Max turned toward the cadets who were standing nearby, trying to shake the sand off their wet clothes. He could see the red welts on the palms of their hands, tell-tale signs of rope-burn.

"We better get movin'," he said gruffly. "There may be other animals like that one out there. Get to your wagons and prepare to cross!"

Everyone had the jitters.

~

After safely making it across the river, the caravan continued on. The land on this side of the river was arid and flat, almost like a desert, with sparse plant life.

Inside the officers' SUV, Horst was using the laptop computer while Adam drove.

"What are you looking for?" asked Adam.

"I'm searching the database of Earth's prehistoric life. Looking for a prehistoric Earth animal similar to the one we just saw."

After a few minutes, Horst chuckled loudly.

"Bingo! I think I have a winner. Okay, get this: There was an animal called Proterosuchus, which lived between two hundred and forty-five and two hundred and forty-eight million years ago. Here's a rendering. Take a look," he said, turning the computer screen toward Adam.

Adam briefly took his eyes off the road and glanced at the image.

"Yes, I agree, that's it—or close to it. What does the article say?"

"It says that it was the largest land animal during the Early Triassic Period."

"It sort of looks like a crocodile. Is it a relative?"

"Hold on . . . haven't gotten that far. Yep, you're right. Says it was an early example of an archosaur, a large group of reptiles that included crocodiles, dinosaurs, pterosaurs, and birds."

Horst looked up from the laptop.

"Fascinating! Too bad Ingrid isn't here to see this!"

After ten hours of travel, it was nearly sunset when they finally reached the border of Area 63. The caravan came to a stop, and the cadets climbed down from the wagons.

Using his binoculars, Chad watched them from a distance. He had arrived the day before on his motorbike, traveling with the sidecar, which was big enough to carry all the supplies he required. Camping by himself was unpleasant, especially as it involved sleeping on the ground. Fortunately, he had found an elevated flat rock, where the bugs couldn't climb into his sleeping bag.

Chad had made his way to Area 63 by using the photographs he had taken of the cadets' maps. He wasn't quite sure what to expect. Fortunately, there seemed to be features he could work with in the area. With their mission to map out the area, surely they would explore the cave, which would be perfect for his plan.

He just needed to wait for his prey to fall into the trap—then *bam!*

Lying awake inside the sleeping bag, he looked up at the magnificent starry sky. Everything was going as planned. *Vater* would have been proud.

Chapter 8

THE NEXT MORNING, AT SIX O'CLOCK, JANU WOKE UP TO THE sound of a bugle playing *Reveille.* He jumped out of his sleeping bag and shook Steve, who was curled up in the sleeping bag next to him.

"Steve! Get up! Roll call!" he said, shaking him.

"Uh?" said Steve, hugging his pillow. He opened his eyes and blinked, staring at the roof of the tent with a puzzled look on his face.

"I said roll call!"

Janu already had his pants on and was putting on his socks. Steve sat up and rubbed his face.

"Okay, okay, I hear ya."

Janu stepped out of the tent into the brisk morning air. Seeing Sergeant Max standing close to the entrance holding a clipboard and pencil, he walked over to him, the first to arrive for roll call. Janu rubbed his arms, trying to stay warm. There was smoke in the air and the smell of frying meat.

"Smells good," said the sarge. "I wonder, bacon or trilobite? Hmm . . . mm! There's one thing I like about camping—breakfast. I especially like drinking coffee outside in the cold morning air."

Hans Groß limped up to them, leaning on a crutch. He was wearing a white cook's uniform, and his face was smudged with charcoal and sweat. He stopped for a minute to wipe beads of perspiration from his face with a rag.

"Excuse me, Sergeant. I'm on mess duty. I need to get back to the Chuck Wagon right away. Can I skip roll call?"

"Yeah, sure, go ahead, Groβ, you're covered," said Max, checking Groβ's name off the roll-call list. "Oh, Groβ: Bacon or trilobite, this morning?"

"Trilobite, Sergeant."

"Thank you. Carry on."

Once the men's cadet group had assembled, Sergeant Max began roll call. All cadets were present and accounted for—except for Cadet Steve.

Sergeant Max was making notes on his clipboard when Steve finally appeared.

"Sorry, Sergeant. I was in the latrine . . . ," Steve stuttered.

Without looking up, the sarge pointed at the ground.

"Right here. Give me twenty."

Steve dropped to the ground and began doing push-ups, as the other male cadets watched. "Doing twenty" had become an almost daily form of discipline for Steve, winner of the "Most Push-Ups" joke award. As a result, his arms had become quite muscular this summer.

"Okay," said Max, once Steve had re-joined the group. "Let's get down to business. I'm assigning your survey group numbers—so please pay attention. After I've assigned the groups, you will have ten minutes to eat breakfast; then, after breakfast, you are to proceed to your group. Each group has been assigned a sector to survey. You will stay on task the entire day, until four p.m. When you have finished, come back *here*, to this location," he said, pointing at the tent site. "Is this clear? I want to see you right *here* when you come back."

"Sergeant, what about lunch?" asked Steve.

"You will each be given a K-rations. Do you know what 'K-rations' means, Cadet?"

"No, Sir."

"Well, neither do I. The meaning of 'K-rations' seems to be another Earth mystery, but you will each get enough prepacked food to get you through the day. It won't be the best tasting, but it will keep you from passing out from hunger!"

They were each assigned their group numbers. Janu was in Group One while Steve ended up in Group Two.

The cadets went to the Chuck Wagon, where Hans Groβ was busy dishing out breakfast to the women cadets. Janu waited in line for his portion of barbequed trilobite, a bowl of oatmeal, and a "cup of Joe." Now that he was sixteen, he had begun drinking coffee on a regular basis, although he wasn't quite sure he liked it. Sometimes, Janu and Steve called coffee, "Java" or "A Cup of Joe."

Once he had been served, Janu saw Olga and Harriet Schuhmacher sitting nearby on the ground, eating their breakfast. Smiling, he walked over to them.

"Hi. Mind if I sit down?"

Olga's mouth was full. She simply gestured to him with the "okay" sign.

"I've never eaten so fast in my life! We have only ten minutes!" she said, looking at her watch.

"Correction—only five minutes!"

"Hi, Jay," said Harriet, giving him a little wave. She attempted to sip her coffee. "Ow! This coffee is too hot."

"So, what group are you guys in?" asked Jay.

"Group One," said Olga.

"I wish I was in Group One," Harriet said, disappointed. "I'm in Group Two."

"I'm in Group One, as well," said Janu, his mouth full of barbecued trilobite. "Steve's in Group Two, too." Then he laughed. "Sounded like I said 'tutu.' Isn't that something ballerinas wear?"

"Stop joking, Jay—we're running out of time," said Olga, pulling herself up from the ground. "I'll see you in Group One."

Balancing her breakfast dishes in one hand, she waved at Harriet.

"*Tschüß!* See you tonight."

Then she walked over to the Chuck Wagon, where Hans Groß was dispensing K-rations.

With little time to spare, Janu and Harriet quickly finished eating. Just as they reached the K-ration line, the sergeants' whistles signaled it was time for the groups to assemble. Janu snatched his K-ration from Hans and darted off to where his group was meeting.

When he arrived, he found Olga standing next to his father and Lieutenant Adam.

"Dad? Are you in Group One?"

"Yes, we are," said Horst, smiling. "Lieutenant Adam and I will be joining you for the first couple of days. We'll be traveling back *Dienstag* [Tuesday]."

"But when you leave, that will leave only Olga and me in our group."

"I believe the plan is to have the sergeants take our place after we leave."

Seeing that some of the other groups were already leaving, Horst looked at his watch.

"We might as well get going. You'll need to be patient with me—I'm a slow walker. Olga, you're Lead Surveyor, please take charge."

Olga flashed a surprised look in Janu's direction. She took a deep breath.

"*Danke,* Captain. I'm leading the way!"

Crouching down, she unzipped her backpack, removing the folded blueprint of a map. She flattened the document on the ground and studied it while Janu squatted next to her.

"This is the map of Area 62, made by last year's cadet squad," she explained, looking up at the officers.

Olga and Janu studied the map divided into a grid of five-by-five sectors, each one-mile square. There was an "X" marked "Camp," somewhat near the center of Area 62. The upper border of the square was marked "Area 63/62."

"For this first week, we've been assigned to survey Sector 3, which is the middle sector. It's the closest sector to the camp, so we don't need to walk too far."

"That's good," said Captain Horst, who was leaning on his cane.

Olga pointed at a mark on the border, near the middle.

"Here's where we will start: 'BM 25,' it's the closest. Janu, can you get out the benchmark field book?"

"*Ja,*" said Janu. He reached in his backpack and removed a field book, marked "Benchmarks." Leafing through the pages, he found the data he needed.

"Okay, got it. Benchmark 25 is a chiseled 'X' on a boulder."

"*Danke,*" said Olga.

Next, she removed a small device from her backpack, which had a little wheel.

"What's that?" asked Adam.

"It's an opisometer—it's used for measuring distances on maps."

She rolled the opisometer across the map, from the campsite "X" to BM 25, then looked at the dial. "Exactly 0.83 miles."

Then, standing up, she took out her pocket compass and aligned her body with the compass's north arrow. "What's the bearing, Janu?"

Janu placed a clear plastic protractor on the map, measuring the angle from the campsite "X" to BM 25. "Bearing is about 10 degrees North-West, give or take a hair."

Turning slightly to her left, she gestured at the terrain in that direction. "Okay, we're headed this way. Let's pick up our stuff and head out."

Janu and Adam hauled the heavy gear—the theodolite, tripod, and gauge rod—while Olga carried the one-hundred-foot tape and two cans of fluorescent spray paint. Since Horst had difficulty walking, he carried the lightest piece of equipment—the plumb bob.

With Olga leading the way, they began their trek. The terrain was hilly, thickly overgrown with many short shrubs that had sharp, spiky needles. To avoid being scratched by the vegetation, they kept to the animal trails as much as possible.

Janu, at the end of the line, noticed rain clouds in the distance.

"Are we expecting rain?" he said to his father, who was in front of him.

Horst looked at the clouds.

"Hard to say. I don't think it rains much here; this place is dry, almost like the desert."

After twenty minutes, they could make out a big boulder in the distance. Janu ran ahead, and when he reached it, he beckoned to the others to join him. When the group caught up with him, they saw the boulder was marked "BM 25" in orange spray paint. This was their starting point for surveying Sector 5 of Area 63. They were at the base of a mountain with a jagged top.

Gazing at the mountain, Janu said, "Ollie, are we surveying this mountain, too?"

Olga, who was studying the field book, looked up at the mountain.

"Not sure about that, Jay. It looks too steep. We'll probably just survey around the perimeter and mark the area as 'Mountain,' then we'll be done with it. I think we can leave detailed surveys for future generations."

"I wonder, is it a volcano?" asked Janu.

Olga shrugged her shoulders.

They divided surveying responsibilities as follows: Olga was the "instrument reader"; Jay was the "rodman" and was responsible for holding the gauge rod; Adam was the "tape man," whose job was to measure the distances from the theodolite (also known in surveyor jargon as "the instrument"); and Horst was the note taker, responsible for recording notes in the field book.

Their first task was to determine their exact coordinates in terms of longitude and latitude. After setting-up the theodolite on the tripod, Olga aimed the device at the sun and looked at her watch. Then she consulted a booklet, which provided longitude and latitude locations based on date, time-of-day, and solar inclination.

"Captain Horst, are you ready?" asked Olga.

"Okay, shoot," answered Horst, pencil in hand, holding the field book.

"Based on our readings, we're at 43 degrees North, 132 degrees West."

"Got it. 43 degrees North, 132 degrees West."

Janu walked to the boulder and held the gauge rod over the chiseled "X." Then Olga looked through the theodolite scope to read the gauge rod marking.

"Ready, Captain?"

"Shoot."

"Instrument Height is 5.6 feet. Angle is 33 degrees 24 minutes and 6 seconds. You copy?"

"Got it. IH = 5.6 feet, Angle = 33, 24, 6."

Adam unrolled the hundred-foot tape while Olga held "the dummy end." He walked to Janu, who was still holding the gauge rod; then, he measured the distance to the instrument. Both Adam and Janu walked back to Olga and Horst.

Horst asked Adam, "Okay—give it to me."

Adam said, "78.25 feet."

"Description?"

"'Boulder.'"

It was in this manner the four-person survey team documented the various topographical features of Sector 5 of Area 63 in the field book. They worked methodically, surveying in hundred-foot-radius circles, recording the locations and elevations of the land features—mostly rocks, hills, dried stream beds, and primitive trees—but staying away from the mountain slopes.

~

After two hours, Horst spotted a cave entrance near the base of the jagged mountain. He was beginning to feel tired. Looking at his watch, he noted it was eleven twenty-three a.m.

"It's almost lunchtime. How about if we break for lunch in that cave up there?"

"Sounds good to me. I'm ready for a break," said Adam, who also appeared exhausted.

"I'll race you!" said Janu to Olga. With that, he sped off toward the cave entrance, with Olga on his heels.

"Hey, guys! Look out for animals up there!" Horst warned them.

Adam began climbing up the foothill, then turned to look back at Horst.

"You think you can make it?"

"Yeah, I think I can make it. It's not too steep."

Supporting himself with his cane, he slowly made his way up the hill, taking small steps. When he arrived at the cave, Janu, Olga, and Adam were sipping noisily through straws inserted in their K-ration bags.

Horst took off his backpack and sat down. The cave was chilly and had a musty odor. He examined the cave floor, looking for evidence of animals, such as animal droppings or bones, but didn't see anything except dried fern branches.

Then he noticed what looked like a large plastic barrel behind them.

"Another cadet group must have left their stuff here last year. See that barrel?" he said.

The others turned to see the object; it seemed out of place in the cave.

"They must have used this place as a shelter," observed Adam.

"*Stimmt zu*," confirmed Janu. "It's a good place to get out of a storm."

Horst unzipped his backpack and removed his K-ration. He took a sip, not quite sure what to expect. The liquid tasted *meaty*.

"Yuck! What is this?" he said, making a face.

"I think it's ground duck, Dad."

"Ground duck? I'm sipping ground *duck* through a straw?"

"It's dehydrated, Dad."

As he ate, Horst looked behind him and saw the cave extended further.

"Janu, do you have a flashlight?"

"*Ja, Vater*—I mean, Captain."

"How about if we do some exploring?" said Horst. "I want to check out the cave—and that barrel!"

"I'm game," said Adam.

"I'm only going in if my flashlight works," said Olga, removing her flashlight from her backpack. "Good, it works. I suppose I'll go in, too—as long as we don't go too far."

After finishing their dehydrated food, the four surveyors got up and began walking further into the cave. Janu was leading the way when he suddenly stopped near the barrel. When Horst caught up, he was surprised to see it was a large yellow plastic garbage can.

"What do you think this is for, *Vater?*"

"I don't know," said Horst. "It must have been left behind by another survey group."

Curious, Horst approached the garbage can as the others watched. He grabbed the lid and tried to remove it, but it didn't budge. He put his nose close to the lid and sniffed; there was a pungent smell of ammonia.

Then he saw something strange: a walkie-talkie taped to the side of the can, with a wire extending inside. The walkie-talkie had a red light blinking rapidly. Horst stared at the contraption.

"How can a walkie-talkie left behind by a survey crew a year ago still be working?" he mused. Realizing what he was seeing, he took a few steps backward, almost stumbling in fear.

"RUN!" he screamed. "RUN INTO THE BACK OF THE CAVE!"

And the group moved as fast as possible, away from the garbage can, into the recesses of the cave.

~

The members of Group Two—Steve, Harriet, Sergeant Max, and Elizabeth, a dark-haired girl from Malta—were in the process of surveying Sector 4 of Area 63 when they heard the explosion.

Steve immediately dropped his end of the tape and ran back to the instrument.

"What the hell was that? Could that be a volcano exploding?" he said to the others.

"It came from over there, in Sector 5," said Max, pointing in the direction of the explosion. They could see billows of reddish smoke rising from the east.

"*Mein Gott,* that's where Group One is working! Come on—let's hope they're okay!"

Leaving their equipment behind, they raced in the direction of the smoke. Panting heavily, they soon arrived at the source of the explosion. Smoke was billowing through what looked like a landslide of rocks halfway up the side of a hill. The smoke had an acrid smell.

Sergeant Max was familiar with this smell, but he wasn't quite sure where he had smelled it before. He turned to Harriet, who was standing next to him.

"Have you ever smelled anything like this?"

"Not sure, Sergeant. It kind of smells like something coming from the fertilizer plant or the steel mill," said Harriet.

"Exactly."

"Sarge, look what I found," said Steve, visibly shaken. He pointed at abandoned surveying equipment at the bottom of the hill.

"That must be Group One's gear!" said Max. He ran up the hill to where the smoke was still spewing from behind large boulders. "*Mein Gott!* It looks like a cave collapsed!"

Chapter 9

WHEN CHAD SAW THE FORCE OF THE BLAST, HE WAS ecstatic. He drummed his feet against the ground and danced in circles, utterly intoxicated by the sweet taste of *rächen* [revenge]. He had created the perfect explosion; there was no way the *Amerikaners* could survive his trap! Absolutely no way!

He blinked, feeling lightheaded. This explosion was the real thing, not just another experiment in his back yard. Four of the enemy were now trapped in the cave, including a bonus prize: the *schrecklish und verdamnt Amerikaner,* Horst Apoteker. Chad was quite surprised to see the old cripple who killed *Vater.*

~

Ever since the day Chad determined his father had been killed by an American, he had hated all Americans. He avoided all interactions with them, even the pretty females. Everywhere he saw them, he cursed the sight of them—at work, the *Apfelwein-Kneipe* [Apple Wine Pub], the grocery store. Eventually, his simmering rage boiled over, and Chad vowed to kill at least four Americans to even the score.

For his weapon of choice, he chose something called a "bomb," which *Vater* had told him about when he was young. Chad's father liked telling secret, terrifying stories about an Earth war called "World War II," which ended with a big bomb explosion. His news announcer father really enjoyed narrating scary stories, always beginning with *"Es war einmal . . ."* ["Once upon a time. . . ."] Chad loved his father's World War II stories, because the bomb was like an impossible-to-defeat monster; it was a special secret he shared with his father. It was something Chad promised to tell no one about, not even his sister, Greta.

However, after deciding to use explosives, Chad had difficulty finding bomb-making instructions: no one had ever made a bomb on this planet before. Fortunately for Chad—but unfortunately for the Americans—he was able to find the information he needed at the New Munich Advanced Institute's Library. It was ironic an American professor named Filbert, a specialist in the History of Technology, was able to locate the information Chad needed. The professor even expressed interest in Chad's "research project."

Once Chad had both the recipe and the ingredients, making a bomb was like cooking. He joked to himself he "baked during the week" and "cooked bombs on the weekends." Building a detonator was the only tricky part, and for that, he converted two old walkie-talkies, which his father had given him on his twelfth birthday. He packaged the bomb inside a bright yellow plastic garbage container, proudly naming it, *"Kleinen Junge"* [Little Boy].

His original plan was to place the device somewhere out in the open near the border of Areas 62 and 63, then simply sit and wait for the pee-wee cadets to be attracted to it, like bees to honey. This plan would yield at least one kill, perhaps four, *tops*. But when Chad discovered the cave, he knew this was the best place to maximize casualties. Most likely, an entire survey crew would want to explore the cave once they saw it. A cave collapse would kill all of them!

Mesmerized, Chad watched the reddish smoke coming from the same spot where the cave opening had existed only moments before. As the smoke began to clear, he could see rocks and boulders now filled the cave entrance. He studied how the smoke seeped uniformly through the cracks between the debris. There was no billowing of smoke through large holes, and this was critically important. *It was perfect: His victims were trapped, with no way for rescuers to reach them.* The massive boulders could only be moved with excavation equipment such as the fork-lifters back in New Munich, a hundred fifty miles away.

He looked to the west, expecting to see cadets from other teams coming to investigate, but saw no one; it was too soon. Then he noticed the abandoned surveying equipment lying on the ground near the cave. It would not take the Americans long to conclude the missing survey crew was buried inside the collapsed cave. No one would suspect his bomb was to blame!

He had to get moving. Chad began to run, still clutching the walkie-talkie detonator, but he was out of shape and quickly became winded. Stopping to catch his breath, he bent over with his hands on his knees, panting. Then, he looked back at the smoking cave, thinking of the four people he had just killed.

He suddenly felt a sense of panic, realizing his fantasy had materialized into reality. *He had just killed four real people.* Placing his hands over his ears, he muttered to himself, trying to silence his scrambled thoughts.

"Hault's Maul!" [Shut up!] he said out loud.

Forcing himself to remain focused, he began moving at a slower pace up a hill, in the direction of his campsite. Close to the top, shiny black rocks covered the slope, which made walking very difficult. Stepping gingerly over the rocks, he finally reached the place where he had left his motorcycle and supplies. Looking back, he could now make out miniature figures in the distance, running toward the smoke; in a matter of minutes, they would reach the cave.

He cleaned up the campsite at a frantic pace, throwing everything into the sidecar; then, finding a fern branch, he swept away his footprints. Instead of mounting the motorbike, however, he began to push it, not wanting its tell-tale roar to give him away. Every twenty feet or so, he stopped to run back and sweep away his tracks with the fern branch, carefully removing all traces of his invasion into the enemy's territory.

After pushing his cycle for almost a mile, he decided he was far enough away to start the bike. Straddling the seat, he kicked the starter pedal, but the engine failed to ignite. He cursed out loud, repeatedly kicking the starter pedal, but to no avail.

In a panic, he got off the bike to check the air intake. He crouched down next to the engine and removed the air filter with a screwdriver. The filter looked clean, so he reattached it, got back on the bike, and kicked the starter pedal again: still no juice.

He had one last option: the lighter fluid in his tool kit. Rummaging through the sidecar, he found the lighter fluid; then, removing the air filter once more, he squirted the lighter fluid directly into the carburetor. Once he was back on his bike, he kicked the starter pedal. This time it worked.

Tears began to well up in his eyes as the bike rumbled forward. He glanced behind him, seized by a rare mood of poetic revelation: Having settled his score over the past, he was now moving toward a better future. He would never tell anyone about this—except, perhaps, Greta. She would appreciate he had avenged *Vater's* death.

He drove the bike slowly through the open wilderness until he came upon the main road. When he was about five miles away from the Americans' camp, he opened up the throttle and looked ahead, toward his future. It was then he broke down, weeping uncontrollably, as he tried to distance himself from the chaos he was leaving behind.

He drove at a steady pace of about thirty miles an hour along the bumpy dirt road. At this rate, he would make it back home by five p.m. As he drove, he thought about his mother and how she probably wouldn't realize he had been away for two days. He hoped she had remembered to feed the dog, Hans.

Gradually, his mood improved as he reflected on his life and what he had just accomplished: After so many years, he had finally gotten his revenge. With malicious delight, he spat on the ground, cursing Apoteker's name. That vermin's life had just gone up in smoke!

He smiled, thinking perhaps, someday soon, he would knock-off Max Baumeister, as well.

As the road became steeper, Chad recognized he was approaching the river. He dreaded crossing the river again. He would have to search for a shallow spot where he could drive all the way across, without having to dismount and push the bike. Unfortunately, when he reached the river's edge, he couldn't find the place where he had crossed before; it all looked the same. Finally, he decided to venture in at the narrowest point where there were the fewest bullrushes.

Cautiously, he drove the motorcycle into the river. As he drove, the water deepened until he was in over his knees. Then the engine stopped.

"*Das pisst mich an!*" [This pisses me off!] he cursed. It was no use—he would have to push the bike to the other side.

As he struggled to push the motorcycle through the water, he felt his feet sinking into the sandy river bottom.

"*Gottverdammt!*" he cursed again.

The more he struggled, the deeper he sank. Standing still, he tried to remain calm. He looked down at his legs and studied the situation. If he let go of the motorcycle, he might be able to free himself; however, he needed it to get back to New Munich.

It was then Chad saw a new danger—a very large animal, with eyes sticking above the water, was swimming directly toward him. He had never seen an animal like this: It had a flat head and a long tail with which it was propelling itself.

Letting out a scream, Chad let go of the motorcycle. He grabbed the submerged bike and, using it for leverage, pulled his legs free from the quicksand. But the creature was only ten feet away now, with its jaws wide open, coming in for the kill.

Standing on the submerged motorcycle frame, Chad jumped backward, landing in a shallow part of the river where the bottom was rocky. As the animal closed in, Chad leaped to the side, unaware a second Proterosuchus was waiting directly behind him. Before Chad had time to react, this second beast clamped its jaws around his torso, then shook him from side-to-side, breaking his neck, killing him instantly. Then the Proterosuchus and his mate locked their jaws onto Chad's head and feet, pulling him like a rope in a game of tug-of-war, until they tore him apart.

Chapter 10

TAKALA FOUND THEM COVERED IN ROCKS. THERE WERE four of them; three were breathing, but he was not sure about the fourth, because he could not see his face. Takala hurried back through the cave, to where there was an opening to the sky. Scaling the steep cave walls, foothold by foothold, he climbed out of the hole, scraping his hands and feet on the rough rocks; then, he ran like the wind. When he reached the village, he slowed his pace and went directly to the Hummingbird Man's dwelling. The old man, Hehewuti, was outside washing one of his hummingbird feeders.

When Hehewuti saw the boy, a smile creased across his wrinkled face.

"Takala—I am pleased to see you!"

"And I am pleased to see you, also!" said Takala, bowing to his elder.

As usual, several hummingbirds had gathered outside the Hehewuti's place, dipping their needle-like beaks into the nectar pots. The little birds seemed to trust the elder; he had a talent for attracting the little creatures and had even given them names.

"Tinker, fly, fly away! You are disturbing me!"

The little bird flew away, as though it understood Hehewuti's request; the old man continued cleaning the pot.

"Why have you come to visit? Surely you are not here to help me wash my bird feeder?"

"No, Hehewuti," replied Takala. "I have found a group of people!"

Hehewuti looked up from the pot and blinked.

"You have found what? My hearing is not as good as it used to be. Did you say you *found a group of people?*"

Takala vigorously nodded.

"Where?" asked Hehewuti.

"I will take you," said Takala, bowing before gesturing for him to follow.

They left his dwelling and headed out of the village. Along the way, they encountered the two strong men, Ciji and Honovi. Takala looked up at the two men whom the tribe used for security in "difficult" situations. Ciji was one head taller than Takala. He kept his jet-black hair in a long ponytail. Today, he was bare-chested and wore his most prized possession: a necklace of polished bones, a reward for his service. Honovi, the leader of the duo, was taller than Ciji by almost one hand's length. The strongest man in the entire village, he had a powerful, muscular body. Honovi was only a little older than Ciji, but his hair, also worn in a ponytail, was showing grey streaks.

"My friends, we have need of your strength," said Hehewuti. "We are going to the Forbidden Entrance—but we do not know what we are going to find."

Ciji and Honovi bowed in unison and, without saying a word, began to walk slightly behind Hehewuti and Takala.

"Takala, what prompted you to go into the Forbidden Entrance?" asked Hehewuti.

"I was near the Entrance when I heard a big noise coming from inside."

Hehewuti stiffened.

"A big noise?"

"Yes," said Takala. "It was like a volcano erupting—there was a lot of smoke and a very bad smell! I went inside to see what had happened."

"I see," said Hehewuti.

They soon arrived at the Forbidden Entrance. Ciji and Honovi used rubbing sticks to light torches of pinewood, handing one to Hehewuti while keeping one for themselves. The four men walked into the cave and came to the deep hole. Peering into the depths of the cave, they could see the only way to reach the bottom was to climb down the walls, using the narrow rock ledges and holes in the walls.

"I am too old to climb," said Hehewuti. "I will wait here on top as you men go down."

While Hehewuti held both torches from above the hole, the three younger men slowly made the descent into darkness, one precarious step at a time. The only light was from the flames reflecting on the cave walls. When they reached the bottom, it was icily cold; the air was thick with pungent fumes.

"What is this smell? Is it pig urine?" grimaced Ciji.

"I do not think so," said Takala. "I have never smelled urine like this before. It smelled much stronger when I got here."

"Look up," called Hehewuti, bending over the hole. His voice echoed around them, bouncing off the walls like a message from another world.

"When I drop this torch, you must catch it before it hits the ground. You are to keep the flame burning!"

As the torch spiraled toward them, Honovi reached up and caught it effortlessly. The flames cast strange shadows across their faces, illumining the darkness.

Brushing the cave dust from his arms, Takala pointed to his left.

"We must go this way!"

He was about to lead the way when Honovi grabbed his arm and stopped him.

"Are they at the Exit to the Outside World?"

"Yes. They are at what *was* the Exit to the Outside World!" corrected Takala. "There is no longer an Exit."

Making their way by torchlight, they trudged through what seemed to be an endless passage. It was as Takala had described: The mouth of the cave was now blocked by a mound of boulders. Under the rock debris were four people, three men and a woman. Takala crouched next to the woman and touched her lips with his fingers.

"Is she alive?" asked Ciji.

Takala felt the neck of the young woman, checking for a pulse.

"She is not dead."

He proceeded to check the pulses of the three men.

"All are alive," he said, "but that one, he is barely alive."

"We must send word to Hehewuti to bring us cots!" said Honovi. "Ciji, come with me! Takala, take the torch—you are to watch these people from the outside world!"

Re-tracing their steps, Ciji and Honovi rushed back through the passage to the bottom of the deep hole. They looked up at Hehewuti, who was standing above them.

"Hehewuti, we have found four people!" shouted Honovi, cupping his hands around his mouth.

"Four?" repeated Hehewuti.

"Yes, four! They are injured. We will need ropes and cots to remove them safely."

"I will get the supplies. Do you need more people to help?"

"Yes!" Honovi stopped to count how many men he needed. He needed five men—the number of fingers on his hand. "Yes, we will need one hand of men!"

Hehewuti began the trek back to the village while Ciji and Honovi waited at the bottom of the hole. In a short time, he returned with five villagers who were carrying ropes, blankets, and poles. Creating a pulley, they lowered the equipment to Ciji and Honovi; then, they climbed down to join them.

Having tied the blankets between the poles, they placed the injured people on the cots and carried them to the base of the hole. With great difficulty, they hoisted the people out of the cave, and then carried them, single file, to Hehewuti's dwelling.

Like all houses in the village, Hehewuti's house consisted of four rooms. He directed the men to place the two older people in the sleeping room, and the boy and girl to go in the eating room, where the cornmeal and flour were stored.

Hehewuti carried a pot of water and a rag to the room with the older men, where Takala was keeping watch.

"Here, take this bucket and rag," Hehewuti said to Takala, handing him the rag. "Wash their faces. I will go to the other room to check on the boy and girl."

"Yes, Hummingbird Man."

Takala washed the faces of the two men. He had never seen faces like these: The men's skin was not dark brown, it was much lighter. They had stubbly hair growing on their faces, and the hair felt stiff.

Takala was worried the Lifeforce had left the one man. He placed his ear next to the man's mouth and listened to his breathing: His breath was very faint. Then he checked the other man: He was breathing more strongly.

When Hehewuti returned to the room, he asked Takala to report on their condition.

"This one is barely breathing," Takala said, pointing at the older man. "Will he survive? Is the Lifeforce leaving him?"

Hehewuti examined the man, listening to his breath, smelling his skin, checking his eyes, feeling his throat and forehead. He stood back, accessing the situation. Finally, he spoke.

"Yes. The Lifeforce may be leaving this one soon."

"Hummingbird Man, why is their skin so pale?"

"I do not know. They are peculiar, these people. I have never seen skin like this."

"And why do they have sharp hair on their faces?"

"I do not know," replied Hehewuti, scratching his own smooth face. "They are very different."

Takala looked at the strange man, worried his condition would upset the Balance of Life. This was not the time of year for a person's Lifeforce to end—that time had passed only three moons ago! Takala wanted to help these strangers so things could return to normal, but what could he do? Perhaps, Gana would be willing to help.

"Hummingbird Man—I know I am bold to ask this question," stammered Takala, "but do you think Gana can help them?"

Hehewuti stood up, looking concerned. As everyone understood, this was not the time of year to see Gana.

Hehewuti squatted down next to the man and listened again to his shallow breathing.

"He is becoming worse. The Lifeforce will leave him soon if we do nothing," he finally said.

"But, it is the wrong time, Hummingbird Man," Takala said, his eyebrows drawing together.

The elder grunted, then wiped his mouth with his hand.

"Follow me—we must think—*together,*" he said, motioning to Takala to follow him.

The two walked outside, through the village, to the water's edge. Upon reaching the water, they stopped and looked at the island where Gana lived.

Deep in thought, Hehewuti wrinkled his forehead. He began pacing, as Takala watched, in silence. It was the custom for the elders to require the *presence only* of younger apprentices to help them concentrate.

Finally, Hehewuti nodded to the younger man, signaling he had made a decision. Now they should walk back.

When they returned to Hehewuti's place, Ciji, Honovi, and the five helpers were standing guard at the entrance, awaiting orders. Hehewuti ordered them to carry the strangers to the water's edge and load them into the canoes.

~

Hehewuti leaned on Takala's arm as they walked through the village, followed by the men who were carrying the cots. When they reached the shore, they placed the strangers in four separate canoes. Hehewuti and Takala got into the one holding the man who was losing his Lifeforce; Ciji gave them a shove, then, once they were launched, he joined them in the stern. The others took their seats in the three remaining canoes, and the group began paddling the short distance to the island.

The island was heavily fortified, surrounded by towering bastions on all sides. After they landed the canoes on the shoreline, the group carried the cots to the entrance gate, walking behind Hehewuti and Takala. As expected, the entrance gate was closed; a large copper gong and heavy mallet hung next to it.

Hehewuti leaned over to whisper in Takala's ear. The boy nodded, then picked up the heavy mallet and swung it against the gong, producing vibrations that reverberated across the river, into the village and back again. The other villagers sat down in the sand with their legs crossed, waiting patiently, saying nothing.

Takala had been to the island many times before, but only on festival days when the entire village was required to attend. Now that Takala was old enough, one of his responsibilities was to row families across the water to the ceremony. But today was not a festival day, and no one knew how Gana was going to react.

Finally, the entrance gate mysteriously swung open, without anyone pushing it. Hehewuti ordered the men to carry the cots into the palace courtyard.

As they walked through the gate, Takala remembered the last festival day, only three moons before. Ahead of them stood a tall staircase with one hundred steps to the top; it was there he had last watched his younger sister, Hola, yield her Lifeforce to Gana.

Takala missed Hola. She had transcended to the Higher Order, leaving Takala behind to continue his life as a mere mortal. Someday he would join her—but that would not be for a long time! He was now seventeen seasons old—too old to be chosen!

The group carried the cots through the courtyard to the palace, which was located directly under the sacrificial staircase. When they reached the entrance, Hehewuti ordered them to stop and wait for a signal. Soon, hearing a bell summon them, they proceeded inside. Hehewuti led while Takala trailed at the end. Slowly, they made their way down a dark hallway lined with flickering torches; the flames created dancing shadows that mimicked their movements on the walls.

Hehewuti stopped at the end of the hallway and turned toward his followers.

"We are about to enter the official chambers," he whispered. "Walk with respect, and remember to keep your eyes focused on the floor. Follow me this way."

When Takala entered the chambers, he caught a glimpse of Gana sitting on his throne holding an enormous golden scepter. Quickly averting his eyes, Takala stared down at the floor. Looking directly at Gana was strictly forbidden.

With eyes lowered, the villagers carried the cots into the chambers and set them down, side-by-side. Then they kneeled, their heads bowed.

As Gana examined the strangers, Takala concentrated on staring at the floor. He had never been so close to Gana before! Noticing Gana's clawed feet, he closed his eyes tightly. He could feel his scorching breath on the back of his neck.

Finally, Gana spoke.

"Who found them?" he croaked.

"I found them, Master," stammered Takala.

"They were inside the Forbidden Exit?"

"Yes, Master," Hehewuti replied. "The Exit collapsed on top of them."

Gana sucked in his breath.

"Don't you think this is strange? Who are they? Where did they come from? And why did the Exit collapse?"

Gana strutted in circles, his tail feathers making a swishing sound. As he walked, he made grunting sounds, breathing heavily.

"We do not know who they are, Master! We have never seen other people!" said Hehewuti.

"I KNOW you have not seen other people!" roared Gana, slamming his scepter against the floor, narrowly missing Hehewuti's head.

From the corner of his right eye, Takala watched Gana examining each of the strangers. When Gana noticed the two younger ones, he became quite interested: They were the perfect age.

Gana examined the two older men. "This one will survive," came the raspy prognosis. "You are to leave them here with me. I will request the proper medicine from my Number Two. We will make them sleep and heal for several days. However, one of these men is ill. The Lifeforce is leaving him in the next six moon cycles. It is unfortunate he is too old."

"Master, shall we go now?" asked Hehewuti.

"Yes, you may go—except for the boy. What is your name?" he trilled, pointing at Takala.

"My name is Takala, Master."

"Yes—*Ta-ka-la*. You will stay here to help administer the medicine."

"Yes, Master," said Takala, his complexion turning white.

Then the other men left the palace.

Chapter 11

WHEN HORST OPENED HIS EYES, HIS BODY HURT ALL OVER. The last thing he remembered was being inside a cave; now, he was in a dark room lit by a flickering torch. Staring at the ceiling, he tried to move his legs, fearing he had broken his back. Fortunately, he was able to wriggle his toes. He pinched his hips and felt the pressure of his fingertips; that ruled out the possibility of paralysis.

Suddenly, a young man appeared in Horst's field of vision. He spoke, but Horst couldn't understand a word he was saying. Nor did Horst recognize him; he wasn't one of the cadets or anyone he knew in New Munich. His skin was dark, reminding Horst of a few Thaws from India, but his features didn't quite fit that mold. He had never seen anyone like him before.

The man continued to babble in a strange language, as he raised the pillow under Horst's head; then he walked away.

With his head elevated, Horst was able to take in his surroundings. He saw Adam, Olga, and Janu were also lying in cots close to the torch on the wall; at the other end of the room was an open entrance leading to darkness.

"Adam! Janu! Olga! Can you hear me?" whispered Horst, barely able to speak.

"*Ja*, Horst," said Adam. "We're all here. You've finally woken up—we were worried about you. Are you okay?"

"What happened? Where are we?"

"The cave entrance collapsed on us, Dad," explained Janu.

"I'm not sure if I can move," said Horst. "Have any of you gotten up?"

"No—none of us can move," said Adam. "We think they gave us something to immobilize us."

"Like a drug? Who do you mean by 'they'? Olga—are you okay?"

"*Ja, ich denke!*" [Yes, I think!]

Then, the young man returned to the room, pushing a cart of food which he rolled directly next to Horst's cot.

The food was unlike anything Horst had ever seen or smelled before. The dishes consisted of pieces of yellow dough or meal that were steaming hot and had a strange aroma.

The man held Horst's head and put a small morsel into his mouth. Horst had no choice but to eat the food, which tasted very spicy. Next, the man held a mug to his mouth, forcing him to sip a liquid. As he fed Horst, he babbled the entire time in a strange-sounding language. When Horst had finished drinking from the mug, the man lowered his head on the pillow and rolled the cart away, presumably to feed the others.

For several minutes, Horst lay still, continuing to stare at the ceiling. Suddenly, he felt a hot sensation in his intestines. His initial reaction was to wonder if he had been poisoned; however, he did not feel sick. Then, very slowly, the hot sensation began to travel throughout his body, starting from his gut, down to his legs and feet, then up his torso, finally reaching his arms and fingers. Horst flexed his ankles, then pulled himself up into a sitting position. Swinging his legs over the side of the bed, he saw Adam, Janu, and Olga were also beginning to move around.

"*Mein Gott!*" said Adam. "What was that stuff? It's like Super-Coffee!"

"Woo! Now I'm awake!" said Janu.

"Me, too!" agreed Olga, rubbing her eyes. "Were we sedated before?"

"Yes . . . I think so," said Horst.

The young man stood near them, watching. He appeared confused by their exchange. He said something to them, which sounded like pure gibberish. Then, suddenly, there was the sound of heavy footsteps walking toward the room. Hearing this, the young man ran over to the entrance and crouched on the floor, bowing in submission.

The light was too dim for Horst to see the features of the new visitor. Judging by its silhouette, he or she was very tall; in fact, taller than anyone Horst had ever seen in his life. Then the visitor began to speak, in a croaky voice, using incomprehensible, guttural words.

The young man responded, using words with staccato sounds and clicks. Then he stood up and left the room. When he returned, he was carrying a torch that illuminated the room, allowing everyone to see his Master's ghastly face.

Olga screamed.

"Olga, be quiet!" shouted Janu.

"It" wasn't human; nor was it like any animal from Earth. Standing nearly seven feet tall, it had green scaly skin and eyes the size of billiard balls, somewhat like the eyes of an ostrich. However, "It" was not a bird because it did not have any wings: "It" was somewhat humanlike—a "bipod," with two arms and two legs—but it was definitely not human.

The creature walked around the room, seemingly assessing the humans. When it reached Horst, it stopped to observe him.

Instinctively, Horst looked down at the floor. The creature stooped down and placed its three-fingered claw-like "hand" on Horst's forehead. Horst submitted to the examination, trying to remain calm, as the claw-like hand touched his forehead, nose, ears, and throat. He kept his eyes closed.

When the creature felt Horst's head, "It" seemed to have discovered something interesting. Horst remembered the eight metal terminals that had been implanted years before at the Einstein-Newton site; they were connected to nanocircuitry in Horst's brain, as an interface with the Genius supercomputer, used in manufacturing.

Apparently, the creature found the metal terminals quite remarkable. "It" croaked something to the young man, who rose to his feet, joining "It" in examining Horst's skull. There was an exchange of croaking, groaning, and clicking, which the humans found utterly indecipherable. Then the young man left the room.

While the young man was gone, the creature grunted, looking at Horst, who then began a rambling monologue, introducing himself and the others.

"Hello, my name is Horst. I'm pleased to meet you. This other gentleman, to my right, is Adam. Say 'Hi,' Adam."

Very nervously, Adam said, "Hi."

The creature stared at Horst, cocking its head to the right side, blinking its ostrich-like eyes.

Horst continued, "And this young man over here, to my left, is my son, Janu. Say 'Hi,' Janu."

"Okay . . . yeah, sure . . . hi," said Janu, giving a little wave.

"And, finally, this young woman is Olga."

Petrified, Olga said nothing.

"That's okay, Olga—we'll get back to her later," continued Horst. "We've come from a place called New Munich. . . . Well, actually, Adam and I originally came from a place called New Eden . . . well, originally, I mean, originally originally, we came from a place called Earth, but I suppose that's beside the point . . ."

The creature lowered its head and looked directly at Horst, sniffing him.

Then it said something: "HOR-IST."

Horst smiled.

"Yes . . . that's right. Yes, my name is Horst—yes, that's me . . ."

"THAAATSRIOT."

"Yes, correct . . . or rather, that's right."

The young man returned to the chambers carrying a box, which he handed to the creature. The creature opened the box, removing a clear glass globe, which glowed with a green light. He held the globe close to Horst's head, slowly moving it in circles; as he did this, the intensity of the light grew, pulsating rhythmically.

Horst watched the pattern of the pulsating light. It was almost like Morse Code: three long bursts, followed by two short bursts, followed by five quicker bursts. Soon the globe was blinking rapidly as the creature watched.

Then, the most unusual thing happened: The creature laughed! It was a deep, croaky laugh, but there was no question that "It" was laughing.

Horst lay still as the creature held the globe, moving it along Horst's body, from his head to his toes. After the process was over, the creature squawked something to the man-servant, giving the globe back to him. The man-servant replaced it in its box, and then the two left the room.

Adam was the first to speak.

"Horst, are you all right?"

"Ah, *ja, ich denke* [yeah, I think so]," replied Horst, gingerly touching the metal terminals.

"Did you experience anything when he placed that thing on you?"

"No, nothing at all."

"I'm scared!" said Olga.

"Me too!" added Janu.

"Me three," said Horst, "although I probably shouldn't admit it!"

Chapter 12

OVER THE NEXT FEW DAYS, HORST, ADAM, JANU, AND OLGA remained confined to their chamber as they recuperated from their injuries. Once a day, the creature visited, always accompanied by the young man-servant. "He" or "She" or "It" continued to examine them with the globe.

Once, when the creature placed the pulsating green light globe against Adam's head, it laughed again, but this time even more loudly than when it had examined Horst.

After the creature finished the examination, Adam twirled his fingers against his temples. Speaking to no one in particular, he said, "I wonder what's so funny about my head?"

"I'm not sure what's funny about your head, either," laughed Horst.

"Seriously," he continued, "we have a communication problem; we don't know their language, and they don't know English."

"I agree, Horst. Their language sounds like gibberish."

"Well, the first thing we need to do is try to learn their language."

"So, how are we going to do that?"

Olga and Janu walked over to Horst and Adam's cots. Throwing their blankets on the floor, they sat down.

"We need to learn to communicate with them. In the very least, we need to know how to say their names and some basic questions," continued Horst.

Olga raised her hand, as though she was in class.

"Yes, Olga, go ahead."

"I've been attempting to communicate with the man-servant. I've been saying my name and trying to get him to repeat it, but he never says anything back to me."

She looked at the young man, who was sitting alone near the entrance, and lowered her voice.

"I think he's afraid to speak when this . . . this . . . *creature* . . . is around."

"You are probably right," said Horst. He turned toward Adam.

"Do you remember learning German in New Eden?"

"Of course. Miss Angelique taught us German. The class was brutal."

Horst laughed. "I was a terrible student in that class."

"Really? I don't remember you being a terrible student."

"Well—yeah. I sort of hated school in New Eden, especially Miss Angelique's classes. Her method of teaching just didn't work for me. Fortunately, my APS grandfather, 'Opa,' explained to me something about linguistics, which I was able to use later when we got to New Munich. This helped me understand language is like mathematics."

"Really? Language and mathematics?"

"Well, there's no math involved, but language has structure," continued Horst. "It has to do with linguistic principles first developed by Noam Chomsky in the 1950s. Fortunately, after we got to New Munich, I was able to improve my understanding of German using these linguistic principles. It's all pretty simple."

He reached in his backpack and found a pencil and paper.

As he began explaining things, the creature entered the room and stood near the entrance. Pretending not to be aware of the creature's presence, Horst continued talking.

"Excuse me, as I put on my 'professor's hat.' As babies, we learn a primitive syntax."

The creature repeated "SIN-TAX" in a deep, croaky voice.

Horst smiled at the creature.

"Yes, that's correct! As I was saying, as babies, we learn a primitive syntax with two-word strings, such as the following words." He scribbled down several two-word phrases:

ALL DRY
I SIT
NO PEE
NO BABY

ALL MESSY
I EAT
MORE CEREAL
BOOT OFF

"This is how babies talk," explained Horst. "Janu, I remember when you were a baby, and you talked in two-word sentences."

Janu cringed. "Thanks for reminding me, Dad! This reminds me of that old *Sesame Street* show."

Olga laughed, then covered her mouth with her hand.

"Yeah, with the puppet, 'Cookie Monster'! This was how he talked!"

"Exactly. Two- and three-word utterances is how Cookie Monster talked," said Horst.

"So, Professor, I don't get it. You want us to teach them baby talk?" asked Adam, who was still massaging his forehead.

"No—you've got it backward. I'm thinking more like, we learn how to talk baby talk to them, in their language."

"Of course. Sometimes I miss the obvious."

"Yeah, I know," remarked Horst, sarcastically.

"But, Dad, don't we need to use more than two words to communicate with them?" said Janu.

Using her best interpretation of Cookie Monster, Olga said, "'Mommy fix,' 'Mommy pumpkin,' 'Baby table.'"

"Did you just say, 'Mommy give the baby, who is sitting at the table, a pumpkin'?" asked Janu.

Olga smiled. "Yep."

"Olga, you've just demonstrated my point brilliantly. Babies get their point across using multiple two- and three-word utterances. I think we can do the same in this foreign language."

The creature had been listening to their entire conversation. Hearing Olga's interpretation of Cookie Monster, it appeared quite interested in what she had to say. It came closer to Olga, saying in a low gurgle, "MOMMIE FIX."

Olga forced herself to grin.

The creature got up and lumbered out of the room.

"That was weird," said Horst.

"Completely," said Adam.

Horst continued with his lesson: "Okay—how do we begin learning their language? To do this, let me explain a few things Chomsky discovered. I love this stuff, by the way."

Janu rolled his eyes. "Yeah, I know, Dad!"

Horst said, "First, let's start with some nouns." He wrote the following:

N → BOY, GIRL, DOG, CAT . . . (NOUNS)

"Next, here are some verbs."

V → EATS, LIKES, BITES . . . (VERBS)

"Now, some adjectives."

A → HAPPY, LUCKY, TALL . . . (ADJECTIVES)

"Finally, there is something we'll call determiners."

det → a, THE, ONE . . . (DETERMINERS)

"Okay, are you with me so far?"

Janu slouched, acting bored. "Yeah, Dad. This is simple."

"Good—I'm about to get to the good part. Any language—even the language used here—all languages have similar structures."

"Really?" said Adam. "I didn't know this."

"Yes, really," replied Horst. "The most basic phrase is called a noun phrase." Then he wrote,

NP → (det) A + N (NOUN PHRASE)

a happy BOY

"So, we have ourselves a noun phrase, 'a happy boy.'"

Then Horst wrote the following:

VP → V + NP (VERB PHRASE)
LIKES
(det) A α N
the tall girl

"As you can see, this one is called a verb phrase, or 'VP.'"

"This is beginning to look like math to me!" remarked Olga.

"Yes, now you're beginning to understand, this symbolic structure is like math—which is probably why it appeals to me. I've added a new noun phrase similar to the preceding example; this one is 'the tall girl.' Now we have a verb phrase, 'like the tall girl.'"

"You're with me so far? I know it's simple and you want to see where I'm going with this. When we add a noun phrase with a verb phrase we have created a simple sentence."

Horst wrote,

S → NP + VP (SENTENCE)
(det) A * N V + NP
the happy boy likes (det) A x N
the tall girl

"Here I've written a sentence, 'S,' adding the noun phrase with the verb phrase."

Olga clapped her hands together.

"This is fascinating! And you say all languages work like this?"

"Basically, yes," replied Horst. "Sometimes, there are differences in word order. When I taught myself German, I used Chomsky diagrams, and I noticed, in many cases, German and English have a different word order. Like, one language uses VP → V + NP, but the other language uses VP → NP + V."

Olga chuckled. "That sounds like the communicative law in algebra. A + B = B + A."

"Good observation—just like algebra. Even if we use the wrong word order—which I probably do a lot when I speak German—the meaning can be understood. Native speakers can usually spot a foreigner when they use non-conventional word order."

Janu began drumming on the floor with his fingers.

"Dad, I still don't get your point. How do you want us to use these diagrams?"

"Here's what I propose: We talk to our hosts and encourage them to tell us their words for things. For example, I'll point at a bed, and they will say their word for 'bed,' then we write down the word. We'll walk around the room, asking them the names of a bunch of objects. Then we'll pantomime like we're running, standing, and pointing. You see where I'm going with this? Hopefully, they can quickly give us a collection of their words for nouns, verbs, adjectives, determiners, and prepositions."

Olga said, "Oh, now I get it! You want us to create a dictionary of their language. And after we learn words for 'N,' 'V,' 'A,' and 'det,' then we can make noun phrases, verb phrases, and . . ."

"Yes . . . and sentences!" said Horst, completing her thought. "Now, you understand. With this approach, we can communicate in baby talk with them. I sense this creature is brilliant. My guess is, it will understand what we are doing."

"What do we call this language?" asked Adam. "Are these people aliens?"

"Aliens—like space aliens?" said Janu. "Are they from space?"

"Perhaps," said Horst, "but we don't know where they're from. I mean, we're from space."

"Good point, Dad."

"I think, for now, we should call them the Natives," said Horst. Everyone agreed that was a good idea.

~

The next time the creature visited them, Horst began pointing at various things in the room: the bed, the floor, the walls, the torch. The creature caught on quickly, appearing to understand Horst's intention to learn its language. Interestingly, the creature was also curious to learn English.

Olga and Janu tried the same approach with the man-servant; but, he seemed reluctant to say anything while the creature was present. However, once the creature exited the room, the man-servant became quite helpful, providing them with vocabulary from his native language.

Within a matter of a few short days, they had created a simple dictionary of words.

The first thing Horst wanted to know was the creature's name. He began by telling the creature his own name: "*Notoka* Horst."

Hearing this, the creature laughed. Then it said, "*Notoka Gana.*"

Horst smiled. "Your name is Gana."

Olga approached the man-servant, to tell him her name: "*Notoka Olga.*"

Aware of Gana's presence, the man-servant looked down and said nothing.

Then Gana turned to Olga and said, "*Nu' umi unagwa'ta.*"

Olga simply smiled. Turning toward Horst, she said, "Captain, are you able to translate that?"

Horst wrote down the words, "Nu' umi unagwa'ta." Then he said, "Let's see . . . using our little dictionary and a Chomsky diagram, let's try translating this." Concentrating on the sentence structure, he concluded: "I think I've got it. This is a simple three-word sentence: S→ NP + VP. That leaves us with two possibilities: Either the noun phrase is one word, and the verb phrase is two words, or the noun phrase has two words, and the verb phrase is one word. I say we go with the noun phrase is one word."

"Sounds good to me," said Janu. "I think the noun phrase is 'Nu,' which is the pronoun that means 'I.'"

"Olga, can you repeat what it said?" asked Adam.

"*Nu' umi unagwa'ta.*"

"Thank you. We understand that 'Nu' is the noun phrase. Then that leaves verb phrase, so we're looking for VP → V + NP or perhaps reversed word order, NP + V. Well, I see here 'umi' means 'you,' which is a pronoun. So '*umi*' is another noun phrase. Which leaves us with '*unagwa'ta*,' which must be a verb."

After studying the dictionary, Olga appeared disturbed.

Adam said, "Okay, I still don't understand. Horst, what did it say to Olga?"

"It said, 'I love you.'"

Chapter 13

TAKALA FAITHFULLY ACCOMPLISHED WHATEVER TASKS Gana required of him. He felt honored to be working for the Master. For almost one full moon, he had tended to the needs of the Unusual Ones. They were getting much stronger now.

One of Takala's responsibilities was to feed the Unusuals. Once a day, near sunset, he left the island by canoe to collect supplies from his village. There, on the shore, he would briefly meet up with Hummingbird Man, Hehewuti, who waited for him with the daily rations, including prepared meals. Today, after Takala beached the canoe, Hummingbird Man greeted him by placing his hand on his right shoulder, calling him by his animal spirit name:

"You have come, Young Turtle Boy!"

"And you're around, Old Hummingbird Man!"

Hehewuti laughed.

"Thank you for adding 'Old' to my name, Takala! Now that you've had some fun, tell me what is happening on the island."

Takala hesitated, looking cautiously behind him.

"Yes, I will share what I have seen, Hummingbird Man, but no one else must hear. I have been by myself so long and have not been talking to anyone."

"Are the Unusual Ones healing?"

"Yes, they have much improved, but I cannot understand them. They talk to each other, but make no sense to me. Sometimes, they make sounds like dogs."

"What do you mean, 'like dogs'?"

Takala tried his best to make the sound of an "r."

"Aarrrgh! It is as though they are growling when they speak. It is very unpleasant, but Master seems to understand them. He has been talking to them. He seems to understand the sounds they make."

"I do not understand how he knows these strange sounds."

"I know," agreed Takala. "But then we do not understand the sounds of animals, either. I mean, a dog barks, but there is nothing to 'understand,' is there? A cat meows, but there is nothing to 'understand,' either."

"Well, when a cat meows, it sometimes means it wants to eat."

Takala snorted.

"I cannot tell what a cat wants, Hummingbird Man! A cat's meow always sounds the same to me, whether it wants to eat or sleep or be petted! But the Unusual Ones make sounds not like barks or meows."

Seeing the bag of pears Hehewuti had brought, he took one and bit into it. It tasted good.

"It has been a long time since I had fruit. We are running low on fruit on the island. Did you bring any honey?"

Hehewuti picked up a clay jar and showed it to Takala.

"Yes, of course. Do you want to eat it now?"

Takala shook his head.

"No, not now—the pear is enough!"

"Tell me, what are they like, other than the fact they do not bark or meow?"

"The young man makes a sound like OL-GAH when he speaks to the young woman."

"It must be her name. What else?"

"They ask me the names of things. When they point at the floor, I tell them the word for floor. When they point at the wall, I tell them the word for wall. Once they pretended to walk, so I gave them the word for walking. They seem to do a lot of pretending."

"This is very interesting. Do they repeat these words?"

"Yes, they say the words. Then they use a special stick to make strange black markings on a material I have never seen before. The material is like a leaf, but it is bigger and whiter than a leaf."

"Are these leaves that have been pressed together?"

"I don't think so. The material is not green. It is much flatter than a leaf, too."

"I remember how strange their clothes are," said Hehewuti. "I noticed their clothes have unusual colors with strange patterns."

"They also have shells on their clothes, about here," Takala said, pointing at his chest. "Their clothes split apart in the front. They put the shells in holes. The shells hold their clothes together."

"What a strange way to wear clothes!"

Hehewuti and Takala began loading the canoe with the sacks of supplies. There were sacks of pears, apples, corn, barley, and, of course, the jar of honey. There was no meat.

"What has Master Gana said to you about the Unusual Ones?" asked Hehewuti.

Takala grinned.

"He says he likes the young man and woman. They appear to be acceptable to him."

Hehewuti nodded in approval.

"They are so fortunate! To think Gana should accept strangers like this! Which one does he like better?"

"It is hard to tell. I overheard him compliment the woman, but she did not seem to understand," said Takala. "The last time he took my sister, so I believe he will want a female again this time. There is still one moon before the offering, so he has time to decide."

Takala and Hehewuti pushed the canoe back into the river. When it was about one foot deep in the water, Takala stepped into the canoe, while Hehewuti continued to shove him into the water.

Turning to look at Hummingbird Man, Takala said, "*Nu' tus payni!*"

The old man replied, "*Ta'a, um ason piw a'ni!*"

As Takala paddled, he felt envious of the young man and woman. Only four seasons ago, Takala had reached the age limit to be chosen. Now he was too old.

Chapter 14

As Horst, Adam, Janu, and Olga learned their host's language, Gana learned English. They referred to Gana as "It," since the creature's gender was indeterminate. "It" had a natural ability for language acquisition, far outpacing the humans' achievements.

Gana and the humans were soon able to understand each other. They developed a process that worked as follows: Gana uttered a sentence, and then Horst repeated the words, writing them down phonetically. The spelling wasn't significant, provided it was consistent. Then came the game of constructing a Chomskian diagram to identify word functions before translating the sentence into English.

As Horst transcribed the phonetic spellings, Gana watched, quickly picking up the sounds of vowels and consonants, learning and retaining words with only one try.

Olga observed how carefully Gana watched Horst write down the words.

"Captain, have you noticed how Gana is trying to read what you are writing?"

"Of course, I have—how *couldn't* I notice?" said Horst as the massive creature peered over his shoulder at his notes. "It's breathing down my neck!"

Olga reached for her backpack and began rummaging inside.

"Ollie, what are you looking for?" asked Janu.

"Just for some simple reading material."

"Like a children's book?"

"Very funny. Can you look in your backpack for something to read?"

Gana turned away from Horst to eye Janu and Olga as they went through the contents of their backpacks. It moved closer to Olga, studying her with its bulging eyes, as she rifled through her belongings, tossing out three pencils, a ruler, three pairs of underwear, K-rations, a plumb-bob. . . .

"Look what I found!" said Janu, holding up his e-reader. "But it doesn't have anything simple to read."

"Okay, I think I've got something: *The Cadet Handbook*," announced Olga, holding a small green book in her hands. She leafed through the manual, skimming through the pages.

"Yes—perfect. I think this is simple enough."

Olga patted on the floor, and the creature slowly lowered itself into a squatting position, balancing on its enormous three-toed feet. As she read the first chapter of *The Cadet Handbook*, which was on the topic of tying knots, Gana listened with intense interest.

After Olga finished reading the first chapter out loud, she passed the book to Horst, who read the second chapter; then, Adam read the third, Janu the fourth, and then it was Olga's turn again. All the while, Gana squatted next to them as they read from the cadet training manual. Taking it in turns, they covered survival instructions on how to make a campfire, how to pitch a tent, and how to purify water.

Having introduced the concept of reading, Olga handed Gana the manual, gesturing to the first page. Still squatting, the creature held the book awkwardly with one clawed hand, tracing over the words with the other. Clearing its throat, it croaked out the words, syllable by syllable.

Gana's reading pace was slow at first but quickly accelerated. After getting through the first chapter on knot tying, Gana grunted something to Takala, who jumped into action and left the chambers. He returned with a piece of hemp, and as Gana translated the instructions into their language, Takala struggled to tie a Figure of Eight with trembling hands. Seeing his nervousness, Janu—who was somewhat of a knot expert—showed him how. Eventually, Takala mastered eight knots: Thumb Knot, Reef Knot, Figure of Eight, Timber Hitch, Clove Hitch, Sheet Bend, Sheep Shank, and Slip Knot.

~

Gana's enthusiasm for reading swelled at an exponential rate. When the creature learned to read silently, it voraciously sped through the Cadet Handbook with minimal assistance. After finishing the handbook, it asked for more reading material. The only other reading material was on Janu's e-reader, on which there were mostly young adult novels.

For the next two days, Gana squatted on the floor underneath the torch sconce, reading. At first, the others made small talk while the creature read; however, this distracted Gana, who became visibly agitated, casting menacing looks in their direction. After that, they decided to remain as quiet as possible.

To hear the creature speaking English in a low, croaky voice was very strange. Gana's speech patterns were also unusual as it pronounced words in a clipped, staccato fashion. Whenever it spoke, there was a lot of starting and stopping, with frequent odd clicking sounds during pauses.

When Janu's e-reader battery finally died, there wasn't anything else for Gana to read. However, the creature's knowledge of English had expanded to the point where it could carry on an adult-level conversation. Gana placed the e-reader on Horst's cot.

"I have read many stories from this device," it said, standing on one foot.

Horst—who was lying on his cot, half-awake, half-sleeping—was startled to hear Gana's voice addressing him. Rubbing his eyes, he pulled himself up into a sitting position.

"Did you find the stories interesting?"

"Yes, although there appears to be a reoccurring theme which I cannot understand."

"Such as?"

"There are many words written about the relationship of human males to human females. Do the two not understand each other? Are there conflicts between the two? I find this aspect confusing."

Horst stifled a smile. They still didn't know if "It" was a male or a female, because Gana wore no clothes and had no sexual attributes.

"Gana, does your species have males and females?"

"We are born either male or female. However, we do not reproduce in the same way humans do."

"How do you reproduce, then?"

"We lay eggs. The female does not carry the embryo, as we have observed with the humans here."

"Gana, there are many things I am curious to learn. Are you the only one here like yourself?"

"No, I am here with my mate, Tresca."

"Are you male or female?"

"I act as the male in the reproductive process."

Good—at least we have that straightened out, thought Horst.

"Gana, where are you from?"

"We will need to leave these chambers so I can show you."

Gana stood up and motioned for everyone to follow him.

Horst was startled to hear they were about to leave. He swung his legs over the side of his cot, but when he tried standing, he lost his balance and almost fell over.

Olga rushed over to Horst and supported his arm.

"Captain, are you feeling all right?"

"I'm okay—just stood up too fast," said Horst. Then, from the corner of his eye, he saw Gana was staring at Olga. Not just *looking* at her, but *staring* at her. With drool dripping from its mouth, the creature leered at her, examining her from head to toe.

Shocked, Horst turned to look at the man-servant to see if he had noticed. Takala, however, seemed used to Gana's strange behavior. It was as though he had witnessed it before: perhaps many times.

The creature continued to stare at Olga, who was still attending to Horst. There was a splash of saliva onto the floor, and Gana snapped out of his reverie. Then he lumbered out of the chamber.

The group followed Gana and Takala out of the chamber, down a long hallway, to a doorway leading to the outside world. When they emerged from the building, it was the first time they had been outside in nearly four weeks.

Horst looked around, noting they were in a courtyard surrounded by very tall walls. As they followed Gana and Takala, he looked back at the building where they had been living: It was a large adobe dwelling with a giant staircase built over the top, leading up to a stage at its summit.

Adam stopped and whistled, looking in awe at the structure.

"This staircase must be a hundred feet high—maybe more—leading to nowhere! What's its purpose?"

Horst shook his head.

"I have no idea—those tall walls are what concern me."

While he was surveying the enclosure, the group moved ahead. Horst tried to catch up, but without his cane, his walking was slower than usual. The others waited for him in the middle of the courtyard. When Horst finally reached them, Gana led them toward a large dome-shaped building.

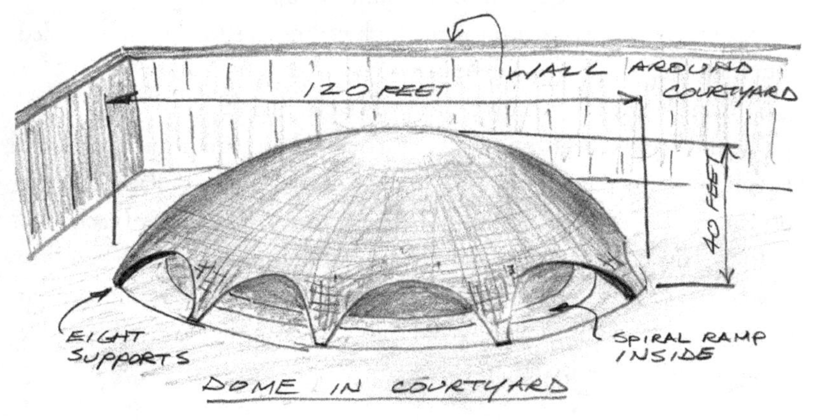

They had never seen a building like this before. It was approximately a hundred and twenty feet in diameter, rising about forty feet high at the center of the dome. The perimeter of the dome was supported at eight narrow points, forming large arch-shaped openings; these allowed the breeze to flow underneath the structure.

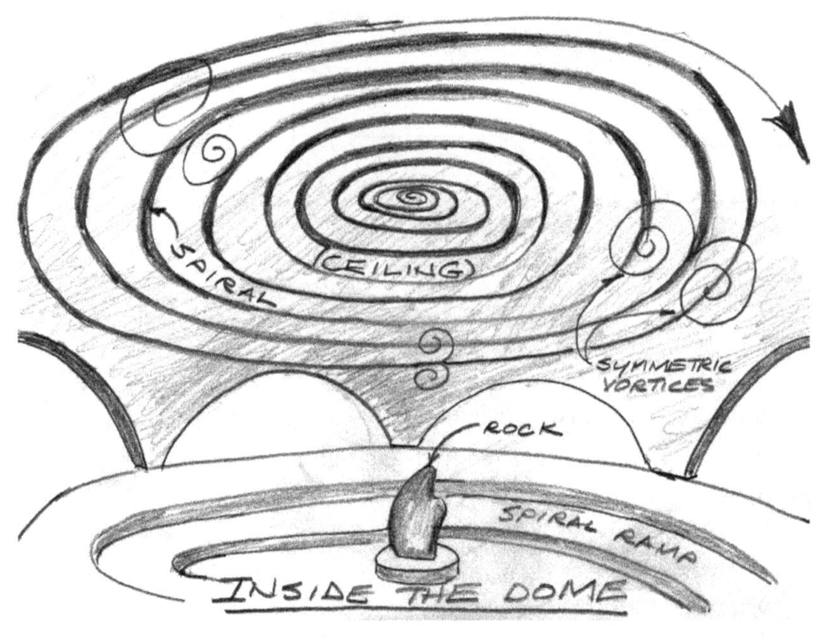

Walking inside, they looked up at the ceiling. Adam whistled again, staring at the underside of the dome.

"*Mein Gott!* Look at this massive column-free span—it's amazing!"

In awe, everyone stared up at the high ceiling: a silver spiral extended from the center to the circumference.

"*Ja! Das ist schön!*" [That is beautiful!] exclaimed Olga.

The floor was equally impressive. Virtually the entire surface consisted of a spiral ramp descending about five feet to a depressed circular area at the bottom. At the center of this depressed area stood a large, shiny black rock.

They followed Gana down the gently sloping spiral ramp. When they reached the bottom, Gana approached the rock. Then, repeating circular gestures with his right three-fingered claw, he began chanting in his native language. Then he bowed.

Seeing that Takala was also bowing, Horst, Adam, Janu, and Olga did the same.

After several minutes, Gana raised his head, lifted both of his scaly arms straight in the air like goalposts, then finished with a quick bow. When his head was down, he looked like a giant bird, pecking for grain.

Following Takala's lead, Horst, Adam, Janu, and Olga raised their heads and straightened up.

Gana turned toward the humans.

"You asked me where we came from. This . . . ," he said, gesturing at the rock, "This is where we came from."

"You came from this . . . this rock?" stuttered Horst.

Gana nodded.

"Yes, we came from this place. This is not simply a 'rock'—it is much, much more. We are tied to its existence."

"I am sorry," said Horst, "but I still don't understand."

"Certainly, it must seem confusing," Gana said. "Notice the image on the ceiling."

"The spiral?"

"*Spiral*? This is another new word for me. Yes, the spiral represents our pathway."

He walked near the center of the dome and glanced up at the ceiling; then he looked back at the rock.

"I will explain more tonight. You are to dine with me and Tresca."

He turned toward Takala, spewing out a torrent of instructions in their language; then he strode away from the dome.

When Gana was out of sight, Takala motioned for the Unusual Ones to follow him back to the palace chamber.

Chapter 15

THAT EVENING, TAKALA ESCORTED THE UNUSUAL ONES TO their dinner engagement with Gana and his mate. When they left the palace, Takala led the way, walking at a brisk pace, which was quite a strain on Horst who labored to keep up.

They made their way through the palace courtyard toward the dome, then, turning right, found themselves in an open field. Continuing along a winding pathway, they eventually stopped in front of an imposing building: an open structure with a curved roof, supported at eight points.

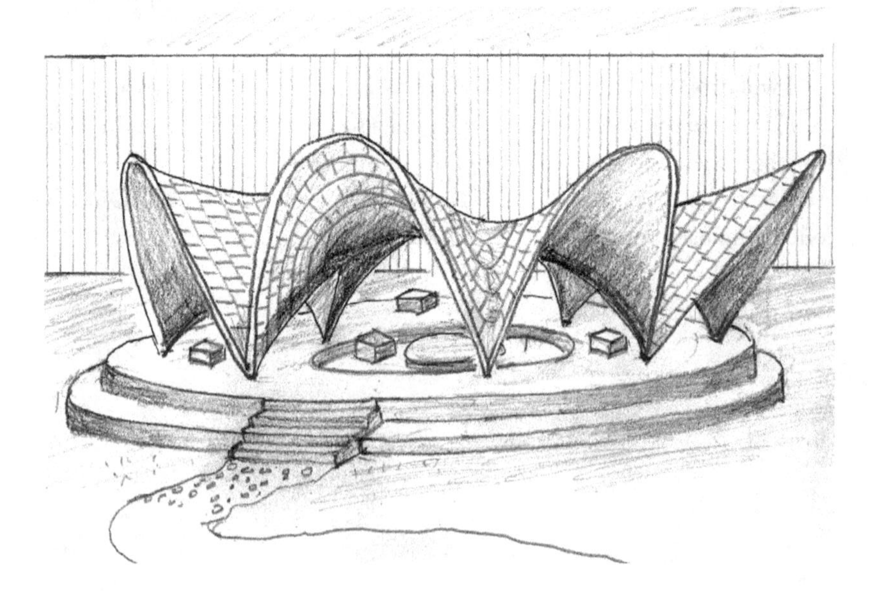

Adam's eyes widened when he saw this architectural masterpiece. For a few moments, he stood still, not saying a word; then, he hurried ahead of the others, reaching the steps leading up to the structure. There, he began examining the engineering details, running his hands over the smooth surfaces while the others caught up with him.

"Impressive, isn't it? It looks like it's floating in air! Can you imagine how advanced this is? It's a hyperbolic paraboloid!"

"Whew! Sorry, Adam—I didn't quite catch what you said," said Horst, breathless from trying to keep up with the group.

"I said it's a hyperbolic paraboloid," said Adam, rubbing his chin. "It's a replica of a structure in Mexico City, designed by an engineer named Felix Candela. A perfect example of structural efficiency."

"Ah, I'm not following you," said Horst, frowning.

"This roof is a two-way membrane: a combination of parabolas and hyperbolas," explained Adam. "The weight of the structure is carried completely by membrane forces!"

Arms folded, he stepped back, admiring all the details. Then, noting everyone's blank expression, he smiled wryly.

"I suppose my explanation didn't help much."

"That's okay, Lieutenant Timoshenko," interjected Olga. "When we get back to New Munich, I'm going to look up 'hyperbolic paraboloid.'"

Horst almost said, "*if we get back*," but he didn't. Instead, he raised his eyebrows and flashed a quick "look" in Adam's direction.

Approaching Takala, Olga said, "*Kalli uey* [House big]. *Tiyah* [We go]. *Titlakuah* [We eat]."

Takala simply nodded.

"*Tiyah?*" [You go?]

Takala shook his head. "*Amo ya.*" [No go.]

"Why isn't Takala joining us for dinner?" asked Horst, who was trying to follow the conversation.

Olga continued to prod Takala with questions.

"*Ken ueue kateh ti?*" [How old you?]

"*Nikaxtolli uan omeyi.*"

Janu laughed. "I think I understood him. Did he say he's eighteen?"

Olga gave a crisp nod.

Just then, two burly male servants who towered over Takala appeared. They had light brown skin and wore their jet black hair tied back in ponytails.

"*Lolma,* Takala. You have done well."

"*Kwakwha,* Ciji and Honovi," replied Takala. "Thank you!"

Ciji was bare-chested, except for a necklace of bones; Honovi was well over six feet tall and was very muscular. The three talked together in hushed voices. Then Takala abruptly turned and bowed, quickly walking away, without saying so much as a simple farewell.

Waving at him, Olga called after him.

"Timoittaseh, Takala." [Goodbye, Takala.]

"He didn't hear you," said Janu.

"Yeah, I know. I'm just practicing."

The two male servants led the dinner guests through one of the openings to a sunken area surrounded by flickering torches. Following instructions, Horst, Adam, Janu, and Olga stepped down, seating themselves on cushions at a massive circular stone table.

Horst felt the top of the table, which was smooth.

"Hmm . . . looks like polished congolomerate rock."

Janu rolled his eyes. "It's a rock, Dad. Isn't a rock a rock?"

"Well . . . no, not exactly, Jay."

Just as Horst was about to launch into a lecture on geology, two female servants appeared carrying steaming trays of food. The young women were barely five feet tall; they wore simple brown dresses and had long, braided jet black hair. They placed various dishes at the center of the table, while the male servants poured beverages into clay mugs for the guests.

Horst looked at the food, eagerly anticipating dinner. He sipped his drink, swirling the liquid around his tongue, but he could not identify the taste; it was like lemonade, but not quite. Before them was an elaborate feast, artistic in appearance, with colorful sauces, vegetables, and fruits: One tureen held a green sauce, another a red sauce, another a sauce that looked like chocolate. The vegetables were a palette of greens, reds, and yellows, unlike any produce available in New Munich.

Adam wafted the steam coming from the hot food toward his nostrils. "Smells good! I'm looking forward to this!"

Janu was about to grab a piece of fruit when his father stopped him.

"Jay, don't eat until our hosts arrive!"

"Sorry, Dad."

"This is good," said Horst, tipping his mug toward Janu. "Try the drink, Jay—it's like lemonade."

There was not much conversation as the four waited; the servants attended to them, keeping their mugs full, until one of the male servants touched Horst on his shoulder, gesturing they should all stand up.

One of the female servants struck a large brass gong, and the sound waves bounced off all the hard surfaces. On that cue, Gana walked into the structure, with his mate, Tresca, following a few steps behind him. She was only a few inches shorter than Gana, but still tall by human standards. The two creatures looked very much alike. Neither had any obvious sexual features, and they wore no clothes over their hairless, green bodies, except Tresca wore one article: a necklace.

Horst was intrigued by the way they walked as a couple. His immediate impression was that they resembled two huge *pigeons*. They walked in a jerky manner, taking a few quick steps, followed by a pause, then a few more quick steps; as they walked, they moved their heads back and forth. Horst also noticed another odd physical trait: When the creatures looked at things, they turned their entire heads rather than merely turning their eyes; apparently, they lacked the necessary facial muscles required to turn their eyeballs.

Gana and Tresca descended into the pit, seating themselves on thick cushions at the empty side of the table.

"Good evening," said Gana in his deep croaky voice. By now, his English had become quite advanced.

To everyone's surprise, his wife also greeted them in English: "Good EVEN-NING." Her pronunciation was somewhat slurred, but still intelligible.

Gana turned toward her. "Very good, Tresca!" He swiveled his head and looked at each of his guests. "As you can hear, I have been teaching Tresca how to speak English. This way, we can more effectively communicate during dinner."

"Yes, we can more EF-FECT-TIV-LEE COM-MUN-NI-CATE during dinner," repeated Tresca.

Horst stood up and gave a quick bow. "It is our pleasure meeting you, Tresca."

As he sat down, one of the female servants topped up Horst's drink; then, she prepared to refill Olga's nearly empty mug.

"*Ömaa* [yes], *hiiko* [drink]," said Olga.

Surprised to hear Olga speaking her language, the female servant smiled. Suddenly, Tresca stood up and lurched at the servant, slapping her in the face with the back of her clawed hand. Terrified, the servant dropped to the floor, prostrating herself, as Tresca continued to chastise her.

Unfazed by this spectacle, Gana slurped from his cup and ate a piece of fruit. He turned his head toward Horst. "I must apologize for our servant's poor behavior. This happens all the time."

"I'm sorry, but what did the servant do?" asked Horst.

"It is good you did not notice. The female had the effrontery to look directly at the young woman in your group."

"You're mad because she smiled at me?" said Olga.

"YES," spat out Tresca. "She HAD the EF-FRONT-TER-REE."

Gana turned toward Horst again. "I'm sure you have run into the same problem."

"I'm not sure what you mean."

"Your servants—bad behavior with your servants."

Gana paused to bite into a pomegranate with his beak-like mouth; purple juice oozed down his face, staining his bone necklace.

"It is a constant problem, isn't it? But this is a part of life—the natural order of things we must constantly enforce."

"Yes, the natural order of things," echoed Horst, looking quite perplexed.

Gana took a swig from his mug, then turned again to speak to Horst.

"We could not help but notice you do not have servants with you. What is your level number? Or do you use letters in your society?"

"*Level number? Letters?* Sorry, but I don't understand."

Gana spoke to Tresca far too quickly for the humans to follow. Then, he spoke again in English: "Perhaps I have not made myself clear. Each of us is assigned a number, based on how we fit within the natural hierarchy of life."

Gana stood up from the table and walked to the edge of the eating pit and stepped up. Then, he began walking around the perimeter, pointing at the ceiling as he talked.

"Observe the stones in this ceiling." He turned his massive head, looking back at his guests, then peered again at the ceiling.

"This structure was built from carefully fitted stones—do you not see them? We instructed our servants to cut each of these stones perfectly, based on exact dimensions."

Stepping down from the edge of the pit, he returned to his place at the table; he placed his three-fingered claw-like hands on his belly.

"Each stone is pushing against its neighboring stone, like this," he said, squeezing his hands tightly together. "Do you not see? The stones are subordinate to this structure. The structure is greater than the stones. The stones are like servants to the structure."

He turned his big head, looking at each one of them, clearly weighing their status. "If we use the number '1' for the structure, we can say the stones are the number '2.'" Finally, he turned to Horst. "What number are you?"

Horst paused.

"We do not assign ourselves numbers in our society. However, for the purpose of our cadet unit, I am called the Captain, Adam is the Lieutenant, and Janu and Olga are both privates."

"So, as the Captain, you are number 1 in your unit?"

"Yes," Horst said.

"And Adam is number 2?"

"Yes, he is," said Horst.

"And, therefore, Janu and Olga are number 3—your servants?"

"No, they are not servants," replied Horst. "We have no servants in New Munich."

"Meaning you are all the same number in New Munich?"

Horst smiled and turned toward Adam. "Do you think you can explain?"

"That is correct, Gana. We do not use numbers—or Greek letters—in our society," replied Adam. "At one time, Earth had kings and queens and dictators who were 'number ones,' but no longer. Of course, Earth probably no longer exists."

Gana and Tresca spoke rapidly to each other. Gana said, "You speak of a place called Earth. What is this place?"

"It is a planet," explained Horst.

"A planet?"

"Yes, follow me, and I will show you."

He climbed out of the eating pit and walked to the edge of the building. Everyone got up from the table and followed Horst, to where he stood, looking up at the sky.

It was a clear, starry night, making it easier for Horst to identify the constellations. When he found what he was looking for, he pointed upward.

"See that star—the third one over?"

Appearing confused, Gana and Tresca looked at each other. Then Gana said to Horst, "What are we looking at?"

"We are looking at the lights in the sky," said Horst.

Gana approached Horst, who was holding his arm out steady, pointing at the stars.

"You will need to follow the length of my arm," instructed Horst.

Gana bent down, following the line of Horst's arm from his shoulder to his extended index finger.

"Good. Now imagine a straight line along my arm. The line is pointing at one of the lights in the sky. Look at the third light."

"Yes, I am looking at the third light," said Gana.

"That third light is our sun," said Horst. "We come from there."

The creature stared blankly at Horst.

"We come from a planet called Earth, which revolves around that star."

Gana said nothing, as he listened to Horst explain about the stars, the planets, the sun, and the Earth. He said abruptly, "We should return to our food and eat." At that, he walked back to the table, followed by Tresca.

Back at the stone dinner table, the human visitors dug into the food as Gana sat quietly, sipping his drink. Each dish was delicious, unlike anything they had ever eaten. Between courses, the humans complimented Gana and Tresca on how delicious the food tasted. The dinner conversation consisted mostly of small talk between the human visitors, while Gana and Tresca listened. The visitors discussed how they were familiar with some of the fruits—the grapes, apples, and small oranges—but that there were many items they had never seen before. They talked about how the fruits and vegetables they ate in New Munich were grown from seeds that had traveled in spacecrafts from Earth.

Horst noticed there was no meat at the table. He found this odd because in the palace chambers, they had been eating spicy foods cooked with chicken and pork. Taking a bite of a pasta dish garnished with a vegetable that looked like asparagus, he savored the taste.

"This is delicious! I can see by these foods you are vegetarians."

"Vegetarians?" said Gana. "I don't understand that term."

"It means this dinner has no meat," said Adam.

"What is MEE-IT?" asked Tresca.

"The word 'meat' means . . . well . . . it means eating other animals," responded Adam.

Tresca and Gana exchanged a few words. Then Gana spoke. "Yes, yes—we understand, but it is not that time of year. We eat, as you say, 'meat,' at the end of the planting seasons. The current planting season will be after the next moon."

At that, he turned his head toward Olga and leered at her. Olga shuddered and immediately looked away, but Gana continued to stare.

"Excuse me, Gana," interjected Horst. "Where did you come from? When you showed us the rock in the courtyard, you said you came from the rock. Can you please explain?"

To Olga's relief, the creature turned toward Horst.

"Certainly. That rock is the location of the passage. Tresca and I were sent here on assignment. We have been at this location for the past two seasons. It is our responsibility to manage this outpost."

"But where were you before this place?"

"We were at another place, somewhat similar to this place."

"You mentioned a 'passage.' We did not see a passage place at the rock. I am sorry, but we do not understand."

"There is much you don't seem to understand," said Gana. "You are being quite difficult!"

"I don't intend to be," said Horst. "It's just all this is very confusing to us. I assume your servants are assigned the number '2,' and you are assigned the number '1.'"

Gana slammed his clawed hand on the table, almost capsizing the remains of the feast.

"The servants are number '4'!" he squawked. "Tresca and I are number '3'! Do you not understand ANYTHING?"

"So if you are number '3,' does that mean you have superiors?" pushed Horst.

Gana pounded on the table once more, breaking his mug into pieces. Rising to his feet, he flung his long arms across the table, sweeping away the plates of food, crashing them to the floor.

The humans jumped to their feet, backing away, cowering at the sight of the enraged creature.

"ENOUGH of these questions! We have talked enough!"

Then he and Tresca stomped away, leaving the humans and servants to themselves.

Chapter 16

WHEN GANA AND TRESCA WERE OUT OF SIGHT, THE GUESTS quietly returned to their seats, exchanging stunned looks. Horst picked at some raw vegetables, which was all that was left of the feast, but nobody else seemed to have an appetite. Eventually, Honovi forcefully tapped Horst on the shoulder and pointed in the direction of the palace.

"Okay, everybody," said Horst. "Time to get moving. Back to our lovely room!"

They followed the men into the darkness, walking in single file, with Honovi and Ciji at the head and tail of the line carrying torches. When they arrived at their chamber, Honovi pointed at their cots and grunted, "*tutskwa,*" meaning "bed."

Following orders, Horst, Adam, Janu, and Olga slipped into their cots. The two servants left the room, carrying the torches with them; the windowless room became pitch black.

Adam was the first to break the silence.

"Okay, Captain, what are you thinking?"

"Let's see . . . I'm still sorting out my thoughts," said Horst. "I think I said a few things that confused Gana."

"Like what?"

"Well, I may have inadvertently exposed him to modern ideas. Sorry—it was my mistake. I just assumed he had a basic understanding of astronomy."

"Like when you talked about the stars and planets?" asked Olga.

"Uh-huh."

"Interesting!" interjected Adam. "Gana may not understand what planets are. He may think the way people thought before Galileo and Copernicus."

"My thoughts, exactly," said Horst.

"Dad, did you see how upset he was when you asked him what number he is? He said he's Number '3'. What's that about?"

"It's simple, Janu. There is someone or something superior to him," replied Horst. "Gana may be a servant to a higher authority."

"*Mein Gott!*" exclaimed Adam. "If he's a Number 3, can you imagine what Numbers 1 and 2 are like?"

"My thoughts exactly," said Horst. "If Gana has superiors, are they superior to us?"

~

Horst slept fitfully that night. The room was poorly ventilated, and he was having a hard time breathing. All he could think about was how much he wanted to get back home to New Munich and to Ingrid; unfortunately, he wasn't even sure where they were! He tossed and turned in his cot for hours, fearing they would never escape.

Eventually, he fell asleep, but for barely an hour. He woke up to the sight of flickering shadows on the ceiling. Exhausted, he lifted his head from the pillow, only to see Takala entering the room, carrying a torch.

Takala announced in a loud voice, "*Um pew ep! Um pew ep!*" which meant they should get up. Walking over to Olga, whose head was still buried under the blankets, he tapped gently on her shoulder. When she finally awoke, they had a brief conversation in Takala's language.

Olga yawned and stretched her arms.

"He wants us to follow him. We're going to the village."

"What?" said Janu. "No *Frühstuck?*"

With barely enough time to pull on their socks, they left the darkness of the chamber and entered the courtyard, which was already awash in brilliant, early morning orange sunlight.

Horst squinted, adjusting his eyes to the abrupt change in lighting. He inhaled the fresh morning air. It was good to be outside. Looking ahead at Takala, he noticed the young man was smiling: It was the first time Horst had ever seen him smile.

They slowly walked across the courtyard, with Horst trailing behind. As they walked, he looked around at the fifty-foot-high walls on all sides, searching for a way to escape. His back was hurting, and he was beginning to feel weaker.

Looking ahead, Horst noticed a gated portion in the wall enclosure, guarded by two men. As they drew closer, he recognized Ciji and Honovi, the servants from the dinner party. Both were leaning against the gates, taking a standing nap.

Takala greeted the men, shouting, *"Lolma!"*

Startled, the two men rubbed their eyes, trying to focus. They jumped into action and began pushing with all their might; slowly, the heavy gates swung open, leaving a gap just wide enough for the travelers to pass through.

It was the first occasion the group had seen beyond the palace walls since their rescue. Horst was surprised to discover they were on an island in the center of a lake encircled by tall, rocky peaks. Squinting from the sun's glare, he saw a village, roughly one hundred and fifty feet across the lake, on the other shore.

Takala led them to a dock where four canoes were tied-up. After untying the canoes, Janu and Olga took one canoe, Adam and Horst another, while Takala took a third canoe by himself.

As they paddled across the lake, Horst looked at the lofty mountain peaks surrounding them. Ever since he was a teenager, he had been a geology buff; now, it seemed apparent to him they were inside a caldera or a dormant volcano.

When the canoes reached the opposite shore, an old man bowed in greeting to Takala, who bowed in return. The elder was a slightly shorter version of Takala; he wore a knitted cap over his grey hair along with a heavy wool vest. When he smiled at the visitors, Horst noted he had gentle eyes.

Horst smiled back. They appeared to be about the same age.

Takala said the man's name was "Hehewuti."

The elder laughed, and corrected Takala, saying, "*Tungwni hoya tsiro taaqa.*"

"He uses the nickname, 'Little Bird Man,'" translated Olga.

"I'm impressed!" said Janu, flashing a grin in Olga's direction.

Takala beckoned everyone to follow him. For a few moments, Horst waited behind, then reached down to pick up a handful of soil, expecting to see volcanic ash or lava; however, upon examining the specimen, all he found was sand. Perplexed, he looked up at the peaks again. *If they weren't inside a volcano, where were they?*

Takala led the procession into a tiny village consisting of one street which was lined on both sides with adobe buildings. Within minutes, the villagers poured out of their homes and filled the street, pressing against each other to have a better view. Takala, however, pushed through the crowd, using his elbows to clear a path.

Horst was the last in line of what seemed like a circus parade. By his estimate, this village was much smaller than New Munich, consisting perhaps of only fifty to eighty people. All around them, children pointed at the strangers: mothers holding their babies gawked, while old men with tobacco-stained teeth, smiled and shook their heads.

When they stopped at the end of the street, next to the small adobe house that was Hehewuti's home, the villagers quickly dispersed. Hehewuti invited the group inside to eat. He walked to the front door, where small clay pots decorated with small holes were hanging on strings next to the entrance to the dwelling. Taking down one of the pots, he peered inside and cleaned the holes; then, having filled it with a liquid, he hung it back up again.

Suddenly, three little birds appeared, flying around Hehewuti's head.

Olga gasped.

"Look! Look at these birds—their wings are so fast, I can't see them!"

"In school, we learned about Earth birds called 'hummingbirds,'" said Janu, marveling at the brilliant blue and emerald plumage.

"Now, I get it! 'Little Bird Man' really means 'Hummingbird Man'!" said Olga, clapping her hands in delight as the birds hovered next to the clay feeder.

Hehewuti made a soft cooing sound. Then, to everyone's amazement, one of the birds landed on his index finger. Hehewuti smiled and whispered something to his little friend; then, it flew to one of the pots, stuck its narrow beak into a hole, then flew away.

Hehewuti turned toward the Americans and waved at them to enter.

"*Um pew*," he said.

Hummingbird Man's house consisted of three small rooms, each about ten feet by ten feet. He led them into a room in which there were many clay pots; stacks of dried corn cobs leaned against one of the walls. There was a square woven rug on the floor, edged with red, white, and black geometric designs.

Horst was still thinking about the hummingbirds they had just seen outside. To his knowledge, the spaceships that landed in New Eden and New Munich had not carried hummingbird embryos—*so how did they get there?* He looked at the woven rug and noticed something interesting in the pattern: an abstract image of a large bird. *Was it an image of a real bird, or was it mythological?* He had heard of large birds on Earth called "eagles"—but there were no eagles in New Munich.

Everyone seated themselves on the rug.

An old woman wearing a white cotton dress and beaded necklace appeared from a side room, carrying trays of food. Barely five feet tall, she wore her long grey hair in a ponytail and appeared to be about the same age as Hummingbird Man. The woman placed the food at the center of the group on the floor.

Nodding to the woman, Takala and Hehewuti began digging into the food, motioning for their guests to do the same. Since the explosion, Horst had become cautious about eating spicy foods; however, seeing a basket of rolls, he assumed they were bland. He took one bite into a roll which tasted like cornbread: until something very spicy set his tongue on fire.

"Wow!" he sputtered, fanning his mouth.

Seeing his distress, the woman immediately came to his rescue, handing him a mug of water. Horst guzzled the entire contents in one swig.

"What's the matter, Dad—food too hot?" laughed Janu. Then, taking a bite out of his roll, he howled in shock, tears streaming down his face. Looking puzzled, the old woman quickly handed him a mug of water as well.

"Ah—I think I'll take a pass on the rolls," said Adam.

Fortunately, there were hard-boiled eggs and melons, which were not spicy.

As they continued their meal, Horst said to Olga, "You're better at their language than I am. Can you ask Hummingbird Man how long he's lived here?"

Olga grimaced, pointing at her mouth, which was full of melon. When she had finished chewing, she wiped her mouth and addressed Hummingbird Man. "*Ken ueyak pia otinen nikan?*"

The old man held his hand about two feet above the floor and said, "*Onikatka tepitsin.*"

"He said he was little when they came?" asked Horst.

"Yes—that's what I understood," said Olga.

"Now ask him where they came from."

Olga turned to Hummingbird Man again. "*Kampa otikuala iuikpa?*"

The old man pointed in the direction of the island.

"*Iuikpa ompa.*"

"Interesting," said Horst. "They come from the island. What did Gana call the place with the rock? A 'passage'?" He shook his head. "I still don't get it."

"Neither do I," said Adam, peeling the shell from a hard-boiled egg.

Looking around the room, Horst noticed a painting on the wall. It depicted a teenage boy who resembled Takala.

Horst smiled at Takala and pointed at the painting, saying "*Ti?*", the word for "you."

Takala nodded. "*Neuatl.*"

Then, Horst asked who made it. "*Akin okiyokoya?*"

"*No tepitsin ueltiu,*" said Takala. Then, abruptly, he stood up and hurried out of the house.

"*No tepitsin ueltiu?*" repeated Horst.

"He said his little sister made the painting," said Olga.

After breakfast, they toured the village with Takala, who had rejoined the group, and Hummingbird Man. They learned the inhabitants spent much of their day tending to small gardens in which they grew corn and beans. They also cultivated fruits that were native to Planet K851b, in addition to some plants the Americans had never seen before. Chickens and pigs wandered freely in a fenced-in area shared by the entire community.

While they were at the gardens, Olga managed to talk to Takala privately. She began by asking him about his family and whether he had any brothers and sisters. Once again, Takala became noticeably upset. Voice trembling, he said that he once had a sister. Her name was Hola, but she was no longer living there. Wiping his nose with the back of his hand, he forced a smile, saying Hola was "the lucky one," and now he was "too old."

When Olga asked Takala where his sister was living, he simply shook his head and looked away. Then his shoulders began to shake, and he broke down and wept.

After seeing the gardens and the livestock, they began heading back down the main street. As they walked, Horst continued to study the geological formations, still convinced they were inside a volcanic caldera. He could visualize a volcano erupting here, leaving these jagged peaks: this image was now cemented in his memory. *But what was it like to live there, in this small place—trapped?*

Was there a way out?

They walked back to Hummingbird Man's house, where Hehewuti excused himself from the tour. It was time for his afternoon nap. Meanwhile, Takala said he was going to take them to the cave where he had found them.

It was only a short distance from Hummingbird Man's house to the cave. Takala retrieved a torch, which was just inside the entrance, lit it, then motioned for everyone to follow him inside.

In less than a hundred feet, they came to a deep hole. Takala stopped and explained how he had heard a loud sound and climbed down this hole; he had found them at the end, where the cave had somehow collapsed. Their bodies were covered with rocks.

"Is the cave sealed off?" asked Horst.

Takala nodded, yes, *"Owi."* The cave was now completely sealed; there was no other way out—except, of course, for the passage on the island.

Horst tilted his head and pursed his lips, confused to hear about a "passage" again. He looked at Adam, who seemed equally confused.

When they exited the cave, this ended their tour of the village. Takala announced it was time for his afternoon nap and left them on their own.

"What is it with these people and their naps?" said Janu.

"They sleep as much as cats!" laughed Olga.

Janu and Olga decided to do some more exploring by themselves while Horst and Adam walked over to Hummingbird Man's house and sat down on the front steps.

Adam scratched the back of his neck and frowned.

"I'm getting bored," he said. "I need to work on something. How are we getting out of here?"

"I'm not sure," sighed Horst who was staring at his feet, his shoulders slumped.

"Are you feeling okay?"

"It's nothing." Horst's voice trailed off. "I just want to get out of here."

He looked in the distance, as though searching for an escape route.

"I just hope Hansel and Jeff get a backhoe up here and try to dig through that cave."

"Do you think they're trying to dig us out right now?" asked Adam, his eyebrows raised.

"How should I know?" snapped Horst, throwing up his hands. "Everything is beyond our control!" With a pained expression, he looked at Adam. "I think we're captives."

~

In late afternoon, after nap-time, the village became active again. Olga and Janu had spent the afternoon swimming in the lake while Horst and Adam had spent the afternoon exploring the perimeter of the caldera, searching for a way out.

They returned to Hummingbird Man's place, just in time for the evening meal. The same old woman appeared, once again carrying plates of food. She must have understood the newcomers did not like hot spices, for she served a chicken dish, which was only mildly seasoned.

As he ate, Horst wrestled with an enigma: *The villagers resembled them and ate Earth foods—they even had hummingbirds! But if they were from Earth, how did they get there?*

~

It was almost sunset when Horst, Adam, Janu, and Olga paddled back to the island in two canoes. After landing, they walked to the gates, where the male servants, Honovi and Ciji, were still standing guard, apparently waiting for their return. They escorted the Americans to the palace chamber, leaving a torch in a wall bracket to illuminate the room.

It had been a long day, and everyone was tired and ready for bed. Olga, Janu, and Adam slipped into their cots. Horst, however, knelt on the floor and rummaged through his backpack.

"Horst, are you going to put out the torch?" mumbled Adam.

Without answering, Horst continued sifting through his belongings until he found what he was looking for: a small hammer, a chisel, and a magnifying glass.

"I'm going outside to use the outhouse," he announced, then walked out of the chamber carrying the hammer, chisel, and magnifying glass with him.

Adam jumped out of his cot, grabbed the torch, and followed Horst. When he caught up with him in the hallway, he said, "Planning on doing some prospecting?"

"If you're coming, you've gotta be quiet—and leave that torch behind!"

Adam extinguished the torch, leaving it near the building exit. When they stepped outside, it was not as dark as they had expected; in fact, there was a full moon, and the sky glowed with millions of stars.

Adam followed Horst, who, instead of heading to the outhouse, set out in the direction of the dome. As they drew closer, they could see torchlight flickering from inside. Crouching down, they walked in the shadows until they reached the perimeter of the dome. They hid next to one of the arched openings.

Cautiously, Horst peered around the wall and looked down into the pit area. He was surprised to see two massive figures kneeling at the base of the rock.

He turned back to Adam, whispering, "It's Gana and Tresca!"

"What are they doing?"

He peeked again, then turned back to Adam.

"Looks like they're praying—praying or having some sort of ceremony to the rock."

"You mean 'at the rock'?"

"No—I mean, they're praying *to* the rock."

Gana and Tresca were kneeling, facing the rock, with their heads down. After almost ten minutes, they stood up and bowed to the rock. Gana picked up the torch, and the two began walking up the spiral ramp, drawing close to where Horst and Adam were hiding. Gana suddenly stopped in his tracks and looked in their direction; fortunately, Tresca pulled his arm, and the two strutted away from the dome.

Horst and Adam watched them until they could no longer see their torch.

"Okay, Horst, they're gone. Now what?"

"You can either follow me or go back to bed, but I've gotta do this."

Not waiting for an answer, Horst walked under the dome, to the spiral ramp leading toward the rock.

When they reached the bottom, Horst studied the rock. It was virtually impossible to see any details despite the moonlight. Judging by its silhouette, he estimated the megalith was about ten feet wide and ten feet tall.

"I can't see a damned thing," he complained. He approached the rock and felt it. "Feels smooth." Turning toward Adam, he said, "We need a small sample. Do you see any loose rocks on the ground?"

Adam looked around.

"I hope I don't fall into a trap door or something! They said there is a passage here."

"Ha, ha—very funny!"

Adam felt the ground for rock fragments. Eventually, he found a small piece and picked it up. When he turned toward Horst, he was shocked to see him holding the chisel and hammer against the big rock.

"Horst—wait! Are you sure?"

But before Adam could stop him, Horst had already chipped away a piece of the rock.

"Got it! Now let's get out of here!"

Chapter 17

THE NEXT MORNING, TAKALA WOKE THEM UP AND TOLD them to get ready for another excursion to the village. This time, Horst took his backpack in which he placed the rock specimens he and Adam had collected the night before.

After paddling the canoes across the lake, they walked directly to Hummingbird Man's house, where they ate breakfast—a flatbread made from cornmeal, fried beans, eggs, fried ground pork, melons, and an unusual vegetable, which they had never seen before. There were two clay pots, one containing a spicy red sauce while the other was filled with a spicy green sauce.

Olga watched Takala prepare his food: he placed the ground pork on the flatbread with the vegetable, then he added some green sauce using a wooden spoon, then he rolled it up. She tried to make a roll using a similar technique, except with less of the spicy sauce. She took a bite, then she nodded as she chewed. "This is good. I like green sauce."

The others made similar rolls. The consensus was the rolls were better with the green sauce.

Janu experimented, trying a mixture of the red and green sauces on his food; however, after the first bite, he was fanning himself. Fortunately, the old woman came to his rescue with a mug of water, which he chugged down quickly.

After breakfast, Janu and Olga followed Takala and Hummingbird Man to the garden, while Horst and Adam stayed behind.

"Okay, what's the plan for today?" asked Adam once the others had left.

Horst grabbed his backpack. "Follow me—we're going to the cave."

They walked the short distance from Hummingbird Man's house to the cave. Horst placed his backpack on the floor, near the entrance where there was enough light to see; then he removed the rock specimens which they had collected the night before.

Adam watched how carefully Horst handled the rocks: as though he was holding precious gems.

"So, you're still interested in rocks? You were always into geology when we were kids in New Eden."

"Yes, sir. Geology has always been a passion of mine," said Horst, examining the smaller rocks with the eye of a jeweler. "Geology is like understanding chemistry on a fundamental level."

He held the rock fragment up to the light and studied it.

"Most people would call this simply a 'rock'—or worse yet, 'dirt'! Not all rocks are the same*, meinen Freund!"*

Horst knelt on the stone floor of the cave, then, reaching into his backpack, he removed the magnifying glass, small hammer, and chisel he had used to collect his rock specimen the night before.

"We're going to take a look at these rocks you picked up off the ground last night, Adam," he said, looking up at his old friend. Taking one of the smaller rocks, which was about three inches in diameter, he placed it on the stone floor. With his left hand, he held the pointed chisel directly on top of the rock; then, with his right hand, he held the hammer and prepared to strike.

"Okay, let's see if I can break this sucker. I'm about to make some noise—this is why I wanted us to go to this cave. You may want to cover your ears."

Adam covered his ears as Horst hammered on the rock several times.

"Good thing everyone's out in the fields—you're making a racket!"

Horst continued pounding, until the rock split. Then he held up the two halves to examine them. "Notice how the inside is the same color and texture as the outside? It's all the same: There are no fossils."

"Fossils?"

"Fossils—you know, dead stuff, like the skeletons of dead fish and sea-life."

"Oh, yeah, I never thought about that. So, we can rule out the possibility this rock came from the bottom of a lake or a sea?"

"Exactly. In other words, this rock is not what's called a 'sedimentary' rock."

Horst retrieved two boxes from his backpack and placed them on the cave's floor.

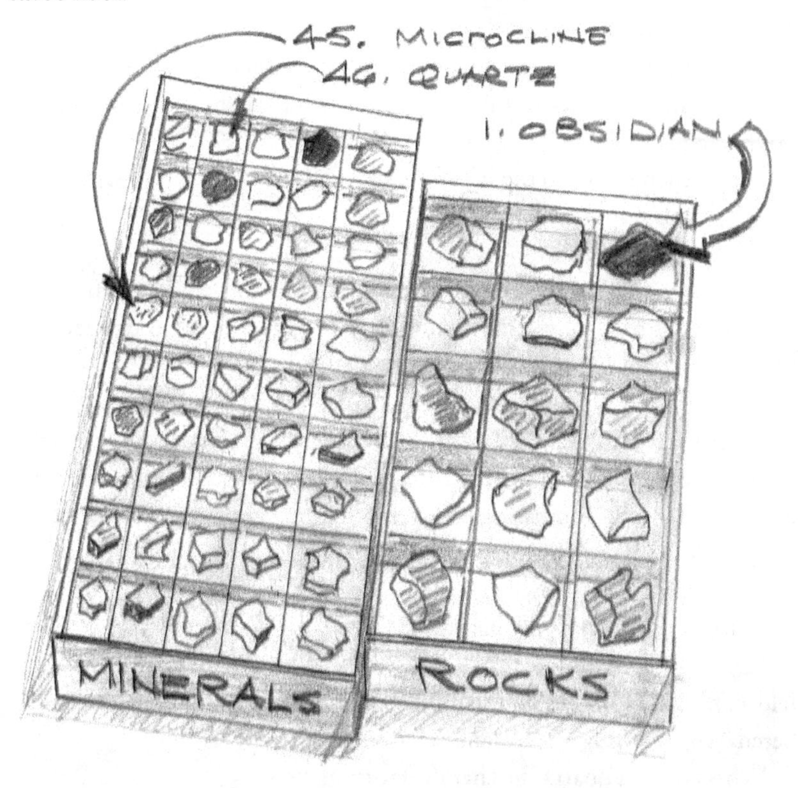

"Okay, don't laugh. These are my collections of rocks and minerals. They took me years to put together."

"You take this stuff with you everywhere?" asked Adam in amazement.

"Don't be ridiculous. I only use this when I'm exploring. I was going to use it on the Cadet expedition, but I never got around to it."

Horst opened the lid of one box. It contained many little pieces of rocks, each of which had a paper label with a number written on it.

"This box has fifty different types of minerals."

"Stupid question: What's the difference between a mineral and a rock?"

"A mineral is a chemical compound found in nature. A rock is made from one or more minerals."

"What are the numbers about?"

"The numbers correspond to a list of mineral names, which I have right here."

Horst removed a piece of paper on the back of the box lid; then he read the faded words:

"We have 'sulfur,' 'graphite,' 'copper,' 'gypsum,' 'quartz,' 'augite'—in total, fifty different elements and minerals with complex chemistry, just inside this box alone."

Horst then removed the lid of the second box.

"Now, this box is my box of rocks."

"And?" asked Adam.

Horst frowned. "No need for sarcasm, Adam. You can see there are sixteen different rock samples, which we'll use to identify the rock specimen I chipped off last night."

"Should I be taking notes?"

Ignoring Adam's remark, Horst reached in his pants pocket and retrieved the rock specimen from the big rock to which Gana and Tresca had been praying. He began comparing it to the samples in his rock collection.

"This looks like obsidian, wouldn't you say?"

He held the rock closer to Adam. "See how it's black on the outside?"

"Sure, it's definitely very black."

"Obsidian is a volcanic rock comprised of the minerals quartz and alkali feldspar," said Horst. From the mineral box, he picked up the sample numbered "46," showing it to Adam.

"This is called quartz. Its chemical formula is SiO_2."

Then he picked up another piece, bearing the number "45."

"And this piece is a type of feldspar called 'microcline.' It's a tectosilicate or aluminosilicate with formula $KAlSi_3O_8$."

"Okay, whatever you say—I trust you. But, yeah, these minerals look like the piece of rock you chipped last night."

"I think that we can conclude this rock is obsidian," said Horst, but his voice trailed off. He stopped and grimaced, his eyebrows furrowed together.

"What's the matter?"

Horst shook his head. "There's something that doesn't make sense, something which has me completely baffled." He stood up and looked in the direction of the lake, rubbing his chin. "When we traveled here in the canoe, my first impression was we are inside a volcanic caldera. I would expect to see obsidian in a volcanic caldera."

"Which you've just proven . . . so, what's the issue?"

"The problem is, the *other* soil around here is not volcanic."

"Uh? I'm not following you," said Adam, staggering to his feet.

"I was expecting to see evidence of old lava flows, but I haven't seen any at all!" said Horst, shaking his head. "I'm not convinced we're in a caldera. What are we missing? What is the piece of the puzzle I'm missing?"

For several minutes Horst examined the rock, holding it up so he could compare it to his samples. "Adam, hold the boxes for a minute—I want to recheck the split rock."

Horst peered through the magnifying glass, examining every facet of the rock.

"Definitely not quartz or feldspar. No, not at all. See the grey metallic interior? This proves this is not obsidian!"

He held the magnifying glass close to the rock fragment so Adam could take a look.

"I have no samples like this in my collection. This seems to indicate a metal alloy, perhaps nickel and iron. . . ."

Suddenly, Horst's mouth fell open. "*Mein Gott!* I don't know why it took me so long! Adam, come with me!" Horst suddenly stood up and began walking away.

Confused, Adam followed Horst as he hobbled down the village path toward the lake. When they reached the lake, Horst looked all around him. "Look! It makes perfect sense! Why did it take me so long?"

"What on Earth should I be looking at?"

Horst pointed at the cliffs surrounding the entire site.

"See the rock edges surrounding us? They form a perfect circle. The circle is centered on the rock on the island. It can only mean one thing: The rock on the island is a meteor that fell from space!"

"You mean we are inside . . . *a meteor crater?*"

Horst nodded.

"Yes, I'm convinced the big rock on the island is a meteor. It must have created this crater."

"But why are they worshipping the rock?" asked Adam.

"I have no idea. Somehow we must find out!"

Chapter 18

HORST SCANNED THE SURROUNDING MOUNTAIN RANGE, HIS eyes widening as he took in the mountains, the lake, the island. . . . Everything emanated from the rock at the center.

"A meteor impact created all of this! It's so obvious," he said to Adam, who was standing next to him.

Suddenly, Adam screamed.

Horst spun around, but someone grabbed him from behind, placing him in a chokehold. He struggled, trying to break free, but his right arm was in a hammerlock; the more he resisted, the harder his opponent pulled his left arm up until it felt like it was about to break.

Looking at Adam, he saw Ciji was restraining him. He couldn't see who was holding him but guessed it was Honovi.

Then he heard Hummingbird Man shouting. "*Honovi! Ciji! Xia!*"

Immediately, the two brutes released Horst and Adam.

Horst fell to his knees, rubbing his arm, which throbbed from his elbow to his shoulder.

He heard Olga sobbing uncontrollably, and he turned. She and Janu had their hands tied behind their backs, held at knifepoint by Takala.

Hummingbird Man tossed Honovi and Ciji two pigskin straps and again shouted at them. "*Kechmekayeuantin ako!*"

Picking up the straps, the two strongmen tied Horst and Adam's hands behind their backs so tightly Horst swore under his breath. He wiggled his hands, trying to loosen them, but Honovi slapped him hard in the face, knocking him to the ground.

Horst landed on his left side, which intensified the pain in his arm.

"Eh man, locker bleiben!" [Take it easy, man!]

Honovi barked a flurry of orders, which Horst did not understand. Infuriated, Honovi grabbed him by the armpits and pulled him to his feet, pointing him in the direction of the canoes, which were beached on the lakeshore ahead of them. He kicked him in the butt.

Bewildered, Horst, Adam, Janu, and Olga trudged across the beach. When they reached the shore, their captives placed each of the prisoners in separate canoes.

They paddled across the lake to the island. After landing, the prisoners marched in single file toward the palace gates, with Honovi repeatedly shoving Horst from behind, trying to get him to walk faster.

Upon entering the palace courtyard, their captors forced them to walk in the direction of the dome. Looking ahead, Horst could see the upper part of the big rock—*the meteor. Gana must have discovered a piece of it was missing!*

When the group arrived at the edge of the dome, Gana and Tresca were standing next to the meteor, looking directly up at them. Honovi and Ciji shoved their prisoners in the back, pushing them down the spiral ramp. Upon reaching the bottom of the ramp, they stood before the two colossal creatures.

Gana paced back-and-forth, examining each of their faces with his bulging eyes. Finally, he turned toward Horst and pointed at the damaged portion of the rock.

"Tell me, which one of you damaged the sacred object?"

"It was me," said Horst, flatly.

Gana stomped on the ground, shouting a flurry of words at Honovi and Ciji, who were standing behind the prisoners.

"Sávikna put!" [Hit him!]

Honovi stepped forward and punched Horst in the stomach so hard he went crashing to the ground, skidding until he came to a stop against the sacred rock.

Infuriated, Gana screamed at Honovi in his native tongue. The manservant cowered, apologizing profusely, while Horst lay crumpled against the meteorite, gasping for air.

Gana turned his massive head toward Adam. "And you?" he said in his raspy voice. "I sense you, too, were involved in this incident. Is this true?"

Wincing, Adam nodded slightly.

Without waiting for orders, Ciji sucker-punched Adam in the gut, and, with one blow, sent him crashing against the rock where he slumped over, next to Horst.

Enraged, Gana threw his long arms up and gave out a primal scream that echoed throughout the dome. By now, Ciji was shaking so hard his knees seemed about to buckle under him.

Gana glared at him, before turning toward Olga, who was sobbing uncontrollably.

"Silence!" he commanded, turning toward Janu.

"And you? Were you and the girl involved in this act?"

Janu emphatically shook his head.

"No, no, sir! We had nothing to do with this!"

Gana stared at the teenagers. After a long pause, he said, "I believe you. Last night I did not *feel* your presence. I should have trusted my instincts; I felt a disturbance. I could tell Tresca and I were not alone."

The creature looked at Horst and Adam, who were still slumped against the meteorite, their arms covering their faces, bracing for the next attack.

"Now, explain why you were in the dome last night and why you damaged the sacred monument!"

Horst didn't respond, so Gana motioned to Honovi, who yanked him to his feet, while holding his left arm in a hammerlock.

Barely able to speak, Horst wheezed out a reply. "We wanted . . . or rather, *I* wanted, to determine what type of rock this is," he panted. "I like rocks—that's all . . . I didn't think it was such a big deal! I chipped off only a small piece! *Mein Gott!*" Then he stopped to catch his breath.

Gana's chest was heaving. With his sharp teeth exposed, he glared at Horst.

"Go on!" he ordered. "Finish what you were saying! You stopped!"

Momentarily confused, not sure what he meant, Horst said nothing.

"I am *ordering* you! What did you determine about the sacred rock?"

Hesitantly, Horst began to explain. "I determined this rock is . . . well, it's quite unusual."

"Unusual? In what way?"

"It is not from this planet. It's my conclusion this is a meteor that fell from the sky."

Incensed, Gana stepped closer to Horst, who flinched instinctively.

"There you go again! You speak of unnatural ideas! What do you mean 'It fell from the sky'? You talk about things in the sky!"

For a few moments, the creature glared at Horst. Finally, he turned toward Tresca and the two disappeared behind the rock, while the prisoners sat quietly, held under guard. After some time, Gana and Tresca reappeared.

"Your presence here has complicated our lives," said Gana. "This exceeds my authority. We have decided to contact our superiors about this matter."

Gana turned toward the guards.

"*Waynuma qatu!*" [Go to the room!]

At that, the strongmen grabbed the prisoners and escorted them back to the palace.

When they returned to the chamber, the guards did not untie their hands. They were to wait while Gana consulted with his superiors. The men sat on their cots, but Olga paced back-and-forth, sobbing uncontrollably again.

"I've got to get out of here! I've got to get out of here!"

"I'm sorry. If I had only known how much trouble I was creating—" interjected Horst.

"Who cares about that stupid rock!" she screamed.

"What?"

Olga stopped her pacing and looked directly at Horst.

"TAKALA SAID I'VE BEEN CHOSEN!"

"Chosen?" repeated Horst. "What does that mean?"

Janu stood up. "Dad, figure it out! Haven't you noticed the big stairs?"

"Big stairs? Oh yeah, the stairs over the palace."

"That's where they have the ceremonies," interrupted Janu. "Takala said they do it twice a year. The last time they chose his little sister, Hola."

"The ceremony?" repeated Adam, his eyebrows squished together.

"THEY'RE PLANNING ON SACRIFICING ME!" sobbed Olga, unable to wipe away the tears streaming down her face.

"*Mein Gott!*" gasped Adam.

"We've got to find something to cut these straps!" said Horst.

Frantically, he looked around the room, searching for a sharp object. Finding nothing suitable, he walked over to Olga and turned his back. "Quick! Turn around! I'll try to untie you!"

Once they were back-to-back, the two worked on untying the straps.

"Hold on, slow down, Olga," Horst said. "Let me free you first."

He turned toward Adam, who looked stunned.

"Hurry up, Adam! Untie Janu!"

The straps were extremely tight. Horst dug his fingers as hard as he could into one of the knots.

"Captain, I've got to get out of here!" cried Olga. "Are they loosening?"

He felt a little movement. "I think I've got a wiggle."

His fingers pried further.

"Yeah, I can feel it loosening . . . just a little more."

Suddenly, they heard the footsteps of guards in the hallway, coming to retrieve them.

When the guards marched them outside, the sun was setting, and the sky had turned a bright orange. Horst squinted, adjusting to the abrupt transition from the dark chamber.

The taller guard, Honovi, walked behind Horst, repeatedly pushing him in the back and pointing at the dome.

"*Ya!*" [Go!] he grunted.

As they walked, Horst searched in every direction, looking for a way to escape. He knew he would never make it out alive, he was too slow, but Janu and Olga must escape—*they had their whole lives ahead!*

"*Ya!*" said Honovi, prodding Horst in the back again. "*Nenemi!*" [Walk!]

Horst walked as fast as he could, but still lagged far behind the others. Looking ahead, he saw the others had almost reached the dome. Then, suddenly, Olga broke away from the group. She sprinted away from her captors with the speed of a cheetah, with Takala chasing after her. Next, just as suddenly, Janu also broke away, running in the opposite direction.

Honovi stopped to watch. He laughed mockingly, his upper lip curling in disdain. Shaking his head, he ordered Horst to proceed.

"*Ya!*"

As Horst limped on, he wondered where Janu and Olga could go: *Could they climb over the wall? Could they swim across the lake and scale the cliffs?*

Behind him, the tall staircase over the palace led to nowhere: It was a high dive to death. *How could he have imagined Gana and Tresca were vegetarians after seeing their sharp teeth? In truth, they were monsters who had a taste for teenagers.*

When Horst and Honovi finally reached the dome, Adam and Hehewuti were standing still, staring in the direction of the rock. Horst followed their gaze and saw something so strange he wasn't sure if it was real or his imagination. The floor beneath the meteorite now resembled a swirling molten silver pool, spinning counter-clockwise with the rock at its center. Both Gana and Tresca were kneeling in front of the meteorite, completely motionless. Then they stood up and tossed something into the pool. Almost instantly, the silver pool vanished, and the ground reappeared.

Speechless, Horst and Adam stared at each other. When they looked at the rock again, Gana and Tresca were both looking up at them. Gana waved his three-fingered claw-like hand, motioning them to come down to the sacred space. Reluctantly, Horst took the first steps down the spiral ramp. Walking stiffly, knees locked, he slowly led the way down the spiral ramp, coiling through two revolutions, until they reached the bottom and stopped at the feet of the towering creatures.

Horst stared straight ahead at Gana's midsection, without seeing. He winced, but, strangely, nothing happened. Gradually, he looked up from Gana's stomach to his face and noted the creature did not appear angry.

"We have just consulted with our superiors," Gana said. "They have made a decision."

He paused, looking up at the image of a spiral on the ceiling.

"The other night, I explained to you I am a 'Number 3.' You seemed confused—were you not?"

"Yes, your statement was confusing; but I also found it quite intriguing," said Horst.

"Intriguing?"

"Yes, intriguing. If you are a 'Number 3,' this leads me to believe you have superiors."

"You are correct. Tresca and I are servants to a higher authority," said Gana, pointing at the ceiling of the dome.

"We are like the stones of this structure."

He pushed the palms of his two claw-like hands together.

"We are servants to something greater than us, but that something requires us. In turn, we, as subordinates, require this greater thing." He turned his head to look at Horst. "Do you understand?"

"Yes—I understand," responded Horst hesitantly. "We are all servants."

"Good—you understand. My existence and Tresca's existence, in fact, the existence of these people who live here, is tied to this rock. You see, we are—what is the word in English?" He paused momentarily. "Ah, yes, the word is 'nomads'—it is a word I read in one of the boy's childish stories."

Gana stopped abruptly, the veins in his eyes turning a livid red.

"Where are the boy and the girl?"

Horst and Adam stared at him blankly, frozen to the spot.

"Where are they, I said?"

He took three steps toward them, but just as he was about to slash their faces with his claws, he seemed to change his mind. Instead, he gave orders to Ciji who bowed and ran off. "*Tsööpölti diyo niqw mana!*" [Catch hold of the boy and girl!]

"We will find them," said Gana calmly. "There is no way they can escape. As I was saying, we are 'nomads.' We go from place to place—from 'rock' to 'rock'—following this path you see on the ceiling."

"But what is the spiral?" asked Horst.

"The spiral is how life unfolds."

"Are you saying the spiral represents time?"

"It is what it is. It is what is given to us. It is something we do not question." Gana looked directly at Horst and Adam. "Our superiors have made a decision: You are to travel to the next camp."

"The next camp?" repeated Adam.

"Yes, the next camp. It has been decided that we have been in this place too long. Tresca and I have been here two seasons; Hehewuti has been here since he was a small child. Now, look at him! He is an old man!"

Horst looked at Hehewuti and estimated he was in his early to mid-seventies. *Could the people have been living there seventy-plus years?*

"You two are to go to the next camp as our scouts," continued Gana. "If it is safe for us to proceed, you will return to let us know."

"Ah . . . what do you mean by, '*if*' it's safe to proceed?" asked Adam.

Gana pointed up at the image of a spiral on the ceiling: "We follow this path, right here," he said, pointing at a segment that seemed to be spinning in a vortex. "This is this group's assigned path. We go places where we have never been before."

He turned to look directly at Horst.

"You will be leading us into an unknown world."

"Listen to me," said Horst, pointing his right index finger at Gana. "We *live* here! We have our own lives here, in New Munich!"

Gana held up a three-fingered hand, signaling to Honovi, who began to advance toward Horst.

Horst planted his feet firmly on the ground, turned his body at an angle as Honovi drew closer.

"*Ueikapa!*" commanded Gana.

Honovi stopped in his tracks and waited while Gana said something to Tresca. She walked over to a box located next to the sacred rock. Carefully, she raised the lid, removing two small bags, which she handed to Gana.

Gana held up the bags.

"These bags contain the means for making your passage."

He reached into one bag and pulled out four small blue pellets.

"You will use these ones to go forward," he said, handing the four blue pellets to Horst. Reaching into the other bag, he took out four red pellets.

"And you will use these to return."

Confused, Horst held up the four blue and four red pellets. They were perfect spheres, each about a quarter of an inch in diameter.

"It is best if you keep them separated. Do you understand?"

"No, I don't understand anything you're saying!" objected Horst.

"Of course, you don't understand!" snapped the creature. "But you will learn!"

Gana looked at Adam then back to Horst.

"Repeat what I just explained."

Horst held up a blue pellet.

"You said we will use the blue ones to go forward in the passage." Then he held up a red pellet. "And the red ones to come back."

Then Gana turned his head toward Adam, awaiting his response.

"Ah . . . blue to go forward, red to return."

"Exactly! This is all you need to know. Do not lose them! It is your only way to come back."

Gana walked closer to the rock, beckoning them to step forward. "Stand here."

Reluctantly, Adam and Horst followed instructions.

"Do not move," said Gana.

He and Tresca backed away, stopping almost twenty feet away from the rock.

"Take out one of the pellets for going forward," ordered Gana.

Horst and Adam each held up a blue pellet.

"Now, throw the pellets at the sacred rock!"

"If we don't throw them, what will happen?" asked Horst.

"If you don't throw them, Honovi will tie you up and throw them for you," sneered Gana.

Hesitantly, they threw the blue pellets at the rock. Suddenly, the floor became like a swirling molten silver disk again, growing larger in diameter, until it was about eight feet across, with its edge only a few feet from where Horst and Adam were standing. Then a small black sphere appeared at the center of the silver disk. The sphere grew and grew, until it encompassed the silver disk.

Mesmerized, Horst and Adam stared into the sphere, completely unaware Gana and Tresca had quietly moved behind them. Before they knew what was happening, they found themselves in a freefall into complete darkness, disappearing from view.

Chapter 19

After Olga broke free, she sprinted to the wall surrounding the island. Gulping down breaths, she pressed her back against the wall and looked up: It was fifty-feet tall, impossible to climb. The wall's smooth adobe surface had no holes or projections to grab onto.

Her leg muscles tightened, ready to run in an instant. Suddenly, she saw Takala's approaching silhouette, and she launched into a full sprint. In less than a minute, she reached the other side of the island, stopped by the wall enclosure.

She was boxed-in, trapped like a hamster in a cage. Everything was happening too fast for her to process. *How long could she keep running like this? All night?* She looked for something to hide behind, a tree or a bush, but the palace grounds were barren of vegetation.

Then she saw something familiar: It was the place where they had dinner the night before with Gana and Tresca—the techy, curved canopy, which Adam called a "hyperbolic paraboloid." And next to the canopy was a round hut-like building: *This must be where Gana and Tresca live.*

She ran behind the house and flattened herself up against the building. Trembling in the moonlight, she listened for Takala.

Suddenly, a door burst open and Takala ran out of the house.

Olga fell to the ground and tried to make herself as small as possible; but Takala easily found her.

He ran to her and stood above her, smiling triumphantly with his hands on his hips, obviously enjoying the chase. Then he reached into his pouch and removed two pigskin straps. Crouching in an aggressive stance, he held one strap between his teeth and the other between his hands, and slowly approached Olga, as though he was about to tie a pig.

As Takala came closer, Olga stood up and faced him. Her eyes locked on to his eyes, preparing for his attack.

Suddenly, Janu grabbed Takala from behind and placed him in a hammerlock. Olga pounced on Takala and covered his mouth.

"Jay, what should I do?" she said, struggling to hold Takala's head.

"Put one of your socks in his mouth!"

Using one hand, she removed a sock and stuffed it in Takala's mouth.

"Good—that'll shut him up!" Janu threw the pigskin straps to Olga. "Now, tie his hands with these!"

Janu held Takala's arms while Olga tied his hands behind his back. Together, they managed to wrestle him to the ground. When they were finished, Takala lay hog-tied on his stomach, with Janu sitting on his back.

"Ollie, can you check if anyone's coming?"

"Okay."

Olga snuck to the side of the hut. Breathing heavily, she looked in the direction of the dome. She was surprised to see colored lights projected against the dome's ceiling. The lights were dancing in swirling, spiraling patterns.

She ran back and reported. "There's something strange happening at the dome."

"Like what?"

"Like weird colored lights."

Janu furrowed his eyebrows. "I hope Adam and Horst are all right."

In a shrill voice, Olga whispered, "We've got to get out of here!"

"What do you want me to do?" Janu threw up his hands.

"I don't know! Maybe we can find a rope to climb over the wall!"

Takala's eyes widened. He was trying to say something, mumbling through the sock.

Olga looked at Takala, then back again at Janu. "Should I take the sock out?"

Janu tightened his hold on Takala. "Okay, take it out. I've got him."

Cringing, Olga reached over to Takala's mouth and gingerly pulled the sock out.

Takala gasped for air. He panted for a couple of seconds, then he said one word: "*Kalakoakisan.*"

Janu grimaced. "*Kalak* . . . ? Did you understand?"

"I think he said 'door' . . . or maybe 'door out.'"

Janu's eyes narrowed. "Why would he want to show us a door out?"

Olga paused, trying to view the situation from Takala's perspective. Then she remembered Takala's sister, who was sacrificed during the last offering. "Maybe he wants to save us from the same fate as Hola."

Hearing his sister's name, Takala looked at Olga and shook his head. "*No-ah Hola! No-ah Hola!*"

Olga repeated, "*Kalakoakisan*? Door?"

Takala nodded. "Ye-es. Doe-ARR," he said, making the 'r' sound like a dog growling.

Olga bit her lip. "Jay, I think we have no choice but to trust him."

They grabbed Takala by the armpits and pulled him up. Then, Takala began leading them in the direction of the palace.

As they approached the palace, Olga searched for an escape door. At the front of the palace stood the sacrificial platform, rising high above the palace roof; and at the back of the palace stood the fifty-foot wall surrounding the island. It suddenly occurred to her, *There must be an exit at the back of the palace through the wall!*

She stopped and faced Takala and pointed at the back of the palace: "*Kalakoayan*? Door?"

Takala nodded. "Ye-es . . . *Kalakoakisan* . . . Doe-ARR."

"Did you guys just say the door is in the palace?" asked Janu.

"Yes. He's saying it's in the back!"

Olga looked at the sacrificial staircase and wondered, do these people willingly sacrifice themselves—or are they forced? She shook her head, as images flashed through her mind of the poor souls who had plunged to their deaths here, including Hola.

Then her gaze drifted to the moon directly overhead: The moon was almost full. Suddenly, her body stiffened, as she realized a terrifying thought: Sacrifices must occur during a full moon! It must be almost time for the next sacrifice!

From the corner of his eye, Takala saw Olga's shocked reaction. He slowed his pace and came to a stop, and looked at Olga and the staircase, ping-ponging between the two. With anger in his eyes, he glared at the staircase. But his anger was momentary, lasting only a few seconds. He broke down, sobbing, repeating his sister's name, "*Hola, Hola . . .*" again and again.

Janu shook Takala's arm and ordered, "Keep moving!" He pointed him in the direction of the palace.

Takala shrugged and began moving.

They walked to the side entrance to the palace, which they had used before. Instead of taking them to the palace chambers, Takala led them down a hallway toward the back. This hallway was dimly lit by small fires in stone bowls on tables.

As they walked, Olga watched their shadows dancing on the hallway walls. She worried the others would be coming soon, and looked behind her. *Was Takala leading them into a trap?*

When they reached the end of the hallway, Takala stopped and turned around. With his back to Janu, he gestured for him to untie his hands.

Janu hesitated.

"Untie him, Jay. We have no choice."

After his hands were untied, Takala began searching for something in the hallway. He walked back and forth, looking overhead, until he stopped and pointed at a rope; the end of the rope was more than six feet above the floor.

Takala stood on his toes and reached for the rope. Barely able to reach, he grabbed the end of the rope and pulled it down; simultaneously, a section of the wall slid upward, exposing an opening in the wall. When he was finished, he tied the rope to a bracket.

Takala grinned and pointed at the opening, saying, "*Kalakoayan!*" Then he got down on his hands and knees and crawled through the opening. Peeking his head through, he waved at Janu and Olga to follow.

Olga grabbed Janu by the arm. "I'm worried—this could be a trap."

Janu shrugged. "I'll go first; you stay here. If things look good, I'll wave you in."

"What if things don't look good?"

"We'll go to Plan B."

Olga bit her lip. "Uh . . . Plan B . . . ?"

But Janu did not answer, and crawled through the opening.

Olga paced up and down the hallway, with her arms folded, waiting for Janu.

It did not take Janu long before he stuck his head through the opening. "Come on through, Ollie. We don't need Plan B."

Olga crawled through the opening and found herself inside a courtyard. At the back of the courtyard, Takala and Janu were standing next to the fifty-foot-tall wall. They were both jumping up and down, trying to grab another rope.

Olga ran over to them. At the bottom of the enclosure wall was a small sliding door—the *Kalakoayan*—their only chance to escape. Dangling above the sliding door was the rope for opening the door. The end of the rope was about eight feet above the ground. She let out a huge breath and hugged Takala. *"Danke! Vielen Dank!"*

Takala was far too short to grab the rope. He looked at Janu and held his hands together, pantomiming he wanted to lift him up.

Janu stepped into Takala's clasped hands and stood up: Unfortunately, they were still about six inches too short.

"Ollie, we need something to stand on!"

Olga turned around and looked for something to use as a step. On the opposite side of the courtyard, she noticed there were many tall rocks.

"I see some rocks over there, Jay. Get down and help me move them."

Olga began walking over to the rocks. As she came closer, she noticed the rocks were shaped like narrow pyramids; each was about four feet tall, with sharp pointed tops. There were many of these pyramids, arranged in orthogonal rows and columns.

Suddenly, she let out a primal scream.

Janu ran to her. "Olga, what is it?"

Holding her hand to her mouth, she shuffled backward several steps and pointed.

Janu jerked his head back. *"Mein Gott!"*

Piled between the sharp rocks were hundreds of human skulls and bones from dismembered skeletons.

With terror in her eyes, she pointed at the bones. "This is where the bodies fall! This is where they butcher the bodies!"

She looked up and saw the sacrificial diving platform overhead.

And, peering down from the end of the platform, stood Gana and Tresca!

Olga grabbed Janu by his arm. Frantic, they turned to escape.

But it was too late: Takala had crawled back into the palace and was closing the door behind him.

They were trapped.

Part III:

New Hamburg?

Chapter 20

WHEN HORST OPENED HIS EYES, HE WAS LYING ON HIS back inside a very dark place. The last thing he remembered was standing next to the silver pool, but he had no recollection of anything after that. It was as if time itself had stopped. Looking to his right, he saw Adam sprawled on the ground, a short distance away.

Slowly, Horst rolled over and, mustering all his strength, crawled across a hard, flat surface. When he reached Adam, he shook him by his shoulders.

"Adam! Adam! Wake up!"

Startled, Adam instinctively raised his arms over his face. Then, recognizing the voice, he looked up and saw Horst peering down at him from only a few inches away.

"*Mein Gott!* You scared me!" he exclaimed, surveying the darkness.

"What happened? Where are we?"

"I think we're inside a building," said Horst, rubbing his forehead. He was feeling pressure in his head, and ached all over.

"Obviously, we're in a building," said Adam, pointing in the direction of flickering lights.

"See—see the windows over there and the walls?"

He attempted to stand up, but, losing his balance, stumbled backward.

"Ow! *Ich habe Kopfschmerzen!*" [I have a headache!] he complained.

On his second attempt, he managed to get to his feet. Horst watched Adam hobble over to the window. Looking out, Adam suddenly stiffened.

"Adam, what's wrong?"

Adam did not answer immediately; he remained transfixed, staring out the window.

"Horst . . . it is like there are stars everywhere. You must come and see," he said, his voice trailing off.

With great difficulty, Horst staggered to his feet. He was beginning to feel nauseous, almost seasick, as he tried to maintain his sense of balance. Nearly every part of his body hurt. Taking small steps, he limped over to the window. When he looked outside, he could see lights in all directions—thousands of them. They were like stars, but they could not be stars, because they were too close.

Adam gazed up into the night sky.

"Look overhead, Horst," he said, pointing at a celestial body. Then he turned to Horst, frowning.

"That isn't our moon."

Horst looked up at the sky. Adam was correct: The object in the sky was clearly not Planet K851b's moon.

"Where are we?" said Adam.

Horst shook his head slightly.

"*Keine Ahnung.*" [No idea.]

Suddenly, a bright light illuminated their surroundings. Now, they could see they were inside a large room with a high ceiling. There were tall cabinets with glass doors against the walls and several tables displaying large rocks.

They heard a man's voice coming from the direction of an open door.

"Okay, if there's anybody in there, come out now—with your hands up!"

Disoriented, Horst snuck over to a wall, signaling to Adam to follow. They stood side by side, holding their breath.

"I repeat, come out with your hands up!" said the voice, this time drawing closer.

Horst looked at Adam and shrugged his shoulders; they had no other choice but to surrender. When they walked out the door, a black man wearing a grey uniform was pointing a pistol at them.

"I said, hands up!" repeated the man, grasping his pistol with both hands.

Horst and Adam raised their hands above their heads and walked forward.

"How did you get in here?" snapped the man.

Horst and Adam said nothing.

"C'mon, how did you get in here? Did you slip-in just before closing time?"

"Yes, sir," said Horst. "We came just before closing time."

"Did you pay admission?"

"*Admission?*" repeated Horst.

The man put away his gun. Then he removed a long stick-like object from his belt, which looked like a miniature baseball bat, and slapped the stick against his palm.

"Okay, guys, you gotta come with me. I don't need to know your story, just as long as nothing was stolen."

They followed the man down a hallway. As they walked, he slapped his palm with the stick. Soon they came to a long open corridor lined with cabinets with glass doors. Horst noticed the glass cases displayed pottery, paintings, clothing, and—weirdly—a few stuffed birds. But the strangest thing he saw was the skeleton of a large animal, mounted on the floor, cordoned off by a thick red rope. Drawing closer, he immediately recognized what it was.

"Adam, is this a . . . sail-back?"

Adam paused to examine the skeleton.

"Yeah, it kind of looks like one."

He saw a sign next to the skeleton.

"It says it's a Dimetrodon. Isn't that what Ingrid called sail-backs?"

But before Horst could answer, the man in the grey uniform turned around and hit the stick against the floor.

"Come on, guys! Time to go!"

Horst and Adam followed the man to a staircase. They walked down four flights of stairs to the ground floor, then out into a central hall. It was an enormous space, with gleaming white marble floors, arched openings, and stately columns.

"*Mein Gott!* This room must be at least 300 feet long!" exclaimed Adam.

He stood still, gazing up at a vaulted glass ceiling four stories above.

"*Schau dort, eine Elefant!*" said Horst, pointing to an elephant standing in the middle of the room.

"It must be dead—it isn't moving," said Adam. "You're quite safe, Horst!"

It turned out to be an elephant carcass, complete with tusks, posed in a fixed position with its trunk raised.

They saw the strangest sight of all standing next to the elephant—a dinosaur skeleton. It was far more massive than the sail-back upstairs.

"Come on, guys! I haven't got all night!" said the man, impatiently jerking his head.

They followed him across the hall until they came to a sign saying, "Exit."

Horst was expecting to see a door, but, instead, there was a cylinder made of glass; inside the cylinder were glass doors forming an "X." He looked over at Adam, who was also clearly confused as to how the door worked.

The man removed a collection of keys from his belt.

"Hang on, guys . . . need my reading glasses."

He removed a pair of bifocals from his pocket and put them on. After finding the correct key, he inserted it in the bottom of the cylindrical entrance; then, he pushed against the glass doors, causing them to rotate around a central axis.

The man looked at Horst and Adam.

"Time to go, guys!" he said, slapping the stick against the palm of his left hand, while motioning with his head for them to walk through.

Horst and Adam remained still, not sure what to do.

"What's the matter with you? I have to complete my route tonight, and I'm already late!"

Seeing Horst and Adam were not moving, the man shoved Adam inside the cylinder. Suddenly, the glass door began rotating, forcing Adam to shuffle around the axis until he returned to where he had started.

"Okay, Mister Funny Man!" snapped the man. "Have you guys been drinking? No more funny business this time!"

Adam stepped back into the glass cylinder, but this time, the man stopped the doors from rotating after a half rotation, and Adam found himself outside the building. Horst joined him seconds later, having made it through on his first try.

They stood outside in the dark. It was bitterly cold, but Horst did not feel cold, despite the fact he was wearing a burlap cotton Cadet uniform that offered virtually no insulation. He felt disoriented, especially by the lights. To his left, he saw swarms of white lights moving toward him and red lights moving in the opposite direction; to his right, there were no lights at all, suggesting they were next to a sea.

Without saying a word, they began walking into this strange new world. Most of the ground was covered in concrete. When they drew closer to the moving white and red lights, they could see they were attached to vehicles traveling on a concrete road.

Horst stared at the vehicles, which were moving faster than the fastest horse and buggy; but these had no horses.

"Horseless carriages?" he wondered aloud. Suddenly, he became nauseous. He bent over, feeling a massive stomach cramp. He began coughing uncontrollably.

Adam grabbed him by the arm, fearing he was about to collapse.

"Horst, are you all right?"

When Horst turned toward Adam, his mouth was bloody and beads of sweat were dripping from his forehead.

"Horst, you look sick."

Horst nodded, wiping the blood from his mouth with the back of his hand. "*Ich habe Magenschmerzen.*" [I have a stomach ache.]

They continued walking on a concrete sidewalk, as hundreds of horseless carriages whizzed next to them. Occasionally, they were able to see the people inside, protected by curved glass enclosures. The people looked straight ahead, as they drove their carriages. However, one of the carriages slowed down, and a man inside looked at Horst and Adam and extended his right middle finger.

Adam imitated the man's hand gesture, holding up his right middle finger.

"A curious gesture," he said. "He must be pointing at the blood on your face."

Horst touched his face, staring at the blood on his hand.

"I must find something to clean this off." He looked around and saw a wire basket at the corner, just ahead.

Horst walked over to the basket and pulled out a paper bag lying near the top. It smelled disgusting. Wrinkling his nose, he said "*Papier.*" [Paper.] How could someone throw away something so valuable? We were just beginning to make paper from Earth trees!"

Adam pulled a face. "*Es riecht!* [It smells!]

"*Stimmt zu,*" said Horst, shaking his head. He touched his face again and looked at the blood on his hand. "What the hell!" he said. He cleaned his face with the bag and then threw it into the basket.

They crossed an intersection, and a short wall appeared next to the sidewalk, extending as far as their eyes could see. As they walked, the road climbed higher.

"We must be on a bridge," remarked Adam. Looking over the wall, he whistled.

"Look at the trains below us, Horst!"

Horst looked down and saw a network of train tracks.

"*Verdammt!* How many trains do these people need?"

As they walked, they counted the train tracks: "*Eine, zwei, drei, funf ...... neun und dreisig Zug!*": a total of twenty-nine train tracks.

At the end of the bridge, they came to a building with an unusual sign made of colored glowing lights, forming the word "Hamburgers." They stopped to look at the sign, mesmerized by the beautiful colors.

"Horst, do you know what 'hamburger' means?" asked Adam.

Horst stared at the blinking letters, attempting to make sense of the words. "Well, I believe at one time, the residents of Hamburg, Deutschland, were called *Hamburgers*."

Adam raised his eyebrows. "Do you think we are in another German settlement?"

"Like *Neuen Hamburg* [New Hamburg]?"

"*Vieleicht.*" [Perhaps.]

Suddenly, a dark-skinned man walked directly up to them, shaking a cup. He was wearing dirty brown overalls that were held up by suspenders.

"Can you spare anything? All I need is a quarter," he said, standing a bit unsteadily.

Horst and Adam stared at the man with blank expressions.

"I said, do you fellows got any change?" repeated the man.

The only thing Horst had in his pockets was the rock and the pellets, which he needed. "*Entschuldigen! Wir haben nicht Geld!*" [I'm sorry! We have no money!]

The man tilted his head to one side.

"*Ent... ?* You from Germany?"

Horst and Adam said nothing.

"*Sprechen Sie Englisch?*" continued the man, with a playful grin. "I was born in Frankfort when my dad was stationed in the US Army. Went to German school there. Still can remember a few words. I can count in German: *Ein, zwei, drei, vier, funf*... ah, I'm not sure what comes after that."

"*Sechs*," said Adam.

"Did you say 'sex'?"

"*Nein*—no. I said, '*sechs*,' the word for six."

The man began to laugh, swaying from side to side.

"There was another word that always cracked me up . . . let me think," he said, pausing. "Oh, yeah, the word was '*farht*'! You know, when you're going somewhere far, you '*farht*'!" This time he laughed so hard, snot dripped from his nose.

"Hey, you wouldn't happen to have something to drink, would ya'?" he whined, drawing closer to Adam.

"*Entshuld* . . . ," said Adam, stepping away from the man's foul breath. "I mean, sorry. No, we don't have anything to drink."

The man slapped Adam on the back. "That's okay, *Herr* . . . you're okay . . ."

He stepped back and looked at Horst's Cadet uniform.

"Very funky clothes—especially your seashell buttons. And your boots are cool!"

"No, they are not cool, sir—they are quite warm."

"Are they alligator?"

Horst was about to explain they were made from Diictodon skin, but stopped himself. "Yes, they are made of alligator."

"Aren't you guys cold? Why aren't you wearing jackets?"

"We have lost our jackets, sir," said Adam.

"Well, in that case, come and follow me," the man said. "Let's find you some warm clothes."

He turned toward Adam and extended his hand.

"Just call me 'Fence'—everyone does."

"Pleased to meet you, *Herr* Fence," said Adam, shaking his hand. "*Ich heisse* . . . I mean, I'm called Adam."

"And I'm Horst," said Horst.

"*Danke*," said Fence, laughing and snorting. "You like that, '*Danke*'?"

They followed Fence to a building where smoke that smelled like cooking grease was pouring from the chimney. He led them behind the building to a large green dumpster filled with garbage.

"You guys hungry?"

"*Ja*," said Horst.

Fence opened the lid and reached inside, rummaging through the waste. It did not take him long to find what he was looking for.

"Got it! Fit for a king."

Triumphantly, he held up three small white containers, keeping one for himself while handing the others to Adam and Horst. Horst looked at the unusual folded box, which was made of a paper-like material. His initial assessment was it was a foamy substance that had solidified. Curious, he broke off a piece and began chewing it.

"No, no!" Fence shouted. "Spit it out, man! Are you crazy? I didn't give you *Styrofoam* to eat! Look inside the box!"

Horst spat out the tasteless Styrofoam. Opening the box, he found a half-eaten sandwich filled with roasted meat. He took a bite and grinned.

"*Ausgezeichnet!*"

"Okay—now you lost me, Chief."

"I said it is excellent."

As they ate their meals, Fence continued chatting, with his mouth full.

"You know, most people around here have a handle. Take me, for example, my handle is 'Fence.'" Then he winked and nudged Adam, with a playful grin, and said, "My lady's handle is Fox. You get it?"

Confused, Adam said, "Should I be getting you something?"

Fence rolled his eyes.

"Ay-yi-yi! You guys don't seem to understand the basics, do you?" He placed his hand on Adam's shoulder. "But you're okay."

"*Ja,*" answered Adam in an uncertain tone.

"Maybe you need a different handle. I mean, 'Adam' is kind of common. How about something with more danger, like 'Klinger'—you know, like on TV show *Hogan's Heroes?*"

"I'm quite happy with my name, *Herr* Fence," said Adam, leaning back. "The name 'Klinger' sounds like '*Klinge*,' which means 'blade,' of course."

Fence spat out his last bite of food and let out a booming laugh. He grabbed Adam by his shoulders and said, "*Blade*—I like it! Yeah, I'm gonna' call you Blade."

"Well, if you insist," said Adam, shrugging.

Fence turned toward Horst. "Your name's 'Horst,' right?"

"Yes, it is."

Fence took another bite and contemplated the possibilities of Horst's name. After a fairly lengthy deliberation, he said, "Ya know, Horst, the problem with your name is people around here are gonna' call you 'Horse.'

Now, don't get me wrong—there must be some advantages to being called 'Horse.' Let me think this over."

He paused, eating his sandwich while evaluating the handle *Horse*; then, he said, "I think it's sort of cool."

"Yes, it is quite cool outside," said Horst. "You said we were on our way to find additional garments, didn't you?"

"Oh, yeah, I almost forgot you're freezing—sorry about that!"

Fence stood up and threw away the remainder of his sandwich. Then he beckoned to his two companions.

"Follow me, Blade . . . and Horse."

The three men walked along the street, past two street intersections, until they came to a building with another large steel container in the rear, labeled "clothes donations." Fence opened the steel lid door, and stood back for Horst and Adam to look inside: It was filled with clothes.

"Just dig in and see what you can find. As they say, 'suit yourself!'" Fence chuckled to himself, noting their blank expressions.

"Get it? I said, 'suit yourself'—like, 'go ahead and find your own suit.'"

"Yes, that was quite amusing, *Herr* Fence," said Adam politely.

"There's another thing I want to ask: Please stop calling me '*Herr*'! It's like calling me a rabbit."

"Why are there clothes here?" asked Horst. "We have no boxes like this where we live."

"No boxes like this in Germany? This is free stuff people have given away. We have a saying in America: 'We're the land of the free'!"

Once again, Fence broke out in laughter, but after noticing their blank expressions, he said, "I give up."

Horst found a blue winter coat, with an emblem of a little bear sewn on the lapel.

"This coat is made from quite an unusual fabric." He looked closely at the threads. "It appears to be a plastic of some kind."

"It's nylon or polyester."

"Interesting," observed Horst. "'Poly,' as in polymerizing, and 'ester' the hydrocarbon molecule, which is usually a gas. You mean to say they have successfully polymerized ester molecules into long strings?"

Fence gave Horst a blank stare.

"I don't know what you're talkin' about. Either take it or leave it."

Both Horst and Adam took two of the polyester fabric winter coats.

"So, where's your crib?"

"Excuse me?" said Horst.

"Translation: Where do you guys live?" asked Fence. Then he placed his hand on Horst's forehead and gently tapped his head. "I said, where do you guys live? *Where do you sleep?*"

"*Entshuldigen, Herr Fence!* We are, in fact, lost and without a place to stay."

"That's what I thought. Come with me. I'll show you a place."

They set off, with Fence leading the way.

"Now, at the place we're going to, you've gotta be careful, but it has a few empty tents. Best of all, there will be mattresses for you to sleep on—you won't believe how many mattresses people throw away!"

After crossing three more intersections, they came to a patch of land next to a very busy road. It was a narrow, triangular-shaped parcel, surrounded by a steel wire fence, a portion of which had been pulled away. The three men stepped through the gap to the other side.

Horst swallowed hard. They were at a campsite, where about twenty tents were pitched. People were standing around campfires, talking; some of them were holding smoking sticks in their mouths. They turned to stare at the strangers.

"*Herr* Fence, are you leaving us here?" asked Horst.

"Sorry, guys, but I have my own place, Horse. Me and Fox live a few blocks away. This is about as good a place that I can offer, since you have no money."

Fence's eyes remained focused on the group of people around the campfire. He smiled and waved at them. They looked back at the campfire, apparently accepting the newcomers.

The tents seemed flimsy, hardly strong enough to protect them from the cold, let alone from any wild animals. Curious, Horst walked up to a tent and began examining it. The fabric was made from a material similar to his coat: A polymerized ester molecules, or "polyester" as Fence had called it. "Fascinating," he said quietly to himself.

Somebody pushed him aside.

"Hey, that's my tent!" said a young man with enraged eyes. "Back off!"

Horst backed away, only to bump into another young man, who also appeared to be angry.

"What the . . . ?"

Fence quickly intervened.

"Horse! Come over here!"

The young man said, "Yeah, back off, Horse!"

"You gotta' stay away from those junkies," said Fence.

"*Junkies?*" said Horst.

"Yeah, junkies! They do heroin. Look at the ground. There are syringes all over the place!"

Horst looked at the ground and saw dozens of discarded hypodermic needles. When he attempted to pick one up, Fence suddenly grabbed him.

"Are you crazy? Don't you ever—*I repeat,* don't you *ever*—pick up a syringe laying on the ground!"

Horst nodded. "What would happen if I touched one?"

Fence rolled his eyes. "You can catch a disease if you touch one of those! You don't know what these people might have!"

"Sorry," said Horst, who wasn't quite sure what "having a disease" meant, since there were no diseases in New Munich.

Fence motioned to Adam and Horst to follow him, away from the crowd.

"Okay, you guys. I've found a place on the north end, near the gas station. They tell me a junkie named Hulk left about two weeks ago and hasn't come back. It's a small two-man tent, with a couple of sleeping bags and an air mattress. You'll probably need to blow-up the air mattress."

He led them to a small orange tent, barely large enough for two people. Pointing at it, Fence said, "It's not much to look at, but it's better than nothing."

Adam and Horst looked at the tent, then at each other.

"*Bitte shone,* Fence!" said Adam, holding out his hand. "We are very grateful for your help."

"Anytime!" said Fence. "*Aufwiedersehen!*"

He disappeared into the night, heading somewhere to his own tent, where he lived with a lady named Fox.

Chapter 21

HORST HAD A FITFUL NIGHT, FINDING IT IMPOSSIBLE TO sleep inside the small tent. The noise from the horseless carriages speeding along the road below the embankment never ceased. He lay awake the entire night, staring at the orange polymerized ester fabric just inches from his face.

Was this a dream? Their current situation was even stranger than "meeting Albert" at the Einstein-Newton site years ago. *Where were they? Would they ever get home?*

For most of the night, he could hear loud chattering punctuated with what sounded like obscenities coming from nearby. Irritated, he opened the tent flap and watched a group of men standing around a campfire, passing a bottle between themselves, enjoying their own private party. Then he saw one of the men inject his forearm with a hypodermic needle, then another. He remembered how Fence had called them "junkies." *Were these men junkies?*

After hours of sleeplessness, he could see a slight change in the sky. It was close to dawn, and the edges of the tent dripped with cold morning dew. Restless, Horst unzipped the sleeping bag and crawled out of the tent. He looked for a bush to hide behind so he could relieve himself, but there was no vegetation. The area was too exposed, especially with the horseless carriages whizzing by, so close. He looked around, hoping to find a communal latrine, but all he could see were piles of filthy clothing, hypodermic needles, and empty glass bottles.

Walking along the edge of the camp, he came across four large plastic boxes with doors. They were too small for someone to live inside, but they were just large enough to be *eine Toilette*. Deciding to take a chance, he opened one of the doors and saw a toilet seat inside. There was a terrible stench, but at least he could relieve himself.

After using the little toilet house, Horst stood outside in the cold, with his arms crossed, attempting to warm up. He looked up at the sky and saw the sun was beginning to come up, with rays of light gradually appearing in variations of orange: red-violet, red, red-orange, then bright yellow-orange. But this sunrise did not stop with yellow-orange; it continued changing colors, in a way he had never seen before. There were hints of yellow-green and green. . . .

Excited, Horst walked as fast as he could back to the tent and shook Adam, who lay curled up in a fetal position.

"Adam! *Aufstehen sie!*" [Get up!]

Adam sat up and stretched. "What a horrible night! I couldn't sleep at all."

Horst pointed at the sky. "Look! Look at the sky!"

Adam's eyes widened. *"Mein Gott! Es ist bleu!"* [My God! It is blue!]

"Is this virtual reality?" asked Horst.

"No, I don't think so," said Adam, scratching his chin. "Although it does remind me of 'meeting Albert'!"

"I know, I was thinking the same thing. Are we 'meeting Albert' again?"

"I have no idea," Adam shook his head. "This . . . this . . . this . . . seems so real."

After Adam visited the little toilet houses, the two men were ready to explore. They walked away from the campground, vowing never to return.

As they walked along a street called "Roosevelt Road," they noticed there was concrete on almost every surface; here and there, weedy patches of grass and plants stuck through the cracks. Just behind the campground, was a building with a green and white canopy, where several horseless carriages were parked. People were standing outside their carriages, holding rubber hoses which were inserted in the side of each vehicle.

While Horst focussed on this scene, Adam stared ahead. Suddenly, he grabbed Horst by the arm, motioning for him to look toward the skyline. Horst was stunned to see a colossal black structure in the distance, soaring hundreds, perhaps thousands, of feet high. The building was made of a cluster of rectangular cubes, tapering in height; at the top of the building stood giant, long, poles, piercing the clouds.

"*Mein Gott!* I know exactly where we are!" said Adam, transfixed by the sight of the building.

"Where?"

Adam turned toward Horst. "*Chicago, Horst! We're on Earth, in Chicago!*"

"*Chicago?*"

"Remember when we were in New Eden, and I told you about my APS Opa, Grandfather Timoshenko? He and Oma, actually *the APS versions of my parents,* used to take me on virtual reality bicycle trips around Chicago. Didn't I ever talk to you about those?"

"Ah . . . it's been a long time, Adam," said Horst. "But, yeah, I kind of remember you telling me about that."

Adam looked at the massive building ahead. "Grandpa called this the Sears Tower. Come on, let's keep walking."

They continued up Roosevelt Road to a street named "Des Plaines" and, turning left, headed over to another street named "Jackson"; then, they turned right, in the direction of Sears Tower. As they drew closer to the massive building, more and more people filled the sidewalks. By the time they reached a street called "Canal," they saw hundreds of people emerging from a building carrying small suitcases and backpacks.

They immersed themselves in the crowd, walking shoulder-to-shoulder with the Chicagoans, who were heading in the direction of Sears Tower. Horst limped along as fast as he could, terrified of being trampled.

Soon they came to a metal bridge spanning a wide, murky river; there were pedestrian paths on each side of the bridge and a central road for horseless carriages. They began following the crowd, but upon reaching the center of the bridge, Adam stopped abruptly to examine the sidewalk.

"*Schau mal!*" [Look here!] said Adam, pointing at a gap in the metalwork. "What can be the purpose of this open joint?"

Looking up the river, he saw many identical bridges, all of which were made of steel and had joints in the center. Horst noticed a large, box-like boat coming down the river, pushed by another boat. It contained piles of gravel and sand.

Horst and Adam leaned over the railing, expecting to watch the boat sail under the bridge. Suddenly, there was a loud clanging, and a red light began to flash. People scurried across the bridge to the other side, with Adam and Horst trailing behind them. Then, a gate came down, preventing any more horseless carriages from crossing the river.

As they watched the large boat draw closer, the most amazing thing happened: the bridge began to move and separate into two halves. The halves pivoted upward until each half stood at a ninety-degree angle.

"*Mein Gott!*" exclaimed Adam, turning toward Horst. "I can't believe what I'm seeing!"

Surprisingly, none of the people standing near them seemed particularly impressed. After the boat had passed underneath, the bridge rotated downward, until the two halves met. A short time later, the gates lifted; then, the horseless carriages and pedestrians resumed traveling across the river.

Turning away from the river, Horst and Adam saw the base of the Sears Tower across the street. In unison, they gazed upward at the skyscraper, almost blinded by the sunlight bouncing off its steel and glass skin.

"*Fantastich!*" said Adam, craning his neck.

"*Ja! Ein großartig Gebäude!*" [Yes! A great building!]

They were standing on a corner, with hundreds of people passing by. As Horst watched the crowd, he noticed something very odd: many people were talking to themselves, waving their hands in the air and laughing out loud. Also, many of them were holding small flat devices, which they punched with their fingers. Nearby, a woman typed words on her device, which looked like an e-reader, but was much smaller. Horst could see she was typing words using her thumbs; then, moments later, new words appeared on the screen. He concluded the woman was having a conversation with someone electronically, via the device.

"*Fantastich!*" he muttered to himself.

When the light turned green, the woman walked away, and Adam grabbed Horst's arm, pulling him back in the direction of the bridge. Now, they were walking against the crowd, struggling to avoid colliding with pedestrians, especially those focused on their little devices. Having crossed the bridge, they came to a black building bearing the words "Union Station."

They managed to find a spot in a sheltered area, underneath the building's massive cantilever roof, away from the stream of people.

From their vantage point, they observed a black man holding a microphone.

"In the name of the Father, the Son and Holy Spirit!" proclaimed the preacher as people walked past him. "GOOD morning, people! It IS a GOOD morning because JESUS LOVES you!"

Adam and Horst listened for several minutes. As he preached, passers-by stopped to exchange a few words with him; some even took leaflets, dropping a few coins in what looked like a metal bucket. In a short time, the man began preaching the same words again.

Adam grabbed Horst's arm and pointed at Union Station. "Let's go inside."

They walked to the building entrance, which had ordinary doors, not cylindrical glass tubes like the first building they had encountered. The doors opened continuously, back-and-forth, due to the constant stream of people. Horst stood behind Adam, holding him by the sleeve of his Cadet uniform. Then, taking an aggressive approach against the multitude, Adam plunged through the entrance, dragging Horst behind him. Once inside, they saw people standing on two moving staircases. Fortunately, there was a stairway between the moving stairs, with fewer people. Adam looked at Horst, signaling him to follow. When they reached the bottom, they found themselves in a hallway. Working their way upstream, they soon came to a door marked "Men."

Adam looked at Horst.

"*Toilette?*"

"*Ja!*"

They entered the men's room, which was quite crowded. Horst and Adam waited in line, conscious of their primitive Cadet uniforms as they stood next to men wearing business suits and ties.

After leaving the *Toilette,* they continued further down the hall until they came to a large room filled with people eating at tables. Horst noticed a group of people who appeared unlike the others: the men had long beards and wore wide-brimmed hats and overalls with suspenders; the women wore bonnets and long dresses. Horst and Adam sat down at a table near them.

Horst looked at Adam and shrugged his shoulders. It was very noisy in this place. Everyone was speaking English, but then Horst heard a few Deutsch words. He tilted his head, pursing his lips as he listened. It was the men with beards talking in a Deutsch dialect.

Horst stood up from the table and approached one of the older men.

"*Entshuldigung, bitte. Sind sie Deutscher?*" [Excuse me. Are you German?]

The man laughed. "*Nein! Ich bin Amish!*" [No! I am Amish!]

"*Aber, sie sprechen Deutsch, nicht war?*" [But, you speak German, don't you?]

"*Wir sprechen Pennsylvania Dutch,*" [We speak Pennsylvania German,] said the man, emphasizing the word "Pennsylvania."

"*Danke,*" said Horst.

After Horst returned to the table where Adam was seated, they heard a voice from behind them. "Blade! Horse!"

When they turned around, it was Fence, the man who had helped them the night before. He was wearing the same dirty brown overalls with suspenders.

Fence approached Horst, holding his fist up. "Horst, my man!"

When Horst did nothing, Fence's shoulders slumped, and he frowned.

"Aren't you gonna' fist bump me?" he asked.

Horst stared blankly at Fence.

"I'm sorry, but I don't understand what you are asking of me."

Fence shook his head. Then he grabbed Horst's hand.

"Here—make a fist."

Horst made a fist.

"Okay. Now bump my fist."

Horst simply blinked and did nothing.

Fence grabbed Horst's fist and bumped it against his own. "Man, do I need to teach you everything! It's like you guys are from another planet!"

Horst and Adam glanced at each other, then back again at Fence.

"Thank you for showing me how to bump fists, *Herr* Fence," said Horst, forcing a smile.

"It's just 'Fence,' okay?" he said, pretending to pull his hair out. "If you guys start calling me 'Herr,' people will make fun of me!"

"I apologize."

"No problem. We're good?" said Fence.

"*Ja, das ist gut!*" said Horst.

Fence looked around the room. "Well, I see you guys have discovered the Food Court. Have you had anything to eat yet?"

"No, we haven't," said Adam.

"Got any money?"

"You mean *Geld?* No, we have none."

"Okay, guys—I'll treat you today. Let's step over to McDonald's and get some Egg McMuffins and coffee. Sound good?"

"Yes, sir, Fence. *Danke.*"

There were many different eateries serving food in the Food Court. They walked over to a counter bearing a sign with the name "McDonald's." Fence ordered them each a tasty biscuit stuffed with egg and sausage, along with cups of coffee.

As they sat inside McDonald's eating their breakfast, Fence asked if they had any plans for the day.

"No, we don't. To be quite honest, we are both lost," said Horst.

"You're lost, and you have no money," said Fence, between bites.

"Yes," answered Adam.

"How was your night in Tent City?"

"*Schrecklich!*" replied Horst. "I mean, it was terrible."

"*Schrecklich,* uh? That sounds like the movie *Shrek.*"

Adam and Horst made no response.

"You two need to get yourselves some money. As the song goes, 'Money makes the world go round.' And there's only one way for people like us to make money—isn't there, Horse?"

"What is the *one* way for us to make money?" asked Horst.

"We beg!" boomed Fence, bursting into snorts of laughter. "That's what I do every day—I'm an expert at begging. Heck, I'll even give you some lessons today!" He wiped his mouth with a paper napkin and stood up. "Come on, guys, let's get to work."

They followed Fence outside Union Station to a sheltered area overlooking the bridge.

"Now, what I'm about to explain is important," explained Fence. "We each have our own territory."

He pointed to a man at the end of the bridge, standing near a bridge house.

"See over there, at the southeast end of the bridge? That's Jack. That's his territory. He's there every day, rain or shine. Panhandles the old-fashioned way, rattling a cup. Never gives a spiel. Jack does simple, honest, cup rattling."

Next, he pointed to the other end of the bridge, where there was a young man.

"See the guy over there, handin' out Krispy Kremes? That's Tom. He's got a sweet arrangement giving out donuts.

"That was funny—a 'sweet arrangement selling donuts,'" he guffawed, but neither Horst nor Adam laughed.

Fence scrubbed his hands over his face.

"Don't you guys get *any* of my jokes?"

"Oh yes, *Herr* . . . or rather, *Mr.* Fence . . . ," apologized Adam. "Donuts are sweet. Ha, ha. Please continue with your lesson."

Fence sighed and then continued.

"Okay—I just gave you the lay of the land. We each have our own territory, and we don't interfere with each other. Do you understand? Good," said Fence as both Horst and Adam nodded in agreement.

"Now, let's find you a spot."

They walked across the bridge, past Jack (who shook his cup, rattling change inside), to a corner where there were no other beggars.

Reaching into a garbage bin, Fence found two paper cups. He handed one cup to Adam and the other to Horst.

Adam and Horst each held the paper cups, scrutinizing them to see how they were made.

Fence reached into his overalls and pulled out a handful of coins.

"Horse, take this. It's about ten bucks."

Horst began to say something, but Fence stopped him. "No need to thank me, Horse! Someday, you can pay me back. Okay?"

He winked at Horst and gave him a fist bump.

"*Danke*, Fence!" said Horst, returning the gesture.

"*Vielen Dank!*" added Adam.

After Fence walked away, Adam grabbed the paper cup from Horst's hand. Crumpling both cups, he threw them in the garbage bin.

"Why did you do that?" objected Horst.

Ignoring Horst's question, Adam motioned to Horst.

"*Bitte*, come with me."

Then he began walking in the opposite direction from Sears Tower.

Horst followed Adam, who appeared to be analyzing their surroundings. More than once, Adam began talking to himself, but Horst did not question him. Eventually, they crossed a bridge spanning an immense road. From there, they could see the awful tent city situated on the east embankment; the very sight of the place spurred them on. Finally, they arrived at a complex of large buildings which appeared to be a school, but it was far bigger than New Munich High School, and the students were much older than high school students.

After what seemed like miles of walking, Horst finally spoke.

"What are you looking for?"

"I'm not sure . . . but I sense it's in this direction," Adam muttered, continuing to forge ahead.

Horst tried to keep up, but he could not walk fast enough.

"Adam, slow down!"

"Sorry," said Adam, reducing speed.

They continued at a slower pace until they came to "Taylor Street." Suddenly, Adam laughed out loud.

"Finally, I recognize something! Horst, check this out!"

He walked over to a building displaying the sign, "Al's Italian Beef."

"This is it! This is the place where we always ended our bicycle trips! Whenever we came here, Clare brought me an Italian Beef sandwich and fries into the virtual reality room!"

There was a large laminated poster displaying pictures of the various meal options and their prices.

"How much do you have, Horst?"

Horst studied his coins.

"I'm not sure how to count these—these aren't Centras." He looked closely at the impressions on the side of the coins, most of which were marked with "25," "10," "5" and "1."

Horst separated the coins into small piles, based on their numbers. It took him several minutes to determine they were carrying a value of 895 of something. Remembering that Fence had used the term dollar, Horst said, "I believe we must have 895 dollars."

"No, I don't think that's right—that seems to be far too much. The cost of an Italian Beef is only . . . let's see here . . . it's *Drei Point Funsig*—three point fifty. How much did you say?"

"895."

"I think we have eight point ninety-five."

Adam walked up to the counter.

"Hello, kind Sir. I wish to order two Al's Italian Beef Sandwiches."

"For here or to go?" said the man behind the counter.

"We will eat our Al's Italian Beef Sandwiches on your premises, sir."

"With fries and a drink?"

Adam hesitated, not sure if they had enough *Geld*. "*Ja, mit fries und trinken*—I mean, yes—with fries and drink."

Once the food was ready, the man rang-up the order on the register.

"Okay, that will be nine dollars and five cents."

Adam gave the man all their coins.

The man counted the coins and said, "I've counted eight dollars and ninety-five cents. You're a dime short. Do you have a dime?"

"No, I'm afraid not."

"No problem," said the man. He took several coins from a little jar near the register and put them in the till.

"*Danke*—I mean thank you!" said Adam.

Exhausted, Adam and Horst sat outside Al's, eating their first *real* Al's Italian Beef, with fries and a Coke. The weather was perfect: the sun was bright, the sky was blue, and the morning chill had disappeared. In the distance, they could see Sears Tower dominating the Chicago skyline. Adam was grinning slightly.

Horst didn't understand how Adam could be content. He had always dreamed of going to Earth, but now he was there, he was living a nightmare.

Chapter 22

A WEEK HAD PASSED SINCE CHARLES AND ELISE TIMOS-henko returned to Chicago from their trip to Arizona. One Saturday morning, Charles sat in his family room reading the *Chicago Tribune* while his nine-year-old granddaughter, Tina, watched TV. Tina's parents were away at Mackinaw Island, Michigan, celebrating their twelfth wedding anniversary.

Reading a *Trib* columnist's op-ed on page 2, Charles shook his head.

"Why does this guy always compare Chicago politics to Greek tragedies?" he said out loud to no one in particular. "The guy's so damned predictable!"

Turning to Tina, he noticed she was watching a cartoon.

"What are you watching?" he asked.

"*Dexter's Laboratory,* Grandpa," said Tina, twirling long strands of flaxen hair around her fingers.

"*Dexter's Laboratory*? Interesting."

Charles put down his paper and began watching *Dexter* with Tina. To his surprise, he enjoyed the show, for the humor seemed to work for both kids and adults. After *Dexter,* they watched *Sponge Bob Squarepants.* Briefly, Charles was able to forget the global catastrophe they would be facing the following week. He was doing better than Elise.

"Breakfast is ready!" announced Elise.

The three sat down in the formal dining room. Lately, Charles had been eating a cereal called *Muesli,* a mixture of corn, wheat, and barley flakes, with raisins, dates, almonds, and puffed rice. He liked stirring plain yogurt into the cereal.

"Tina, you want to try some?" he asked.

Tina examined the cereal. "Not sure, Gramps. Give me a spoonful."

Tina tried the Muesli. "Yuck!"

Making a face, she walked to the garbage can and spat it out.

"Don't you have anything *good* around here?"

"Like what?" asked Elise.

"Like *Frosted Flakes* or *Captain Crunch,*" said Tina, throwing up her hands.

"I doubt if we have those," said Elise. She walked over to a cabinet above the refrigerator and pulled out a box of *Honey Bunches of Oats.*

"Is this okay?" she said, showing Tina the box.

Tina hesitated.

"You've got two choices: *This* or oatmeal," repeated Elise.

"Okay, I'll take the *Honey Bunches,* Grandma."

The three ate quietly for a while until Charles broke the silence.

"What's your favorite movie?"

Tina closed her eyes and concentrated.

"Ah . . . ah . . . Oh, yeah. I like *Superman.*"

"I love that one, too," said Elise. "You mean the original 1978 movie with Christopher Reeve?"

"I don't know about that one," said Tina. "I just like it."

"Why do you like it?" asked Charles.

"It's a lot like us. You know, how we sent my brother up into space four years ago."

Tina was referring to her fraternal twin brother, Adam. Four years ago, Adam had been sent as a frozen embryo to Planet K851b on a mission to save the human race from extinction.

"Interesting observation," said Charles, pausing to push up his glasses. "You're saying your brother was sent from our planet, just like Superman was sent from the planet Krypton?"

"Yeah, that's what I mean," said Tina. "Do you think Adam has super-powers, like Superman?"

Elise burst into laughter. "Charles, I guess that makes you Marlon Brando!"

"You mean Superman's father? Ha, ha, very funny," replied Charles. It was the first time he heard Elise joke in a long time.

"Grandpa, I said, do you think Adam has super-powers?"

Charles wrinkled his nose. "Interesting question. It depends on the gravity of the planet. If the planet where Adam lives has lower gravity than Earth, then I would say he definitely has super-powers. In that case, Adam will be able to jump very high. If there are alien beings on the planet, Adam may be relatively stronger than them."

"Has he gotten there yet?"

"No, it's far too soon. The spaceship won't get there for a very long time."

"And that's why they sent him as a frozen embryo?"

"Correct."

The phone rang, and Elise went to answer it. Charles and Tina continued eating breakfast. As they ate, they overheard Elise talking on the phone: "Uh-huh . . . yes. . . . Can you repeat that? Okay, I'll tell him. He'll be right over." Her voice trailed off, and she hung-up.

When Elise returned to the table, she stared at Charles, frowning.

"What was that all about?" asked Charles, sipping his coffee.

Elise's voice trembled. "Charles, have you been truthful to me all these years we've been married?"

Charles choked in his coffee. "What are you talking about?"

"That was the police. They told me the strangest thing. They want you, specifically, to go down to the police station as soon as possible. They've arrested two men," she said, looking directly at Charles.

"One of them says he's your grandson. I don't have a grandson—*do you?*"

The idea Charles had a secret grandson created a very uncomfortable situation in the Timoshenko household. Elise asked Charles if he had been living a double-life during their forty years of marriage. Charles emphatically denied any such possibility, but, nevertheless, Elise remained quite shaken. She insisted on going along with him to the police station.

Charles, Elise, and Tina made their way to the police station, which was only two blocks from their house. Inside the entrance, a female officer sat behind a bullet-proof double-glass window. Charles walked over to the officer while Elise and Tina stood near the opposite wall.

"Hello, what can I do for you?" asked the officer.

"Ah . . . I was called to identify two men," said Charles.

"Can I see your ID?"

Charles removed his Illinois Driver's License and passed it through a metal trough under the window.

Having examined his license, the officer then said, "Please take a seat. Officer Klemke will be right with you."

Charles, Elise, and Tina sat down in the waiting area. Tina immediately opened her "Search and Find" book, *Where Are You, Maria Taylor?* Elise fidgeted and smoothed down her clothes.

"Officer Klemke? Wasn't that a character in *West Side Story*?" whispered Charles.

Elise furrowed her brows. After a momentary pause, she whispered, "No . . . that character was '*Sergeant Krupke*,' not '*Klemke*.'"

"Well, I was close," said Charles, smiling. "Don't I get a point?"

Elise didn't respond.

"Guess not," Charles said to himself.

Soon Officer Klemke arrived. "Please come inside," he said, holding open an ultra-secure, bullet-proof door, leading to the inner sanctum of the police station.

They followed him to a small room with a table and four chairs. Officer Klemke sat down in his swiveled chair and leaned back. When everyone was seated, he said, "May I get you some coffee or water?"

"No, thanks, Officer," said Charles.

Elise and Tina simply shook their heads.

Klemke leaned forward, placing his elbows on the desk. "I apologize for bothering you on this nice Saturday morning. Let me explain the situation. We have two gentlemen here, and one of them claims to know you, Mr. Timoshenko. These men were caught riding stolen Divvy bikes, all the way from Chicago."

"Divvy bikes?" asked Elise, narrowing her eyes.

"You know, those blue bikes that people rent in Chicago."

"Oh, I've heard of them," said Elise. "You say people rent them?"

"Yes, people are supposed to use their credit cards to rent them. However, in this case, these two men stole the two Divvy bikes. These bikes have tracking systems on them. The Divvy company alerted us to the whereabouts of their stolen property, using their tracking software. We arrested them when they rode into town."

Charles leaned forward and cleared his throat.

"Officer, my wife said one of these men claims to be my grandson." He quickly looked at Elise, then back at the officer. "I don't have a grandson!"

"Yes, he is obviously not your grandson!" said the officer, swiveling in his chair. He shook his head, laughing out loud.

Charles sank back in his chair.

"If it's obvious, why did you ask us here?"

"Unfortunately—or fortunately, depending on your position—we are obligated to verify all statements. You know that saying, 'To assume is to make an ass of you and me.'" Officer Klemke looked at Tina, "Sorry for my language, little lady."

Tina, who was engrossed in her book, said nothing.

"Would you mind taking a look at these felons?" said the officer. "We have a viewing room which allows you to look through a one-way mirror. It will be in-and-out, they will never see your face. Would you mind doing that? Then we can wrap this case up for processing and send them to the County Jail."

"Okay, show us where to go. I was going to Lowes today, so I'd like to get it over."

"Good," concluded the officer. He stood up. "Please follow me down this hall. Unfortunately, there are a lot of homeless people who should probably be in a mental institution. However, due to Illinois State budget cuts there are fewer mental institutions these days—but who am I to judge?"

They went to a room with a gallery of chairs facing a window, looking into another room.

Officer Klemke pointed at the window. "Are you ready?"

"Yes, Officer. As ready as I'll ever be," said Charles.

The officer picked up a phone. "Okay, Scooter, you can send 'em in."

A door in the other room opened, and two middle-aged men walked in.

Officer Klemke spoke into the microphone.

"Okay fellows, you can stand right there. Just look ahead at the mirror."

The first thing Charles noticed was their unusual clothes. Both men were wearing Chicago Bears jackets, which wasn't surprising, but it was the rest of their clothes that were strange. Their clothes were old fashioned—actually primitive—and drab, with little color and devoid of patterns. Their shirts had small seashells instead of buttons, and there were no front pockets. Their pants were fashioned of thickly woven cotton, almost like burlap, while their boots appeared to be made from alligator or a reptile's hide. Their hair was fairly long, and they had not shaven for at least a couple of days.

Suddenly, Elise let out a gasp. With an incredulous stare, she pointed at one of the men.

"Oh, my God! Look—look at his face!"

Charles immediately saw the resemblance of one of the men.

"I'll be damned . . . he looks—"

"Exactly like you—only younger," said Elise, completing his thought.

Officer Klemke looked back-and-forth at the suspects and Charles. "I'll be damned! Even I can see the resemblance! But there's no way he could be your grandson—he's too old. They must be in their late fifties or early sixties."

"Sixties, would be my guess," said Charles, standing closer to the window, examining the man's face.

"As I said, I don't have a grandson." He rubbed his hands through his hair, then he looked at Elise and repeated, "*We* don't have a grandson!"

At that moment, little Tina, who had been quiet the entire time, walked up to the glass. She looked at the man standing on the left. She said, "I think that's Adam."

"Adam?" said Elise, glancing at Charles.

"I can feel it," said Tina.

"What do you mean, 'you can feel it'?"

"It's just something I can feel. I think he's my twin brother, Adam."

Officer Klemke laughed, "He's your brother? I'd say that's quite an age difference, little lady!" He paused to read his clipboard, then looked at the Timoshenkos.

"Now, this is interesting: One of the suspects says his name is Adam."

Charles and Elise exchanged puzzled looks.

"If you're interested, you can talk to the suspects in a private room," said the officer. "Otherwise, you can leave."

Charles took a deep breath and shrugged his shoulders.

"Okay, we'll meet them."

Officer Klemke took Charles, Elise, and Tina to another room, where they were seated on one side of a table. After a couple of minutes, the suspects came into the room with their hands cuffed behind their backs.

When the men were seated, Officer Klemke said, "I'll excuse myself and stand outside the door so you can talk privately. When you're finished, please press the intercom button."

He left the room and closed the door.

When Charles looked at the one named Adam, it was like looking into a mirror, except this man was a slightly younger version of himself.

The one named Adam was the first to speak. "Charles, Elise—where should we begin?" he said, sounding very nervous. "I know this must seem extremely unusual to you. We should first start with introductions: *Ich heiße Adam.* . . . I mean to say, my name is Adam."

"And my name is Horst," said the other man, forcing a smile.

Flustered, Adam continued, "I know you must find this confusing—we ourselves are finding this situation even more confusing! I am not sure where I should begin."

"Well, I think I know where to begin," interrupted Charles. "The officer said you claim to be my grandson! What the *hell* is that about, *huh?*"

Adam hesitated. "Please, bear with me, sir . . . I fully appreciate how uncomfortable this must be for you. The fact is, I know you quite well—or, rather, I know the *Artificial Personality Simulator version of you* quite well."

"The APS version of me?" Charles sighed heavily and crossed his arms. "Okay, now you've got my attention. Hit me with your best shot. Please explain."

"As I was saying, I know the APS version of you quite well; in fact, I've known you since I was a teenager. Your APS version taught me many things. I am also a structural engineer, like you—"

"And I was taught to be a chemist by the APS version of my grandfather, Dr. Frank Erbstoesser," interrupted Horst.

Charles opened his mouth, then stopped himself from saying anything. He stood up and began pacing the room, trying to grasp what he was hearing. *Had Frank arranged a joke on him?* Pranks were uncharacteristic of Frank—he was a serious guy—and why now?

The door opened, and Officer Klemke came into the room. "Is everything okay?"

"Yes, Officer, we're doing fine. Still getting to know each other," said Charles.

"If you have any trouble, remember to use the intercom."

"Thank you, Officer," said Charles. "We'll call you when we're ready."

"You know," said Charles, "it's possible you saw my APS simulation at the University of Illinois at Chicago, or at the University of Michigan. Both of those colleges were involved in the APS program."

The one named Adam said, "I do not know of these places."

"Adam," interjected Horst. "I think we may have seen one of those places. We walked through a large school in Chicago this morning. Remember seeing all the young adult students?"

"Oh, yes, I remember. We were on our way to that gentleman's Italian Beef restaurant."

"You mean, you went to *Al's Italian Beef* on Taylor Street?" asked Charles.

"Yes, we found that restaurant today. I believe Al was behind the counter."

Charles and Elise exchanged looks.

"What is the term the poet used? It's sounds like 'A willing suspension . . .'"

"It's 'A willing suspension of disbelief,' Charles," said Elise. "Like when you read *Harry Potter,* you allow yourself to get into it." She gave a slight nod to Adam, signaling him to continue.

Tina said to the one calling himself Adam, "Did Buzz make it?"

The one named Adam said, "*Buzz?* Oh, yes. When I was small, Miss Clare gave me a doll which was named *Buzz Lightyear,* although I never understood the meaning of that name."

"I gave Leader Graham that doll when the spaceship was launched," said Tina, smiling shyly.

Charles pressed the intercom button. "Officer, we are finished here. We would like to leave now."

Officer Klemke opened the door, "Okay, everybody. Thank you for your time. You may leave now. Just take the corridor to your left—"

"Officer, how much would it cost if I cover the expense of the Divvy bikes that were stolen?"

The policeman looked at him incredulously. "You are offering to pay for the bikes?"

"Yes," replied Charles. "This is really a minor theft, isn't it? Will $300 cover the expense?"

~

It took another two hours to process and release the men. Officer Klemke contacted the Divvy Bicycle Company and explained Charles's offer to reimburse the cost of the bikes. Divvy accepted the offer and dropped all charges.

When Adam and Horst were finally released, they walked outside the suburban police station. Now they were in a town even stranger to them than Chicago.

"Now what?" said Horst.

Adam shook his head. "I'm not sure what to do. I suppose we need to walk back to Chicago."

"And do what?"

A car pulled in front of the police station. It was Charles and Elise Timoshenko, waving at them to come over.

From the front seat of the car, Charles said, "I assume you have no place to stay."

Adam began to explain, "No, sir. We have no place here."

"The first night we were here, we slept outside in a tent in Chicago. It was a horrible place next to a very busy road," interjected Horst.

"A tent?" repeated Elise. "You must have been in the homeless camp next to the Dan Ryan."

"We assumed you had no accommodations," said Charles. "We would like to offer you a better place to stay. Would it be acceptable if we put you up at the Super 8 on Milwaukee? I checked, and they have a room available with two queen size beds."

Adam and Horst looked at each other, clearly elated.

"Yes, we accept the offer, Opa and Oma—I mean, Mr. and Mrs. Timoshenko," Adam corrected himself.

"Good," said Charles. "Please get in the back seat."

After they pulled out of the police station parking lot, Charles said, "As far-fetched as your story sounds, a lot of things you said make sense to me. I still don't understand how you got information about the APS, Miss Clare, Leader Graham—you have me baffled!"

He shook his head.

"Your story is bizarre. If your intent is to snooker me—well, you've done a damn good job! A damn good job!"

"We are not snookering you, sir," insisted Horst.

"Here is my plan," continued Charles. "I don't care what your issues are, but something about you appeals to me, and I'd rather not see you live outside. Given the dire circumstances we're all in, *nothing matters any longer, does it?*"

Adam and Horst looked at each other with blank expressions.

Charles continued, "I can pay for your stay at the Super 8 until . . ." then he stopped himself. "Suffice it to say, I can pay for a couple of weeks."

"Thank you, sir," said Adam.

"Good. But, before we go to the Super 8, I want to make a little detour. While you were being processed at the police station, we made arrangements at my doctor's office to have a few tests—that is, unless you have objections. Is that okay with you?"

"No, sir, I have no objections. Do you have any objections, Horst?"

"No—it's fine with me," said Horst.

Charles and Elise drove Horst and Adam to the doctor's office where the two men were each given a variety of tests: blood samples, urine samples, EKGs.

After Doctor Sugar listened to Adam's chest he said, "Your heart and lungs sound good. Are you up to date with your shots?"

"Shots?" said Adam in an uncertain tone.

"Vaccines. Have you had your yearly flu shot?"

"No."

"Have you had your shingles shot?"

"No."

"Covid-19 shot?"

"No."

"Tetanus?"

Adam shook his head.

"Have you had any shots in your life?" asked the doctor, with an incredulous stare.

"No," said Adam.

The doctor instructed the nurse to give Adam and Horst three vaccines for this visit. He said they would need to come back the next week for the remainder of their shots, and their arms would hurt.

Charles was most interested in having DNA tests. The doctor agreed, and so the group provided saliva samples. Because the bloodwork was done in-house, the test results would be available the next day. The doctor said he would need to send the saliva samples by messenger to Northwestern Medical Center for DNA analysis.

"For the DNA test, you're simply trying to determine if you're related? You're not looking for ethnicity breakdown?"

"Correct—we just want to know if we're related," said Charles.

"That should be no problem. I'll ask Dr. Berguson to keep it simple."

After the doctor's visit, Charles drove the men to the Super 8. He gave them each $100, explaining there was a Wendy's on the corner where they could get something to eat. For her part, Elise promised to buy them some new clothes at Kohls, which she would leave at the front desk. They would stop by the next morning.

Chapter 23

THE NEXT MORNING, CHARLES AND ELISE ARRIVED AT THE Super 8 and went directly to Horst's and Adam's room. Charles knocked on the door. They heard Adam's voice as he struggled with the door chain.

"*Ich komme! Entshuldigen, bitte!*"

Charles looked at Elise. "German?"

"*Ja.*"

Charles could not suppress his laughter; the 'Mission' had, in fact, been a joint effort of America and Germany.

The door opened, and Adam greeted them. There was a significant improvement in his appearance since the day before: Hair washed, face clean-shaven, and wearing the new clothes Elise had purchased at Kohls.

"How did you sleep?" asked Charles.

"Much better than the night before, when we slept next to—*what did you call it?*—I believe you said it was 'the expressway.'"

"Yes, the expressway," said Charles. "Based on the description you gave, you slept next to the Dan Ryan Expressway."

"A terrible place!" uttered Adam. "Once again, we must thank you for putting us up."

They heard Horst coughing in the bathroom, hacking away for nearly a minute. When he emerged, he saw Charles and Elise standing next to Adam.

"*Guten Morgen!*"

"*Guten Morgen!*" replied Elise, with some hesitation.

"Sprechen Sie Deutsch?" [Do you speak German?] asked Horst.

"Ein bischen," [A little,] said Elise, pinching her fingers together. "I took a few years in high school, but that was decades ago."

"The doctor called last night," said Charles. "Some of the test results are back, and he wants to go over them this morning. We have an appointment in his office at eleven ten a.m. Have you eaten breakfast yet?"

"*Nein*," said Adam.

"I'm sorry," said Charles, "but I don't speak German. Are you from Germany?"

Adam and Horst both shook their heads.

"Our mistake," apologized Adam. "We will not *sprechen Deutsch*—I mean, we will not *speak German* in your presence in the future. Please forgive us."

"No problem," said Charles.

~

They drove a couple of blocks to Wendy's for breakfast. Both Adam and Horst ordered *Sausage, Egg, and Swiss Croissants,* along with *Junior Chocolate Frosties,* while Charles and Elise enjoyed *Senior Discount* coffees. *"Ausgezeichnet!"* said Adam appreciatively; then, catching a reproving look from Horst, he quickly added, "Excellent!"

From Wendy's, they drove directly to the doctor's office. After about twenty minutes, a nurse escorted them into a small room containing a table and six chairs.

"Good morning!" said the doctor, greeting Charles and Elise by bumping elbows; however, when he tried bumping elbows with Adam and Horst, they looked at him blankly.

The doctor gestured in the direction of the chairs.

"Please sit down. I have some very interesting results for you," he said, smiling. "You are Adam—correct?"

"*Ja*—I mean yes."

"Well, based on your DNA results, we've determined with 99.99% accuracy you are directly related to both Charles and Elise. However—and I hesitate to say this—our tests indicate that Charles and Elise are your grandparents!"

He shook his head slightly as he studied the results.

"There is definitely a glitch. Charles, how old are you?"

"I'm seventy, Doctor," answered Charles.

"And, Adam, you are sixty-two?"

"Yes, Doctor."

The doctor shook his head, "An eight-year difference in your ages. I'm baffled by these results! Obviously, a glitch somewhere."

"I simply can't believe this," objected Charles. "We came to you because this man—Adam—claims to be related to us. I assumed he could be a cousin, but this is simply ridiculous! Elise and I have only one grandchild, and she's nine years old!"

"Yes, he does look like you, in fact, quite a bit," said the doctor. "I'm as baffled as you are, but let's move on. Excuse me, are you Horst?"

"*Ja*," said Horst. "I mean, 'Yes.'"

"You are the first person I've met named 'Horst.' Are you from Germany?"

"No, sir," answered Horst.

"Normally, these blood tests are confidential. Should I discuss the results with each of you privately?"

Adam and Horst looked at each other, then shrugged their shoulders.

"We don't mind sharing your findings with Mr. and Mrs. Timoshenko. They can stay," said Adam.

The doctor continued to read the report.

"Your bloodwork came out normal, Adam: Healthy cholesterol levels . . . triglycerides are exceptionally low—in fact, some of the lowest I've ever seen . . . Urinalysis looks good."

Then he turned toward Horst, "However, your blood test concerns me. In particular, your immunoglobulin antibodies are quite elevated."

Horst winced.

"Sorry for my ignorance, but what are immune—whatever—antibodies?" asked Elise.

"Our bodies make antibodies to protect us from infections. There is one type of immunoglobulin antibody called 'IgA.' Typically, when we see high IgA levels like Horst's, we are concerned about the possibility of an infection in the lungs, sinus, stomach, or intestines . . ."

Charles looked at Horst. "Have you had this test before?"

"Yes. I'm fully aware of this test."

"Good. I assume you've consulted a doctor?"

"Yes, I have. Back home, in New Munich."

~

As Horst sat in the back seat of the Timoshenkos' car, he looked up at the blue sky and thought about how badly he had wanted to see the *real* Earth, not just a virtual reality recording of the Earth. But now he was here, he wanted to be home. *How he missed the orange sky of Planet K851b! How he missed Ingrid and New Munich!*

Adam turned to Horst, speaking to him in a low voice.

"Kennst du sich kranken?" [Did you know that you were sick?]

"Ja." [Yes.]

"Wie lange?" [For how long?]

"Sechts wochen." [Six weeks.]

"Kennen Ingrid also?" [Does Ingrid know, too?]

"Ja, sie kennt." [Yes, she knows.]

Horst turned toward the window. He didn't want to discuss his health any further. Nothing made any sense to him. His entire life had spun out of control.

~

Charles drove the car back to the Super 8 parking lot and parked the car. "Okay, guys. Go inside and get your stuff."

Once the surprise had sunk in, Elise turned around and said to Horst and Adam, "Looks like you're staying with us! We have plenty of room."

Adam and Horst grinned at one another. Thanking the Timoshenkos profusely, they went inside the motel and returned to the car with their belongings.

~

When they arrived at the Timoshenko household, Elise gave Adam and Horst a tour of their home. It was a modest, brick, two-story, four-bedroom house. Adam would be staying in their daughter Jennifer's old bedroom, while Horst would be using the guest room. After seeing their bedrooms, Adam and Horst followed Elise downstairs to the dining room, where Charles was sitting at the table with a pad of paper and a pencil. Tina was sitting next to him, playing on one of the small hand-held devices they had observed in Chicago.

"Okay, everybody, please sit down! We have a lot to discuss. Adam, based on the DNA test and based on the fact you look a hell of a lot like me, I think we can conclude you are related to Elise and me."

"Yes," agreed Adam.

Charles leaned back in his chair, staring at Adam and Horst over the rims of his bifocals.

"I want to hear your story. Please start at the beginning."

Horst and Adam began to describe their lives on Planet K851b, explaining how they had been brought there as frozen embryos, how they had been raised by robots, and how they had traveled to New Munich and met their German counterparts.

After hearing their story, Charles looked at Elise, stunned. "My God! It actually worked! The mission actually worked!"

"I know . . . even the part about the robots. Charles, do you remember meeting Clare at Washington Cathedral?"

Adam looked dazed. "You met Miss Clare?"

"Yes," said Elise. "We met her at the *Embryo Blessing Ceremony* at Washington Cathedral. She came up to us when we were sitting in our pew."

"I remember her, too!" said Tina excitedly. "I thought she was human!"

"Miss Clare saved my life," said Horst quietly.

"What?" said Charles.

"It's a long story . . . I don't want to overwhelm you with too many facts, if you don't mind."

"Some other time then," said Charles. "My head is already spinning. This is beginning to sound like science fiction."

Everyone laughed. It was the first time Adam and Horst had laughed since arriving on Earth.

"Okay, guys—I believe your story. It all makes sense. I was involved in planning the mission, after all. But what I don't understand is how you got back to Earth?"

"This is a question we've been asking ourselves," said Horst. "And this leads us to the part of our long story we have not yet explained to you."

He fumbled in one of his pockets and brought out a rock, two red spherical pellets, and two blue spherical pellets which he placed on the table.

"These are the things that brought us here," he explained. "We were given these things by Gana."

Horst held up one of the red pellets. "He told us to use this red pellet to return."

"Unfortunately, we don't know how to use the red pellet to return! We don't know what to look for!" he said in a voice choked with emotion.

"Who is Gana?" asked Elise.

"Gana is—well . . . suffice it to say he is someone we encountered on our planet," continued Horst. "He gave us these things."

"You're saying Gana gave you this rock and those pellets?" asked Charles.

"No, he did not *give* me this rock. I stole it. It's a piece of a much larger rock. This rock has, somehow, allowed us to travel to Earth."

"May I take a look?" asked Charles, reaching across the table.

Horst handed the rock and a red pellet to Charles.

Charles examined the rock, turning it over in his hands; then he handed it to Tina. "Horst, why is this rock black?" asked Tina.

"I think it's a piece of a meteor."

Charles held the red pellet, and then he began tossing it in the air.

Horst jumped up and caught the pellet in mid-air.

"Please be careful with these, sir! We need them to get back!"

"You need *these pellets* to get back?"

"Yes, Opa. When we came here, we threw a blue pellet at the big rock on our planet. Gana has told us we need to use the red pellet to go back."

"Let me get this straight: You threw a blue pellet at a big rock on your planet, then, like *whoosh*, you popped-up here on Earth?"

Adam and Horst nodded.

"Now, you're supposed to throw the red pellet at something to go back?"

"Yes."

"But you don't know what this other something is, correct?"

"That is correct. You see, we were sent as scouts into uncharted territory. Gana does not know what is here. We are leading the way."

"I see. You're saying you came to Earth as scouts—" Charles stopped himself mid-sentence, then said, "You know, at this point, I think we all need a drink. How about a beer?"

Charles retrieved a mini-keg of *Stiegl* from his basement refrigerator, placing it on the oak table. As he poured, Adam and Horst watched him tilt each glass at a forty-five-degree angle until it was about half-full; then he straightened the glass, allowing a two-inch head to form.

"Interesting—very interesting. This stuff is way beyond me," muttered Charles. "There is only one person I know who might be able to help us, that is, if he's still alive—Professor Kalinsky, from the University of Chicago."

Elise's eyes sparkled with excitement. "Oh, I remember him! Wasn't he the man we ran into at the Snail Bar in Hyde Park years ago? Wasn't he wearing one of those owl pins from your little secret club?"

Charles frowned. "That 'little secret club' you're referring to is the National Academy of Science's advisors to the President!"

"Sorry," replied Elise. "But he wore the cute little owl pin, right?"

"Yes! Yes! He wore the 'cute little owl pin'!" said Charles, wiping the back of his hand across his forehead.

"As I was *trying* to say, Professor Kalinsky was, or may still be, a member of the National Academy of Science. He taught physics for many years. He's quite charming but, intellectually, quite a bit over my head."

"And you were also a member of the National Academy of Science?" asked Horst.

"I'm not sure if I told you, Horst, but my grandfather was an expert advisor on structural engineering issues," explained Adam.

"Correct, Adam—except you said, 'I *was*.' I'm still alive, and I'm still an engineer."

"Charles, you retired!" protested Elise.

"But I'm still an engineer!" said Charles, snapping his pencil.

"Sorry," said Elise. "Horst and Adam, Charles is still an engineer, but he's retired."

It was getting late. Tina, who had been listening to the grown-ups, had gotten bored. "Grandma, isn't it time for bed?"

"Oh my! It's late! Let's go up to bed right now. You first need to take a bath."

"Can I have a bubble bath?"

"I'll need to check if I have any bubbles. Now, scoot!"

Tina ran up the stairs with her grandmother following behind.

Charles waited for Tina and Elise to be out of earshot, then turned to Adam and Horst. "There's something we need to talk about, and I don't want Tina to hear."

"What is it, Opa?"

"Do you remember the reason why you were sent to your planet?"

"Of course," said Horst. "An asteroid or meteor was about to hit the Earth. Obviously, that did not happen!"

Charles slightly shook his head. "Not yet," he said.

Adam leaned forward, listening intently. "What are you getting at?"

"The asteroid will be hitting the Earth in two weeks, on April 5th at precisely two thirteen p.m.!" said Charles flatly.

"*Mein Gott!*" said Horst.

Chapter 24

THE NEXT MORNING, HORST WOKE UP AT SEVEN A.M. AND went downstairs to the family room, where Adam and Tina were sitting on the floor in front of the TV, watching a cartoon show; it featured a yellow talking sponge named Spongebob.

"*Licking doorknobs is illegal on other planets!*" said the sponge.

"Hey, I take offense to that!" said Adam. "We lick our doorknobs all the time!"

"You're funny!" laughed Tina.

"Yeah, I know," replied Adam, pulling one of her pigtails. "You're sort of funny, too."

Tina snorted.

"Shh, Tina! You sound like a pig!"

Tina jumped on Adam's back, wrestling him to the floor.

Horst watched the two fraternal twins, ages nine and sixty-two, playing together as if they were both nine years of age. He wondered, are siblings hard-wired? Already, they were so close and relaxed, despite their age difference.

But his thoughts turned to the asteroid. Before the cave disaster, his life with Ingrid in New Munich had been so simple. Now, he had to get back to his planet before the asteroid hit and before Gana sacrificed Olga. He felt for the rock and the pellets in his pant pockets: They were still there—*but at what was he supposed to throw the pellets?*

Walking into the kitchen, Horst helped himself to a bowl of cereal. It was fortunate they had found Charles and Elise, but he had no idea how to explain the situation about Gana and Olga. Lost in thought, he didn't notice Charles enter the kitchen.

"I see you found the Grape Nuts."

"The what?" said Horst, startled out of his reverie.

Horst looked at the cereal box.

"Oh, yes. Grape Nuts. It is delicious, but it does not taste like grapes or nuts to me."

"Yeah, I know. I'm curious, how would you say Grape Nuts in German?"

"Well, it's not a real word, but we make a lot of compound words. We would say *die Traubenuss*."

"*Die Traubenuss!*" repeated Charles, smiling.

"Perfect!"

"When I was young, I spoke Ukrainian."

"Yes, I know. Adam has told us many times about his Ukrainian ancestry," said Horst. "He is one of the few people on our planet who has kept his Earth family name."

"Interesting. And what is your last name?"

"*'Apoteker,'* which means pharmacist or druggist."

Charles's eyes widened as he scrutinized Horst's features.

"Is *Frank Ebstoesser* your grandfather?"

"You know *meinen Opa*?"

Charles nodded.

"We used to be best friends! We go way back, to our days at Los Alamos."

"What happened?"

"Well, let's see. I was the best man at his wedding. But Frank and Cynthia eventually got divorced. A very brilliant man—a true scientist—one of the smartest people I've ever met. I haven't seen him in years. I'm an engineer, so he and I are in different worlds."

"I'm from a different world."

"Yes, you certainly are!" laughed Charles. "Sometimes, I think I would have loved to be a chemist myself, but I'm not sure if I would have cut the mustard. I understand construction, though."

Charles's cell phone rang, interrupting their conversation. Looking at the caller ID, he held up his finger.

"Gotta' take this."

A few minutes later, Charles ended the call.

"We're in luck! That was Professor Kalinsky. We're going to meet him today at his apartment in Hyde Park at noon—be sure to bring your rock and those pellets!"

~

Charles, Adam, and Horst drove to Chicago's Hyde Park neighborhood, famous for its museums, lakefront, and the University of Chicago. After parking the car on 55th Street, they walked along a tree-lined street not far from Lakeshore Drive. Charles pointed ahead at a high rise.

"The Professor and his wife live up there, in Promontory Apartments. It's a twenty-two-story skyscraper designed by Ludwig Mies van der Rhoe. It was the first building Mies designed that featured an exposed structural skeleton."

"*Opa,* did you know this architect?" asked Adam.

Charles smiled, shaking his head.

"No, Mies was a bit before my time."

They took an elevator to the twentieth floor, then headed down a corridor to the professor's apartment. After pushing the doorbell, Charles whispered, "It's been ten years since I've seen Professor Kalinksy. Their apartment has breath-taking views of both Lake Michigan and the Museum of Science and Industry."

They could hear the professor shuffling to the door.

"Coming! Coming!"

When the door opened, Charles immediately noticed how much Professor Kalinsky had aged. He was using a walker, with two yellow tennis balls attached to the bottoms of the front legs. A small stuffed bear was attached to the walker with a twisty.

When the professor saw Charles's reaction to the stuffed bear, he burst out laughing.

"Ha—you appear confused, Charles!"

He placed his hand on Charles's shoulder and ushered him inside.

"This is Dorothy's walker! How are you doing, Charles? Please come inside."

"I'm doing fine, Professor. And how are you? I see that you have some mobility issues."

"Ah, yes. Hip problems. What can you expect, I'm eighty-three years old! Haven't lost my mind yet, though!"

Adam and Horst remained in the hallway, just outside the door. Charles motioned for them to join him.

"Come in, guys—you're the stars of the show! Adam and Horst, I want to introduce you to Professor Kalinsky from the University of Chicago."

"Well, *formerly* of the University of Chicago," said the professor. "I'm retired and no longer teach. I still have some old contacts there, but I'm afraid the entire field of physics is moving along nicely without me!"

A short elderly woman with silver-white hair shuffled into the room, leaning on a walker that was evidently too high for her. She glared at the professor.

"Boris, why are you using my walker?"

"Sorry, Dorothy. I grabbed the nearest one when the doorbell rang," apologized her husband. "Gentlemen, this is my wife, Dorothy."

"Good afternoon, Dorothy, it's so good to see you after all these years! This is my . . . eh . . . my cousin, Adam and his friend Horst."

"Cousins, huh?" remarked Professor Kalinsky, looking at Charles and Adam. "You two could be twins!"

With some difficulty, Dorothy switched walkers with her husband. "Excuse me, I will make lunch, while you gentlemen talk about science."

"*Danke!*" said Horst.

"German?" exclaimed Dorothy. "We love visiting that part of the world—absolutely beautiful! *Sehr shone!*"

Horst pulled a face.

"Sorry, but I've never been there."

"Oh, I just assumed you are German," she replied, looking confused. "But please, don't tell me where you're from—let's wait 'til lunch!"

After Dorothy left the room, the professor turned to his guests. "What brings you fellows here on this fine Sunday, when you could be outdoors?"

"To begin," said Charles, "We need your opinion about something belonging to my cousin and his friend. Horst, please show Professor Kalinsky the rock and the pellets."

Horst handed the rock to the professor who rolled it around in his hand, quickly examining it.

"Sorry, Charles, but I'm a physicist, not a geologist. This looks just like a rock to me."

"Do you know a geologist who could help us identify what this rock is?"

"We think it's a piece of a meteor," interjected Horst.

"A meteor, really?" said the professor. "In that case, I can ask Dr. Davis. He works at Argonne National Labs, but, conveniently for us, lives in this building. Charles also mentioned something about pellets?"

"Yes," said Horst, removing a blue pellet from his pocket. "Please be careful handling it—I'm afraid I can spare only one."

Professor Kalinsky quickly glanced at the pellet, "I'm sure Dr. Davis can determine exactly what these things are, he's quite a capable laboratory man. I'm a numbers guy, a theorist. I was always clumsy in the lab. In fact, that's how I met Dorothy: We were chemistry lab partners, freshmen year in college."

"Boris, are you talking about me?" came a shrill voice from the kitchen.

"I was just saying, Dear, that we met each other when we were lab partners in college," said Boris loudly.

"Ah, yes—chemistry. I remember I did most of the work in the lab—similar to how I do all the cooking now. Oops! My pot of water is boiling over!"

The professor turned his attention back to the men.

"Please take a seat—I'm forgetting my manners here. Anything else, besides this rock and pellet?"

Charles cleared his throat. "Professor . . . ah . . . do you think time travel is possible?"

Professor Kalinsky smiled and crossed his arms.

"Come on, Charles! Have you been watching science fiction movies lately? Is this what you three grown men drove all the way down here to ask me? Time travel! Hah!"

Then, noticing the deadpan expressions of his guests, he stopped laughing. "Seriously, Charles?"

Charles rubbed the back of his neck and nodded. "Yes, we are quite interested in your opinion. Excuse our ignorance, but, yes—seriously—is time travel possible?"

The professor paused. "Well, in a nutshell, I'd say 'no.' Or let me reframe my response: In my opinion, a time *machine,* like the one in the classic book by H. G. Wells, is impossible. Remember that movie, *The Time Machine*, with that actor named 'Rod'—what's his name?"

"Rod Taylor," answered Charles.

"Yes, Rod Taylor. What a great movie! Wasn't it about a time machine going into the future 80,000 years? He met 'Weena' and the Morlocks. God, how I loved that movie when I was a kid!"

"You say that, specifically, a time *machine* may be impossible. Why not?"

"There have been several proposals for building time machines: What I would classify as 'thought experiments' only. Some very brilliant and respected physicists have explored this as an intellectual exercise. I recall one idea called a 'Tipler Cylinder,' proposed by Dr. Frank Tipler of Tulane University. A Tipler cylinder would need to rotate at nearly the speed of light! Can you imagine!" he chuckled. Seeing there was no response from his guests, he continued.

"Another very prominent physicist in the field is Kip Thorne—a colleague of Steve Hawking's. He suggested the construction of wormholes for traveling instantly through space; they could also be used for time travel. Kip has a fascinating book on this subject, which I can give you."

"No, I don't think that's necessary, Professor," said Charles. "I'm sorry we've wasted your time on this silly subject of time machines."

"Now, Charles, I didn't mean to blow you off," said the professor. "I'm just warming up! I was about to mention an intriguing topic in modern physics and cosmology. I said I don't believe that *manmade* time machines are possible. However, many physicists believe that *natural* time machines exist throughout the Universe."

Horst and Adam looked at each other, suddenly attentive, but before they could ask another question, Dorothy entered the living room.

"Lunch is ready! Everyone, come into the kitchen!"

~

They went into the kitchen and sat down at a round dining table.

"I hope you like quesadillas," said Dorothy, placing a large plate on the Lazy Susan in front of them.

Horst looked at the flat, triangular pieces of food called quesadillas. He reached for one and bit into it: it was filled with meat and cheese. The spicy taste was like the food they had eaten with Takala and Hehewuti. He glanced at Adam, who was nodding at him, apparently thinking the same thing.

"I hope it's not too spicy," said Dorothy. "I only buy Old El Paso with the mild sauce. Like it?"

"*Ja,*" said Horst. "I meant to say, 'yes.'"

"If you're not from Germany, are you from Austria?" asked Dorothy.

"*Nein*, I mean, 'no,'" said Horst, once again slipping into Deutsch. "We're from a very small place where they speak both Deutsch and English."

"*Liechtenstein?*" asked Dorothy.

"Good catch, Dorothy. Yes, Horst is from Liechtenstein," said Charles quickly.

"Dorothy, wasn't there a Peter Sellers movie about Liechtenstein?"

"No, Boris. You're thinking of *The Mouse That Roared.* That was about a fictional country." Returning her attention at Horst, she said, "I suppose you don't have Mexican food in Liechtenstein."

"Is this what this food is, Mexican food?"

"Yes, it's Mexican food."

"What's it made of?" asked Adam.

"Well, it's pretty simple. Flour tortillas, ground beef, frozen corn, chopped green onions, chili powder, shredded cheese, and, of course, Old El Paso *Thick and Chunky* salsa. I can write down the recipe, if you want."

"Thank you, Dorothy. We must take the recipe back to Liechtenstein!" said Horst.

Just then, a black and white tuxedo cat ran into the kitchen, chasing a marble across the floor. Everyone watched the cat playing with the marble, as though it was catching a mouse.

"That's Misses 'O,'" laughed Dorothy. "She loves that marble. She can play with that thing all day long."

Charles said, "Misses 'O'?"

"Well, her official name is 'Oreo Cookie,'" explained the professor.

Eventually, the cat lost interest in the marble and left the kitchen.

"Young man, can you please pick up that marble and hand it over to me?" said the professor, turning to Horst.

"Thank you. I think I can use this as a prop to explain time effects."

He placed the marble on the table next to his plate. "Okay, let's get back to the fascinating topic of time. As I was saying, there are, in fact, *natural time machines* in the Universe. One such theoretical possibility is called a 'closed time-like curve' or 'CTC,' for short. CTCs were predicted in the 1920s by Paul Dirac. Later, in the late 1940s, Kurt Gödel wrote a paper proposing a special CTC manifold where time-reversal would be possible.

Incidentally, Gödel and Einstein were best friends in Princeton, New Jersey. They had many long talks about such things as CTCs, as they strolled across campus."

Horst's eyes widened. "This is fascinating! How is this possible?"

"Closed time-like curves can happen around very massive celestial bodies—principally black holes."

"What's a black hole?" asked Adam, helping himself to some tortilla chips.

"Black holes form when massive stars collapse into something called a *supernova*. Then the mass of the celestial body is compressed into a volume smaller than the 'Schwarzchild Radius.' This quantity was derived in 1916 by Karl Schwarzchild, using Einstein's Theory of Relativity."

Picking up the marble, the professor tossed it back and forth in his hands, then held it up. With everyone's attention on the marble, he said, "This marble is about the size of the Schwarzchild Radius for the Earth."

Incredulous, Horst stared at the marble, then turned his attention back to Professor Kalinsky.

"So, you are saying, if the mass of the Earth were somehow squished into the size of a marble, it would be a black hole. But how? How could something like that ever happen?"

The professor helped himself to a quesadilla and took a bite.

"Sorry, this is the trouble of lecturing while I'm eating, it's one or the other. In answer to your question, 'no,' the Earth will never form a black hole and nor will the sun, although there is presently some debate about this. Black holes form when stars about three times the mass of the sun collapse. You see, all stars are sustained by nuclear fusion in their innermost core. When nuclear fusion ceases, the star's outer mass falls toward the center of the star, compressing the matter together."

"Fascinating, Professor," said Charles. "I've heard of *supernovas,* before."

"It's a historical fact the Mayan Indians living in Guatemala and Mexico were expert observers of the galaxy," continued the professor. "They kept track of a supernova in our galaxy called the *Orion Nebula*. The ancient Mayans understood the motions of the sky better than most people today!"

"Are the Mayans still around?" asked Adam.

"No, they vanished. It's one of those great mysteries."

Horst whispered to Adam, *"Hören das? Wieder Mexico."* [Hear that? Again Mexico.]

"I find it remarkable to eat this delicious Mexican meal as we talk about the Mayan Indians of Mexico," said Horst, nodding appreciatively at Dorothy.

"Speaking of Indians," said Charles, "Elise and I just returned from a trip to New Mexico, where we met—" He suddenly stopped himself in mid-sentence, distracted. Then he continued, "I'm sorry, Professor Kalinsky, but you were about to explain natural time machines."

"Ah, yes, we seemed to be getting slightly off course, but we haven't strayed too far. What I was saying is, closed time-like curves exist around black holes. Now we've finished lunch, I propose we go back into the living room to continue our discussion."

~

The group moved back into the living room. The professor and his wife sat on the couch while their guests sat in armchairs, facing them.

Professor Kalinsky held up the marble. "Returning to this marble in my hand, let's say it represents a black hole. Some extraordinary things happen with time and space around black holes and massive objects. This has to do with Einstein's Theory of General Relativity. Are you familiar with Einstein?"

Adam looked at Horst. "Well, yes, both Adam and I are quite familiar with Einstein as a personality."

"Yes, we are quite familiar with him," confirmed Horst.

"But are you familiar with his Theory of General Relativity?"

"No," replied Horst. "I never got that far in my physics studies."

"Well, Einstein's Theory of General Relativity states that mass curves spacetime."

"You mean it curves time?" asked Horst.

"No, not 'time,' but something called '*spacetime.*' It is a combination of space and time, called 'spacetime.' It is not something we can see, but something which is a sort of 'fabric' of the Universe."

He held up the marble and said, "Okay, here's our black hole. Now, let's suppose we have a piece of matter entering the event horizon of a black hole. For this, I need something to demonstrate. Horst, can you give me that rock again?"

Horst reached into his pocket and retrieved the meteor, handing it over to the professor.

"Thank you, Horst."

He held the rock near the marble. "Now, if the rock is in the event horizon of a black hole, something astounding happens to the measurement of time: From the perspective of an outside observer, the orbiting rock appears to slow down until it stops."

Horst frowned.

"Ah . . . I didn't quite understand that last part."

"Of course. When the rock reaches the Schwarzchild Radius, the rock appears to slow down until it freezes."

Charles's eyes widened. "So, will the rock ever fall inside the critical radius?"

"Yes. If you were on the rock, you would experience no delay in time." The professor smiled, "I know, it's confusing. Time is something that is measured differently by different observers. To an outside observer, the rock appears to stop; but to an observer on the rock, time seems normal."

Perplexed, Charles continued, "What happens if we take things one step further? What happens if the rock descends into the black hole?"

"Well, we call the region of spacetime inside the event horizon 'Finklestein spacetime.'"

"Finklestein . . . ?"

"It is a region of spacetime that is separated from the rest of the Universe."

"Will time be reversed in this Finklestein guys's spacetime?" asked Charles.

"There's really no point exploring if time is reversed inside a black hole, because nothing can survive going into a black hole."

Horst raised his eyebrows and interrupted: "But you said there are natural time machines."

The professor paused, then said, "I'm cautious—"

Dorothy interjected, "Boris is very cautious."

The professor closed his eyes and grimaced. "Darling, please allow me to finish."

"Sorry, dear."

The professor paused and took a breath. "What I'm trying to say is, I'm cautious in my viewpoints—*about physics.* At the risk of tarnishing my scientific reputation, I admit there are theoretical manifolds in spacetime called *wormholes,* which could be used as a means of time travel—and space travel, for that matter. In my opinion, wormholes are physically impossible, but that's just me. There are some very bright physicists who are quite serious about the existence of wormholes."

"I think you've answered our question, Professor," said Charles. "Thank you for your time. I found this fascinating!"

"Yes, fascinating!" agreed Horst.

"*Fantastich!*" said Adam.

Professor Kalinsky picked up the rock. "I will give this to Dr. Davis. I'm certain he will understand what it is."

"And, please, don't forget the pellet," said Horst.

"Yes, of course! Just one more thing, I want you to have something."

He hobbled over to his bookcase. "Ah, hah! Found it!"

He removed a book which he handed to Horst. "Here it is—Kip Thorne's book, *Black Holes & Time Warps*. Very interesting reading."

"Danke!"

The professor turned toward Charles, laying his hand on his shoulder. "I'm sorry that this is the end of the line, Charles. We go back a long time, since we were both members of the National Academy."

"Yes, we go way back—at least twenty years!" said Charles.

"And to think we planned that crazy mission: Sending frozen embryos into space to save human civilization! It's unfortunate we will never know if the Mission will be successful!"

"It was," said Charles.

"Say again, Charles?" said the professor, cupping his hand to his ear. "Sometimes, I can't hear."

"I said, the Mission was successful," said Charles, looking at him directly.

After closing the door, Professor Kalinsky turned to his wife. "Did I hear him correctly? He said the Mission '*was*' successful! How can that be? The journey to that planet will take 80,000 years!"

Chapter 25

AFTER EXITING THE KALINSKYS' CONDO BUILDING, CHARLES, Horst, and Adam walked to the car and drove away from the Hyde Park neighborhood. They took a different route back, driving past the Museum of Science and Industry, then heading north on Lake Shore Drive.

"We're taking the scenic way home," explained Charles. "I want to avoid the Dan Ryan, it's always a mess at rush hour."

He glanced at Adam, who was sitting next to him in the front of the vehicle.

"Sorry, guys, I didn't mean to get your hopes up. But look at it this way: At least we now know time machines aren't possible unless, that is, we can somehow travel into a wormhole!"

He chuckled to himself, then looked in the rearview mirror at Horst, who was engrossed in Professor Kalinsky's book. "So, Horst, what's the name of the book?"

Horst looked at the cover. "It's called *Black Holes & Time Warps* by Kip Thorne."

"Black holes! Time warps!" Charles shook his head. "You heard the expert: Time machines are impossible."

Horst's eyes narrowed. "But somehow Adam and I got here, Charles."

"Yes, somehow, you got here, but not in a time machine!" agreed Charles, keeping his eyes on the road.

Horst flipped through the book and felt the paper. "*Sehr interassante!*"

"Let me guess: You just said that something is interesting?" said Charles.

"Yes, it's interesting to feel and read a real *bound* book."

"What do you mean, a *bound* book? As opposed to what else?"

"We have no printed books on our planet, only e-readers."

Adam turned around to face Horst, "*Bitte*! May I see the book?"

"*Nehmen Sie!*" said Horst, handing him the book.

Adam ran his fingertips over the paper. "I like this! I like the way it feels."

Charles listened in silence. Here was yet another minor detail that corroborated Adam and Horst's story: Only e-readers were sent on the Mission because printed books would have taken up too much space on the shuttle-craft. *Could Professor Kalinsky be wrong?*

They continued along Lake Shore Drive and soon passed McCormick Place Convention Center and Soldier Field stadium. Suddenly, Adam pointed at a large building and shouted, "*Schau dort!*" [Look over there!]

Horst looked at the large building. "Ah, Adam, what am I looking for?"

"Don't you see it?" said Adam. "See the tall columns, over there on the left? The Greek Ionic columns?"

Then Horst sat bolt upright. "*Mein Gott!* I see the revolving glass door we used when we arrived here!"

"Uh, what are you guys looking at?" asked Charles.

"That's where we came from!" said Adam, pointing to a massive building.

"Ah, that's the Field Museum, guys." Charles spoke slowly, stretching out the words. "You're saying you came out of the Field Museum?"

"*Richtig*—I mean, 'correct,'" said Adam. "That's where we found ourselves on the floor! A man discovered us and made us leave!"

"Really?" said Charles, swerving sharply to avoid an Uber driver who was distracted by her GPS. He pressed down on the horn, muttering under his breath.

Soon they came to an intersection with stoplights. As they waited for the light to change, Horst pointed at the intersecting road.

"Adam, this is where we walked to that awful place with tents where we slept!"

"I did not sleep at all!" said Adam, shaking his head.

Charles looked at the street sign. "Roosevelt Road." *Had they walked from the Field Museum down Roosevelt Road?* That's how they must have reached the tent city next to the Dan Ryan Expressway.

When the traffic light turned green, Charles accelerated ahead of the other cars at fifty miles per hour, then, catching himself speeding, slowed down. Time was running out: In only nine days, on April 5th, at two thirteen p.m., the asteroid would be hitting the Earth, just west of Wichita, Kansas. Any day now, the US government would make a press announcement.

For the remainder of the ride, they sat quietly, enjoying the impressive skyline and scenery, although Horst seemed more interested in reading *Black Holes & Time Warps*. They continued north on Lake Shore Drive, past downtown Chicago, Navy Pier, Lincoln Park, and the Zoo. Eventually, they reached the northern suburb of Wilmette, and while they were driving on Sheridan Road, they came across an extraordinary, beautiful building.

Adam's eyes widened as he stared at the twenty-story domed structure, surrounded by gardens and fountains.

"*Sehr schön!*" [Very beautiful!]

"Oh, that's the Bahai Temple," commented Charles. "It's one of eight Bahai temples in the world. The construction took over thirty years—"

"Excuse me, Charles and Adam, but I am trying to concentrate," interrupted Horst, holding up the book on black holes for them to see. "Black holes are my immediate concern."

~

For the next two days, Horst threw all his efforts into learning as much as he could about General Relativity and black holes. When he had almost finished reading *Black Holes & Time Warps*, he asked Charles if he had access to other books with explicit mathematical derivations of General Relativity or "GR." Charles borrowed a textbook on GR from Northwestern University's technical library, titled *Spacetime and Geometry: An Introduction to General Relativity*. Horst dove into reading about General Relativity, working out the mathematics step-by-step at the dining room table.

~

On the morning of the third day since their visit to Professor Kalinsky, Horst went downstairs to the family room to find Adam, Tina, and Grandma Elise all wearing bike helmets. Charles was sitting in his chair, reading the *Chicago Tribune*.

"Going on a bike ride today?"

"Yes, indeed we are," said Adam, who was adjusting his helmet strap. "I am looking forward to going on a *real* bicycle trip, as opposed to an APS bicycle trip!"

"And I get to use my new bike!" squealed Tina, jumping up and down.

"So, where are you going?"

"We're going up the North Branch Trail to the Botanical Gardens," said Elise. "I would invite you to come along, but we don't have any more bikes."

She turned toward her granddaughter and said, "Tina, did you remember to pack the trail mix?"

"Y-e e-s," Tina sighed, making a one-syllable word sound like a two-syllable word.

"And your water?"

"Y-e e-s. Come on, Grandma, let's go!"

"Just one more thing." Elise took out her cell phone and opened a phone app, *Map My Ride*. "Okay, now, I think we're ready!"

Charles barely looked up from his paper. "Have fun!"

As the three walked outside to their bikes, Adam turned back and said, *"Tschüs!"*

Charles's eyebrows scrunched together. "What did he say? Sounded like 'choose.'"

"He said, '*Tschüs.*' It means 'good-bye,'" said Horst.

"I thought you would say '*Aufweidersehen.*'"

"Not always. '*Tschüs*' is an informal way of saying good-bye."

While the others were on their bike ride, Charles and Horst remained in the family room. Charles continued studying the *Chicago Tribune*, while Horst was reading books about GR and Einstein's life. After nearly an hour, Horst broke the silence.

"I'm getting tired. This is fascinating stuff, but the mathematics is overwhelming. I only understand a small portion of this theory."

"Can you elaborate? It may help if you try to explain what you've learned."

"Sure, I can try," said Horst, standing up. "How shall I begin? Hmm. . . . Let's first talk about light." He began pacing back-and-forth, as though giving a lecture.

"When Einstein was a young man—a teenager, in fact—he was fascinated by the speed of light. He tried to imagine what it would be like to travel close to the speed of light. His basic assumption was nothing could travel faster than the speed of light."

"I remember that from my college physics."

"Charles, do you have a piece of paper and something I can write with?"

"Of course."

Charles handed Horst a pad of paper and a pencil. Then Horst quickly drew a sketch:

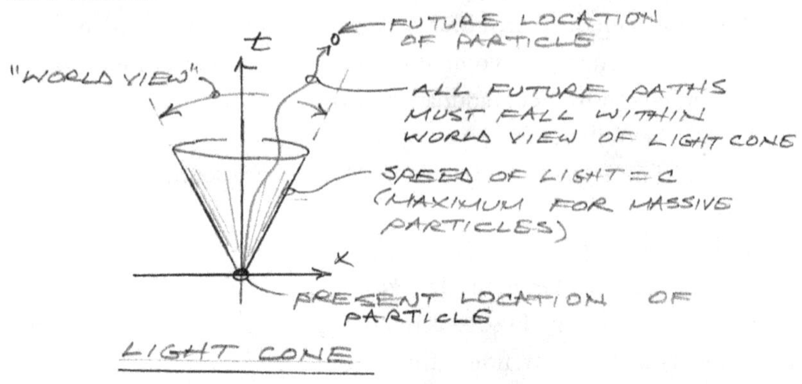

"In this sketch, I've drawn what is called a 'light cone.' Everything inside the light cone represents the collection of all possible future positions a particle can have."

"Now, you've lost me."

"Okay, let's think of a practical example. Currently, you are sitting in your chair. In this sketch, see where I've written 'present location of the particle'?"

"Yep, that's me: a particle."

"Your sense of humor reminds me of my wife!"

"I hope that's a compliment. What's your wife's name?"

"Her name is Ingrid. She's a physician, but Charles, if you don't mind, I would like to remain focused on physics. I can discuss Ingrid and my children another time."

"Sorry . . . maybe another time."

Horst closed his eyes, as if in deep thought. When he opened them again, he flipped to a clean sheet of paper and made another sketch, this time of a triangle.

"I think it would be helpful if we draw a practical example of a light cone. Here I've drawn a light cone, and I want us to fill in some information. Let me first ask, how far is Chicago from here?"

"Ah, I'd say about twelve miles."

"How long does it take to drive there?"

"If I go down Waukegan Road at thirty-five mph, I'd say it would take about twenty minutes."

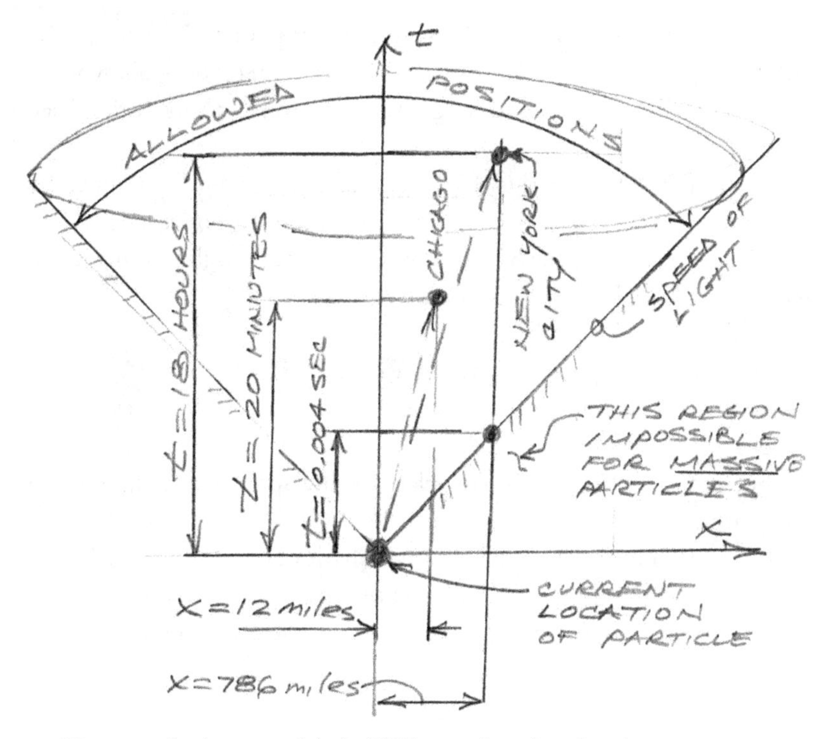

Horst marked a point labeled "Chicago" on his sketch.

"Good, we have one point inside the light cone: x = 12 miles at t = 20 minutes. Give me another place to go to."

"New York City."

"How far is New York City from here?"

Charles pulled out his phone and Googled the distance from Chicago to New York City.

"My phone says it's 786 miles."

"How long would it take to drive there?"

"Well, it's a long drive. Once, when Jennifer was looking at colleges, it took us about eighteen hours."

"Good enough. We have a second point inside the light cone: x = 786 miles at t = 18 hours." He labeled the point "New York" on the sketch. "Next, imagine you have a rocket ship that can travel almost the speed of light. How long would it take to get to New York?"

"How fast is the speed of light? I'm a 'miles per hour' person."

"Of course: The speed of light is 186,000 miles per second."

Charles turned on the 'calculator' app on his phone. "Let's see . . . it's 786 miles from Chicago to New York, divided by 186,000—oh, wow! It would take only 0.004 seconds to go from here to New York at the speed of light!"

"Good. Let me insert this third piece of data in your light cone: x = 786 miles at t = .004 seconds." He drew a point directly under the previous "New York" point. "Notice how I've placed that point right on the boundary of the light cone?"

"Yes."

"Do you think you can get to New York in half that time?"

"Well, no, that would be impossible."

"Because . . . ?"

"Because I would need to travel twice the speed of light, which is impossible."

"Correct!" Horst smiled and patted Charles on the shoulder. "Good, we're making progress. Technically, no *massive* particles can travel faster than the speed of light, although I'm not sure what an *anti-massive particle* would be."

Then Horst drew another sketch:

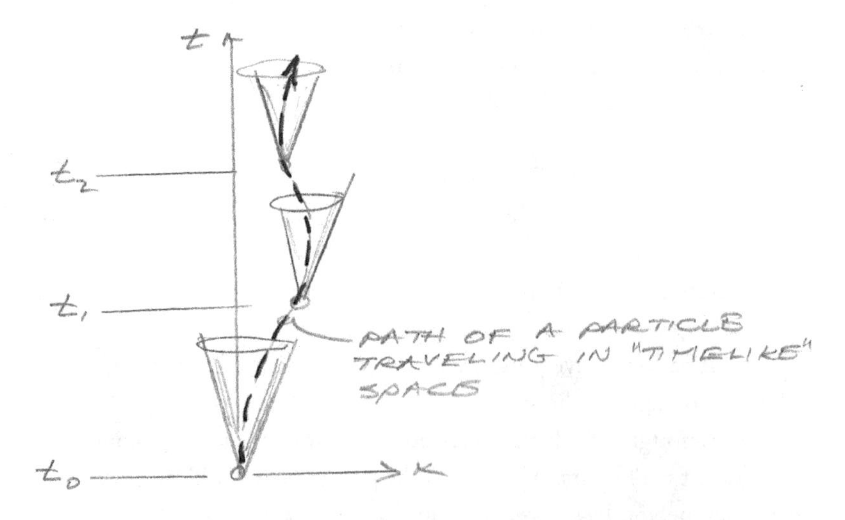

"This next sketch may seem a bit pedantic, but trust me, I'm leading up to something. This sketch shows the path of a massive particle during a particle's life. Notice how the particle always stays inside light cones?"

"Yes, I think I get it. Let's say the particle goes from here to Chicago, New York, Iowa, Los Angeles, China, Hawaii, Europe—any place it can possibly go, as long as its speed is less than the speed of light."

"Exactly," said Horst, his eyes gleaming.

"Ready for the interesting part? Mary, my daughter-in-law, uses an expression: 'It will blow your mind.' Do you say that here, too?"

"Well, yeah, it's sort of a 1960s' expression. I sometimes use it."

This time, Horst drew a sketch, showing a group of light cones traveling in a curved closed path:

CLOSED TIMELIKE CURVE (CTC)

"What I've drawn here is called a 'closed time-like curve' or 'CTC' for short," explained Horst. "A physicist by the name of Paul Dirac determined CTCs are possible due to General Relativity. In this sketch, I am showing how there is the possibility the path of a light cone can *circle back to its starting place.*"

"But, can light curve like that?" objected Charles. "Doesn't light always go in a straight line?"

Horst shook his head.

"No, light doesn't always travel in a straight line. Light—specifically, photons—are influenced by gravity. This is something that was predicted by General Relativity."

Charles furrowed his eyebrows. "You're saying it may be possible for photons to make a closed loop and go backward in time?"

"Yes. It would be an infinite cycle, always returning to the beginning, over and over. It would appear frozen in time to an outside observer."

"Is this what Professor Kalinsky meant when he said natural time machines exist?"

"I believe so," said Horst. "There may be time machines in nature."

He rubbed his eyes and stretched. "I've got to take a break," he said, walking over to the window.

"Honestly, this stuff is way over my head! It would take me months to understand the mathematics. The fact is, Adam and I somehow got here. How else could we get here but by time travel?"

"I don't know what to tell you," said Charles.

Horst turned to the window again. Only a few feet away, outside the window overlooking the backyard, birds were feeding from a bird feeder, which was hanging from a tree branch extending over the patio. Then he noticed a little grey furry animal sitting on the wooden railing of the patio deck. As the birds feasted, the animal watched them, moving its mouth rapidly as it chewed their seeds.

Fascinated, Horst asked, "What is this animal called?"

"Let me take a look," said Charles. He stood up and walked over to the window.

"Oh, that's just a squirrel."

"We don't have squirrels on our planet."

"We have a lot here. Squirrels are smart; I call them nature's engineers. I've watched that squirrel sit there every single day, trying to figure out how to get into the bird feeder!"

"Has he ever gotten in?"

"Yeah, sometimes, but not often," laughed Charles. "If there's a will, there's a way!"

Rubbing the back of his neck, Horst walked back to the sofa.

"How long do we have? Only a week?"

"Unfortunately, just seven days," said Charles, returning to his armchair. "To be exact, the time of impact is two thirteen p.m. on April 5th."

"We've got to return—they're expecting us!"

"Who?"

Horst winced and closed his eyes for a few seconds before replying.

"Charles, you and Elise have been so kind to accept Adam and me into your lives, but there is another aspect to our story. I'm afraid that you may find this part impossible to believe."

"Go ahead," sighed Charles, leaning back in his chair. "Get it all out."

Looking steadily at Charles, Horst said, "There are . . . how shall I say? . . . there are creatures on our planet who sent us here."

"*Creatures?* Do you mean, like, aliens? Like aliens from space?"

Horst nodded.

Charles sat up, leaning forward on the edge of his seat.

"What are they like?"

"They are somewhat humanoid in appearance; they have two legs, two arms and a head, but they are not humans. They are very intelligent in some ways, possibly even more intelligent than humans," said Horst, beginning to shake uncontrollably.

"Calm down, Horst. Let's take this one step at a time. Explain what happened before you came here."

"It happened all so fast! Olga and Janu managed to escape because Gana wanted to kill them! Then Gana gave us the pellets."

He reached into his pocket and pulled out the pellets, holding them in the palm of his hand. "Gana told us 'use the blue ones to go forward' and 'use the red ones to go backward'! Then he pushed us into a swirling pool next to the meteor, and, *whoosh,* we found ourselves in the Field Museum!"

"Olga? . . . Janu? . . . Gana? . . . I don't understand," stammered Charles.

"We must get back! We must use the red pellets to get back!"

Horst fell backward in his chair, his shoulders slumped. He stared at the red pellet, holding it close to his face.

"The question is: How am I supposed to use this?"

Chapter 26

WITH ONLY SIX DAYS BEFORE THE MASSIVE METEOR WOULD hit Wichita, Kansas, everyone in the Timoshenko household was on edge. In just six days, the meteor would wipe Wichita off the map and half the United States along with it. After this impact, there would be another mass extinction of most life on Earth. Elise did her best to keep Tina occupied, while the men—out of earshot—discussed how the country would respond once the news of the approaching catastrophe was made public.

Their conversation dragged on into the afternoon, accomplishing little except to heighten their fears. The "worst-case scenarios" they imagined were grounded in fact, not fantasy. As an engineer, Charles was keenly aware of how the impact would destroy all infrastructure, bringing down electrical generators, gas lines, nuclear power plants, and water filtration facilities; as fires raged, roads and bridges would become impassable, with panicked drivers heading in every direction. Whole cities would topple, and what was left standing would soon fall victim to the inevitable tsunamis and earthquakes.

Their conversation was interrupted by a phone call from Dr. Neal Davis, the geologist colleague of Professor Kalinsky. They were to meet the next morning at nine a.m., at Argonne National Laboratory.

"*Fantastich!*" said Horst.

~

The next day, Charles, Adam, and Horst drove to Argonne National Laboratory, located west of Chicago in Lemont, Illinois. They drove up to the guardhouse entrance, where an officer took their names and checked their IDs before allowing them to enter the compound. He then directed them to a security office for further screening, where they each received a name tag with a bar code to be used for clearance protocols inside the vast complex.

They waited for Dr. Davis in the security office, sitting on uncomfortable fiberglass seats. Horst was sweating through his shirt; Adam fidgeted nervously.

"Cool it, guys," whispered Charles. "I'll take the lead when they meet us here."

They heard the voices of several people walking down a hall. When the door opened, a man wearing a white lab coat appeared, accompanied by two military officers. One of the officers wore an army general's uniform.

Charles immediately stood up from his chair.

"General *Mitchell!* I didn't expect to see you here!"

"Charles!—the *original* Planner of the Mission! So good to see you!" said the general.

The man in the white lab coat approached Charles.

"Good morning, Mr. Timoshenko. I'm Neal Davis, Chief of Material Science at the Lab, and this is Colonel Ned Zroka, General Mitchell's assistant."

While the other men were introducing themselves, Adam and Horst stared at General Mitchell, unable to believe their eyes. They had received cadet training on Planet K851b by the simulated APS version of General Mitchell, and now they were about to meet the real person.

Noticing Adam and Horst were staring at him, General Mitchell turned his attention toward them. "Excuse me, but haven't we met before?"

"Ah, hello . . . General," stuttered Horst.

Adam smiled but said nothing. He glanced at Charles, who shot him a warning glance.

"General, this is my . . . cousin, Adam and his friend, Horst . . . from . . ."

"Liechtenstein," said Horst.

"I've never been to Liechtenstein," said the general, looking at Horst directly. "My apologies. I must be confusing you with someone else."

Dr. Davis motioned toward the door. "Please follow me to the conference room."

Leaving the security office, they walked into the main complex of the lab. The building was a massive, five-story structure, with labs and offices overlooking a spacious atrium. Their footsteps echoed through the halls, as Dr. Davis led them through a maze of corridors.

"As you can see, I get a lot of exercise working here!" he said. "We are going to a Security Level B area."

"Excuse me for asking, Neal, but what's your security clearance here?" asked General Mitchell.

"Oh, me?" said Dr. Davis. "I'm only a Level B. I guess that working with rocks is not considered sensitive information," he laughed. "The top-level here is 'Q.' There are places I can never get close to!"

Finally, they reached a conference room with a sign saying, "RESERVED" on the door. Dr. Davis ushered them into a small, windowless room, about twelve feet by twelve feet, with four long tables arranged in a square. Once everyone was seated, he began the meeting.

"Again, welcome everyone. Let me get straight to the topic of this meeting. You have brought us some very interesting specimens, I must say—very interesting."

"Quite phenomenal," added the general, looking squarely at Adam, then Horst.

Dr. Davis held up the rock specimen. "First of all, let's discuss the rock specimen. This rock is a piece of a meteorite, identified as *Canyon Diablo*."

"We suspected it was a meteorite," said Horst.

"Yes, you are correct. It is a fairly large specimen you've found, too. Most of that region has been thoroughly picked over."

"What region?" asked Charles.

"Well, *Canyon Diablo Crater,* in Arizona. It was renamed '*Meteor Crater*.'"

Charles jerked his head back. "Meteor Crater? What a coincidence. My wife and I were there only a couple of weeks ago!"

"Did you see the *Holsinger Meteorite* in the Visitor Center Museum?" asked Dr. Davis. "That's the most significant piece of the meteorite discovered to date."

"Unfortunately, not. We were in kind of a hurry," said Charles apologetically.

"There are little slivers of the meteor all around the crater. As I was saying, the sample you provided is quite large. Many, many years ago, before the white man came to America, the Ancient Puebloans knew about this crater. People have found arrowheads dating back to ancient times. I haven't been there in years, but my wife and I have been talking about visiting that area next year on our anniversary."

"Next year? I highly recommend you see Sedona, too," said Charles, catching a warning glance from General Mitchell.

"Oh yes, Sedona—we love it there!" Dr. Davis's expression became more serious. "Back to the meteorite. It's a *Canyon Diablo* meteorite, no doubt about it. This rock, like all meteorites, entered from outside our solar system, as the product of a supernova."

"An exploding star?" asked Horst, his eyebrows furrowed.

"Yes. Based on the elements in this meteorite, it is a product of a second or third-generation star. There is no way to tell which supernova it came from, possibly the Orion Nebula. We can pursue this further—"

"Thank you, Dr. Davis," interrupted the general. "I think you've covered your findings regarding the meteorite quite thoroughly. Please proceed with the more interesting finding."

"Certainly, General Mitchell," said Dr. Davis, clearing his throat. "The second specimen you gave to Professor Kalinsky was astounding."

"You mean the pellet?" said Charles.

"Yes, the pellet," Dr. Davis said slowly. "We did initial testing here at Argonne. Of course, our facility has some of the most advanced equipment in the world."

"Of course," said Charles.

"We first examined the pellet using an electron microscope. It became immediately apparent the exterior consisted of an advanced material composed of *Buckminsterfullerene.* Are you familiar with this?"

Horst raised his hand. "Yes, I am familiar with this chemical. By the way, I am a chemist by profession. I recall Buckminsterfullerene is a fullerene with formula C60. It has a cage-like structure, like a soccer ball."

"Do you mean like a geodesic dome?" interjected Adam.

"Exactly," said Dr. Davis. "This allotrope was named after Buckminster Fuller, who designed geodesic domes. C60 is a geodesic dome-like assembly of interconnected carbon atoms."

Taking a deep breath, he continued. "My job is usually easy, but I thought we were working with a C60 material, probably a metal complex. I assumed it was a complex of C60 and titanium: possibly a titanocene complex, which would be quite rare. We usually approach identifying materials by first doing some nondestructive testing, because, really, who in their right mind would want to destroy a nice C60 Bucky Ball?"

He paused, evidently amused by his joke, but no one laughed. "As I was saying, usually our next step is to put the material in the Bruker 700 MHz nuclear magnetic resonance spectrometer, which is exactly what we did. Unfortunately . . ."

His voice trailed off as he raised his hands and shrugged.

"What happened?" asked Charles, frowning.

"Zilch!"

"Zilch? I'm not familiar with that word," said Horst.

"Don't you use that word in Liechtenstein?" remarked the general, looking at Horst intently. "I find this very strange."

"'Zilch' means, we got nothing," explained Dr. Davis. "We didn't get *any* reading for the material inside the pellet!"

"The nuclear magnetic resonance spectrometer couldn't detect what was inside it?" asked Horst. "Isn't that impossible?"

Dr. Davis nodded. "That's exactly what I'm saying. We thought there might be something wrong with the Bruker, but there wasn't. We tested the Bruker on a few other materials, just to make sure the thing was working right, and everything was A-okay. But every time we tried testing the pellet in the Bruker, there was no magnetic resonance."

"A very curious finding. It defies everything we know about matter, doesn't it?" observed Horst.

Dr. Davis looked directly at Horst. "My point exactly. All matter has a magnetic resonance which we should be able to detect in the Bruker."

"I'm curious: Did you do any other testing?" asked Charles.

"Yes—I was leading up to that, Charles. The next step was to do a destructive test. My suspicion was there was some bizarre stuff inside the pellet. So—*get this*—we got clearance to do a test using our linear accelerator!"

"I don't quite follow you," said Charles.

"As I said, I only have a Level B Security clearance, but, somehow I was granted a Level Q clearance to bombard the pellet using Argonne's Tandem Linac Linear Accelerator System—the ATLAS! Essentially, we bombarded the pellet with high energy particles, to observe the behavior of the particle collisions."

By now, Horst was leaning on the table, sitting on the edge of his seat. "This is amazing! You bombarded the pellet using a *linear accelerator?*"

Dr. Davis nodded. "Yes, we certainly did. But this is where things got even more bizarre."

He took off his glasses and rubbed his eyes. "I'm not sure if I can explain this correctly: We're talking about particle physics now, and I'm a materials scientist. All I can do is paraphrase what the particle physicists explained to me. During this test in the ATLAS, they observed behavior none of them had ever seen before. In fact, they said this behavior has never been seen at any laboratory, not even at CERN."

He took a deep breath, then continued. "This is how the test works. The Atlas is a high energy machine, which bombards a target with particles traveling at nearly the speed of light. The impact of this collision imparts significant energy into the target object, creating all sorts of inter-particle interactions. I assume most of you have seen photos of particle collisions?"

"Yes," said Charles. "I recall seeing photos of particles colliding in college physics. The particles spin off in spirals after a collision, in a bubble chamber, don't they?"

"Yes, normally they do. The particle physicists use the movements traced in a bubble chamber to analyze the particle interactions. All pretty standard stuff at our lab. But that's not what happened. What happened was just plain weird."

"*Weird?*" said Horst.

"When the collision particle hit the target, the collision particle disappeared."

"It disappeared?" repeated Horst. "What could have caused this?"

"Well, that's what we've been trying to figure out. Tentatively, we have a theory—well, I'm not even sure if I should be telling you this stuff."

General Mitchell waved his right hand impatiently. "Dr. Davis, please go ahead and explain your conclusion. These people have the proper clearance."

"Well, then, here goes: We've concluded . . ." he paused, then spoke in almost a whisper. "We've concluded the material inside your pellet may have had *negative mass*! This is a theoretical possibility which no one has ever observed before."

"Why negative mass?" asked Horst.

"Because when the high energy collider particle hit this stuff, it was annihilated into pure energy. It's like, +1 and −1 equal zero. Our particle physicists think this material has properties that are the opposite of the matter in our world."

Horst looked blankly ahead and uttered two words: "Exotic matter."

"Why, yes—that's a term used by Steve Hawking," said Dr. Davis.

"Both Kip Thorne and Steve Hawking used that term," continued Horst.

Dr. Davis looked at Horst with narrowed eyes. "Now, you have me curious. Did you know what was inside these pellets?"

"Absolutely not," answered Horst, folding his arms and leaning back in his chair.

As the two men stared at each other, Charles broke the silence. "This is why we went to Professor Kalinsky, to learn what the rock and pellet are."

"Well, the rock was an easy one—it's the pellet which has us baffled," said Dr. Davis, rubbing the back of his neck. "This one has me stumped. I'm sorry I haven't been more helpful."

Horst smiled. "You've been helpful. Absolutely!"

"Dr. Davis, if you don't mind, Colonel Zroka and I want to discuss several security issues with these gentlemen from Liechtenstein," said the general. "Would you mind if we use this room to talk to them alone?"

"Why, not at all."

Dr. Davis stood up, but before he left the room, he turned to Horst, handing him the meteorite specimen.

"Please don't forget your meteorite. That's quite a sizeable piece you have there. The last time my wife and I were at Meteor Crater, they were selling slivers of the meteor for $10 each. As I mentioned earlier, the largest piece of the meteor is the Holsinger specimen, which weighs 1,406 pounds. It's at the Visitors' Center of the Meteor Crater. The second-largest is 1,050 pounds, and it's in the New York Museum of Natural History." Then, opening the door, he turned toward Horst again. "We're also quite lucky to have a piece in Chicago. We have the third-largest piece, weighing 1000 pounds, at the Field Museum.

"Nice meeting you, everyone!"

Charles, Adam, and Horst stared at each other, speechless.

Chapter 27

AFTER DR. DAVIS CLOSED THE DOOR, COLONEL ZROKA LOWered himself from his chair and climbed under the table. Horst leaned forward to watch as he fumbled with an electrical line attached to a phone on the table. After disconnecting the phone, the colonel methodically began examining every surface—the walls, the ceiling, under the tables and chairs—until, suddenly, he stopped and stared at something on a wall. Horst noticed it, too. It was a very small circle, only about one-tenth of an inch in diameter. It would have been undetectable unless someone were explicitly looking for it.

The colonel quickly walked over to the general and whispered something to him. After a few moments of consultation, the colonel removed a small can from his briefcase. He carried his chair to the wall and, standing on the chair, applied a putty-like substance over the circle. Then he stepped down and placed the chair back in its spot at the table.

"Thank you for your patience. We needed to make sure this room was secure," he said, wiping his hands with a handkerchief.

"Are you sure that was the only one?"

"Affirmative, General. Only one microphone."

"Good work, Colonel," said the general. Then he turned to Horst. "*Liechtenstein,* huh?" He chuckled, slapping him on the back. "I almost laughed when I heard that! Good one!" he said, removing his glasses. "*Liechtenstein!*"

Horst stared at him blankly.

The general shrugged. "Okay, perhaps you are not amused! Let's move on. First of all, gentlemen, Colonel Zroka is not my assistant." He turned toward the colonel. "Ned, please explain to these gentlemen who you really are and why you are here."

"Certainly, General. Sorry for the ruse, guys, but I'm actually with the NSA—the National Security Administration—in Washington, DC. Not a lot of people know about us, but it's NSA's function to monitor the nation for suspicious activities."

"In other words, your job is cyber-security?"

"Exactly, Charles. Using a supercomputer, with very sophisticated algorithms, we are constantly searching for terrorist activities in the digital world. We have a vast database of information on nearly every US citizen, including facial definitions, fingerprints of people with criminal records, and profiles available on social media.

"That's enough about me . . . now let's talk about you two," he said, looking directly at Horst and Adam. "You seem to have presented an anomaly in our system."

The colonel placed his briefcase on the table and removed a document. He paused to skim the first page and circled something. When he had finished, he looked up at Horst and Adam.

"This dossier is a record of your activities. Almost a week ago, you were red-flagged as suspicious through our network of security channels."

He studied the document again, flipping to the second page.

"We were first alerted of your activities when security at the Field Museum filed a report with the Chicago Police Department. The museum provided the CPD with a surveillance video, showing you being escorted from the museum. The next day, you were arrested by suburban police for stealing Divvy bicycles."

He flipped through more pages, muttering to himself as he skimmed.

"Uh-huh . . . blah-blah-blah . . . Okay, found it."

Leaning forward in his chair, he scribbled something on the document.

"This is where things get interesting. The police submitted your photos and fingerprints into their system, which ultimately uses the FBI's criminal database. We found no matches of your fingerprints, so we can check a criminal history off your resumes. Even more interesting, our facial recognition software showed no matches of your faces in any database. In fact, your identities do not appear in any of our systems. There is nothing on you—no credit cards, no birth records, no past addresses, no history. I might as well use Dr. Davis's expression: We have 'zilch' on you!"

Turning to the last page of the document, he looked in Charles's direction.

"The final piece of information was entered when Charles Timoshenko came to the police station to release you, thus raising a red flag. The NSA's computers warned us of a possible 'situation' with a particularly important person."

"Excuse me for interrupting, Colonel," said General Mitchell. "That's when the NSA alerted me, because I am—or was—Charles's boss. Don't worry, Charles. As a Planner of the Mission, you are quite an important person. The NSA was able to pick up an . . . *what's the word Dr. Davis used?* . . . ah, yes, an '*anomaly.*' The NSA picked up an anomaly. Let's face it, guys," he continued. "We know you're not from Liechtenstein. And I have a wild hunch—*a really wild hunch*—about where you came from."

"I doubt it, sir," said Horst. "Liechtenstein is as good a place as any."

"I agree," added Charles. "There is absolutely no way you could guess where Adam and Horst are really from, absolutely no way!"

The general smiled. "We'll see about that. This is why we secured the door: I don't want anyone to hear what I'm about to tell you."

He stood up and began pacing back-and-forth across the small room, his hands behind his back.

"You know, sometimes I can't believe how many smart people I get to work with! You see, I'm just a regular guy, but I manage a team of people who are a heck of a lot smarter than me!" He stopped, placing his hands on the back of a chair. "I work with PhDs who are perpetual students in every conceivable specialty. The National Academy has a network of experts on just about every topic. The US government has think tanks of geniuses who study every possible angle, every possible strategy on just about any subject."

He gestured toward Colonel Zroka.

"As a perfect example, we have the NSA. We have computers simulate game theory and predict the outcomes of things like battles, hurricanes, earthquakes, floods; we have cybersecurity systems which analyze literally millions of suspicious emails and social media accounts every day. The average American citizen has no idea about just how much we know about almost every person living in our country. So, my people—actually, *your* people, the US taxpayer's people—have been developing a theory for a long time now."

"And what is your theory?"

"I was about to get to that, Charles. You were in New Mexico recently?"

"Yes, just a week ago."

"Of course, I know you were there—we sent one of our men to meet you."

"You mean Professor Day of the University of Illinois?"

"Yes, Professor Day." The general returned to his chair. Steepling his fingers together, he looked at Charles. "Please tell us what happened that day in New Mexico."

Somewhat embarrassed, Charles explained how he and Elise had traveled to Sedona, Arizona, where they had met a mysterious tribe in Winslow. He described meeting the ninety-six-year-old Chief Hototo, and then how they had traveled to the great kiva in Chaco Canyon during the lunar eclipse.

"And what did you observe from the great kiva?"

"We focused our telescope on a rock structure which the Ancient Puebloans had built."

The general nodded, watching Charles closely. "And . . . what did you see?"

Charles's lips parted, then, after a moment's hesitation, he said, slowly, "The Ancient Puebloans had created a rock structure marking Planet K851b."

Appearing confused, Horst frowned and shook his head.

The general leaned on the table, practically shouting at Horst. "You're not from *Liechtenstein,* damn it! You're from Planet K-8-5-1-b!"

Triumphantly, the general looked at Horst and Adam; both seemed relieved, and neither of them attempted to contradict him. They listened intently while the general explained how Professor Day and his team—all experts on the Ancient Puebloans—had developed a theory about how these ancient people had somehow vanished.

"Our people, experts like Professor Day, have taken images of many ancient pictographs, trying to make sense of them. For the most part, the pictographs are fairly primitive. However, there were several sets of pictographs which we could not decipher: not until they were shared with an interdisciplinary group of experts in one of our think tanks."

"What did they find?" asked Charles.

"When our physics experts saw the pictographs in question, they immediately noticed the pictographs looked like *Lie Diagrams.*"

"What does that mean?" asked Horst.

"Lie Diagrams are mathematical symbols used by theoretical physicists to analyze spacetime."

"You're saying the Ancient Puebloans were analyzing spacetime?"

"Not exactly, Horst. We believe an alien race lived with them a thousand years ago and they were the ones who were analyzing spacetime."

"For what purpose?" asked Charles, clearly mystified.

"General, shall I show them the video?"

"Yes, I think it's about time, Ned."

Colonel Zroka opened his computer and booted it up. After he had entered a series of commands, a video appeared, which was stopped at "pause."

"This is the surveillance video which was given to us by the Field Museum. This particular camera is located in the permanent 'Meteorite' exhibit at the museum. It is pointing directly at the *Canyon Diablo Meteorite* from Meteor Crater, Arizona. I'm about to click 'play.' Please observe what happens."

When the colonel clicked "play," the video showed a swirling silver disk appearing on the floor. The silver disk rotated in the counter-clockwise direction and was about ten feet in diameter. Then, suddenly, two bodies appeared in the disk, and just as suddenly, the silver disk vanished.

Seeing this, Horst jumped up, pointing at the screen. "There . . . look, Adam . . . it is us!"

"Mein Gott!" exclaimed Adam. *"Wir sind da!"* [My God! We're there!]

Charles shook his head in disbelief. "Now I've seen everything! But how . . . how is this possible?"

The general turned to Horst. "Horst, you made a very curious comment when Dr. Davis explained the nature of the pellets. He said he thinks the pellets are '*exotic matter.*' I was watching your reaction: You appeared to understand him completely. Can you explain to us what you're thinking?"

"Certainly, General. There has been speculation that something called a wormhole in spacetime can be held open by exotic matter. This would be a type of matter we don't normally see in our part of the Universe, or perhaps it's something we can't normally detect. Again, I am no physicist, this is simply what I've read."

The general nodded. "This is exactly what Professor Kalinsky explained to me the other day."

"You've been talking to Kalinsky?"

"Affirmative, Charles. After you met with Professor Kalinsky, he called me. You had raised his curiosity. Horst, you're an intelligent man. Do you have a theory about how you got here?"

Horst paused, as he tried to put all the pieces together. He thought about Gana and how he called himself a "No. 3." He thought about the meteor, and how it was the product of a supernova. He thought about how the Mayan Indians were aware of the Orion Nebula. He thought about closed time-like curves.

Finally, it all made sense to him. "I believe that the meteor that fell on my planet and on Meteor Crater are pieces from a larger meteor, created from a supernova. The piece that fell in Meteor Crater broke into fragments upon impact. Most pieces are still at Meteor Crater, but one of the larger pieces is now on display at the Field Museum."

"And what is the significance of the meteor?"

Horst grinned with excitement. He looked at Adam, then at Charles, then at the general. "It now seems obvious: The meteor and all its pieces are a part of a closed time-like curve. When the pellets of exotic matter are thrown at these meteorites, a wormhole opens, creating a pathway for traveling instantly through space and time."

The general let out a deep breath. "This is amazing, my team of experts didn't get this far at all! But, were we correct to assume an alien race is involved in this time travel device?"

Horst nodded slowly. "Yes, you are correct—there are aliens involved. We have met two. Their names are Gana and Tresca."

"And what are they like? Can you describe them?"

Horst quickly explained the aliens' bird-like appearance.

"What about the humans who live with the aliens?"

"They speak neither English nor Deutsch. We learned a few words of their language. They seem to have a living arrangement with Gana and Tresca."

"I still don't quite understand your purpose here. Now that you're here, are you supposed to go back?"

"Yes, General. We were sent as scouts to see if this is a safe place for the next camp. Gana told us to use the red pellets to go back, but I didn't understand what he meant by that. I didn't understand how to use the pellets! When we arrived at the Field Museum, we had no idea where we were!"

Adam's eyebrows furrowed.

"*Mein Gott!* It's so obvious—don't you see? We must go back to the Field Museum and throw the pellets at the meteorite exhibit."

Chapter 28

THEIR MEETING ENDED AT CLOSE TO FIVE P.M., RUSH HOUR. Charles, Adam, and Horst hurried to the parking lot which was already jammed with the cars of Argonne employees. Charles edged his vehicle to the end of a long line of cars creeping toward the exit. Finally, they passed through the security entrance gate and were on their way.

"I'm famished," said Charles. "How about if we find a place to eat before we hit the road home?"

"Sounds good to me," said Adam.

"Ja, auch mich," added Horst [Yes, me too.]

Charles opened the navigation screen. After punching-in the "show restaurant" function, he saw a Buffalo Wild Wings located near the entrance to Interstate 55.

It was a relatively short drive to Wild Wings. When they entered the restaurant, there were television screens everywhere, all showing baseball games. Soon they were seated in a booth, and, having ordered beers, they studied their menus.

"*Entshuldingen*, but what are Buffalo Wings?"

"Chicken wings that are kind of spicy, Adam; the recipe came from Buffalo, New York. I think you'll like them."

The waiter arrived with their beers and then took their orders of Buffalo Wings.

Charles took a good swig of beer. "Man, that tastes good!"

"Ja! Ausgezeichnet!" [Yes! Excellent!] agreed Adam.

"Ja! Das stimmt!" [That's right!] echoed Horst.

Charles shook his head, listening to the two speak German. "When I was a boy, I spoke Ukrainian for the first few years of my life."

"We know, Grandpa. There are a lot of things I know about you."

"I forgot," said Charles. "Adam, it's amazing you've had a relationship with my APS self, while I'm only getting to know you now!"

Horst burst out laughing and slapped his hand on the table. "Let me tell you something truly amazing: We had a relationship with the APS version of General Mitchell, too, but today was the first time we met!"

"I was thinking the same thing myself, Horst!" laughed Adam. "I mean, wow, I was shocked!"

"What was the APS General Mitchell like?"

"He trained us to be Cadets, Grandpa! We went through five years of Cadet training with him! He was really tough on us!"

"There is so much I've learned from him—I mean the APS version of him," said Horst, savoring his beer. Now he no longer felt pressured, his eyes brightened as he remembered Cadet training.

"And you say you've learned a lot from the APS version of me, too?" asked Charles, turning toward Adam.

"Of course, Grandpa!"

Horst looked at the televisions mounted on the walls around them; they were so much larger than the black-and-white TVs they had in New Munich. He noticed no one seemed to be particularly interested in watching the games; the televisions appeared to be there for background noise, or perhaps for scenery. He grinned, satisfied with what they had accomplished. It had been a long day; now was the time to relax.

Charles interrupted his musings.

"I think it's time to discuss your next steps. Obviously, we need to get you to the Field Museum. I suppose you simply throw the pellets at the meteor. It might be housed in a glass case, so we should probably bring a hammer and . . ."

"Excuse me, Charles, but there is the issue of my health," said Horst.

Adam almost choked on his beer. He slapped his hand on the table and glared at Horst. "Are you feeling so bad that you can't continue?"

"I have cancer, Adam." Horst swallowed and looked down at the table.

"Cancer?" said Adam, tapping a fist to his lip. "I didn't know it was this serious."

Horst nodded. "It was the reason I went on the Cadet Training Mission . . .to spend some time with Janu."

"How is Ingrid taking it?"

"Well, it's hard on her, I can see. She's a doctor, but she's also my wife."

Charles scooted closer to Horst. "Are you undergoing any treatment?"

Horst shook his head. "Unfortunately, no. On our planet, doctors are unable to give me chemotherapy. We have nothing like that."

"And, on Earth, we could give you chemotherapy, but, unfortunately, we've run out of time," said Charles slowly.

"Exactly," said Horst, looking at Adam. "I don't think . . . I don't think it makes any sense for me to go back."

"What?"

"So, I'm proposing a plan. We have only two red pellets for going back. I propose Tina goes back with you to our planet."

Charles's face grew red. "Hey . . . wait a second!" he snapped, pounding his fist on the table. "This isn't your decision! She has parents!"

Adam said, "But Horst, if she goes with me, Gana and Tresca are there! You saw what they were about to do to Olga!"

Horst sighed, avoiding eye contact with Charles. "Charles, if she stays here, she faces certain death!"

He ran his hands through his hair and looked steadily at Adam. "Considering she faces certain death here, at least she will have a chance with you."

"Well, yeah, if you put it that way," said Adam.

Charles fumbled with his napkin.

"It's not my decision. We will need to discuss this with Tina's parents."

"Of course," said Horst. "Let's assume Adam and Tina use the two red pellets to go back. That leaves us with the blue pellets. Gana explained we use them to 'go forward'—wherever that is! We gave one of the blue pellets to Dr. Davis, who destroyed it. That leaves only one blue pellet. Charles, do you or Elise want to use that one?"

Charles gave Horst an incredulous stare. "What does it mean to 'go forward'?"

"We have no idea," said Horst, crossing his arms across his chest. Then he moved to the edge of his chair, looking Charles square in the eye.

"This form of transportation involves jumping between pieces of the meteors in the closed time-like circuit. Let me make this clear to you: There is the distinct possibility of transporting to a piece of the meteor that is in empty space! The fact is, we know nothing about these pellets and this wormhole thing, nothing at all!"

Charles paused to think about this option. What a choice! Either he or Elise, transporting themselves into what? Nothingness in space or to a different planet?

He said nothing for several seconds; finally, he took a deep breath and smiled at Horst.

"Thanks for the offer, Horst. I've already lived a full life. I can't leave Elise behind, and I can't subject her to something potentially dangerous. I guess that leaves just you."

"Thank you," said Horst. "I will use the blue pellet to go forward."

"And I will need to talk to Tina's parents tonight when we get home—they already know the situation we are about to face."

"Grandpa, I will need something to defend myself against Gana and Tresca! Do you have a gun?"

"No, Adam—I've never owned a gun in my life!"

Adam frowned. "Then, I will need to find something else."

The conversation stopped when the waiter arrived with their Buffalo Wild Wings.

"These are quite good," said Adam, licking the hot sauce that was dripping over his fingers.

"When we get home, I'll find you a recipe you can take to Planet—"

"K851b," said Horst, tearing into a wing with his teeth.

Suddenly, all the television screens in the restaurant went black; then a message flashed across each screen, accompanied by a screeching sound: "EMERGENCY MESSAGE FROM THE PRESIDENT! EMERGENCY MESSAGE FROM THE PRESIDENT!"

When Charles heard this, he swore under his breath. He knew this was coming, but the timing couldn't have been worse. Some of the people in the restaurant stopped eating and turned toward the televisions, while others continued chatting. A man wearing a Harley Davidson jacket walked up to one of the screens, carrying his beer. He turned around and whistled, which got everyone's attention. He yelled, "Would ya' all SHUT THE HELL UP!"

A few seconds later, the President of the United States finally appeared on the fourteen televisions in Buffalo Wild Wings, sitting at her desk in the Oval Office, wearing a dark suit with an American flag on her lapel, looking grimly at the camera. On her right stood the American Flag; the Flag of The President of the United States and a map of the United States were displayed on her left.

A booth full of teenagers continued giggling and making wise-cracks. The Harley man turned around and glared at them, gesturing with his two fingers, using the "Hey-I'm-looking-at-you" sign. The kids immediately got the message and became quiet.

The President cleared her throat and began her address to the nation: "My fellow Americans, in this grave hour, the most fateful in our history, we are facing a catastrophe the likes of which humanity has never witnessed. Nearly ten years ago, the space satellite, New Horizons, discovered a massive asteroid on the edge of our solar system. NASA has been following this asteroid for ten years."

She stopped for a moment, trying to maintain her composure. When she spoke again, her voice shook. "I have just received a briefing from the Head of National Security, General Zroka, that I am going to share with you now: Next week, the asteroid will be impacting the Earth."

Harley Davidson dropped his beer. "What the hell?" Men and women pushed past one another to get closer to the television screens, upturning chairs in their haste. Parents shouted at their kids to "shut up" while the teenagers repeatedly uttered, "Oh, my God!"

Charles Timoshenko quietly sipped his beer, observing everyone's look of shock. Now, after ten years, all hell was about to break loose.

The President continued, staring into the camera as she spoke. "Our planet is routinely hit by small asteroids and comets that burn-up. However, the size of this particular asteroid is enormous: It is almost a hundred miles in diameter, far exceeding the size of typical space debris. Unlike a comet, which typically consists of ice, this object is rock, and we expect it will cause significant damage."

The camera zoomed in on the map of the United States directly to her right. The President stood up, pointing toward the middle of the country.

"NASA has determined the asteroid will be hitting just to the west of Wichita, Kansas, on April 5th at two thirteen p.m. Central Standard Time."

She returned to her seat behind the desk, the camera now focusing on her face. She removed her glasses, revealing her reddened eyes. "Unfortunately, we expect . . . we expect, due to the colossal size of the object, massive destruction will occur. What I'm trying to say is the consequence of this collision will be . . . the obliteration of most life on Earth."

By now, there was chaos in the room. Almost all the diners had huddled around the television screens. Some were clinging to each other for support, while others were wailing out loud—and no one, not even the Harley Davidson man, told them to stop.

The President continued, this time reading from her teleprompter. "Near the point of impact, winds will be in excess of 1,500 mph, wiping out everything within a 1000-mile radius; there will be a catastrophic upheaval of the Earth's surface, causing seismic accelerations a thousand times greater than the worst earthquake ever recorded.

"The impact will throw billions of tons of soil into the atmosphere, plunging Earth into complete darkness for five years. Temperatures will drop, and most life forms will be unable to survive, including the human species."

She stopped, looking up from the teleprompter, directly at the American people.

"As your President, I encourage you now to return to your homes, say goodbye to your loved ones, and spend your last moments on Earth doing something positive for somebody else. If you are a person who prays, then pray; if not, then take some time to reflect with gratitude on all the good things you have experienced during your lifetime. May God Bless America, and may God save the world!"

Just as suddenly, the television screens switched back to baseball, but the game had stopped. Crowds of terrified fans were frantically pushing their way out of the stadium, trampling one another in their haste to escape. There was no sound, just dead air, as sports announcers had simply stopped covering the game.

At first, everyone in the restaurant stood in shock, staring incredulously at each other. By now, some were crying hysterically, while others whimpered. Young children tugged on their parents, asking, "What's happening?" Finally, the group of teenagers left the building, followed by the remaining customers, waiters, and cooks. Everyone stumbled out of the restaurant in a daze, leaving Charles, Adam, and Horst behind, sitting in their booth.

"This was a little sooner than I had expected!" said Charles.

"You knew they were going to make this announcement?" said Adam, biting his lip.

Charles nodded. "Yes, I knew it was coming. Let's face it, guys, I've known it for years!" He took another bite of chicken wings. "Now, I suggest we finish our dinner so we can get out of here! You guys want another beer?"

"Yeah, sure," said Adam.

"Sure," said Horst.

Charles stood up and walked to the bar. Behind the counter, he found three clean mugs and two beer taps.

"Which one would you like?" he asked. "We've got Blue Moon or Sam Adams."

"Charles, you can pick," said Adam.

"Okay, we'll go with Sam Adams—again."

After filling the mugs, he carried them back to the table. "I hope we don't run into a lot of trouble outside."

Adam gulped down half his beer, wiping his mouth with his sleeve. "Did the President need to announce this to everyone?"

"Yeah, I think it was the right thing to do. The government doesn't have the right to withhold information like this from the public. I just hope we will make it back to the house. I need to call Tina's parents."

Charles took a bite of wings and wiped his mouth with a napkin. "You know, from this point on, I'm more-or-less just your chauffeur. Unfortunately, Elise and I will be going down with the ship. It's important you guys and Tina—especially Tina—get out of here alive!"

He stood up and stretched. "Okay, I'm done. Everybody use the men's room while you can, I expect this will be a long drive home!"

As the three men drove north on I-55, they witnessed other vehicles racing to get ahead, rampantly disregarding traffic laws. Cars were running traffic lights, speeding more than 100 mph down the expressway, weaving in and out of lanes, even occupying the shoulder. They heard several gunshots as drivers cut one another off. Eventually, traffic came to a grinding halt due to an accident. Everyone began honking their horns impatiently until the driver of a full-size pick-up truck—a Ford F-150—rammed the crashed vehicles into a roadside ditch, clearing-up the entire mess. Then, traffic began moving again.

"*Mein Gott!*" exclaimed Adam. "What about the poor people in those cars?"

"I'm afraid it doesn't look good for them," said Charles, tightly gripping the steering wheel while watching for erratic drivers on every side. Reaching into his pocket, he handed Adam his phone.

"Here, Adam. Please call my wife."

"How do I use this?"

"Enter the password 'MISSION.' Now, look for a little green icon that looks like a phone."

Adam looked at the screen. "Oh . . . yes, I think I see it."

Charles glanced over. "Yes, that's it. Now push the icon, and I'll give you the number to punch in."

When Elise answered, Adam gave the phone back to Charles. "Hi, honey . . . Yeah, we heard the President. Yeah, we're on I-55. Traffic's a mess. At this rate, maybe one or two hours . . ." Charles stopped talking. He said, "Damn it! The phone's gone dead!" He handed it back to Adam. "I guess we can't use that anymore!"

They took the exit to I-294, north. It was here Charles observed traffic on the other side of the expressway was much heavier—in fact, it was jammed with vehicles, bumper-to-bumper.

"People are heading toward Indiana," he said. "They're all driving east! Everyone is driving as far as they can from Wichita, Kansas!" He shook his head. "They have no idea! They simply can't escape . . ." Then his voice trailed off, and he became quiet. "What the hell—I wish them all luck."

"Grandpa, do you think any of them will make it?"

Charles shook his head. "I'm sorry to say there is no place to escape, even if they drove all around the Earth to China!"

It took them nearly three hours to drive home: a drive which, under normal circumstances, should have taken an hour.

When Charles, Adam, and Horst opened the door, Elise greeted them. "You're home! We were so worried about you!"

Tina was holding Freddy, her stuffed frog.

"The TV doesn't work anymore, Grandpa! It stopped after the President was on!"

"Yes," confirmed Elise. "All the channels are dead."

Charles took off his coat. "That makes sense. No one is staying at their jobs—not even at the television stations! No one is maintaining phone service! Everyone is dropping everything!"

Then the lights began to flicker. Elise walked from the living room to the kitchen to the family room, checking the lights.

"The electricity is going out!"

"Christ! The workers at the power plant must be leaving their jobs, too," said Charles. "The power plants are shutting down!"

Then the lights went out, and the house became dark.

Charles looked out the front window and noticed the streetlights had also gone out. Opening the front door, he walked into the street; there were no lights in the neighbors' houses, either. The only source of light was the full moon. He walked back inside.

"Elise—please check your phone."

"The screen says 'no signal.'"

"I wanted to call Jennifer and John, but, without a phone . . ." His eyebrows furrowed. "When were they supposed to come back from Mackinaw Island?"

"They were coming back in a couple of days."

Charles scratched his chin. "I don't think we can wait that long."

"What?" said Elise.

"I'll explain later."

Charles went into the garage and came back with an electric camping light. He placed the light in the center of the family room, and everyone sat in a circle on the floor, staring at the light. Through the family room window, they could see the full moon.

Tina held her stuffed animal and snuggled next to her grandmother. "Freddy's scared!"

Elise looked at Charles, who was sitting on her other side. "What are we going to do?"

"Tomorrow, we're going to the Field Museum."

Elise's eyes narrowed. "The Field Museum?"

"Long story." Charles wiped his face with his hands. "I'm completely exhausted. Do we still have that camping tent?"

"I think it's out in the garage, still unused after twenty years."

"I need to get the tent tomorrow. We need to pack enough for a week. Do we have any camping bags?"

"I think there are a couple in Jennifer's old room."

"Good—two is enough."

"Why only two?"

Charles looked directly at his wife and squeezed her hand. "They're for you and me, Elise. Adam, Tina, and Horst won't need the bags," he said quietly. "We need to get them to the Field Museum. They'll be able to escape all this if we get them there."

Elise gasped.

"But . . . I don't understand . . . why?"

Charles shook his head.

"It's too hard for me to explain right now. Suffice it to say, Adam, Tina, and Horst will be able to escape if we get them to the Field Museum."

Elise stared at Charles but said nothing.

Charles stood up. "There's no use staying up any longer tonight—it's late. We don't have any power, and we all need to get some sleep. Tomorrow we'll load-up the Dodge Caravan and drive to the Field Museum."

Adam turned to Tina, placing his arms around her shoulders. "Tina, we're taking you to a safe place. You need to be strong."

Tina twisted and broke away from Adam. She began screaming, "I don't want to go! I don't want to go! I want Mommy and Daddy!"

Adam shook his head and grabbed her tiny wrists. "Tina . . ."

Tina planted her feet and pulled herself from Adam's grip. "Where are you taking me?" she screamed.

Charles watched, feeling helpless. He realized he did not have the right to make this decision, but it was impossible to reach Jennifer and John. There were no other options.

Suddenly, he remembered the APS versions of himself, Elise, Jennifer, and John were on Planet K851b. He turned toward Adam and said, "We don't have to 'be there' to 'be there,'" he said, gesturing the universal quotation sign with his fingers.

Adam nodded slightly.

Calmly, Charles looked at Tina, and said, "When you go with Adam, we will be there, too."

"And Mommy and Daddy, too?"

Charles forced himself to grin. "Yes, your mommy and daddy, too."

Tina immediately calmed down and allowed Adam and Horst to help her up the dark staircase leading to her room.

"I still don't understand," said Elise when she and Charles were finally alone.

"It's simple, Elise. Tomorrow, they're going back."

"Going back? Where?"

"To Planet K851b."

~

First thing in the morning, Charles, Elise, Horst, Adam, and Tina left the house. As they drove away, Elise looked back at the home where they had lived for the past thirty-five years, and began to cry, trying not to let Tina see her tears. When they approached the Edens Expressway heading to the city, they found the traffic was gridlocked. Charles immediately took a different route, along Lincoln Avenue, running through the town of Skokie.

As they drove toward Chicago, they witnessed mayhem on every block: cars left abandoned on the street; vandalized gas stations; broken storefront windows; gangs of drunken young men, rampaging, out of control, slashing tires, breaking into liquor stores and supermarkets; women diving into clothing stores, emerging with armfuls of merchandise.

Worst of all, arsonists were setting buildings on fire. Hundreds of buildings were burning in every neighborhood, creating an enormous black cloud of smoke, rivaling the Great Chicago Fire. The fire departments had given up, simply because there was no point, no reason, to salvage anything.

Through this hazy, smoke-filled environment, Charles drove the Dodge Caravan along Lincoln Avenue, until they finally reached Lake Shore Drive.

~

As they drove along Lake Michigan, Horst looked ahead toward Chicago's downtown, The Loop. Smoke blanketed the city, making it look like a burning hell.

He checked the pellets in his pants' pocket. Still there, good: One red one for Adam, and one for Tina; one blue one for himself. But where would this blue one take him? Was he about to transport into empty space?

Looking at Charles and Elise, he felt selfish he was about to leave them behind. But he had no choice—this would save Tina. He forced himself to stop thinking about Gana. He needed to remain focused: First things first. At least he now understood the nature of the meteorite. Now he knew how to get back!

They continued driving south along Lake Shore Drive, toward the John Hancock Building, toward the big turn next to Navy Pier. After that, they would go past Millennium Park, then drive the final stretch to the Field Museum.

Charles said nothing as he concentrated on driving the van. Elise was crying, holding Tina in her arms. But when they made the turn, it looked like the entire South Loop was up in flames, including the Field Museum.

"Mein Gott!" screamed Horst.

"Now, hold on, hold on, everyone—let's not jump to conclusions!" urged Charles.

They continued driving south on Lake Shore Drive until they reached the Field Museum. As they had feared, the building was on fire, and the blaze was raging out of control. Even the wooden dinosaur replica in front was burning.

Adam looked at the entrance, from where they had emerged only a few days before. "Everything has been destroyed!"

It was true, the entire south side of the building was now a mass of molten metal and blackened stone. There was nothing left of the meteorite section. They would never be able to find the Canyon Diablo meteorite in the rubble.

Confused, Tina said, "What's wrong? What are you all looking at?"

Charles pulled the van over, onto the Roosevelt Road overpass. He slumped down, placing his forehead against the steering wheel.

Horst hit his fist against the seat cushion. "We were so close! How could this happen?"

Charles slowly raised his head. He started the car, pulling it out into traffic, before turning north on Michigan Avenue.

"Charles, where are we going now?" asked Elise.

Without saying a word, Charles drove north on Michigan Avenue. When they reached the intersection of Jackson and Michigan, he stopped the car. There was a sign, "Beginning of Historic Route 66."

He pointed at the sign. "See this?"

"Charles—you want to drive down Route 66? That will take us west! Everybody is driving east, away from Wichita!"

"Elise, Route 66 will take us directly to Meteor Crater, Arizona. How many days do we have?"

"Four days," said Horst.

"Good. I think we can make it in three."

Part IV:
Route 66

Chapter 29

They attempted leaving Chicago by taking Interstate 55 south, but this proved to be impossible. Frantic to leave the city, drivers were heading east on both the eastbound and westbound lanes, and the resulting chaos had brought traffic to a standstill. Horns blared into the night, while drivers hurled obscenities at one another; some passengers had already begun to ditch their rides, choosing to walk instead to wherever they were heading. Seeing the exit ramps from Lake Shore Drive were completely backed up, Charles continued heading south. The only way to get out of Chicago would be to take the back roads through the south side, then through the southern and southwestern suburbs.

It was slow going, inching their way through the crazy traffic, but, eventually, they made their way to the farm country, south of Joliet. As they traveled through Illinois, they followed long stretches of the old Route 66, running parallel to I-55. When they reached the towns of Normal and Bloomington, they drove along a remnant of the old Route 66 called "Veterans Parkway." It was a bumpy ride as many of the small-town main streets were in a state of disrepair.

Charles focused on driving and said little. He was worried they weren't traveling fast enough as their average speed was about forty-five mph. Fortunately, a few stores had remained open for gas and food. Many of these establishments were quirky-looking, restored to vintage condition from Route 66's heyday. There were hot dog drive-ins, whippy-dips, and Mom and Pop family restaurants, where a person could get a "cup of joe."

These store owners were the diehards: the ones who had stuck it out after the rest of the world left Route 66 behind. More than one store owner said the asteroid was a hoax, something contrived by the US government, a "Deep State" conspiracy. One old codger spat out, "It's the damn government! You'll see!" Charles warned his passengers not to contradict the locals, or things could turn ugly.

The first night they "occupied" an abandoned farm where there were enough beds for all of them. In the morning, they collected eggs from the chicken coop and made omelets in the farmhouse kitchen, where they found a skillet, spatula, and even some butter. The next night, after crossing the Mississippi, they camped in the Missouri Ozarks, next to a stream. Adam and Tina went fishing, and each of them caught four trout. It was Tina's first-time fishing; Adam had never seen a trout before. Meanwhile, Horst constructed a small fire pit with Charles's assistance, placing dry branches at the bottom and kindling on top. Once the flames were hot enough, Elise took care of grilling the fish.

Traveling slowly from small town to small town, they worked their way south through Illinois, Missouri, Oklahoma, and Texas, until, finally, they reached the last leg, the "Land of Enchantment": New Mexico. It had been a grueling forty-eight hours, especially for Charles, who had done all the driving.

When they reached Gallup, New Mexico, they stopped at the famous El Rancho Hotel. Tina screamed when she saw an eagle perched on the roof of the portico, but Elise assured her it was just part of the western décor and that it was plastic. Above the main door was a sign which said, "Charm of Yesterday . . . Convenience of Tomorrow." Charming or not, the place was deserted, and since the main door was unlocked, they went inside to freshen up and scavenge for supplies. Horst and Adam were surprised to see beautiful rugs and baskets with similar designs to those in Hummingbird Man's house. They were also startled at the sight of two deer heads with massive antlers mounted on columns on either side of a central fireplace.

"There are lots of hunters around here," explained Charles. "They would have eaten the venison and kept the heads as trophies."

Tina pulled a face, then went scampering up one of the red-carpeted staircases leading to a landing overlooking the bar and central dining area. The walls were lined with old black and white photographs of the many celebrities who had visited the hotel. While the adults headed to the kitchen, she discovered some of the guest rooms were still wide open, as if housekeeping had been about to clean them. Better yet, the rooms each had a mini-refrigerator filled with snacks.

"Not exactly healthy," observed Elise when she joined her granddaughter upstairs. "But there's no food left in the kitchen."

Everyone was grateful for the sodas, potato chips, and candy bars. After an hour's break in Gallup—enough time to take a shower—they hopped back into the Dodge and took Old Route 66/Interstate Route 40, west toward Arizona.

Charles recognized the scenery from only two weeks before. The hills had distinct bands of grey and red strata; some were completely white or dotted with green shrubs.

"We're near the Painted Desert," Charles said to Elise, pointing out a shop's sign. "See, they're selling petrified wood."

"Do we have time for a detour?" asked Elise. "I want Tina to see—"

Charles shook his head. "No, we're running out of time."

"Charles, do you even know why we're here or where we're going?" snapped Elise. "I honestly don't understand why we've come on this wild journey."

"Yes, of course. We're heading to Winslow."

"You mean, where we met that Indian gentleman?"

Charles nodded.

"Yep. I have a hunch that old Indian chief, Hototo, can help us."

Chapter 30

IT WAS NEARLY SUNSET WHEN THEY REACHED THE BEST WESTern in Winslow. As they expected, the parking lot was empty. Charles got out of the car and walked inside the hotel, soon returning to the van.

"Nobody's there."

"How are we going to find the old man?" asked Elise.

Exhausted, Charles hunched over the steering wheel. "I have no idea. No idea whatsoever."

Suddenly, Horst rolled down his window and looked at the horizon. He pointed south. "Smoke! Look over there—I can see smoke!"

True enough, there were white puffs of smoke in the distance.

"Good eyes, Horst."

Charles put his key in the ignition and started the van, speeding out of the Best Western parking lot. They immediately took the ramp onto Interstate 40 and headed west, in the direction of the smoke. There were no other cars on the road. Charles stepped on the accelerator and shot the speed up to eighty mph, but was afraid to go faster. Following the smoke, they took the first exit, an isolated road appropriately named "Desert Hills Drive." They drove south, through West Winslow, past rows of pre-fabricated houses, rusty trailers, and dilapidated ranches.

"My God, we're in the middle of nowhere," said Elise. "It's like we're chasing a rainbow."

"Yes, that's me—the rainbow-chasing leprechaun!" retorted Charles.

Elise stared at her husband. "Do you know what we're supposed to do when we get to the smoke?"

Charles shrugged. "I have a gut instinct we're supposed to talk to the chief."

He looked at Elise, wrinkling his forehead.

"Don't you ever get feelings, like you're supposed to do something, but you don't know why?"

"I get hunches many times," said Horst, from the back seat. "So many times things have worked out for me. Perhaps I've just been lucky . . ."

". . . or smart," said Charles, looking at Horst in the mirror.

"May the Force be with you," said Tina, holding her right fist over her heart.

Adam looked at his sister. "What does that mean? Did Buzz Lightyear say that?"

Tina rolled her eyes. "OMG! Haven't you ever seen *Star Wars,* Adam?"

"Sorry, I haven't, Sis."

"You're supposed to say, 'May the Force be with us all' back at me!"

"Sorry."

"Say it!"

Adam shook his head and held his lips tightly together.

They came to the source of the smoke—a ranch, with a wooden sign saying "Chocolate" hanging from a rusty chain between two posts. Charles turned onto a gravel road leading onto the property, kicking up dust until they came to a cattleguard at the entrance; then, he slowed down as they rattled over the metal grid. Once past the cattleguard, they found themselves in a parking lot full of old pickups. A large metal storage building stood on one side; on the other, a corral with chickens and pigs. Next to the corral, there was an open ball court with faded paint lines and old basketball hoops at either end.

Charles pulled the van to a stop.

"I think this is close enough. Let's get out and walk the rest of the way."

When they slid the van's doors open, they could hear loud drumming and chanting in the distance.

The group walked in single file along a narrow path in the direction of the smoke. Though there were no street lights, they could see on either side of the path stood buildings made of natural or painted dried mud. Some were single-room dwellings while others consisted of a sprawling network of rooms that must have been added to the original structures over time; the more elaborate buildings had external ladders or staircases leading to upstairs quarters.

Adam walked up to one of the buildings and ran his hands over the surface, feeling the mud and twigs. He looked at Horst.

"Reminds me of the huts in New Eden, but this one is orange with turquoise trim."

Horst nodded, furrowing his eyebrows.

Eventually, having left the dwellings behind them, they reached an arched entrance leading into what looked like a ceremonial courtyard. Hundreds of people clad in brightly woven ponchos over leather leggings sat in concentric circles around a bonfire, chanting the same syllables over and over again, with deep resonating solemnity. Close to the fire, a group of male and female dancers wearing wooden masks swayed hypnotically to the rhythm of drums, flutes, and whistles, their ankle rattles creating the sound of heavy rainfall. One of the men whose head was concealed by a preserved deer's head leaped amongst them, imitating the movements of a live deer with all the grace of a ballet dancer.

Quite unexpectedly, all the people who were seated stood up, turning toward the visitors. The circles broke apart, and they stepped aside, making an opening for the strangers to walk through.

As he followed Charles and the rest of the group, Horst observed the faces of their hosts. He was shocked at how closely they resembled the Natives on his planet: both the men and women were short and stocky, with broad faces, prominent hooked noses, and deep black eyes. Their hair was black, coarse, and straight.

The people's response seemed choreographed, as though they expected them. The drumming and chanting grew louder; the dancers bobbed their heads, up and down, shifting their weight from one side to another as they stomped in unison to the beat.

With Charles leading the way, the visitors walked toward an elder who, holding a hand-carved cane, was sitting on a ceremonial chair—a rectangular stool carved from a single block of wood in the shape of a turtle; over it lay the skin of a black bear. Charles motioned for Adam and Horst to wait while he and Elise, holding Tina's hands, approached the elder.

Fascinated, Horst and Adam watched as Charles knelt at the elder's feet. Then the two men briefly exchanged words, which they were unable to hear. Suddenly, the chief struck his cane against the ground, commanding the drumming and chanting to stop. Charles turned around to face them.

"Horst and Adam, Chief Hototo wants to speak to you."

Slowly, Horst and Adam walked toward the ceremonial chair, kneeling to the right of Charles, Elise, and Tina.

The elder spoke slowly. "Horst and Adam, you are finally here."

Confused to hear his name, Horst looked up at the chief. He was shocked to see it was Hummingbird Man.

"Hehewuti?" said Horst, confused.

"Hehewuti is the name I used when I was Hummingbird Man. I am now Chief Hototo."

The elder was much older than they remembered, but there was no doubt he was Hehewuti. Only a week before, when Horst had last seen him, he was a man in his sixties or seventies. This man, the very same man, was in his nineties.

"But you are so much older!"

"We arrived here almost twenty years ago. Now, I have seen ninety-six harvests."

"Ninety-six? But we saw you only a week ago!" said Horst, blinking rapidly.

Then he stopped, suddenly understanding the confusing possibilities of traveling through a wormhole. In a perplexing sequence of events, Hehewuti had come back to Earth at a point in time before Horst and Adam had arrived.

"You can now speak English," observed Horst.

"Of course. We have been here a long time," replied the chief.

Then another man approached them. He was much younger than Chief Hototo but looked strangely familiar.

"Horst and Adam, you have come. We have been expecting you!"

Horst stared at the man.

"Takala?"

"Yes, it is I," said Takala, who was now in his forties.

"You were expecting us?" said Adam.

Takala turned to Adam and Tina. "You two play a critical role in our story. It is because of you, we are here."

Then he looked directly at Horst, placing his hand on his shoulder. "And you, my dear friend, you play the most important role of all: You are here to save us."

Horst flinched. He studied Takala's face, searching his eyes, attempting to find a glimmer of meaning.

Takala smiled. "I have made many mistakes in my youth. Some I cannot take back. But I can help you to stop Gana and Tresca from taking more lives."

Then Chief Hototo motioned to Takala to draw closer. "Brother Takala, can you bring me my scooter? The night is getting dark, and we must be on our way."

Takala walked over to a red electric scooter chair, the type commonly seen in grocery stores; then he drove it next to the ceremonial chair and assisted the chief into the driver's seat.

"Does anyone wish to ride with me? There is a little seat in the back."

"Ah, no . . . I'm good," said Horst. "Adam, do you want to ride on the scooter?" he said teasingly.

Tina squealed with excitement. "I do! I do! I want a ride!"

"Please jump on!" said the chief, smiling. "I thought you might want to join me!"

Tina climbed onto the back of the scooter, wedging herself into a narrow seat that faced outward. From its proportions, the seat was intended for a rather small child, but Tina didn't complain.

"Please follow me to my home. We must not delay," said the chief. Then he drove away with Tina in the back, while the crowds bowed to him, before returning to their chanting and dancing.

~

The chief steered the electric scooter chair at a fairly good clip down the narrow path leading to one of the more intricate adobe dwellings. Though built on only one level, the house had multiple rooms. It was set back slightly from the path, leaving enough space for a narrow driveway and a patch of yellow chocolate flowers, desert marigolds, white sagebrush, purple thistles, and agave plants. Having parked near the clay pot hummingbird feeders hanging close to the entrance, he and Tina waited for the others to arrive. To her delight, Tina saw an emerald-throated hummingbird hover over the chief, before resting briefly on his shoulders; then, in a flash, as the other humans approached, it was gone.

Takala helped Hototo off the scooter. Leaning on the younger man's arm, the chief walked into the house, as the others followed.

After Takala had lit some candles, they could see the interior of the main room. It contained many decorative artifacts—hand-woven wool rugs with geometric designs, multi-colored yucca baskets of various sizes, ornamental ceramics, and a magnificent fireplace built from fieldstones. The furniture, hewn from cypress branches and logs, looked as though it had just come from the forest.

Charles examined a clay pot sitting on a shelf.

"Chief, is this Hopi?"

Hototo shook his head.

"Hopi? No, I am not of that tribe. At one time, my family belonged to a people known as the *Hohokam*. My father was a long-distance trader called Pochteca. He brought chocolate to this area, in exchange for turquoise."

Tina saw a stuffed buffalo toy sitting on the stone hearth of the fireplace. She walked directly to the hearth, and, sitting on the ledge, began petting the buffalo.

"He's so cute!" she said to the chief. "Can I pick him up?"

"Of course," said Hototo. "If you like, you can have him."

"Thank you!" said Tina, clutching the buffalo tightly. "What's his name?"

"Buffalo Wiseman," responded the chief.

After everyone found a place to sit in the living room, Takala excused himself and walked to another room. A few minutes later, he returned with a box which he presented to Hototo.

"We ordered this online from Dick's Sporting Goods. It's a Barnett Whitetail Hunter II," said the chief as he opened the box. Inside was a crossbow and some "all-purpose" arrows.

"Have you ever used one of these before, Adam?"

"Ah . . . yeah, sure, Chief," stammered Adam. "We learned how to use crossbows in New Eden during Cadet training."

At a signal from the chief, Takala took the crossbow from Hototo and handed it to Adam.

"Now you must take a few practice shots before you go," said the chief.

"Practice? Before I go?"

"Bows and arrows!" exclaimed Elise shrilly. "What's going on? Will Tina be in danger?"

Charles put his arm around Elise's shoulders, attempting to calm her. "Elise, we talked about this . . ."

"But . . . bows and arrows?"

Takala left the living room and returned, carrying a satchel filled with arrows. He gave the satchel to Adam.

"These arrows are hand-made by our best craftsmen. You will see the arrowheads are made of pure silver. The feathers are raven pinions, and the wood is cypress. We will use the arrows from Dick's for practice."

Adam examined the Barnett Whitetail Hunter II crossbow, along with several of Dick's all-purpose arrows. Seeing Adam prepare for battle, Horst was at a loss for words. Why was Hehewuti—Hototo—preparing Adam to kill his own people? Then, he understood: Adam's mission was to kill Gana and Tresca.

Horst looked at Hototo, and their eyes connected. Almost imperceptibly, the chief nodded, then spoke slowly.

"You will learn there is no past or present to your story—yours is like a twisted rope, Horst. The end of your story loops back to the beginning."

Takala grabbed Adam by the shoulder and pushed him toward the door. "Adam and I are going to take a few practice shots before you guys leave."

"Okay, Takala, but don't take too long! Dawn is almost upon us!" warned the chief.

He turned toward Horst. "Do you have the pellets?"

"Ah, yes, I certainly do. They're right here in my pocket," said Horst.

"Show me."

Horst reached in his pants pocket and pulled out two red pellets and the one remaining blue pellet. "Tina will be going back with Adam; they will use the red ones. I will be using the blue one."

"You are going forward into an unknown region. Are you afraid?"

"Ah, yeah," admitted Horst.

"I understand. We have always used the blue ones for the scouts; they go to the next place."

"Do the scouts always come back?"

"Not always," said the chief, shaking his head. "There is always a risk."

"That was our purpose, remember? We came here as the scouts, to check if this place is safe, but it's not safe."

The chief smiled but did not answer immediately. Finally, he said, "Yes, Horst. Adam and you came here as scouts. But only Adam and Tina will be returning. This is the story."

"But, Chief, how do we use the pellets? Do we go to Meteor Crater, break into the Visitors' Center, and throw them at the Holsinger meteorite?"

"The Holsinger meteorite? I know of no such thing," said the chief. "Listen to me carefully! You are to go to the Canyon Diablo Crater, the place where my father took me during ancient times! It is the same place where we returned here twenty years ago."

"I'm sorry, Chief. Specifically, what do we need to do?"

"You are to climb to the top of the crater, then throw the pellet into the crater!"

"Then, do we jump into the crater?"

The chief took a breath, changing the pace of his narrative.

"Our story—your story—is already written. We are re-enacting what must occur, again! When you throw the pellet into the crater, you will see—you will know—where to jump!"

The door opened, and Takala and Adam returned.

"He's a good shot," said Takala.

"I think I'm ready," said Adam. He held the crossbow firmly, feeling its weight.

"It's a good bow—way better than what we had in New Eden, for sure."

Elise was leaning on Charles's shoulder, crying softly.

Tina approached her grandmother and hugged her.

"Don't worry, Grandma—we'll be all right! Adam and me are going to have an adventure!"

The chief smiled, as the little girl kissed both her grandparents. Then he turned toward Horst. "Remember—your story is already written."

Horst nodded. He had no choice but to go ahead and jump into Meteor Crater, and possibly die.

Chapter 31

THE MOOD INSIDE THE DODGE WAS GRIM AS THEY DROVE the last leg of their journey, to Canyon Diablo Crater—Meteor Crater. Everyone was quiet, except for Tina, busily at play with her Buffalo Wiseman stuffed animal. Charles glanced at Elise, who was sitting next to him in the front passenger's seat, body half-turned so she could watch little Tina. He shook his head and sighed, regretting how they had taken Tina from her parents. But the phones were out, they couldn't reach Jennifer and John, there was no choice. He hit his hand forcefully on the steering wheel.

"Damn it!" he said as the van swerved across lanes.

Elise jerked forward, then sank back as her seat belt saved her from hitting the dashboard.

"You scared me half to death!" she complained.

"Sorry," said Charles, squeezing her hand. "I'm as tense as you are, but this is the only hope for Tina. Maybe, just maybe, she will get to have a life on Planet K851b. As for us, this is the end of the line."

"I'm so afraid," whispered Elise. "I don't want to die!"

"Nobody wants to die, Elise. It is the fear—the anticipation of death, the anxiety of knowing—that's the hardest part!"

Charles glanced in the rearview mirror at Horst, who was looking out the window, lost in thought. Perhaps he was thinking about his triple death curse: Death by cancer, death by asteroid, or death by wormhole! As for Adam, he was sitting bolt-upright like a WWII paratrooper about to jump from a plane during the invasion of Normandy. What would he and Tina face when they popped up out of nowhere on Planet K851b?

They headed west on Interstate 40, and, in a few miles, saw the sign to Meteor Crater. Turning at the exit, they drove the last few miles along Meteor Crater Road.

Horst turned away from the window and looked at Adam, his lifelong friend: the best friend he ever had. They had known each other their entire lives, since they were infants. They had shared so many experiences and adventures growing up together. Even their wives and kids were friends. Together, they and the other Third Thaws had done nothing less than rebuild human civilization on their planet. Now he was facing the most challenging task of all.

Adam forced a grin, but his eyes welled up with tears. This was it; it was almost time, the very last time they would ever see each other.

"When you get home . . . when you see Ingrid, tell her I love her," said Horst, barely able to get the words out.

Adam nodded, unable to speak.

"And tell all our brothers and sisters of the Third Thaw that I love them." Horst reached out and grabbed Adam's hands in his. "You need to be strong, Adam," he said in a firm voice. "I'm counting on you to save Janu and Olga—and Tina."

"Yes, sir—Captain."

Horst laughed. "We had some good times, didn't we?"

"We certainly did, my friend," said Adam.

When they arrived at the crater, they found the security gates leading to the parking lot were open.

"Good," said Charles as he parked the van. "Let's see if we can get into the Visitors' Center."

It turned out the building was locked.

"Damn! We can't get in the easy way. No food for us at the Blasted Bistro, it seems!"

"You're not thinking of food at a time like this, are you, Charles?"

"Just joking, Elise. And we're not going to watch Collision in the 4D experience room, either!"

Surveying the metal railings at the rear of the Visitors' Center, they could see the stairs leading to the viewing platform.

"We'll need to get behind the building and then climb over the railings. Adam, you can lift Tina onto the steps while I help Elise. Horst, let me know if you need a hand. It shouldn't be too difficult to swing ourselves over the handrails. Everyone follow me!"

With some effort, they scrambled over the railings, then climbed the stairs leading to the observation deck overlooking the crater's jagged rim. Charles led the way, followed by Adam, carrying his crossbow and satchel of arrows. Tina held onto her grandmother's hand, tightly clutching onto Buffalo Wiseman, while Horst, the slowest walker, lagged behind.

When they reached the top of the stairs, a powerful wind blew them against the handrails. Tina screamed, almost dropping Buffalo Wiseman, but Elise stood in front of her to shield her from the strong gusts. Charles and the others gripped the rails to brace themselves. Then, noticing the viewing platform just a few feet away, they proceeded to inch their way forward, clutching on to the railings to stay grounded.

"Adam! Are you ready?" Charles shouted into the wind.

Adam gave the thumbs-up, then quickly grabbed the railing again.

Charles turned toward his granddaughter. Closing his eyes, he tried to regain focus. "Tina! Come and say goodbye to Grandpa!"

Little Tina walked up to him, still clinging to both Elise and Buffalo Wiseman. "Opa! I will see you again, won't I?"

"Adam will show you how to contact me when you get there," said Charles gruffly.

Tina pursed her lips in thought. She narrowed her eyes. "I will see you again, won't I, Opa?"

Charles leaned away from Tina. Clearing his throat, he said in a shaky voice, "Tina, you and Adam must be brave. Your brother will take care of you now. You're going to a safe place."

"But Opa!" shouted Tina, her lips trembling.

Elise stepped between Charles and Tina and quickly hugged her granddaughter.

Tina attempted to squirm away, but Elise held her tightly.

"Grandma! I don't want to leave you!"

Elise continued holding her. Looking directly at Tina, she said, "Sh . . . sh . . . I know, it's scary, but you have to go!"

Tina hugged her grandmother, burying her face in her chest as she sobbed.

Elise patted her back, soothingly.

"There, there . . . Shh, everything's going to be all right."

Gradually, as Tina began calming down, Elise walked her over to Adam, who was standing at the end of the platform, which extended directly over the crater. There was only one more person to wish them goodbye. Horst hugged Tina; then, he reached out to shake Adam's hand.

Adam grabbed Horst in a bear hug.

"Good-bye, my friend!"

Then Horst walked away, joining Charles and Elise, on the other side of the observation deck. Adam said something to Tina before giving her one of the red pellets. Then they counted out loud, "One, two, three!" and tossed the red pellets into the canyon.

Nothing happened.

Horst peered down into the crater.

"Do you see anything—anything at all?"

"Nein! Verdammt!" [No! Dammit!]

Then Tina pointed toward the north part of the crater where there was a faint orange glow. Gradually, the orange light enveloped the entire cavity, and as it did, its color intensified, becoming a rhythmic, pulsating pattern. Then the pulsating transformed into an orange wave, slowly sweeping around the crater in a clockwise direction.

They watched as the wave revolved around the nearly one-mile-wide Meteor Crater. The first revolution was relatively slow, the second revolution faster, the third became faster still, eventually stabilizing at about ten cycles per second. Soon the wave morphed into a spiral, its color changing to silver. Then a small black sphere appeared where the red pellets had landed. The sphere grew in diameter until it was about eight feet across.

Adam slung his crossbow and satchel over his shoulder, then picked up his sister, holding her in his arms. Climbing over the platform railing, he leaned against the metal bars, holding Tina, who was clinging to his neck.

Together, they looked down at the sphere hovering just a few feet below.

"I'm counting to three, Tina!"

Tina nodded and closed her eyes.

"Eins, zwei, drei!"

Then Adam and Tina jumped. Almost immediately, the sphere and spiral vanished, along with Adam and Tina.

Horst, Charles, and Elise ran to the edge of the observation deck and looked down.

Pulling out a pocket flashlight, Charles scanned the crater below.

"Nothing... I see nothing at all! If I hadn't seen it with my own eyes...!"

For the first time since leaving Chicago, Elise smiled. "They're gone! It worked! It actually worked!"

Charles smiled, hugging Elise. "I know—I can't believe it myself. It worked!"

Then Charles turned to Horst. "It's your turn. Are you ready?"

"I suppose I'm as ready as I'll ever be," said Horst in a flat voice. "I can't thank you both enough—"

"It has been an honor knowing you, Horst. I am very proud of what you have accomplished on your planet," said Charles, shaking his hand vigorously.

"It has been an honor knowing you, too, sir," said Horst, pulling away to hug Elise.

Then Charles and Elise walked across the platform. From there, they watched as Horst climbed on top of the railing. Staring down into the crater, he retrieved the blue pellet from his pocket and looked at it one last time.

Then he hurled it into the crater.

This time, a faint blue appeared on the south side of the crater, becoming a blue wave that spun around the cavity in a counter-clockwise direction. As before, the wave became a spiral, gradually becoming silver. Another black sphere appeared, where Horst had thrown the blue pellet.

Horst looked back at Charles and Elise one last time and waved.

Then he jumped into the wormhole, vanishing forever from the face of the Earth.

~

Arm in arm, Charles and Elise slowly walked down the stairs to the parking lot. Once they were back in the van, Charles checked the gas.

"I think we need to fill-up," he said. "There was a gas station along Meteor Crater Road. Hopefully, I can jerry-rig the pump."

"Where are we going now, Charles?" asked Elise.

"You haven't guessed yet?" he said, smiling. "You've always been good at games."

"Ah, let me think," Elise said, pondering possible locations. Then she stopped. "Oh, no, Charles! Tell me we're not going to . . ."

"Wichita," he smiled. "We're going to Wichita."

Part V:

The Future and Present

Chapter 32

WHEN ADAM OPENED HIS EYES, HE WAS ON PLANET K851B lying under the dome in the pit next to the meteor. He couldn't remember anything that had happened after leaping into Meteor Crater, back on Earth; it was as though someone had pushed the pause button in his life. Slowly, he sat up. His whole body ached, and he had a tremendous headache. Next to him lay his crossbow and satchel of arrows.

Rubbing his head, he looked up at the dome's ceiling and saw the enigmatic image of the spiral. Now, he understood its meaning: The meteor was a natural time machine, while the spiral suggested that Time must, somehow, turn in gyres, going backward and forward, even spinning-off into random eddies.

Then, he remembered Tina. He looked to his left and right but didn't see her. Twisting around, he saw her lying on her back only a few feet away, not moving. Slowly, he crawled over to her and shook her shoulders.

"Tina! Tina! Wake up!"

Tina's eyes suddenly opened, as though she had suddenly been jolted by an electric shock. Gasping for air, she sat up, her eyes darting in every direction.

"Adam? Where . . . ? Where are we?"

Adam held a finger to his mouth.

"Shh, Tina! We made it!"

"We made it?" she repeated in a shaky voice. She tried standing up, but Adam grabbed her arm, pulling her toward him.

"Tina, you've got to stay down!"

"Ouch!" she whimpered, rubbing her arm. Then she sniffed the air. "Why does it smell like a campfire here?"

Adam also noticed the burning smell. Cautiously, he stood up, and, having checked around the dome for guards, he tried standing on his toes to see outside. The meteor pit, however, was too deep for him to see anything at ground level.

Suddenly, hearing the sound of drumming and chanting, he dropped to the floor.

Tina lowered her voice to a whisper. "It sounds like the drums at Chocolate Ranch."

"Chocolate Ranch?"

"Chocolate Ranch is where the nice old man gave me Buffalo Wiseman."

She grabbed the stuffed buffalo lying next to her, clutching him tightly. "Remember?"

Of course—Hehewuti's ranch!

"Tina, we need to get out of here," said Adam. "We have to get back to New Munich—but, first, we need to escape from this place."

"Escape?"

Adam nodded. "Yes, escape. The good news is, we made it here; the bad news is, we're in a dangerous place with some very bad . . . eh . . . people."

Tina hugged Buffalo Wiseman. "I'm scared."

Adam grabbed his crossbow and satchel of arrows and slipped them over his shoulder; then he took Tina's hand.

"Come with me. We first need to find you a hiding place. Keep your head low."

They crouched down and walked up the spiral ramp, out of the pit. Upon reaching ground level, they ran to the nearest dome support column and knelt behind it. From this vantage point, Adam had a clear perspective of the entire island compound.

The courtyard teemed with people. It appeared the entire village had assembled at the base of the sacrificial staircase, except for four individuals standing on the platform at the top. Two of them were twice as tall as the others.

Gana and Tresca, thought Adam.

Adam and Tina watched the crowd dancing, swaying, and chanting to the rhythm of the drums. The music was intoxicating.

"It's just like the party at the Chocolate Ranch!" said Tina.

Adam shuddered. That night's ceremony was a preparation for a sacrifice! Who would be the victim: Olga or Janu, or both? Desperately, he searched the crowd, looking for them, but it was impossible to see clearly from that distance.

There was a massive bonfire behind the crowd, its flames flaring at least thirty feet into the air. Adam assumed the sacrifice would occur after sundown. He looked at the sky. Judging by the orange tint, it was almost sunset. Perhaps he had an hour's window to do what he had to do, but, first, he needed to hide Tina.

He scanned the perimeter of the compound. Fifty-foot-high walls surrounded the island, their smooth surface making them impossible to climb. The entrance gate was the only way in and out.

"*Verdammt!*" he cursed.

He motioned for Tina to follow him. Then, they crept like panthers, keeping low to the ground, looking for a place to hide in the direction away from the ceremony; unfortunately, the island had no trees, bushes, or big rocks—except, of course, for the meteor.

Then, Adam saw the hyperbolic-paraboloid structure where they had dined with Gana and Tresca. If he could get Tina on top, she could hide there.

Momentarily, he worried the edifice might not be able to support her weight; the membrane could support uniform loads, not concentrated loads. There was a risk it would collapse. "What the hell," muttered Adam, under his breath. Then he began walking, pulling Tina by her hand.

When they reached the structure, Adam stopped and looked up. Judging by the steepness and curvature of the roof, it would be best if he lifted her.

He turned toward his sister. "Tina, I need you to hide on this roof, while I go do something."

Tina was shaking, clutching her stuffed animal. "You're going to use that bow and arrow, aren't you?"

He frowned. "Yes . . . that's what I need to do."

"Adam, I'm afraid—don't leave me!"

"Shh! You have to keep your voice down!"

Adam crouched next to her. "After I lift you up there, I want you to stay there until I get you, okay?"

Tina nodded, her chin trembling. "But what if you don't get me?"

He paused to think for a few seconds.

"If I don't get you before dark, you'll need to climb down by yourself and ask a guard for help. They will take you to the village."

He wiped a hand across his forehead, which by now glistened with beads of sweat.

"Sooner or later, the Thaws will find this place and save you."

"Adam! I'm afraid!"

"I know, Tina. I'm afraid, too."

Adam walked next to the structure, put his hands together, and said, "Get up!"

Tina put one foot into her brother's clasped hands, and then the other, trying her best to keep her balance so he could raise her onto the arch. The incline was steepest near the bottom, so he continued pushing her up as far as he could while standing on his toes. From that height, her feet were able to get a grip, and she managed to climb higher still. Then, crawling behind one of the roof humps, she sat down, with her back leaning against it.

Adam lifted the crossbow, feeling its weight. Then he pulled a silver arrow from the satchel and loaded it into the crossbow. Holding the crossbow chest high, he stared through the instrument's crosshairs, feeling its deadly power and accuracy. He felt ready. No longer Gana's prisoner, he was now the hunter while Gana was his unsuspecting prey.

He looked up at Tina and gave her the thumbs-up. Then he turned and ran in the direction of the palace courtyard.

~

When the sun went down, Adam approached the ceremony, his senses acutely sharpened by the rush of adrenaline. He crept along the perimeter wall, staying within the shadows, away from the flickering bonfire lights. Keeping low to the ground, he held his crossbow on the ready.

As he drew closer to the ceremony, he stopped a few feet from the towering flames of the bonfire. He waited there, watching the villagers dancing and chanting to the hypnotic rhythm. The drumming and chanting were becoming louder, building to a crescendo.

At the base of the steps, Adam saw Janu tied up with ropes and gagged. Then, looking up toward the top of the staircase, he could see Gana and

Tresca, preparing something at a long stone table. Next to them, the two strongmen, Honovi and Ciji, were holding Olga by the arms. She was standing at the edge of the platform, swooning like a limp rag doll, apparently drugged.

Adam watched as Tresca removed a gleaming knife from its sheath. She held it above her head, displaying it to everyone, while Gana read from a scroll he was holding. Given the distance from the steps, it was hard making out what the creature was actually saying, but Adam could hear a guttural chant that sent chills down his spine.

With no time to spare, Adam made his move. Stealthily, he edged forward, behind the crowd. When he was about ten feet behind the last row of people, he stopped and prepared to aim.

Holding the Barnett Whitetail Hunter II crossbow like a rifle, Adam sighted through the telescope. Tresca handed the knife to Gana, who bowed slightly. Tresca's back was in full view; she was blocking Gana, making her the easier target.

With one hundred and sixty pounds of force, Adam pulled back the bowstring. Steadying himself, he focused the crosshairs on Tresca's head. Although she was about a hundred and fifty feet away, it was not too far for this lethal weapon. If he didn't make the shot, he'd go for another, then another, until he ran out of arrows. He would fight to the death, if necessary.

He pulled the trigger, launching the twenty-inch-long silver arrow at 350 feet per second. At this velocity, it took less than half a second to reach Tresca, piercing straight through the base of her neck.

Tresca staggered backward. Seeing the arrow sticking out almost a foot from her neck, she grabbed it with both claw-like hands, then reached toward Gana, begging for his help.

With Gana now in full view, Adam loaded a second arrow into the crossbow and began setting up for the next shot, aiming at Gana's heart.

"Hold still, you bastard," he said under his breath.

But Gana suddenly moved, reaching toward Tresca. Quickly, he grabbed the arrowhead, pulling it from her neck. Blood spurted from the wound, drenching them both. With a terrible squawk, Tresca clutched at her throat before collapsing, falling backward, down the staircase—all one-hundred steps—to the bottom.

Gana stood still, watching his mate fall to her death.

During those few seconds, Adam shot the arrow. This second arrow went into Gana's right arm.

Grabbing the arrow, Gana tried to pull it out, but the barbed arrowhead lodged beneath his skin. With a terrible roar, he looked down at the villagers, searching for his attacker. His laser-sharp eyes quickly focused on Adam, standing alone behind the villagers.

The entire ceremony had stopped; all the villagers were now staring at their master.

Still standing at the top of the staircase, Gana screamed into the night: "*Petlachuilistli!*" [Attack!]

Expecting the worst, Adam loaded another arrow, ready to take on the entire village.

But the villagers, never trained as soldiers, did not understand their master's command. They simply stood still, not sure what to do. Adam, meanwhile, was holding his crossbow, pointing it in their direction.

Gana continued screeching orders: "*Petlachuilistli! Petlachuilistli!*"

Still, no one moved.

The tables had turned. Seeing the villagers were no threat, Adam carefully began to set his aim on Gana, who, howling in rage, had started descending the staircase, jumping three and four steps at a time. When he reached the ground, he was gasping from the effort. Still holding the sacrificial knife, he looked at Adam savagely.

Expecting a head-on attack, Adam held the Barnett chest high, preparing for a close-range shot. To his surprise, Gana took off, with long, birdlike strides, toward the dome.

Looking up at the sacrificial platform, Adam could see that Honovi and Ciji were still holding Olga. He pointed his crossbow at Honovi, then Ciji. The two strongmen looked at each other, shrugged, and then slowly began carrying Olga down the staircase, taking care not to slip in the trail of blood left by Tresca's mangled body.

The next task was to free Janu. Adam ran over to where Janu was tied-up. Takala was standing next to him, evidently guarding him.

Adam pointed the crossbow at Takala.

"Untie him!"

Takala shook his head slightly. Adam raised the crossbow, aiming at Takala's face. Pointing with his left hand at Janu, he repeated, "Untie him!"

With shaking fingers, Takala immediately untied Janu and removed his gag.

"You made it! You actually made it!" gasped Janu, hugging Adam in relief.

"Okay, Janu, we're not finished. First, we need to grab Olga. Then we need to get Tina."

"Tina?"

"It's a long story."

~

Moaning loudly, Gana lumbered along, leaving his mate behind. There was a stabbing pain in his right arm. He looked backward and saw he was alone. *Was there no one chasing him?*

When he drew near the dome and the sacred rock, he stopped to examine his wound. Something straight, like a stick, was jutting out from his torn flesh. He pulled hard on the stick, but there was something at the end of it, like a hook. The more he pulled, the more the piece tore into his body, hurting him even more.

He gave up his attempt to pull the stick from his arm. His superiors could mend the wound, *but they would not be able to fix Tresca—her Lifeforce had already left her!*

Moisture welled in his eyes as he looked down at the sacrificial knife which he was holding like a weapon. Of course, it was not a weapon; it was a sacred artifact he used only twice a year, to satisfy his primitive urges. Long ago, his kind were carnivores, but not any longer. His kind had developed an arrangement with the No. 4's, who willingly sacrificed one of their number every six months.

He thought about how essential it was to have order: *No. 4's understand the natural order of things and how important it was to preserve the old ways.* New ideas were dangerous. The strangers had interfered in his life, talking about ridiculous things, like planets and stars in the sky. No. 4's had never discussed such things before. Now the one named Adam had invaded the sacrificial ceremony carrying a weapon. Worse still, he had assassinated Tresca.

He stared at the sacrificial knife, his only means of defense. With only a knife against Adam's powerful stick shooter, he was defenseless. He looked at his damaged appendage, which was oozing blood and pus. If this Adam attacked him again, he would lose his Lifeforce, like Tresca.

He was starving: The urge to eat meat was strong. For many days, he had been fasting, preparing to gorge himself at the ceremony. His wound was weakening him; he must eat soon.

When he reached the dome, Gana stopped, suddenly realizing he did not have the correct pellet for transport. Changing directions, he headed toward his house where they were stored.

Taking great strides, Gana lolloped through the dark, but as he approached his home, he saw something unusual on the roof. As he drew closer to the open-air structure, he saw it was a young No. 4 female who was holding a toy of some kind.

He had never seen this No. 4 female before. She was just what he needed—she would make a good sacrifice, a very good sacrifice. Gana licked his jagged teeth at the thought. That girl-child would satisfy his craving for meat. Then, suddenly, he realized the girl must belong to the No. 4 named Adam. Sacrificing her would be the perfect revenge.

Gana looked for a way to reach the top of the roof. He could not climb up the sides of the structure because the roof slope was too steep. He needed something to stand on, so he could hoist himself up.

Still nursing his injured arm, Gana looked around for any objects on which he could stand. His eyes soon rested on the many chairs and tables he and Tresca would use on the rare occasions when they invited the villagers to dinner. Panting heavily, he pushed several chairs against the side of the structure. He stood on one chair, but it did not give him sufficient height; then, he stacked a second chair on top of the first, but the chair pile was impossible to climb. Carefully, he began constructing a pyramid of chairs, with three at the base. By placing a table next to the chairs to launch himself, he was able to climb on top of three chairs. This gave him almost enough height to climb on top of the roof.

~

Adam and Janu walked away from the ceremony space, placing Olga between them, her arms over their shoulders. She was barely conscious, so the three moved slowly, heading toward the palace residence where Tina would be waiting.

As they walked, Adam scanned the horizon for Gana, preparing himself to attack. He would have to finish him off, and he had to do it now: That was the only way to escape. He was tempted to rush ahead and hunt him down but didn't dare leave Janu and Olga alone.

Eventually, they left the flickering light of the bonfire behind them; the only illumination was Planet K851b's moon. In the darkness, Adam was finally able to make out the Candela structure, where Tina was hiding on the roof.

Suddenly, he stopped in his tracks. Gana was at the bottom of the edifice, attempting to climb up to reach Tina. Immediately, Adam let go of Olga, and before Janu could understand what was happening, he sprinted forward, holding the crossbow in both hands. Because of the poor visibility, he would have to be close enough—say, fifty feet—to get a good shot. Otherwise, he might accidentally shoot Tina.

When Tina saw Gana's head and arms appear, she let out a piercing shriek. Defenseless against the monster, she scooted backward until she found herself blocked by a hump in the roof. Crumpling into a ball, she held her stuffed buffalo and screamed.

"Adam! Adam!"

"Adam will not save you, little girl!" croaked Gana, leering at her.

Convulsed with sobs, Tina watched as Gana repeatedly tried to hoist himself on top of the roof, sliding back every time.

Then she saw Adam in the distance. Standing up, she waved, frantically.

"Adam! Adam!"

At this point, Gana was standing on four chairs. Hearing Tina's cry, he spun around and saw Adam charging toward him. Gana looked at the sacrificial knife in his hand, then at the No. 4 female. He had to get her, she was his only chance. Just the thought of meat energized him.

There was no time to stack a fifth chair, so Gana leaped from the chairs, landing on the roof with his arms and legs splayed. This time he did not slide backward. Using his claws, he gradually climbed higher, until the roof slope was nearly at a forty-five-degree angle. As he raised himself upright, he caught sight of Adam on the ground below, holding his stick shooter.

Muttering to himself, Gana turned toward the screaming No. 4 female, who was now only a few feet away, and stepped toward her. Suddenly, a shooting stick narrowly missed his head. Enraged, he lunged toward the female child with knife raised, but just as he was about to stab her, Tina rolled sideways, narrowly avoiding the serrated blade. Her sudden move caused Gana to lose his balance and fall, his knife lodging in the roof membrane. The shock waves from this impact jolted Tina from her perch; still clutching Buffalo Wiseman, she began sliding down the sharpest incline of the roof, eventually tumbling to the ground.

Gana lay still, flat on his back, in the very center of the structure. Suddenly, the roof began to sink under his weight. As the center gave way, the sides curled up and folded together, burying Gana under a massive pile of rubble.

Rushing over to the collapsed structure, Adam found Tina lying on the ground, shaken but unharmed. He hugged her tightly.

"You're all right now! We're safe!"

Looking at the debris, he saw the creature's motionless claw-like hand sticking above the rubble.

By now, Janu and Olga had joined them and were staring at Gana's hand.

"Don't worry—he's dead," said Tina. "This is Buffalo Wiseman, and I'm Tina!"

Behind them, the villagers appeared and inspected the collapse. At the head of the crowd stood Hummingbird Man, Hehewuti. He approached Adam and bowed, saying, *"Kwakwhay."*

"That means, 'Thank you,'" said Janu.

"In that case, *Bitte!*"

~

Within an hour, once the drugs wore off, Olga's mind cleared. She clung to Janu, unable to let him out of her sight after the trauma of nearly being sacrificed. Likewise, Tina was also in a state of shock. Just a few days earlier, she had been living in a Chicago suburb; now, she was on a different planet, light years from her parents and grandparents. That night, Olga, Tina, and Janu sat quietly together, traumatized by their experiences, yet happy to have survived.

The villagers crowded around Adam. Hehewuti and Takala bowed before him, prostrating themselves at his feet, as though they expected him to be their new master. It was not a role that Adam wanted. Nevertheless, that night, Adam allowed the villagers to treat him like a king, and everyone enjoyed a sumptuous feast around the bonfire in the palace courtyard.

~

In the middle of the night, Gana's claw suddenly moved. Slowly, his three-fingered hand removed the rubble, stone by stone. Eventually, having removed enough pieces to free himself, he was able to stand up.

He was severely injured. His left foot and right shoulder seemed to be fractured; the arrow shaft had sheared off, leaving the head embedded in his arm. Gana felt his head, expecting to find blood, but there was none. It appeared that his brain had survived the collapse of the building.

Bloody and battered, he limped toward his palace home. In the front room, he went to the special box, which held the pellets, and took out a blue one. He had to get to his superiors immediately.

Dragging his left foot, Gana made his way to the dome, to the sacred rock. Looking out at the palace yard, he could see the bonfire and hear the laughing. He had failed; he was no longer in charge. Never again would he be able to regain control of these No. 4's.

He dreaded seeing his superiors again and having to explain his failure; now, however, he had to escape from this place.

Gana threw the blue pellet at the big rock. Suddenly, a blue spiral appeared, which began turning counter-clockwise; then, the color of the spiral changed to silver . . .

Summoning his remaining strength, Gana jumped in, vanishing forever from Planet K851b, never to return.

Chapter 33

When Horst opened his eyes, he saw millions of stars. It was just as he had feared: he had popped-up on a meteorite in empty space. Instinctively, he gasped for air, but, to his surprise, was able to breathe. Inhaling deeply, he concluded the atmosphere was the right mix of oxygen and nitrogen; wherever he was seemed safe.

Regaining his senses, he realized he was lying on a flat surface, looking up at the sky through a thin, glass-like membrane. To his left stood a massive meteorite, evidently the time portal at his location. Apparently, he was inside a structure that sealed in the environment from the emptiness of outer space. On closer examination, he noticed the structure was made up of interconnected triangles; it was a geodesic dome, like the Bucky Ball molecule C60. His eyes followed the lines of the dome, curving down to a bottom ring. Its diameter appeared to be almost four football fields: about a thousand feet.

Horst's entire body ached. Just as was the case with his previous time travel experience, he had a tremendous headache. He rubbed the back of his neck vigorously, but this did nothing to alleviate the throbbing. When he attempted to stand, he felt nauseous and fell backward. He waited for almost a minute before trying again. On his second attempt, he managed to maintain his balance, but with great difficulty.

He looked down at his feet until the vertigo gradually passed. When he could eventually straighten up, he saw twelve stone seats arranged in a circle around the meteorite, like the five-minute marks of a clock. Beyond the circle, massive boulders formed a wall, in the middle of which was an opening, perhaps the entrance to a cave.

Suddenly, Horst heard a sound coming from behind the meteorite. Cautiously, he edged his way around the rock, only to discover Gana, sitting on one of the stone chairs. The creature was rocking back-and-forth, mumbling to himself. There was an arrow stuck in his arm.

Horst slowly approached him.

"Gana?"

Gana looked up. "Oh—now you have arrived! I hope you're happy now!"

"Happy?"

"It is because of you and your kind I am here!"

Horst wrinkled his nose. "You mean, Adam?" repeated Horst, straining to hear clearly.

"Yes, Adam!" croaked Gana. "He has taken the Lifeforce from Tresca!"

"So Adam made it back and killed Tresca?"

"Yes—that is your word: 'killed.' He killed her with his stick shooter! Because of him, I have lost Tresca—and I have failed!"

"I'm sorry to hear about your loss," said Horst, not knowing what else to say.

Horst sat a safe distance from Gana as he listened to his account of Adam's attack during the sacrificial ceremony. From what he was hearing, he concluded that Janu and Olga were safe.

"That Adam," continued Gana, "he stopped the sacrifice with his stick shooter. Instead of that No. 4 woman giving up her life-blood, my Tresca lost her Lifeforce. Then he took the girl-child from me."

"The girl-child?"

"Yes, a small, tender girl-child who would have satisfied my hunger," spat Gana, grinding his teeth.

"So you weren't able to eat her?"

"No, unfortunately I was not—thanks to that Adam. She slid off the roof before I could plunge my knife in her. Then that Adam took her and all the No. 4's followed him, leaving me for dead."

Stifling a sigh of relief, Horst cleared his throat. "Where are we now?"

"We are where our superiors live."

"You mean your superiors," corrected Horst.

"No—*our* superiors. They will repair my arm. After that, I expect a reassignment."

"A reassignment?"

"Yes, a reassignment." Gana shook his head, rocking back-and-forth. "I cannot go back! Adam is now Master of my No. 4's. The last place was my second outpost! I have failed, again! They will demote me to pathway maintenance!"

"Pathway maintenance?"

"Do you not understand somebody maintains this system? It is huge!" Gana cradled his head between his claw-like hands. "It is a lonely and dangerous job, traveling from place to place, eating only prepackaged food!"

At the word "food," Gana's stomach began to grumble loudly. He bared his sharp teeth.

"I have been fasting too long," he snarled. "I must eat soon. I am beginning to feel faint."

Seeing Gana's deadly incisors, Horst sat up straight, ready to move further away. Then he noticed someone—or something—emerging from the cave entrance. It was a beast similar to Gana and Tresca, well over seven feet tall. The creature, walking in a jerky, bird-like manner, headed straight toward Gana. It momentarily stopped and stared at Horst for several seconds, before speaking to Gana.

Horst wasn't able to understand a single word of their dialogue, which consisted entirely of guttural sounds and some gestures. At one point, Gana raised his raspy voice, holding up his wounded arm and pointing at the arrow. The other creature inspected the injured arm, then motioned to Gana to follow. Then they disappeared into the cave, leaving Horst by himself.

Once he was on his own, Horst explored his surroundings. He walked around the meteorite a few times and looked behind the boulders. Then he made his way to the edge of the dome, peering through its translucent skin. Judging by the curvature of the horizon, Horst conjectured that he was on a small planet or a moon. To test the force of gravity, he tried jumping a few times, but he could not jump any higher than usual. This suggested the gravity was about the same as on Planet K851b and Earth.

When Horst returned to the circle of stone chairs, a woman was waiting for him. She was wearing a colorful hand-woven poncho over a long white dress; around her neck was a necklace of turquoise and silver beads from which hung a magnificent pendant of inlaid turquoise. As he came closer, Horst noticed her features were like those of the village people. However, there was something ethereal in her appearance, not quite human.

The woman spoke.

"Notoka Toot."

Horst thought she said, "My name is Toot," but he wasn't sure. He could not remember many of the words from the village. In response, he simply smiled and said, "Hi."

She tilted her head to one side. Then she stood up and walked back to the cave, leaving Horst alone.

Nearly fifteen minutes later, she re-emerged from the cave. She walked up to Horst and sat on a chair next to him.

"Otto is surprised you have come here." She spoke almost in a monotone, with minimal inflections to her words.

"Otto?"

"Do you not know Otto? Have you not been here before?"

"Ah, no . . . I've never met Otto."

The woman stood up and came closer to Horst. She looked closely at his face, then she took his chin into her hands, tilting his head up and down, left and right, as she studied his features.

"Ah . . . what are you looking for?" spluttered Horst, trying not to gag.

She stopped her examination, still grasping his head firmly. "You are not like the others. When I said, 'Notoka Toot,' you did not appear to understand."

Then she went back to examining him, now running her hands down his neck.

"Did you say your name is Toot?"

She stopped and looked at him.

"Yes. I am Toot."

"How is it you can speak English?"

"Gana explained your language to Otto. I am using the words Gana provided." Then she stepped back. "Please stand up."

She continued to run her hands over Horst's body, but this time, barely touching him through his clothing. Warmth radiated from her fingertips, traveling from his neck along his extremities.

"And what is your name?"

"Horst."

While the woman examined him, Horst was studying her. Her skin was like a human's, but smoother, without pores or body hair. Her eyes had solid blue irises, without marbling; her pupils were not circular but were vertical slits, like a cat's. Her hair was blue-black, without any highlights, reminding Horst of the polymerized ester fabric he had seen in the jackets and tents in Chicago.

"Are you giving me a physical?"

"I do not know that word, 'physical.' I am looking for damage to your body." She stood back and pointed to the ground. "Please come over here and lie down."

As directed, Horst lowered himself to the ground and lay on his back. Then Toot kneeled next to him, feeling his stomach and chest.

"Please roll over and face down," she said.

Horst turned on his stomach. She felt his back, moving her hands deftly, beginning with his neck, then his shoulders, moving lower. Upon reaching the lumbar region—where Horst had once broken his back—she paused, rotating her hands above his clothing. When she finished, she motioned for him to sit up.

"Have you found damage?"

"Yes, damage has been confirmed. You have an uncontrolled growth of aberrant cells dividing in your body. There is one colony of aberrant cells in this part of your body," she said, pointing at Horst's right lung.

Horst's eyes bulged, as he realized his cancer was metastasizing throughout his body. "You mean there is a tumor in my right lung?"

"If your word 'tumor' means an aberrant cell colony, 'yes,' you have a tumor right here," she said, pointing again at his right lung. "I have also found damage in your spinal cord. However, it appears the spinal cord has been partially repaired."

"Yes, my spine was repaired using nano-surgery."

"I do not know those words," said Toot, placing her hands on his head again.

"Please relax. I will be examining your head. This may require several minutes. You may feel nauseated while I do this."

"Ah . . . okay . . ." he said in a shaky voice.

For several minutes, Toot held Horst's head. She moved his head from side to side, back and forth, feeling every part of his skull.

As she did this, Horst periodically saw flashes of light. Also, for no apparent reason, random disassociated thoughts and memories from his past began to surface.

When Toot removed her hands, Horst felt exhausted, entirely drained from the experience.

"What were you doing with my head?"

"I was examining your brain structure." She pointed at a chair. "Sit."

As instructed, Horst sat down. Suddenly, he remembered what Gana had said about his superiors: He had said his superiors were No. 1 and No. 2.

"Are you a No. 2?"

"Yes, I am a No. 2," she said flatly.

"That is what Gana explained. He said he was a No. 3."

"Correct, Gana is a No. 3."

"And I am a No. 4?" asked Horst.

"Yes, of course."

"Is Otto a No. 1?"

"Correct."

Horst tilted his head and raised one eyebrow. "Are you a robot?"

"I do not understand what that word means," said Toot.

"Were you born from an animal life form or were you constructed by an animal life form?"

"I was constructed."

A robot—exactly as Horst thought.

Toot continued, "I was constructed to function as an interface for No. 4's, like you. We have another who was constructed to interface with No. 3's. You saw him take Gana away."

"Yes, I saw him take Gana away," said Horst, fascinated. "You say you are an interface. Do you mean that you are an interface with Otto?"

"Yes, that is my purpose," said Toot. "I communicate with lower species on their level; then, I provide the information to Otto."

Interesting, thought Horst. This robot was an intermediary, a liaison, between animal life forms and Otto, whoever or whatever he may be. But if Toot was a No. 2 and Gana was a No. 3, was Toot superior to Gana? Was it possible for a robot to be superior to a living thing?

"Will I be able to speak to Otto?"

"That will not be possible," said Toot. "You cannot speak directly to Otto, he does not communicate that way. My primary purpose is to communicate for you to Otto."

"Where are you from?"

"I am from Otto."

"Where is Otto from?"

"That is information of which I have no knowledge."

"Okay, but can you answer this: Where is Gana from?"

"We retrieved his species from a place sixty-five million years ago, based on your units of time."

Hearing 'sixty-five million years ago' immediately jogged Horst's memory: It was sixty-five million years ago when an asteroid had hit the Earth, causing a mass extinction of most species, including dinosaurs.

Horst raised his eyebrows.

"Are you saying you retrieved Gana's species from Earth?"

"I do not understand the name 'Earth.' We found Gana's ancestors near one of the sacred rock pathways. The rock's collision caused that place to become very dark. Many life forms could not survive in the darkness. We took several of Gana's primitive ancestors. They have since evolved."

"When you say, 'we,' who are you speaking of?"

"Other No. 2's like myself, but older models. During that time, only No. 2's traveled between the sacred rock pathways. Currently, No. 3's travel the pathways."

"By 'No. 3,' you mean Gana's species?"

"Correct," said Toot. "As Gana's species evolved and became more intelligent, they were assigned to travel duty. Later, when the No. 4's arrived, they were also assigned to travel with the No. 3's."

"By 'No. 4,' you mean the humans from Earth?"

Toot tilted her head to one side.

"Again, you use this word 'Earth.' Yes, we found the 'humans,' as you say, in the same place as Gana's species, near a different sacred rock portal."

Was the 'rock portal' she spoke of Meteor Crater? Had robots like Toot found the No. 4's—Hehewuti's tribe—near the meteorite that created Meteor Crater? Sixty-five million years ago, had they found Gana's ancestors near the meteorite that caused the mass extinction of dinosaurs? These meteorites must be entries and exits to the same closed time-like curve, created by the same supernova.

"Fascinating," said Horst.

"Fascinating? What does that word mean?"

"It means 'interesting.' For the first time, I understand your pathways. I find it interesting. . . . Actually, the word 'interesting' is an understatement. I find the pathway, and you and Otto, absolutely fascinating."

He leaned forward.

"What is your purpose? Why travel across the galaxy using the sacred stone pathways?"

Momentarily Toot stopped and closed her eyes, as though in a trance. When she opened her eyes, she looked directly at Horst.

"I am communicating with Otto. He finds this conversation interesting. He says no other No. 4's have asked these questions before. Otto says he likes you."

"Thank you," smiled Horst.

"You have asked, why do we go from place to place? Otto says he is an explorer. He and his kind have explored long before the time of Gana's ancestors. Otto's kind have great powers. They have learned to control material objects and influence events. Otto says you will not be able to understand."

"Why not?" asked Horst." I have so many questions! I want to understand."

Toot paused, silently listening to Otto, interpreting his thoughts.

"Perhaps an analogy will help you. Otto says, for you to understand him would be like a dog trying to understand a No. 4."

Disappointed, Horst slumped in his seat.

Toot smiled. "Otto finds your curiosity amusing. He likes you. He says you remind him of another No. 4, named Plato."

"You mean the ancient Greek, Plato?"

Toot nodded. "Yes—a No. 4 who was very inquisitive. He spoke of a world of abstractions that exists outside the visible world. He talked about things like straight lines and circles, numbers, truth, and falseness, which have an existence of their own. He believed mathematics is a path to the abstract world, a separate world."

"Is it?" asked Horst, raising his eyebrows.

"Obviously," said Toot. "Mathematics works because the physical world uses the same principles. Mathematics can predict the outcome of all physical events, except on microscopic scales."

Horst wanted to ask her about the pellets, but when he reached in his pocket, it was empty. He had used the last one. Disappointed, he said, "I wanted to ask about the pellets that Gana gave me. Do you know what I am referring to?"

"Of course."

"Are the pellets negative matter?"

Again, Toot paused to communicate with Otto. "Otto says, there is always a positive and a negative, a black and white, an up and down, a left and right. There is always a balance and tension between these qualities. Yes, the pellets are the opposite of what you call 'matter' on this side of things."

"And it all adds up to nothing: zero, doesn't it?" concluded Horst. "On the other side of a black hole, there must be a white hole . . . but we will never know, will we?"

"Otto is intrigued by you," replied Toot, without so much as a smile. "He enjoys your questions. He again says you remind him of Plato."

"Is that good or bad?"

Toot tilted her head.

"How is Otto's statement good or bad? His statement is an observation. Otto's species is many millions of years old. Your species is only a few million years old."

She paused and closed her eyes. When she opened them again, she said, "Otto has a question. He does not understand how you found Gana and his people. Were you always living near Gana and his people?"

"It is a long story," explained Horst. "We originally came from Earth."

"But how? Did you use the sacred rock pathway? We did not detect your presence on the pathway."

"We came on a spacecraft. We were sent as frozen embryos to the planet where Gana lived. We were raised from birth by robots who acted as our parents."

"Robots? You mean like me and other No. 2's?" asked Toot.

Horst nodded. "Yes, robots similar to you, but not as advanced as you. These robots acted as our parents and raised us. We did not know they were robots until our sixteenth birthday."

Toot paused.

"Otto is impressed. He said perhaps you are more advanced than he assumed."

Rubbing his neck, Horst looked at Toot sadly.

"Unfortunately, the Earth has probably been destroyed by an asteroid. . . . My species may no longer exist," he said, his voice choking.

When Toot heard this, she closed her eyes. She stood still for several minutes, as Horst waited.

Finally, she opened her eyes. "Otto now understands. Our pathways are very large. He has just traced to a portal occupied by a No. 4 named Hehewuti. This No. 4 has verified he is stationed at a place called 'Earth' by the inhabitants. Otto considers this place one of the more interesting portals."

Toot waved her hand, motioning Horst to follow her to the cave. "Please come with me."

The cave was lit by sconces hanging from the walls, shining in a kaleidoscope of greens, blues, and oranges. They walked along a narrow path, past flowing underground streams, springs, miniature waterfalls, and huge, cavernous chambers with precious crystal gems hanging from the ceilings.

Finally, they arrived at a room much like a hospital operating theater. There was a large silver metal table in the center.

Toot pointed at the table. "Please lie down."

As instructed, Horst lay on the table. Then Toot adjusted an overhead apparatus, which looked like a giant ray gun. She carefully moved the contraption into position over Horst's chest. After making a series of adjustments to the device, she finally said, "Please do not move. This procedure will take some time."

Horst remained as still as possible.

For the next two hours, Toot pointed the apparatus at various parts of Horst's body, repeatedly asking him to hold still. Quickly and efficiently, she manipulated the equipment, aiming it at specific locations of his body.

Having rolled away the ray-gun apparatus, Toot returned with an even larger machine on coasters; it had a donut hole similar to that of an MRI or CT scan machine. For this part of the procedure, Horst lay on a sled-like table on wheels, as Toot rolled him into the donut hole. When his spine's lumbar region was aligned with the donut, she stopped and said, "Please do not move. This will take one hour of your time measurement."

In total, the procedures took nearly three hours to complete. Finally, Toot said, "We are finished now. You can expect to feel tired."

Already, Horst was beginning to feel very tired.

"Also, you can expect your hair to turn white."

Horst's eyes narrowed. "You mean, I will grow to be old, that I am cured?"

"That is correct."

She motioned for him to follow her. They walked out of the labyrinth of cave tunnels to the outside, returning to the meteorite.

Toot retrieved a blue pellet from her pocket and inspected it. Then she held it up, showing it to Horst.

"I assume you will be returning to Earth, correct?"

Horst held up his hands, in horror.

"No . . . no, I don't want to go back to Earth! Please . . . please send me back to the location where Gana came from. I want to see Ingrid—my wife—and my son, Janu. My life is on Planet K851b with my family and friends, not on Earth!"

"Very well."

She put the blue pellet back in her left pocket, before retrieving another pellet from her right pocket.

"You will be returning now. Do you have any further questions?"

Horst frowned, then smiled. "Ah . . . yes, I have a question. I was wondering about your name and Otto's name. They seem very similar. Is there a meaning to your names?"

Toot closed her eyes for several seconds, then she spoke.

"Otto says both our names are symmetrical. The names are spelled the same way, left-to-right or right-to-left, up or down."

"Interesting," said Horst. "The world's most symmetrical names." Then, he remembered what Otto had said: *There is always a positive and a negative, a black and white, an up and down, a left and right.*

"Is that all?"

Horst nodded. "I have no more questions. I'm just happy to be going home."

"Then, prepare yourself."

She tossed the blue pellet at the large meteorite, and the ground turned into a spinning spiral, changing in color from orange, eventually to silver; then a black sphere appeared, which grew larger and larger. When the sphere was about six feet in diameter, Horst looked at Toot. She nodded, motioning with her hand for him to jump.

Then, for the third time in his life, Horst jumped into a wormhole and vanished.

Chapter 34

AFTER CHARLES AND ELISE LEFT METEOR CANYON, THEY took Interstate 40 east. The road was empty, so they had the entire interstate to themselves.

Charles set the Dodge van's cruise control to eighty mph. They blasted through Albuquerque, New Mexico, into the panhandle of Texas, then through Oklahoma. When they hit Oklahoma City, they took a left on Interstate 35, toward their destination: Wichita, Kansas, only one hundred and fifty-eight miles to the north.

Finally, they reached the asteroid's bull's eye: Wichita. It was one twenty-eight p.m., just forty-five minutes ahead of the predicted time of impact, two thirteen p.m. The city was empty. There were neither cars nor people on any of the streets; the only signs of life were a few stray dogs behind an Arby's, scavenging for food amongst the garbage spilling from a dumpster. Charles and Elise had never been to Wichita before. They were aware of its reputation as the "Air Capital of the World," a major center of the aircraft industry. Textron Aviation and other firms, including Bombardier Learjet, Airbus, and Spirit AeroSystems, operated design and manufacturing facilities there. However, when they drove past the industrial complexes, they saw no traces of activity.

Charles stopped the van and surveyed the aeronautical factories; then, he shook his head.

"Think of all the jobs, all the people making stuff, all of it gone! Humankind succeeded in making so much stuff out of nothing. We brought so much—*what is the word I'm searching for?*"

He paused, rubbing the back of his neck. "We brought so much *order* to our lives."

Elise's eyes narrowed. "*Order?* Is this what humanity achieved?"

"Yes, order. It's what drives us, we cannot stop ourselves from creating order from chaos. It is why we build things and create things. Order is the ultimate aesthetic: it's what we mean by 'perfection.'"

With a far-away look, Charles gazed in the distance. "Some people become obsessed and are consumed about bringing order to things. They are driven to create: I know because I'm one of them. For me, it wasn't about money, it was about the excitement of designing and working on construction projects."

He looked at Elise, forcing a smile. "Did I work too much?"

Elise leaned back and laughed. "In all our forty-two years of marriage, I've learned you have only two modes: You're either working on something full blast, or you're sleeping—there's no in-between!"

She placed her hand on his arm. "We made a good team, Charles. Yes, you worked hard. While you were at the office, I was home raising the kids."

"But, I mean . . . did I help you enough?"

"Well, not always, but nobody's perfect," she said, hugging him. "You were a great example for the girls. Both of them followed in your footsteps and got tech jobs, didn't they?"

His eyes welled up with sudden emotion. "This sucks."

"Yes, it certainly does," said Elise, nestling closer to him. "But I'm curious. When the asteroid hits, will it leave a crater like Meteor Crater?"

Charles shook his head.

"Meteor Crater? *Pfft!* How about a hole the size of Lake Michigan—or bigger!"

Elise shivered.

"The size of Lake Michigan? You never explained this to me—"

"That's because I've spared you the gory details! What would telling you have accomplished?"

"But I want to know!"

He paused. "Well, if you really want to know. . . . What I'm about to explain was classified material. The boys at Los Alamos made real-time simulations of the asteroid's impact using the Cray XC40 supercomputer. They modeled the asteroid's exact shape and path of descent, using geophysical data of the Earth in the Wichita area. There was an immense amount of digital information they entered. Such things as the Earth's crust thickness here, the theoretical formation of magma . . ."

Then, noticing Elise's terrified expression, Charles stopped. "Perhaps I'd better not continue."

"I get it. These studies determined there will be nothing left," she said flatly.

Charles nodded. "Yes, nothing."

Nervously, Elise began to brush her clothes off with her hands.

"I think we need to find a church."

Charles raised an eyebrow. "Isn't that how the movie War of The Worlds ended, in a church?"

"Never saw it, but I have a strong urge to find a church."

"Okay, let's start looking—but we don't have much time." He turned on the van's ignition.

"We'll have to find a neighborhood away from these factories. If we're lucky, perhaps a few people stayed behind."

Driving away from the industrial zone, they soon came to a shady street lined with houses. It was not long before they saw an Episcopal church. Its architecture was Tudor style, with a half-timbered church and stone ancillary buildings. Surprisingly, the parking lot was full.

Charles pulled the Dodge into the church parking lot.

"Looks like we're not alone," he said, turning to Elise. "You ready?"

"Ready as I'll ever be," she said, forcing a smile.

Charles grabbed her hand as they hurried across the parking lot.

"It's a long time since we've been to church," he remarked.

"Yes, hasn't it? The last time was four years ago, at Washington Cathedral for the Blessing of The Embryos ceremony."

The front doors to the church were wide open. As they drew closer, they could hear strains of "Amazing Grace."

"Amazing Grace, How sweet the sound
That saved a wretch like me
I once was lost but now am found
'Twas blind but now I see . . ."

They entered the building and stood in the doorway for a few moments. Almost all the pews were full. In the sanctuary, a woman priest, vested in an almond-white linen chasuble and an emerald green stole, was bowing to the cross. Charles and Elise slipped into a pew, just as the congregation was finishing "Amazing Grace."

As the priest walked to the pulpit, the entire community quieted down. She adjusted her electronic headset and microphone and looked out at the assembly. Noticing Charles and Elise, she said, "I see we have some visitors! Welcome!"

Charles and Elise gave a slight wave.

Then the church bells rang twice. The priest looked up in the direction of the belfry. "It is two p.m. We have thirteen minutes," she said, her voice sounding surprisingly calm.

Many of the parishioners began sobbing.

"In this short remaining time, I will not be giving a sermon. Instead, I think it best we say goodbye to each other; then we will finish with a prayer."

She stepped back from the pulpit and raised her hands. "Please, everyone, stand. Let's take these last few minutes to share our love for each other!"

The entire congregation stood up and turned to their loved ones and neighbors. They shook hands and hugged, going from pew to pew, saying their goodbyes. Several young children, apparently unaware of what was about to happen, scurried about, visiting their friends, laughing and giggling.

The priest walked down the aisle, greeting all her parishioners. Upon reaching Charles and Elise, she introduced herself as Reverend Sue. They introduced themselves, smiling politely.

When the minister returned to the pulpit, the church became very quiet again.

Charles looked at his wristwatch: It was two eleven. Only two minutes remained.

The priest said: "Join me now in reciting Psalm 23. Please turn to page 612 in *The Book of Common Prayer.*"

The congregation read the Psalm in unison:

"*The Lord is my shepherd; I shall not want/ He maketh me to lie down in green pastures/ he leadeth me beside the still waters. . . .*"

Charles read from the prayer book but chose not to recite the words out loud. He glanced at Elise, who was beginning to cry as she read the prayer:

"*. . . He restoreth my soul. . . .*"

Suddenly, looking through the windows, Charles saw the sky had become very dark. A few seconds later, the wind whipped-up, rattling every beam and joist in the building. He stared at the ceiling, thinking the roof might blow off from the suction. As for the parishioners, all seemed unfazed by the storm outside. They continued reading the prayer in unison:

"*. . . he leadeth me in the paths of righteousness for his name's sake. . . .*"

Through the windows, he saw flashes of lightning. Seconds later, there were deafening booms of thunder.

"*. . . Yea, though I walk through the valley of the shadow of death, I will fear no evil: for thou art with me; thy rod and thy staff they comfort me. . . .*"

In that instant, Charles decided he could no longer sit inside the church: the pull from what was happening outside was too strong.

He turned to Elise. "I've got to go."

She turned and stared at him, her eyes filled with tears.

Charles grabbed Elise by the shoulders. "I've got to go! I've got to see it!" He hugged her one last time, said, "I love you," then ran from the pew.

She screamed, but he was already out the door.

Reaching the parking lot, he looked up at the sky. To his surprise, he could see the asteroid with his own eyes. It was a monstrous black object, completely eclipsing the sun. Elise, meanwhile, had run out of the church to be at his side. In this final moment, they stood clinging to each other, bracing themselves against the wind, staring at the asteroid as it came closer, becoming larger and larger, until—

Epilogue

IN 1964, A SOVIET ASTRONOMER NAMED NIKOLAI KARDASHEV proposed a scale for measuring civilizations. Kardashev categorized civilizations as "Type I," "Type II," or "Type III," depending on how much power the civilization is capable of accessing. "Type I" civilizations access power only from the planet they live on; "Type II's" gain access to power from planets and stars; finally, "Type III's" access the energy available in the entire galaxy they inhabit.

Some have said—most famously, Carl Sagan, the late astronomer—that human civilization is currently a Type I civilization in its adolescence. But it would be difficult to determine where, exactly, Otto's civilization fell on the Kardashev scale spectrum: His civilization seemed somewhere between a high-end Type II and an early Type III. Otto and his kind had learned to utilize wormholes as natural time machines; this would qualify them for possible entry into the "Type III club" of the most advanced civilizations in the entire Universe.

It was quite fortunate for Earthlings when Horst met Otto. Horst impressed Otto as a potential replacement for Gana. In Otto's opinion, after sixty-four million years, Gana's species seemed to have peaked-out.

It was because of Horst's warning about the asteroid Otto contacted a No. 4 named Hehewuti, who was stationed on a planet called Earth. After Hehewuti confirmed his No. 4's lives were in danger, Otto decided to save them. It was child's play for Otto to make the asteroid disappear.

We humans may never understand how Otto did it; however, there are theories. Coincidentally, near the time of the predicted impact, several eyewitnesses in Canada described an extraordinary event: In Canada's Hudson Bay, the Nastapoka Arc is one of the most massive meteor craters on Earth. Residents of a nearby village reported seeing an enormous expulsion of material ejected from the bay at a high velocity. In their words, the material "flew upward into the sky."

Publicly, US and Canadian scientists have offered no comment about the Canadian incident. However, NASA has confirmed satellite imagery recorded the expulsion of material or energy of some kind; this material followed a direct course toward the asteroid. Moreover, some scientists theorize the material ejected from the Nastapoka Arc was antimatter coming from a wormhole. In effect, when the antimatter collided with the asteroid, both disappeared. To paraphrase Horst, ". . . it all adds up to nothing: zero, doesn't it?"

In the aftermath of what came to be known as "the Big Dud," many people thought the asteroid was a hoax concocted by a conspiracy. Consequently, the director of the *When Worlds Collide Operation,* General Leslie, had to face Congressional hearings. Eventually, there was an investigation into the whereabouts of Hehewuti's tribe: Unfortunately, investigators found no trace of the tribe's existence at the Chocolate Ranch near Winslow, Arizona.

Charles and Elise Timoshenko were baffled to see the asteroid vanish before their eyes. For the remainder of their lives, they firmly believed that, somehow, Adam, Horst, and Tina had saved the Earth. They also had no doubts Adam and Tina were living safely together on Planet K851b, some 80,000 years in the future.

Acknowledgements

THE INSPIRATION FOR THIS STORY CAME TO ME DURING A 2018 trip to the Grand Canyon with my wife, Lisa. When our tour guide described the disappearance of the Anasazi civilization as one of the greatest mysteries in archeology, I sensed a whiff of a plot.

In developing this story, the challenge of getting the characters back to Earth was a formidable one. Since *The Third Thaw* stories are works of "hard" science fiction, a semi-plausible means of time/space travel was required, based on real physics.

Like the hero of this story, Horst, I dived into books on General Relativity. By pure lucky coincidence, my research retraced the path of the astronomer Carl Sagan, when he wrote his great sci-fi novel *Contact.* Sagan consulted with the prominent physicist Kip Thorne for a scientifically plausible method of time travel. In response, Kip Thorne mailed him fifty relevant equations on gravitational physics! In writing *The Final Thaw,* I have relied heavily on Kip Thorne's book, *Black Holes and Time Warps.* The concepts presented in this novel about spacetime, black holes and wormholes are to the best of my understanding. Although readers will require some "willing suspension of disbelief," it is my hope this story will serve as a pedagogical adventure in science for people who like to learn such things.

There were several people who helped me develop this book from start to finish. After I finished the first two drafts of the manuscript, once again I used the writing coach services of Dr. Elizabeth-Anne Stewart, who lives and teaches in Chicago. It was a great pleasure to work again with Elizabeth in this venture.

I also must thank WiDo Publishing for accepting this manuscript. It was a pleasure working with WiDo's Content Editor, Stephanie Procopio, and Managing Editor, Karen Gowen.

Some References Used:

1. *House of Rain* by Craig Childs, copyright 2006, published by Back Bay Books/Little, Brown and Company: About the vanished civilization of the American Southwest. Interesting account of Childs' experiences hiking through remote sites, archeological digs and dealing with Hopi tribal elders. Describes the remains of ancient archeological sites. Especially interesting information on Chaco Canyon, where the great buildings are arranged as architectural calendars. Interesting reference about Chaco during the time of a supernova in 1054 AD (p. 40).
2. *The Meteor Crater Story* by Dean Smith, 2nd Edition Revisions by Neal Davis, copyright 1996, Meteor Crater Enterprises, Inc. We visited this crater on a separate trip, and it was extremely windy—perhaps due to the shape of the crater. Several interesting bits of history were used from this book.
3. *The Road to Reality: A Complete Guide to the Universe* by Roger Penrose, copyright 2004, published by Vintage Books: A very enlightening, broad and conjectural tome by an authority on physics. Demonstrates how mathematics, especially complex numbers, reflects reality. Heavy into topology and manifolds. Explains the concept of "light cones," which was used in this plot.
4. *Spacetime and Geometry* by Sean M. Carroll, copyright 2013, published by Pearson: A thorough textbook on the mathematics of General Relativity. Explains Minkowski space and closed time-like curves, which was used in this plot.
5. *Black Holes & Time Warps* by Kip S. Thorne, copyright 1994, published by W. W. Norton and Company: An amazing reference, explaining the history and backstories of how physicists have deduced the existence of black holes in the Universe. Many interesting stories about physicists as people. Thorne explains highly complex phenomena, using virtually no mathematics (perhaps so as not to turn-off readers).

6. *Contact* by Carl Sagan, copyright 1985, published by Simon and Schuster: Kip Thorne's contributions to this story appear on pages 347, 358 and 408, and Author's Note.
7. *The Stubbornly Persistent* by Anderthal Kord, copyright 2018: This short, thoroughly researched book postulates the existence of a fifth dimensional Universe. Very interesting idea that spacetime is comprised of space coordinates (x, y, z), "normal time" (t), and another time dimension (at right angles to normal time). The idea of a spiraling nature of time, which is used in the plot, was influenced by this book.
8. "An Example of a New Type of Cosmological Solutions to Einstein's Field Equations of Gravitation" by Kurt Gödel, *Reviews of Modern Physics,* July 1949. A classic paper describing a manifold in which time travel is possible. Contains a fascinating quote: "It (the manifold) is theoretically possible to travel into the past, or otherwise influence the past."
9. Webpage: "Did the Native American in North America know about Aztec and Maya Civilizations?" by various contributors. (https://www.quora.com/Did-the-Native-American-in-North-America-know-about-Aztec-and-Maya-civilizations). The last piece of the plot puzzle: The Aztecs and Mayans sent foot traders to trade chocolate with the Ancient Puebloans in exchange for silver and turquoise. The Ancient Mayans were experts in celestial bodies, particularly the Orion Nebula, which is a result of a supernova (exploding star). Theoretically, the Orion Nebula may have a black hole at its center.
10. Webpage: "A Primer on Time Travel" by Damon Shavers (http://www.readmag.com/Columns/timetravel.htm). This short webpage describes all the various ideas for time travel. Excellent, common sense discussions, particularly about "Closed Timelike Paths."
11. Webpage: "The Return of the Dinosauroid Man" (Troodon Sapiens - Dinosauroid Sculpture by Dale Russell and Ron Seguin, 1982 - Canadian Museum of Nature, Ottawa, Canada (thelivingmoon.com). The amazing sculptures of Dale Russell and Ron Seguin, speculating how dinosaurs could have evolved if they had not gone extinct. I used these as inspiration for the characters of Gana and Tresca—with some feathers added.

About the Author

Karl Hanson, a structural engineer, earned degrees from Colorado State University and the University of Illinois. Since 1980, he has helped design buildings and bridges throughout the country. In Chicago, he is involved in everything from small projects to high profile projects such as Millennium Park and McCormack Place.

Since 1991, he has developed a suite of structural engineering software by the name of "DCALC" (DesignCalcs), used by structural engineers across the country.

His hobbies are piano playing, learning German, and riding bikes with his wife Lisa on the weekends. Karl and Lisa have two daughters and a family of avid readers. Visit the author at kjhanson.net for information about his current writing projects.

CPSIA information can be obtained
at www.ICGtesting.com
Printed in the USA
LVHW091955300721
694063LV00023B/22